Frances Paige has made herself
writers working today with the publication of her ongoing saga about the McGraths of Sholton, but she has always had a large following for her many novels, written under a number of pseudonyms. Under the name Frances Paige she published two novels before embarking on her saga: *Three Girls* and *Lost Time*. The first book about the McGraths, *The Sholtie Burn*, was published in 1986, to be followed by *Maeve's Daughter* in 1987 and *The Distaff Side* in 1988.

Born in Scotland, Frances Paige is married to a psychiatrist whose thinking, she admits, has greatly influenced her approach to characterization. She and her husband live in Lancashire and travel regularly to southwest France, her second love.

By the same author

Three Girls
Lost Time
The Sholtie Burn
Maeve's Daughter
The Distaff Side

FRANCES PAIGE

Men who March Away

This edition published 1993 by
Diamond Books
77-85 Fulham Palace Road
Hammersmith, London W6 8JB

First published in Great Britain by
Souvenir Press Ltd 1989

Set in Times
Printed and bound in Great Britain by
BPCC Paperbacks Ltd
Member of BPCC Ltd

I would like to thank Messrs. A. P. Watt Ltd., on behalf of
Michael B. Yeats and Macmillan London Limited, for
permission to quote two lines from 'Down by the Salley
Gardens', from *The Collected Poems of W. B. Yeats*.

To Archie

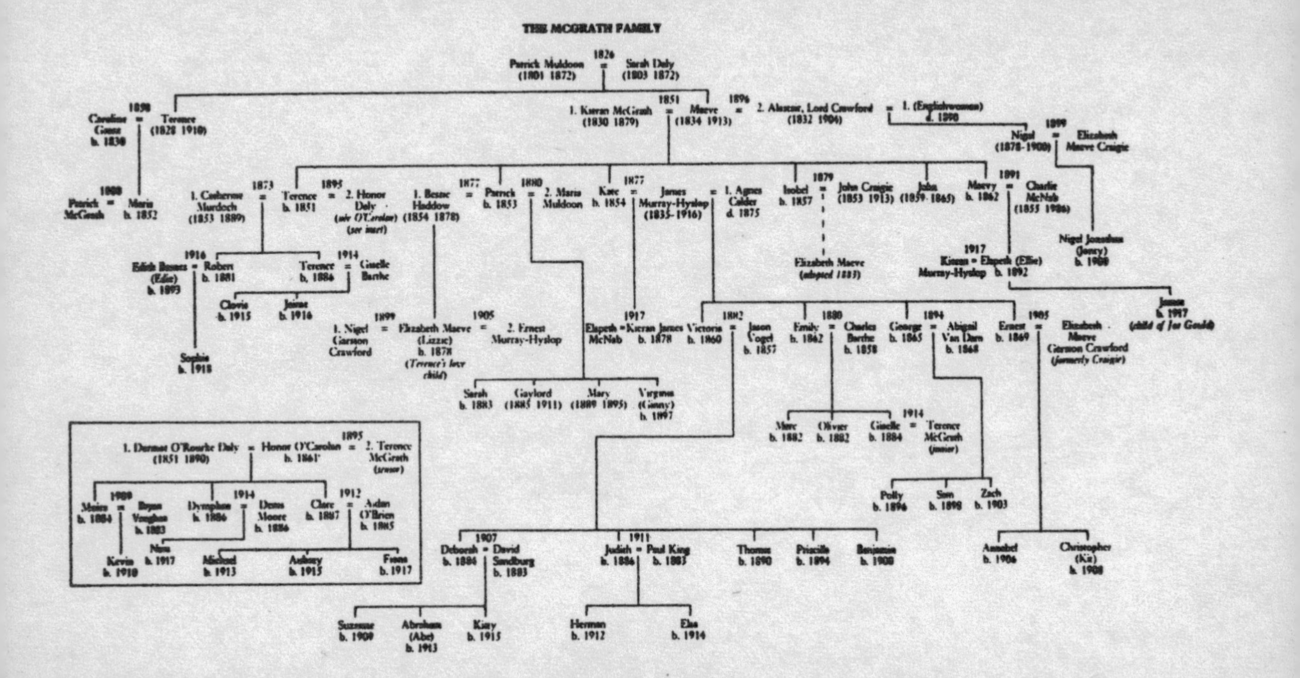
THE MCGRATH FAMILY
Patrick Muldoon (1801 1872)
1826 =
Sarah Daly (1803 1872)
Caroline Gosse b. 1830
1850 =
Terence (1828 1910)
Patrick McGrath
1880 =
Maria b. 1852
1. Kieran McGrath (1830 1879)
1851 =
Maeve (1834 1913)
1896 =
2. Alastair, Lord Crawford (1832 1906)
= 1. (Englishwoman) d. 1890
Nigel (1878-1900)
1899 =
Elizabeth Maeve Craigie
Nigel Jonathan (Jonny) b. 1900
1. Catherine Murdoch (1853 1889)
1873 =
Terence b. 1851
1895 =
2. Honor Daly (née O'Carolan) (see inset)
1. Bessie Haddow (1854 1878)
1877 =
Patrick b. 1853
1880 =
2. Maria Muldoon
Kate b. 1854
1877 =
James Murray-Hyslop (1835-1916)
= 1. Agnes Calder d. 1875
Isobel b. 1857
1879 =
John Craigie (1853 1913)
John (1859 1865)
Maevy b. 1862
1891 =
Charlie McNab (1855 1906)
Elizabeth Maeve (adopted 1883)
Kieran Murray-Hyslop
1917 =
Elspeth (Ellie) b. 1892
James b. 1917 (child of Jas Gould)
Edith Barnes (Edie) b. 1893
1916 =
Robert b. 1881
Terence b. 1884
1914 =
Giselle Barthe
Clovis b. 1915
Jaime b. 1916
Sophie b. 1918
1. Nigel Garston Crawford
1899 =
Elizabeth Maeve (Lizzie) b. 1878 (Terence's love child)
1905 =
2. Ernest Murray-Hyslop
Elspeth McNab
1917 =
Kieran James b. 1878
Victoria b. 1860
1882 =
Jason Vogel b. 1857
Emily b. 1862
1880 =
Charles Barthe b. 1858
George b. 1865
1894 =
Abigail Van Dam b. 1868
Ernest b. 1869
1905 =
Elizabeth Maeve Garston Crawford (formerly Craigie)
Sarah b. 1883
Gaylord (1885 1911)
Mary (1889 1895)
Virginia (Ginny) b. 1897
Marc b. 1882
Olivier b. 1882
Giselle b. 1884
1914 =
Terence McGrath (junior)
Polly b. 1896
Sam b. 1898
Zach b. 1903
Annabel b. 1906
Christopher (Kit) b. 1908
1. Dermot O'Rourke Daly (1851 1890)
= Honor O'Carolan b. 1861
1895 =
2. Terence McGrath (senior)
Moira b. 1884
1909 =
Bryan Vaughan b. 1883
Dymphna b. 1886
1914 =
Denis Moore b. 1886
Clare b. 1887
1912 =
Aidan O'Brien b. 1885
Kevin b. 1910
Nora b. 1917
Michael b. 1913
Aubrey b. 1915
Fiona b. 1917
Deborah b. 1884
1907 =
David Sandburg b. 1883
Judith b. 1886
1911 =
Paul King b. 1883
Thomas b. 1890
Priscilla b. 1894
Benjamin b. 1900
Suzanne b. 1909
Abraham (Abe) b. 1913
Kitty b. 1915
Herman b. 1912
Elsa b. 1914

BOOK ONE

Commitment 1916–1917

1

'Well done, Miss McNab,' Ellie's Chief said. The patient had been wheeled away by the nurses. 'The neatest little appendectomy I've seen for a long time.'

'Thank you, Mr Ledbridge. My mother nearly died of an inflamed appendix, a long time ago. Things have moved on since then. Maybe it's thanks to Lord Lister.'

'Lord Lister?' His eyebrows raised. 'Do I know him?' She was never sure when he was teasing.

'No, he was before your time.' She wanted to add 'just' but stopped herself. You could go so far with your Chief, even Mr Ledbridge. 'My father worshipped him.' She stripped off her rubber gloves and walked towards the sink.

'Was he medical too?'

'Yes, the family doctor in Sholton, where I live, but he did part-time surgery here. My mother was a nurse here too.'

'Ah, that explains your skill.' He joined her at the sink, a handsome man in his late fifties with quiffs of grey hair on his temples which had the effect of broadening his narrow face. 'I hear you may be going to France soon. Are you sure you want to get into the midst of the fighting, a young girl like you?'

She saw admiration in his eyes. He was suave, an English suaveness, unusual in Glasgow. And he had a reputation amongst the nurses, nothing scandalous, just a capacity for making them feel like women. 'Mr Heart-throb' they called him.

'Oh, I'm sure.' She dried her hands carefully and pulled

off the green skull-cap, thinking that the heat of the operating lights would have made her fair hair damp and curl in tendrils on her brow. She was susceptible to his susceptibility. 'I'm very lucky to be taken on as a surgeon. It's no ordinary war hospital, you know. It's run entirely by women.'

'Really?' A Scotsman might have said, 'Wummen! A never heard the like!'

'I'm hoping they send for me soon. Surgeons are badly needed out there.'

'No doubt, but I thought a pretty girl like you would have been thinking of getting married instead.' At the operating table Mr Ledbridge was cool efficiency personified. Away from it his one aim seemed to be to tease. She tried to dampen down the flicker of annoyance, decided to drop a verbal bomb.

'No, once bitten, twice shy. I was jilted four years ago. He skited off to Australia.' There was a small triumph in being able to say that, considering how besotted she had been with Colin Thomson, a young assistant in the Sholton practice. It had nearly wrecked her career.

Mr Ledbridge was shaking his head in pretended amazement. 'The foolishness of some young men! Ready? After you, Miss McNab.' He held the swing door open for her. 'Still,' he went on as they walked along the tiled corridor together, 'I imagine there are plenty eager to take his place.' She had shot her bolt. She wouldn't tell him of Kieran, her American cousin who had asked her to marry him when they had met in Paris two years ago, at the wedding of his niece, Giselle Barthe.

It had been on the same day as the murder at Sarajevo of the Archduke Franz Ferdinand, and she had made the unsettled state of the world her excuse. 'The times are out of joint,' she had said, 'I couldn't settle down as a married woman . . .' ('In America, of all places,' she had wanted to say.) 'I have to be here, ready, but after that, I'll see . . .' She found herself explaining to Mr Ledbridge.

'Ever since the outbreak of war I've been desperate to be in it. That's why I trained as a surgeon, like my father. You could see it coming. Everyone I know seems to be involved. You know how many young doctors have gone from the Royal. Even my cousin Lizzie's running a convalescent place for soldiers. She gave over her house, Sholton Hall. You may know it.'

'Of course I do. Is Mrs Murray-Hyslop your cousin?' His grey quiffs rose with his eyebrows in surprise. 'A charming woman. I've had dinner there. Mr Ernest Murray-Hyslop is a director of a big transport firm in Glasgow, I believe.'

'Yes, it's the family firm.' She was amused because he looked impressed. 'My grandfather and grandmother McGrath started it. Ernest was brought up in America, but his stepmother is a McGrath, and he got roped in too. The war has made them busier than ever.' She was enjoying this.

'Ah.' He nodded. 'McGrath's Carting Company. A household name. Please give my regards to Mr and Mrs Murray-Hyslop when you next see them.' They had reached the end of the corridor and he stopped. 'I have one or two patients to see in Ward Nine.' His eyes were kindly on her, no teasing now. 'A hospital in France, run entirely by women, eh? Your father must be proud of you. I expect he's like me, too old to volunteer.'

'He died ten years ago.'

'Oh, I'm sorry. The Boer War?'

'No, not long after it. A stupid motor accident. . .' Surprisingly she felt her throat go thick. 'Yes, he'd be pleased. Good-night, Mr Ledbridge.'

She walked past the smoked grey bulk of the Cathedral

and down High Street to the Trongate. She enjoyed the walk and the fresh air after the stuffiness of the Royal. Sometime in the future she might buy a motor car. She had discussed it with Belle Geddes who had taken her father's place in the practice and drove about Sholton with great aplomb in her Bullnose Morris.

'Were you afraid, Belle, after the . . . accident?' She remembered the look from those strange silver-grey eyes, the wry curve of her mouth. She could almost hear the low-pitched voice.

'More than afraid. Physically ill. Waves of fear. I made myself drive – part of the punishment . . .' She had loved Father, of course. Ellie had jaloused that long ago. And to have been at the wheel when the car went out of control . . . She had often imagined the agony of the woman having to crawl up the Brae to get help, shaken and bruised, but knowing that Charlie was lying dead, his neck broken. Mother, at least, had been honoured and supported in her grief. It was no wonder Belle had become a confirmed spinster.

Still, perhaps a village doctor could be a spinster with impunity. Would *she* become the same now that she had more or less turned down Kieran, Ernest's half-brother and the beloved son of Aunt Kate and Uncle James in Wanapeake, New York State? Uncle James Murray-Hyslop, that wry and courtly man who was dying of emphysema.

But she didn't *love* Kieran. Her affection for him was not to be compared with her obsessive desire to be involved in the War, nor with that long-ago passion she had felt for Colin Thomson whose touch had made her tremble and sigh. Was it that Kieran was too good, too predictable? Should men have in their make-up a 'bit of devilment', like Colin or even Mr Ledbridge, or again like Ernest with his mischievous gaiety?

She was in the Trongate now, and the tram-car was

swaying towards her. She jumped on to the platform when it stopped, paid her fare to the green-skirted conductress, and followed her upstairs to the upper deck, admiring her sturdy legs in the green stockings which her shorter skirt displayed. The War had given some women the chance to get out of their houses and they had jumped at it.

She settled into the wooden-slatted seat against the window and looked out at the shuttered darkness of Anderson's Royal Polytechnic. In its wide entrance, a one-legged man, his shabby trouser-leg pinned round the stump, was playing a melodeon. She heard the plaintive notes floating up, 'There's a long, long trail awinding. . .' A sad song. But life was sad for so many people now, with anxiety and often bereavement and always men marching away, some never to come back. She thought of their terrible cheerfulness as they swung along, their poignant songs, 'Keep the home fires burning . . .'

How desolate the war-time Glasgow streets looked in the early evening! There was litter blowing about on the pavements, swirling in the puddles in the gutters. May was a chancy month: it could be sunny one day, raining the next. The people hurrying along had grim faces. Had there ever been a happy time?

Perhaps because she had been talking of Lizzie and Ernest to Mr Ledbridge, her mind went back to the many Sunday afternoons she had spent at the Hall. How pleasant it always was there, what an aura of happiness Ernest and Lizzie created, even on that particular afternoon two years ago, the first Sunday after War had been declared. Lizzie was the last person to let a war spoil tea in the garden.

She saw her in her mind's eye, serene, beautiful, copper-haired, seated at the lace-covered table with its fine china and silver spirit kettle; Ernest near her on a deck-chair, dapper as always, Jonty sprawled on the lawn at his feet. A family portrait, as if she had arranged it herself. Although he was Lizzie's son by her first marriage, Nigel Jonathan Crawford, he and his step-father were the best of friends. 'I say, Ernest – ' she remembered the Crawford elegance although still a schoolboy – 'look what Bottomley says in this rag . . .'

She wouldn't dare say 'Maevy' to Mother, nor, indeed, 'Isobel' to Aunt Isobel. They'd been there too, seated together on an upright wooden seat, having primly dismissed the offer of deck-chairs, long skirts arranged with decorum, parasols propped, flower-laden hats securely anchored . . .

She looked out of the streaming window beside her. They were passing York Street where McGrath's opulent offices were, and where Mother went every day. Strange, when she had just been thinking of her . . . 'My right-hand man,' Ernest called her. Everyone respected Mother, a well-known figure in the Movement. When she had more time, she would join, too.

The tram-car gathered speed as the crowds thinned; now the driver was careering through Anderston with the Finnieston Docks on the left. City slums always seemed worse than the poorer quarters of a village like Sholton, like Colliers Row, where, unbelievably, Grandmother had brought up her family. A far cry to the Hall with its spacious lawns and razor-edged flower-beds, its tall chestnuts making a haven for Lizzie's Sunday tea-parties . . . her mind went back again, lulled by the gentle motion of the tram-car which had slowed down. You had to be careful of the children playing on the streets . . .

She remembered Ernest flicking over the pages of *John Bull*. 'When it gets to pillorying a poor German because he sells Waldstein pianos . . . it'll be the Royal Family next.'

'At least Kitchener isn't a muck-raker.' Ernest and Mother thought alike.

'Nor James Dalrymple, the Tramway manager. He has illuminated tram-cars going about the town, and bands and parades . . .' It was amazing how Aunt Isobel had found her voice since Uncle John had died.

Jonty was not to be left out. 'We had a debate about it at school and everybody wanted to go.'

'Oh, Jonty! All those shining young men going out to be killed, perhaps. And from Eton, too.'

And Mother bristling. 'They're no better than our HLI. Do you know their marching song, Jonty? "Ta-ta, Bella, I'll no' say goodbye, Although I'm leavin' Glesca wi' the HLI." There now!'

'Oh, jolly good! "Ta-ta, Bella, I'll no' say goodbye . . .".'

Ellie giggled, looking out of the tram-car window to hide it. That upper-class English voice of his! She sobered when she thought of Lizzie's face when Jonty had said, 'Anyhow, I bet they all think it's glorious to die for their country, like my father . . .'

Where was she now? Ah, yes, coming to the gushet of Argyle Street and Sauchiehall Street, with her Alma Mater up there on Gilmorehill. Hard work, but there had been great *tares* . . . And Colin Thomson at nights in his darkened motor, new feelings, strange excitement, and the guilt when she had crept into the house.

There were two children dancing along the pavement hand in hand, reminding her of Annabel and Kit, Ernest and Lizzie's children, scrawny and badly-dressed where they were plump and kitted out by R. W. Forsyth. She remembered how they had come running across the lawn that Sunday: 'Mammy! Mammy! Jane's crying because her Billy Boy has been called up!'

It had killed for her the pleasure of the sunny garden,

the company. She shouldn't be here, she should be in her room at Hillhead studying, or in the wards of the Royal. She had to be qualified as a surgeon first. She had to put Colin out of her mind. *Then* she could join up. When she saw Lizzie coming back from comforting Jane, shady-hatted, white-organdied, she had waved and gone to meet her. She would ask her if she would like to go for a walk.

Even when you were twenty yards away you could tell Lizzie was a seductive woman, just as you knew Mother wasn't, never would be. Mother with her proud walk was Today's woman, Lizzie's walk proclaimed that she was Ernest's.

They had walked past the stables which were quite grand, an ensemble of courtyard cottages with mullioned windows and rounded towers, stone archway, parapet crown – 'I've got plans for these,' Lizzie, the planner, had pointed, then they had climbed the stile and gone across the field where the soft wind blew cool on their faces.

'I sometimes envy you your happy marriage, Lizzie.'

'Don't. Colin wasn't the right man for you, Kieran probably is. Colin was self-centred, Kieran is caring. Look how he has supported his mother through Uncle James' long illness . . .'

'Why did you say "probably"?'

'Because you seem able to wait.' That enchanting smile . . .

They had skirted Brow Farm and gone through the wood to emerge from the gloom of the trees at the old monastery, with its standing walls of rough stone and its tower with the broken steps running round it. And as they threw themselves down on the short dry turf, Lizzie, who could always surprise, had said, 'Did you know this was a trysting place of Grandmother's and Nigel's father?'

'When she was still married to Grandfather McGrath?'

'Yes, an illicit affair!' Her eyes had sparkled with

mischief. 'But, of course, she did marry Lord Crawford when Grandfather died!'

She had been lost in admiration. Trust Grandmother. Even when she was no longer with them she could still surprise you. 'It was our favourite place, too, Nigel's and mine,' Lizzie had said. 'Knowing that they had been here before us gave an edge to our lovemaking!' Oh, Lizzie . . .

How her mind was wandering! Where were they now? She looked across the aisle of the tram-car and recognized the bulk of the Western Infirmary. She was smugly glad she had done her training at the Royal and that they had kept her on. It had been Mother's and Father's place, and Joseph Lister's too, she told herself, Father's mentor. But two years ago she had been less dedicated. She had thought more of love, lost love, and love offered but refused . . .

'Did they . . .?' she had said, turning on her stomach and burying her face in the warm grass, 'Did they . . .?' And Lizzie had hummed a tantalizing little song, looking away, smiling. Love. Love . . . she had thought. Nigel and Lizzie lay here, and before that Maeve, my grandmother, and Alastair Crawford, her lover. She had pressed her body into the ground and wished for a tempestuous love, wished there was no war, no indecision . . .

It was then, as if to shake her out of her maundering, that Lizzie had dropped her bombshell – that she was planning to turn the Hall into a hospital. She had sat up, astonished, saying stupidly, 'A hospital, a *war* hospital! I never guessed!'

'Well, you're only in Sholton occasionally with your own flat in Hillhead, and you're so busy coming out for a surgeon . . . Oh, Ellie,' the peals of laughter seemed to be echoing in her ears, 'Do you remember that silly joke about the Royal and the man in a white coat?'

'No . . .?'

'It's about a woman who was visiting a patient. And there was a man in a white coat at the door. So she said to him, "Are you a doctor coming out for a surgeon?" And he said, "No, I'm a painter coming out for a pint!"'

She laughed aloud as she remembered and, realizing where she was, put her hand over her mouth. 'No, I'm a painter. . .' If she wasn't careful with all this day-dreaming she would miss her stop. But, they had been *helpless* . . .!

Suddenly, with a loud, double 'ting-ting!' the tram-car stopped. There was silence for a second, then a loud clatter of voices around her. One, louder than the rest, was so close that she jumped in her seat. 'In the name o' Goad,' the voice said, 'whit is it?'

If she had been laughing, it hadn't been noticed. People were craning their heads at the windows, and those on the opposite side had crossed the aisle to get a better view. She looked down on the street to see what the commotion was, fearful, yet bracing herself. She might have to help . . .

A woman, wearing a shawl, was shaking a small boy like a rat, and shouting so loudly that the words reached Ellie. 'A *telt* ye, didn't a? A *telt* ye a hunner times . . .!'

The tram-driver was climbing down from his platform, majestically, gauntlet-gloved. Ellie thought his face looked white under the green-visored cap. He put an admonishing hand on the woman's shoulder. 'Don't kill him, Missus, after me savin' his life!' He looked around and upwards as if making sure of his audience before he went on. 'But . . . let that be a lesson to you. Don't let him run wild if you want him to grow up to be a sodger!' There was a murmur of appreciation on the upper deck.

'Aye, aye, Mister, a will that. The wee devil! Ye jist hev to turn yer back . . .' The woman abased herself to

Authority. She scooped up the boy and huddled him in her shawl. His small face peered from its folds like that of a gnome, a tearful gnome.

'Puir wee soul,' a woman behind Ellie said. 'A hope she disnae gie him a good leatherin' when she get him hame. He's had a big enough fright.'

'Not to mention the driver,' Ellie said.

'Presence o' mind there.' A man beside her took the floor. 'Banged his fit on the coo-catcher, that driver did. A ca' that presence o' mind.' He sat down suddenly as the tram-car gave a peremptory 'ting!' and moved off with a jerk. Ellie heard the conductress shouting, 'Next stoap Byres Road!'

She was suddenly tired. When she got into the flat she would have a bath, then make a light meal and read the paper. The fighting would still be going on at Verdun, she supposed, and then there was Ireland. She had seen a placard outside a newsagent in High Street. 'Rebels Executed After Easter Rising.' The sooner the French hospital sent for her, the better.

If she could keep her eyes open she would write to Kieran. In his last letter he had said his father was sinking. Poor Uncle James. He was a much-loved father to all his family – the two daughters, Emily Barthe in Paris and Victoria near him in Wanapeake, and his sons George and Kieran who were also with him. And there were the Vogel and Murray-Hyslop grandchildren. It was a pity Ernest was so far away.

It was a pity, too, that she couldn't say to Kieran when she wrote that she would marry him. But it was no good. The passion wasn't there, that passion Grandmother had known with *her* Kieran and Lord Crawford, Lizzie twice also – so like Grandmother – with Jonty's father and now Ernest. It had been there between Colin and herself, however briefly.

2

Wolf House was very quiet because it was a house of death. That was how Mrs Vanaressi put it to Irma, the Polish maid. Being Italian herself she had a fine feeling for death. She liked the thought of white flowers and black crêpe and much weeping. If you made a friend of death there was a kind of comfort in it, of being part of the Universe.

She well remembered when Guiseppe, her husband, had died, how she had wept non-stop for three days, and the refreshment of it, and how at the end of the three days she had dried her eyes and said to the sorrowing family around her, 'Now, that's enough. Back to work.' And how she had found this wonderful place with Mr and Mrs Murray-Hyslop and had known a quiet kind of happiness ever since.

She had two families now, and her three sons doing well in New York City, her married daughter in Wanapeake, and her employers, and without asking questions but being quietly observant one could have a rich and satisfying life. And where in all the world would one have found two better people to work for than Mr and Mrs Murray-Hyslop, she with her beauty and tranquillity and he with his drollery? Had he been Italian, that wry smile of his would have been the equivalent of a pinch on the bottom. Ah, it was sad to see such a man of fun fighting for breath and unable to joke any more.

'Irma,' she said sternly, 'do not stand there as if there was nothing to be done. Miss Emily will be here soon with her husband from Paris – that is to say, Monsieur and Madame Barthe.'

'What about their daughter with the interesting name?' Irma patted a dark plait. 'Will she come too?'

'Giselle? No, I understand from Madame that she is *incinta*. On you go.' Mrs Vanaressi waved her rolling pin. 'I have much baking and cooking to be done. The house will be full soon – Miss Victoria and her husband, and Master George and his wife, and their bambinos. Madame loves them.'

'Shall I take Master Kieran and Madame some tea before I start?'

'No, no, it is for me to do that. On you go.' Yes, it was for her to do. Almost a member of the family. She knew how to conduct herself in the presence of death, moving silently but showing her sympathy in every gesture. She only hoped the tears would not escape from her eyes and spoil her composure, especially with Madame so brave. Like that mother of hers with the ramrod back and eyes like the Calabrian sea in summer, and that extra something in them which seemed to say that life was a joke . . . what a character, what a loss!

'Yes, Mrs Vanaressi?' Kate Murray-Hyslop looked up. She and Kieran were sitting in James' dressing-room where she had had two easy chairs placed. The door into the bedroom was open. She could see James' head on the pillow and hear the painful stertorous breathing which all the doctor's sedatives could not subdue. 'We must try and make his passing as easy as possible for him,' he had said.

'I brought you some tea and some of those almond tarts you like, still hot from the oven.'

'It's kind of you, but, no . . .'

Kieran interrupted her. 'You must be sensible and eat

something, Mother. The family will be here soon and you need your strength for that.'

Almond tarts and my dear husband dying next door, slipping away from me . . . 'Yes, we'd both like some tea, Mrs Vanaressi. Just leave the tray on that little table. Thank you.' How black her hair was against the white of her collar and she must be over sixty now. Perhaps the oiliness . . . Why did one have such irrelevant thoughts?

Mrs Vanaressi straightened. 'Would you like me to bring your shawl from the closet, Madame?'

'Yes, please. It has gone a bit chilly.' She had seen the black eyes swimming in tears, the sternness of the mouth because of the effort of control.

'Is there anything else I can do for you?' The woman had placed the shawl round her shoulders. Such kindness . . .

'No, thanks. I'm sure you've plenty to do downstairs. You've enough food? Cookies for the little ones?'

'Plenty, Madame.'

'I engaged her when we first came here,' she said when Mrs Vanaressi had gone. 'Agnes was poorly – your father's first wife.'

'I know.'

'She asked me to call her that. We became good friends.'

'You're good friends with everyone. Now, drink that,' he handed her a cup, 'and have one of the famous tarts because I'm going to have one. She used to roll the same paste for me to make little soldier men. . .' They were both harping back because they couldn't face the present.

'Kieran,' she said, 'I want to talk to you before the others come. Your father has left you the house in his will.'

'Ah, but it's yours first and always, you know that. I have the apartment in New York. And I might . . .'

'Enlist? I know. I don't think I'll be spending much time here either . . .'

'Why?'

'You know Lizzie has turned over Sholton Hall to the Red Cross?'

'Yes, Ellie told me in a letter. It's just like Lizzie. She has a busy brain.' You should know, she thought, you were in love with her once. Was it inadequacy that he couldn't see beyond his cousins, or . . . how could one hope ever to understand one's children?

'I'll go back with Ernest and Lizzie to help in her hospital, after . . .' I'm talking in a dream, she thought. Reality is in the next room. 'Maevy will have me at Braidholme. I started as a children's nurse, I might as well end nursing soldiers.' She still couldn't accept it.

'Don't talk about ends,' he said, 'a beautiful young woman like you.' He was like her father when he smiled, that gentle man, that gentleman . . .

'Ach . . .' She got up and went into the bedroom, gazed down at her sleeping husband. Dr Melvin, Dr Studebaker's young successor, had said that his breathing would quieten towards the end. It was he who had suggested that she and Kieran should watch from the adjoining room so as not to use up the air . . . the young were factual. She stood, a pillar of grief, watching the heaving chest. Agony was sharp like a sword. Her teeth cut into her lower lip. Pain worse than this was impossible to imagine. When she felt able to speak she went back to Kieran.

'How was he?' His uplifted face seemed to reflect her suffering.

'Peaceful, but his chest . . . So uncomplaining for so long! "Must get that young doctor to fit me up with a new pair of bellows," he'd say. He would have liked to see you married, son, and bringing up a family here.'

'There's only Ellie.' He turned away from her. 'But you know what she's like. The War comes first with her. She can't think beyond that, or doesn't want to . . .'

'She's young yet.' James had once said, 'It's a paper romance, all letters. Wouldn't have satisfied us. Perhaps the War will end sooner than we think.' She didn't think so. The terrible slaughter at Verdun was still going on, and the Somme offensive had just begun.

'They need us in with them! What's President Wilson thinking of? Is he too busy with Pancho Villa? I thought if the sinking of the *Lusitania* didn't convince him, the gas at Ypres might . . .'

'Shh.' Her head went up. 'Not so loud. I think he's stirring.' She put down her cup.

'Let me go.'

'No, you finish your tea. You were up all night.' She braced herself. 'Oh, Kieran,' she wanted to say, 'Don't you leave me too,' but in the end you couldn't lean on anyone. Or at the end.

The room was quiet when she went in, too quiet. She listened for a moment to the quietness, the sword turning in her breast. She went swiftly to the side of the bed, knelt down and took his hand. She saw his lips move.

'Yes, my darling,' she said, 'it's Kate. I'll never leave you.' His hand was cold, the nails blue, the pulse flickered only feebly. 'I'm here. Don't be afraid.'

His head moved. He was looking at her. His eyes, although clouded, had love in them. Only death would dowse that. 'Speak to me, Kate,' she had to bend close to hear the whisper, 'to ease the p . . .' She didn't catch the last word. It wasn't 'pain' . . .

She stroked his hand softly. What had the word been? 'The good years we've had together, isn't that so? And our lovely and loving family who became mine as well as yours and Agnes's, along with our own dear son, Kieran.

And the grandchildren. We've been lucky, haven't we?' She saw his head nod slowly, the faint smile.

'I remember you in Scotland when I first came as a nursemaid to your house in Blythswood Square. I'd never been in such a grand house with its cornices and its crystal chandeliers, but you know Mother! Said she was only coming along to see if it was good enough for me!' She saw the faint smile again.

'The children loved you coming up to the nursery. You could always make them laugh with your droll remarks. But I saw you as young and anxious with an ailing wife and four children, and that's when my love for you began. Oh, but I'm tiring you, dear heart!' She saw the greyness of his face. His hand moved under hers.

'You want me to go on?' Not 'pain'. The word hadn't been 'pain'. 'Do you remember my navy-blue dress with its white collar and cuffs? I never felt that to wear a uniform was anything but a privilege. And the girls with their white frilled pinnies and shiny black buttoned boots, the boys in their Norfolk jackets . . .' She stroked his hair, subduing the anguish. 'Parting'? Could the word have been 'parting'?

'When I used to visit Mother in Colliers Row, what a sensation we caused, arriving in your carriage. "The little gentry!" And Mother, not a bit bowled over because *she* was gentry herself, would dispense tea in the kitchen with its stone floor, the deal table covered with an Irish lace-trimmed cloth . . .' She waited, saw the eyelids flicker.

'You loved her too, didn't you? Oh, the parting was sad, leaving her and my gentle father in Scotland, and yet nothing would have separated me from you. I was a wicked girl. I loved you for years illicitly, Mr James Murray-Hyslop, did you know that?' He beckoned her with a movement of his head, raised a finger to his mouth and pointed. She laid her lips on his and felt their coldness. They moved faintly. What passion there had been in that mouth, but the small movement said as much as before. His love for Agnes, he had once told her, had been a boyish love; he had taken her in his maturity, the best of times.

'But you made an honest woman out of me, didn't you? Not that there was ever any hanky-panky, even after poor Agnes died.' A smile twitched his mouth. He'd taught her his light way of speaking. Ernest had it. 'We'll have no ponderosity in this house,' had been one of his favourite sayings, making her laugh at the concocted word.

'Then the right time came as I think we both knew it would. You went to see the girls off to Paris to that finishing school and drove through the night to be back with me. You were so pale and tired and dishevelled. I shall never forget what you said to me.'

She bent forward and laid her cheek against his. It was colder surely than his cold lips had been, or perhaps it was the contrast with her cheek, hot with unshed tears. 'You said,' she turned her mouth towards his ear, 'you said, "I had only one thought in my mind and that was to get home, because therein lay my happiness, the only cure for my desolation . . .".'

She lay against his cheek, feeling that word ache in her, feeling the yawning darkness of grief, and loss. Bear it. Show him you can bear it. It will ease his passing. 'Passing'. That was the word.

She raised her head and smiled, saw his eyes on her cloud, the brief nod of his head as his spirit left him.

Behind her she heard the soft scuffling of people filling the room, the murmurs, knew they were all there. She could imagine them, like one of those family portraits with the canvas full of faces, and the proud progenitor in the centre . . . on his deathbed. James, with his pawkiness, would have appreciated that.

She hadn't been a great procreator herself – only Kieran James, the best of sons, but unlucky in love so far. Ellie was Maevy's daughter, as resolute and dedicated. It would be a long time, if ever, before she chose the soft option. She was too like her parents for that. She must get up . . .

'Mother. . .' It was Kieran's hand on her shoulder. 'Could you try to rise?' His voice was tender. 'Mother, Father's gone.' She moved her head from side to side, resisting him.

She was making an exhibition of herself. She got to her feet with his help, staggered once and righted herself. 'I'm trying not to weep, Kieran.' It must be a poor smile. 'I can't take it in . . .'

'I know.' He was weeping. He had a gentle heart.

She turned and saw them all as a blur. 'I'm glad you were all here in time . . . to pay your respects.' She saw Emily's bright painted face masked by her black veil – always a little too much, Emily. Giselle, that lovely daughter of hers, had got it right, even to marrying the right man, Terence, the namesake and son of her brother in Ireland. Lizzie was here – she knew by that expensive perfume which was masking the sickroom smells – with Ernest. And dear, reliable Patrick, her other brother, with Maria . . .

Maria, accustomed to sorrow, came forward. 'Come downstairs, Kate. You're exhausted.' Her arm encircled her shoulders. Maria was at home in rooms of death: first that poor little handicapped child, Mary, then Gaylord . . .

But it couldn't be! Emerging from the blur – Mother, a young, slender Mother, coming forward to meet her as she had done in that kitchen in Colliers Row so long ago; the same flaming hair, the same deeply blue eyes, the usual radiant smile subdued by the sorrowing expression on the lovely face, 'Oh, Aunt Kate!' She felt the embrace, 'I'm so sorry. You'll miss him so much.'

Her vision cleared. 'Ginny,' she said, she must have been lightheaded for a moment, 'it was good of you to come.' She turned to the girl's mother. 'Yes, Maria, I'll come downstairs.'

3

Maevy was reading the *Glasgow Herald* as she travelled in the train to the city that Saturday morning. It's certain carnage, she thought. Those brave lads, and every one a volunteer . . . She raised her head and looked out at the dreary industrial landscape as they crossed the bridge, as desecrated as any Picardy battlefield, except that it was in the name of 'progress'. Crawford's Iron and Steel Works hadn't spread its tentacles as far as this until Sir Edward Hamilton got his hands on it, worming his way into Lord Crawford's affections when the poor soul was ill, and cutting Jonty out. 'Progress', she thought, but was McGrath's entirely guiltless with its heavy lorries thundering about the countryside?

Fourteen years since she had started to work with them during the Boer War, and now they were in the midst of another one, far more terrible. Now it was Ellie going away, not Charlie. But he would have been proud of her, as she was. No regrets: Mother had taught her that. Live for the present, but what a present! The losses of the French Army at Verdun were bad enough, 250,000 Frenchmen killed, but now this. Where was it she had read that the British would fight on to the last drop of other people's blood?

Politics and war. You couldn't separate them. Men dying by the thousands and McGrath's making more money than they had ever done. She remembered that champion of the carters, Hugh Lyon, saying that the 1913 Strike was the making of their society all over the country.

Would there be further strikes while many of them were laying down their lives for their comrades?

'The Big Push Began on the Somme Today,' she read. 'Severe Casualties Feared.' And, underneath, 'France's promised support drained by the savage five-month German attack on Verdun . . .' Ellie would be in the thick of it any minute.

If only the Americans would come in and turn the tide. The sinking of the *Lusitania* last year, Kate had said in a letter, was the last straw. Over a hundred Americans had lost their lives. But she had been wrong. And now James was dead and she was here in Sholton helping in Lizzie's hospital and living at Braidholme. 'It's not called Braidholme now,' Isobel had said in her new, pawky fashion, 'it's the Widows' Retreat.' Kieran, as she had expected, had joined an American Field Ambulance and was stationed at Neuilly Hospital in Paris. What would Ellie think about that?

Still, it was none of her business. Ellie had always known her own mind, except when she'd been moonstruck over Colin Thomson who couldn't be compared with Kieran. Her sadness went. The three sisters, all together as they'd been in that little house at Colliers Row so many years ago! There was a rare bond between women, as she had discovered in the Movement. There they had been sisters under the skin, now it would be real sisters. They would work together and laugh together and not talk too much about the old days, but make the most of the present and look forward to the future.

Aye, she thought, getting up as the train drew into the smoky murk of Central Station, we'll have some rare *tares* together, but what wouldn't I give to have Charlie back, my own dear love.

She walked through the forecourt of the station and hailed a taxi in Gordon Street. She had learnt not to be penny-pinching in the last few years – or rather, Ernest had taught her. 'Take a taxi to York Street, Maevy,' he had admonished her often. 'It can be quite a step on a cold day. It will be all the same in a hundred years.' True enough, and they were making enough money.

It was a damp, drizzling day, the kind that dirtied your shoes and stockings with sticky Glasgow mud and sometimes the hem of your skirt, although she had taken to wearing them shorter in the last year or two. After all, there was a war on, and McGrath's even had women driving some of their vans.

This was a Women's War. They had rushed into industry and the services like lemmings to the sea, delighted to get out of their houses and take the place of their husbands fighting for them. And to be earning money. Some of the girls in the factories spent it on themselves – 'the fur coat and no knickers brigade', she had heard them called!

She got into the taxi, smiling at the thought, and gave the office address. 'Aye, right y'are, Missus.' she liked the man's admiring look. It was one of the bonuses of being out in the world working. What would he say if she told him she had a daughter who would soon be going out to France as a surgeon? Her anxiety was momentarily dampened by her pride.

She sailed through the main office on her way to the board room, smiling to the 'good mornings' coming from right and left. She would never have the beauty and charm of her mother, but they seemed to like her. 'We can always rely on you, Mrs McNab,' one of the clerks had said to her. It wasn't as good as a magical presence, but it was better than nothing.

Ernest greeted her, correct in his dark, well-cut suit and crisp white shirt, his hair sleeked close to his skull – brown, thin hair like Annabel's. His mischievous smile was in place. 'Here's the lady we were waiting for to bring some glamour to our dull lives.' He drew out her chair with a flourish.

'You talk a lot of rubbish, Ernest,' she said, seating herself and looking round. 'Good morning, everybody. A dreich day.'

'Aye, that it is,' Dan Johnson, Tom's son said.

'*You're* looking chirpy in spite of it!' Even his rimless spectacles were shining. Certainly his face was. She saw him blush, to her surprise, a rare event.

'And so he should be,' Ernest said, 'he's just got himself engaged to Ruby Carter.'

'Have you, Dan? Well, I couldn't be more pleased!' She got up to shake him warmly by the hand. 'Congratulations!' She sat down again. Ruby was the younger of the two Carter girls, she remembered, thirty-five to her sister's thirty-eight, if you could call that young. She chided herself, looking round at the other members of the board. 'Some of you won't remember Bob Carter, but he and Dan's father were the two stalwarts of McGraths in the old days. My mother and father used to say they couldn't have done without them.' There were nodded heads round the table, pleased expressions.

'Now to business,' Ernest said crisply. 'The Minutes, if you please, Mr Richardson.'

There was no doubt the War had saved McGrath's bacon, Maevy thought as she listened, first to the Minutes read by Jack Richardson, and then to Ernest's report. Certainly they had lost a lot of the younger carters to the Forces, but on the other hand the carting industry was no longer based on local needs and local outlooks, and carters and motormen were at a premium.

'Although the parcel delivery trade has declined,' Ernest was saying, 'and our morale slumped badly in the early years of the War, we have made up in other directions. As in every war, there has been a great amount of movement both in goods and people, and this has meant a steady demand on our heavy vehicles, such as transporting aircraft frames.

'And now to an important, and I might say, historic matter. . .' He paused and looked round the table, his glance resting on Maevy for a second. 'You all know that for some time a merger has been on the cards with our two competitors,' he smiled, 'Bannister and Craig, and Naylor's.

'I think you all realize how carting has changed, expanded and become more complex. There is, for instance, the question of affiliation with the Labour Party, which was first raised in 1914. There is a gradual loss of the . . . patriarchal element. The men have become more aware of their rights. Then, our firm has become, shall we say, unwieldy. Because of the numerous outlets we are in danger of chasing our own tails, or chasing the same business as our competitors . . .' There were nods around the table.

'The question of this merger has come up before, but I think you'll agree that our experience during the War has clarified our ideas. And there has been a further development.' He lifted a letter from the table. No one moved. All eyes were fixed on him. Trust Ernest, Maevy thought, he's got what he wanted.

'I have here in writing an offer from these two firms that, in the event of amalgamation, I should be chairman of the joint board. Perhaps you'd read it and pass it on, Maevy.' He slid it across the table. There was no doubt about it. She passed it on and waited in the silence while it circulated. She judged by the murmurs that everyone was impressed.

'Just a point, Ernest,' she said. 'If you were chairman, would that assure us of a finger in the collective pie?'

'Yes, and I think I could pull out the plums as well. I would make it a condition that we continue with the heavy carting during the War, that to be reviewed when hostilities cease; but the household removals, shipping and travel would remain with us. As transport improves I see a great increase in travel, for pleasure. As for shipping, with Patrick in America that is definitely our concern. I know he wouldn't hear of relinquishing it.'

'Have you approached him?' Dan asked.

'Yes, a long time ago. I know his views. If we can keep the shipping he's agreeable to the merger. Young Robert, Terence's boy, feels the same. That's his forte. And for myself, I would insist on household removals staying with us. I see great possibilities in that direction.'

'We have that big place at Parkhead,' Maevy said, 'there's plenty of room for storage there.'

'Yes, that was a wise move of yours.' His eyes congratulated her. 'With so many people moving around we need storage facilities. Later it could be converted into refrigerated space. Or even auction rooms. Some of the furniture will never be claimed, more's the pity.'

There was a rustle of surprise. She knew the board's opinion of Ernest. Sandy Gregg had said to her once, 'He's that quick he'll meet himself coming back one of these days.' As if he knew she was thinking of him, she saw the man's hand go up.

'Would the parcel trade go?'

'Yes, Mr Gregg.' Ernest nodded. 'It's never been lucrative and we need a large fleet. We've tended to concentrate on the heavier vehicles, and in any case we never got much credit for the smaller runs with most of the companies and the Railway insisting on having their own name on the vans and carts. One of the conditions would be that where any member of the merger has sole monopoly they would trade under their own name, but if it's a joint effort we'd trade under Globe Express Deliveries.' His mouth went up at the side. 'That would please Patrick on the other side of the world.' He sat down. 'Talk amongst yourselves for a minute. There's no rush.'

John Drummond, sitting next to Maevy, said, 'It's a sad day to think of McGrath's going the way of all flesh. What would your mother and father have said?'

She turned to him, an old friend of her brother Terence who was now happily out of all this decision-making, living the life of Larry in Ireland with a woman he loved, and doing what he liked most, breeding horses. 'Father wouldn't have liked it, John, but then he didn't even like the thought of motor or steam. Horses were his first and last love.'

'Aye, his last. He lost his life saving them in those stables at Sholton.'

She nodded, sighed. 'But, Mother. She was a different kettle of fish. She wouldn't have minded. She was forward-looking. She had no time for nostalgia. Besides, nothing stands still. My father fought for the men over truck – you're too young maybe to remember that – but now the men have organized themselves and can do their own fighting.'

'Bob Cranston still talks about your father. He wrought with him in the pit.'

'Yes, he did. Over eighty now, and still going strong. No, it's changed days. After the War they'll demand more than ever. And it's *time* they'll demand as well as money. Leisure time. You'll see.'

'That sounds like Arthur, Bob's son, talking. Rights for the individual.'

'And I believe in it.'

Ernest called them to order. They took votes. Seventy-five per cent wanted the merger, one hundred per cent were in favour of Ernest being chairman if it went through.

Maevy had a word with him after the others had gone. 'Are you happy about it, Ernest?' she said.

'Yes. I've no regrets. You can drive too many horses. I think we'll do very nicely with what we've got.'

'You said "horses". There will be precious few of them, I'm afraid. That's sad.'

'Yes. But who can say what it will be like after the War when the men come back. There will be unrest, Maevy. We've all been shaken up too much. There will be disappointment, frustration and unemployment, too many men chasing too few jobs . . .'

'Provided they aren't all killed. Have you seen the papers?'

His face was grim. 'Yes, I have. I can tell you, I don't feel so happy about being chairman of Globe Express Deliveries with all that slaughter going on.'

'Still, you've always taken a cool look at things.'

'You're right. I try to be objective, and I've no desire to be scattered needlessly amongst the poppies. Does that sound too cool? But, if you've something to offer, maybe you shouldn't hold back.'

She looked at him, puzzled. 'What do you mean?'

'Thinking aloud.' He smiled, shaking his head. 'Shouldn't do it. Well, I expect like me you've a hundred things to do . . .' He paused. 'There's something I want to say, Maevy. Believe it or not, I was thinking of you in this merger.'

She laughed. 'Thinking of me!'

'Oh, yes, I was. You're very dear to us, Lizzie and me. You should be beginning to take things a little easier now. You don't spare yourself. Look at the fuss you made about taking a taxi.'

'You've cured me of that. I'm beginning to get quite well known amongst the drivers.'

'I'm pleased to hear it. But Lizzie tells me about the sterling work you're doing at the Hall, and that you've done night duty as well when they're stuck.'

'Is that so? Well, there's a little poem I'd like you to say to that Lizzie of yours. "Tell-tale tit, your tongue shall be slit, And all the little puppy dogs shall have a little bit."'

He laughed. 'I'll tell her.' He surprised her by bending and kissing her on the cheek. 'Who said I wasn't sentimental?' he said.

She stood, watching him going away with his swift step.

4

Ellie was spending her last weekend at home before she went off to France. After morning church she, her mother, Aunt Isobel and Aunt Kate walked to the Hall where they had been invited for lunch. They were greeted downstairs by Lizzie, crisply beautiful, her copper hair burnished and shining against the white overall she was wearing. 'Here's the contingent from Braidholme,' she said, giving each one a warm embrace. 'My goodness, Ellie,' she said, 'you'll be a tonic for the men. A sight for sore eyes.'

'What about *you*, sailing about like a queen!'

They stood talking at the entrance to the drawing-room, now converted into a ward, with eight beds down each side, neat with their red blankets folded on top of the white counterpanes. The long windows were open, the gauze curtains moved in the light breeze, she could smell the summer scents from the garden.

'A full complement of patients,' Ellie said.

'Yes, and more on the way, we've been told. Every hospital has been warned to stand ready. The casualties are being shipped home by the boat-load.'

'Oh, the poor souls,' Isobel said. 'They say some are only out for a day before they're back.'

'They're lucky if they're back and alive.' Maevy was taking off her coat and hanging it up. She looked every bit as crisp as Lizzie, Ellie thought with pride. Any soldier would be the better for being nursed by her.

She noticed that some of the patients were propped up on pillows, but others were lying down, their heads turned away. She knew that attitude well, a withdrawal from the world. Once that had been conquered, recovery would begin. You weren't long in medicine before you saw how strong was the influence of mind over body.

'It makes a lovely ward,' she said. 'And look at that floor, polished to perfection.' The Persian rugs had been taken up and stowed away, revealing a shining expanse of wood.

'We've a small army of Sholton women who come in every day,' Lizzie told her. 'I had no difficulty in finding volunteers.'

Maevy nodded. 'Sholton's rallied, there's no doubt. Miss Coates at the school has the children knitting for them and writing letters. They've each adopted a soldier.'

'It's a pity we have to have wars to bring out the good in people,' Isobel said. 'Well, I'll away to the office. I expect there's plenty to do.'

'There's a pile of paper-work.' Lizzie laughed. 'It seems to grow when you turn your back, Aunt Isobel.'

'That's fine. The better the day the better the deed.' She scurried away, her thin body lanced forward in her eagerness.

'Just look at her,' Maevy said, 'she wouldn't see even the Kaiser in her way!' They laughed.

'The flowers are beautiful, Lizzie,' Ellie said. 'I expect you do them.' She pointed to a large crystal vase of delphiniums and roses.

'Yes. I have to keep old James McFarlane happy. He's only got a wee lad to help him now – the rest are called up – but he's anxious to do his bit.'

'I remember being sent to the greenhouses by your father-in-law,' Maevy's face was soft, 'to get some orchids for Mother. It was before they were married. They told Charlie to go with me. A ploy . . . Well, come on, Kate, we shouldn't be standing here gassing . . .'

'Who's gassing?' Kate smiled at her sister.

'How are you feeling, Aunt?' Lizzie's voice was tender. 'We're not giving you much time to rest.'

'I didn't come to rest, Lizzie. I could have done that at home. And sat thinking about James all day. You're doing me a service.'

'Well, there are more beds to be put up, and there's a nurse off sick . . .'

'Come on, then.' She hung up her coat beside Maevy's. 'You be the boss.' She smiled at her sister. 'You always are.'

'What a thing to say, Kate! You've got cheeky since you went to America.'

'They're lovely together,' Lizzie said to Ellie as they stood watching them walking down the ward. 'They're happy, the three of them, at Braidholme, like returning to their childhood, but armed with their maturity. Kate and Isobel never miss a day here, and most evenings your mother looks in, as well as weekends.'

'You're a good organizer. You make them feel wanted. I expect if you're a widow it's grand to *feel* wanted.'

'Yes, that's the sum of it. Come on, then, we'll go to the other ward.' She said, as they walked through the hall, 'You're sharp, Ellie, always were. I *have* found that I have a bit of talent for organizing. I can see an overall plan . . . I don't think when this War's over we'll ever live in this place again, as a family. Now, here we are. Come in and give the men a treat.'

'As if I could hold a candle to you!'

'Will you listen to yourself! You're like one of old McFarlane's roses this morning. *My* petals are beginning to fall . . .' She raised her voice, 'Good morning, everybody!' Ellie stood beside her, seeing the heads turn.

The men in this ward, formerly the dining-room, were up, some hobbling about on crutches, others manoeuvring themselves about the floor in wheelchairs. Their blue suits and red ties gave them, even with their infirmities, a look of uniformity and smartness.

'Come and speak to two of my favourites.' She led Ellie to one of the large windows where two men were seated in wheelchairs. 'Now, then,' she said when they reached them, 'here's a special treat for you. My young cousin, Miss McNab, a fully-fledged surgeon, come to say hello. This is Jock Galbraith, and this is Willie Rintoul.'

Jock Galbraith, a curly-headed youngster who looked no more than eighteen, laughed and looked at his friend. 'We've had enough of surgeons, haven't we, Wullie?'

'Aye, enough.' The other man's voice had bitterness in it.

Neither of them had any legs. They had been amputated above the knee, and the stumps stuck out like infantile limbs in front of them, uncovered. The patient and the onlooker had to get used to them.

'When do you get your artificial ones?' she asked them. No pity must show in the eyes. That would be an insult. She herself would be hacking off arms and legs before long . . . The awful futility of war struck her, made her sick to her stomach. She wanted to use the ugly language she had often heard in the wards.

'When they've got room for us at Erskine,' Jock Galbraith said.

'And not before time. We'll be glad to get rid of these two!' Lizzie was better at it than she was with all her medical qualifications. 'They're worse than Annabel and Kit upstairs with their antics.' She smacked the younger man's left stump. 'Do you think you could keep them in order, Miss McNab, while I go to the office?'

'I'll do my best.' It was like a charade. How was she going to work over there without making a fool of herself? She sat down beside the two men. Could they see through her, or was her profession like a cloak covering her inadequacies?

'If you're a doactor, whit fur does she call you Miss McNab?' Willie Rintoul had a grudge against life, and no wonder.

'Surgeons are always called "Mr",' she said sweetly, 'but I'm not a man so it's got to be "Miss". See!' She shrugged her shoulders and his companion let out a loud laugh.

'That's pit yer nose oot o' joint, Wullie!'

'He was quite right to ask. I'm going to a hospital in France next week. I thought you might give me an idea of what to expect?'

'That's no' fur a young wumman like you.' Rintoul frowned.

'It's no' for anybody,' she said, 'but the need is there. My father was a surgeon in the Boer War. He'd want me to do what I could if he were alive.'

'Was he killed there?' Jock Gillespie asked.

'No, in a motor accident when he came home.'

'Ye dinna tell me! That's fate, sure it is, Wullie?'

'Aye, there's no rhyme nor reason.' He glanced briefly at his stumps. 'It was the CCS for us first – that's the Casualty Clearing Station – where they stick on a lump o' cotton wool and tell ye to haud it. Then you're taken to the hoaspital, the rocky road to Dublin, sure it wis, Jock? The hoaspitals are no' that bad in spite o' aw the screamin' an' shoutin'. At nights it was awful! Cryin' fur their mammies, some o' them great grown lads! The relief o' gettin' oot o' that bluidy mess at Ypres was great all the same.'

'Aye, you're right there, Wullie,' Jock Galbraith said.

The older man seemed to relax. 'A'll tell ye, doactor, a mean, Miss McNab, ye get to the stage o' offerin' bribes to Him up there to get ye oot o' it. At least *A* did. "Gie's a Blighty yin, Goad," I used to pray in they stinkin' trenches wi' ma taes drapping aff yin by yin. "You've got a Blighty one, soldier," this doactor said to me, la-de-da, English, a toff. A didnae think they'd take aff ma bluidy legs to make sure!'

'If it was gas gangrene,' Ellie said, sounding to herself sickeningly false, 'it was your life or your legs.' She smiled to hide the sickness. 'You both look like healthy chaps to me. What do you do in Civvy Street, Jock?'

'A went doon the pit here.'

'So did my grandfather.' He looked disbelieving. 'But they'll get you a better job when you're fixed up. What about you, Willie?'

'A had a wee shoap in Dennistoun wi' the wife. She says she'll get me a stool and I can sit on it behind the coonter, gie the customers a laugh. She's took it well, Maggie, I'll say that aboot her.'

'You're lucky,' Jock said. Now she saw the agony in his eyes. 'Ma lass took yin look at me and ran oot o' here screamin'. D'ye mind that?' He laughed. 'Mrs Murray-Hyslop spoke to her for a long time and came in and saw me. Said Bella was willing to come back. But a telt her to go to hell.' He was still laughing.

'That was cruel,' Ellie said. 'You think it over. My cousin could send her a note.'

'No bluidy likely. Excuse my French, Miss.'

'I told you I was going to France on Wednesday. It would be like a lucky charm to me. Would you think about it?'

'It's nae good. She was mad aboot dancin'.'

She put a hand on his. 'You're a fine-looking lad.' She met his eyes and made herself smile. 'My cousin said I wasn't to flirt with you and here I am doing it. You'll be a smasher with your artificial legs. Able to do the Highland

Fling.' She hadn't looked at a man like that since Colin. She saw it work. He looked sheepish.

'Well, maybe. . .'

She got up after a time and made a round of the ward. They needed to talk about their disablement, and she listened at each bed. All of them said that what they couldn't take was how people wouldn't talk about it.

'Well, start the ball rolling,' she said. 'I've been in wards where they keep the lights lowered all the time. Where half their faces have been blown away. Just think that you at least are intact there, you can speak, and use your eyes . . .'

One armless man said to her, 'Ma wife put oor wee Totie on ma knee and the wee thing put her arms roon ma neck. A wusny ony different to her, ye see.'

She guided a blind man round the garden and wrote a letter for him, and when she took him back to the ward the nurse reminded her that she had to go upstairs for lunch. 'They're waiting for you,' she said. And then, severely, 'Come on, Jimmy, I know you. You've been trying to get on Miss McNab's soft side. You know the way to the garden well as she does.'

She looked at the young girl in her VAD uniform. She, like Lizzie, was better at it than she was. Pity was the thing you had to watch. That was what separated the disabled from other people.

5

She went upstairs for a late lunch with her mother and the two aunts and found Lizzie and Ernest in the airy drawing-room dispensing sherry. Lizzie had taken off her overall and was wearing a white lawn dress with ecru lace at the neck and flounced sleeves. She had a blue velvet ribbon at her throat, emphasizing the brilliant blue of her eyes. 'A bonny face fits the dishcloot – ' Ellie remembered one of her grandmother's sayings, although the beautifully-cut dress could scarcely be called that.

Ernest was no less elegant in his light suit of fine broadcloth, his honey-coloured shirt and the brown bow-tie which he had lately affected. And how trim his waist was with the gold fob emphasizing it. One of Pharoah's lean kine. He would never be fat.

Redfern had placed the sherry decanter on a silver tray, but Ernest passed round the filled glasses himself. 'A reward for your labours,' he said.

'And what if we bent too near a patient and he got a whiff?' Aunt Kate always brightened when she was with her stepson.

'Oh, they're used to it,' he said. 'They get a tot to brighten them up from time to time.'

'They must think they've landed in paradise when they come here, a real family concern.'

'It's the least we can do, but we didn't reckon on having three beautiful ladies dancing attendance, not to mention a lovely young surgeon! I can see some of their temperatures shooting up.'

'Have you heard from Jonty yet?' Ellie asked, laughing at him.

'Yes, just a postcard. Their school camp is near Salisbury Plain. He's a bit of an individualist. I don't know how he'll like all the route marching, but it's only for a fortnight.'

'Still, he's in the Corps at school, Ernest,' Lizzie reminded him. 'He's proud of the uniform. Just you wait and see, he'll have Annabel and Kit forming fours when he comes back. They copy him in everything.'

'Are you still taking them round the wards with you on Sunday evenings?' Maevy asked Ernest.

'Yes, it's a great treat for them. They take little gifts which they've managed to accumulate during the week.'

Lizzie laughed. 'I caught Annabel slicing the nursery soap in two and wrapping it up. And Kit wanted to take his white mouse in a matchbox to show them.'

'They're popular with the men,' Ernest said. 'Probably they remind them of their own children, but I think the principal thing is, they have no connection with the War. Children accept people as they are, disabilities included.' He shot a mischievous glance encompassing the three aunts. 'Though I'm in no way trying to decry the efforts of the Three Musketeers.'

'I'm certainly no D'Artagnan,' Maevy said, and Ellie remembered how she had always enjoyed reading, especially in bed. Her light would be on for hours. 'Charlie educated me,' she had once said, 'I knew nothing about music and books till I met him. They've proved a great solace.' Now she said, looking at Ernest, 'If you're casting anyone for *that* role, Lizzie's the most likely.'

'No, no,' Lizzie laughed, 'I'm sure Dumas *Père* would say I wasn't the type.' Her French education, Ellie thought, impressed. . . 'The main thing for someone like me, with no talent for nursing, is to see that everybody is as happy as possible, and that the place runs on oiled wheels. Luckily we have a fine body of VADs and Red Cross nurses. What did you think of them, Ellie?'

'I was impressed. If the hospital I'm going to is half as well-run, I'll be in clover.' Redfern was at the door, announcing lunch, grizzled and bent now. She remembered him as part of her childhood when Grandmother had been here, Lady Crawford.

'Come along everybody,' Ernest said, 'and Ellie can tell us all about it.' She liked the way he went to his stepmother, took her glass and gave her his arm. And when they were seated in the dining-room – one of the guest bedrooms converted by Lizzie with her usual flair – 'Now then, Ellie, let's hear all about this French hospital of yours.'

'Well,' she said, looking around the table, 'it's run entirely by women from the lowliest occupation to the highest – stretcher bearers, women drivers, doctors, all equally important. It's the brainchild of Dr Elsie Inglis.'

'Oh, we know of her!' Maevy said. 'Remember, Isobel? We heard her speak at an NUWSS meeting.'

'Yes, of course I do. At Kingsway Hall, in London! We went with Belle.'

'That's right. She's well known in the Movement, and a great organizer.' Maevy looked at her niece. 'I never knew why you didn't join, Lizzie. You have the same capabilities.'

'It wouldn't suit Lizzie,' Isobel said, 'she's an individualist.'

Lizzie raised her eyebrows comically. 'If that means I get my own way by other means,' she smiled at Ernest, 'Aunt Isobel's right.'

'My Lizzie,' there was a quirk at his mouth as he applied himself to carving the roast, 'is a manipulator of the first degree. But she does a lot for your Cause in her own way.'

'Well,' Ellie laughed, 'as I was saying, Dr Elsie Inglis set up through sheer perseverence – with men blocking her path in every direction, I may say – the Scottish Women's Hospitals for Foreign Service, and the NUWSS has given it its full backing.'

'What can I do but applaud when I'm the only man amongst five women! Try some of this roast beef, Maevy. It may be your last chance before it's rationed.' He handed her a plate with a few delicately pink slices on it, richly creamed with fat.

'Thanks, Ernest. Too much, but it looks delicious. You haven't a leg to stand on, you know. Ellie's got it right. All our fund-raising machinery, which was concentrated on getting us the Vote, was switched towards the financing of Dr Inglis's scheme. My, she got a great reception that night. Belle Geddes clapped louder than anyone else, I think.'

'I must look in and see her before I go away,' Ellie said.

'Yes, don't forget. You're a favourite of hers.'

'She'll be as proud of Ellie as we are,' Isobel said.

'Oh, Aunt Isobel, you'll make me die of embarrassment.'

'No, I'm serious. To think of you being one of the surgeons! And she told us that women even bury the amputated limbs!' Ellie looked at her, thinking, my goodness, that fragile wee thing, but her aunt was sitting straight in her chair, her eyes shining. 'It made me realize how little *I* do.'

'If keeping the books for this whole place is little,' Kate said, 'then I've another word for it.'

'We're all being so nice to each other,' Ernest smiled at them, 'that it will be tears before bedtime. Do you remember that's what Ingrid used to say, Kate?' And to Ellie, 'Go on about the hospital. We're interested.'

'Oh, I'll bore you. All right. The one I'm going to is in an abbey near Chantilly, about seven hundred years old. A large part of it hadn't been used and all the women, doctors included, lent a hand, scrubbing, scraping, cleaning floors and walls, setting up beds. There wasn't even a water supply and that had to be carried all over and along endless corridors in buckets. Nor any blankets. The doctors and nurses had to wrap themselves in rugs and overcoats until they arrived.'

'Thank goodness that was all done before you go,' Aunt Isobel said.

'Yes, I'm lucky, I suppose. It was the French who sent them their first patients. Verdun. They were desperate. Our lot were a bit slow. Women! The very idea!' Amid the laughter she turned to her Aunt Kate. 'I've a good chance of seeing Kieran, so I'll be able to give you first-hand news of him.' Was it chance that he had been stationed at Neuilly? She chided herself. Of course she would be glad to see him . . .

'I'm beginning to be envious,' Ernest said. His tone was light, but she saw his eyes.

'It's not over by a long chalk yet.' Aunt Kate had noticed, too. 'Be thankful you're still at home with Lizzie and the children. Where are they, by the way?'

'Jane asked permission to take them home with her. It's her afternoon off,' Lizzie said.

'How is she?'

'She looks . . . blighted, since Billy was killed at Ypres. Her only solace is the children, so I let them spend a lot of time with her. She left her postcards for you to see, Aunt Kate. She said you understood . . .'

'Oh, I understand all right. But so do many others. So do you.'

'Ah, that's a long time ago.' She looked at Ernest. 'And who could be sad with this man teasing me all the time?'

Ellie was touched by the postcards. When she thought of France she saw herself saving lives, but those were poignant memories of a young man who had lost his life there.

Patching up men to send them into battle again . . . was it all pointless?

They were hand-embroidered on organdie or muslin, very French. 'From your darling Billy Boy,' she read. 'We'll be together soon.' The pansies were sewn in coloured silks. Women were the peacemakers. Better to embroider with silk than have your hands stained with blood . . .

The four women were quiet as they walked home together. 'Do you remember,' Isobel said, 'the excitement at the beginning? How we cheered those men going away? Now all we can think of is the pity of it, the pity of it . . .'

The day of her departure arrived. She had visited Belle Geddes, thinner now, but still with that sensual air about her which attracted men. The mouth was less curved, but those silver-grey eyes still gave her a look of distinction, of being 'different' from the run of the mill.

'I envy you, Ellie,' she said. The voice hadn't lost its seductive slowness. 'I'm supposed to be indispensable here since the others were called up. Besides, I haven't the guts now. I used that up in Holloway long ago. Force-feeding. Humiliation.' She shrugged. 'The memory's slipped away like snaw aff a dyke . . . but not the memory of your mother's kindness. She wrote me such grand letters, far more than one suffragette to another. She's a fine woman.'

'I know that,' she said, but Belle was her old mocking self again.

'I'm past my best now, Ellie. An old hack.'

'Rubbish. Besides I don't want you to go. I'm relying on you to keep an eye on Mother. I know the aunts. It'll be, "Oh, nothing must worry our Ellie!" She laughed. 'Ernest calls them the Three Musketeers.'

'He'll be the next one to go, but I don't see him lying bleeding to death in the front line. He'll pick and choose.'

'He should stay where he is. McGrath's are doing a lot of war work. That should satisfy him.'

'Stay, just the way you did? It won't satisfy him any more than it satisfied you.' She got up from her chair and kissed Ellie, which was a rare thing for her. 'Have a good time if you can. You'll get dull if it's all work and no play and turn into one of those awful, worthy Scotswomen. I had an aunt like that. She had a moustache.'

'Oh, Belle!' She left the surgery smiling.

She wouldn't let her mother come to Glasgow with her, but Maevy insisted on driving her to Sholton Station in the pony and trap. 'I'll never take to motor cars,' she said.

No wonder, Ellie thought. 'I know. Still, this is far better. Plenty of room for my luggage.'

Maevy was determinedly cheerful, a smile fixed firmly on her face as if she had adjusted it that morning. She was almost coy with the station-master when he came to help with the valises. 'Now, don't you be lifting too much at one time, Mr Cox. How do you like Ellie's outfit? Isn't she a sight for sore eyes?'

'Aye, she's that, but I don't hold with it all the same.' He muttered to himself as they followed him with his trolley, 'Nae wummen in the last yin . . .'

'How do you feel about Kieran?' The question popped out of her mother's mouth so suddenly that Ellie knew she had been trying to raise the subject since they left home. 'You don't talk about him much.' They were sitting on a bench on the platform, and beside them were two men in shiny suits and bowler hats, who looked like commercial travellers.

'There's nothing to say, Mother.' She tried to keep the impatience out of her voice. 'We're leaving it . . .'

'But you love him?' Her voice was hoarse with embarrassment.

She lowered her voice. 'If I do, it's a different love from . . . the last time. Quieter . . .'

'Colin Thomson? Maybe it will flame brighter when you spend time together. I know mine did, right to the end, right to the end. . .' Her voice went softer. 'We went to Dundee for our honeymoon, to see Charlie's folks. Well, it wouldn't have mattered where we went. I just think of the flames flickering on the ceiling of the bedroom . . . she kept good fires, that woman.'

'That's as good as Jane's postcards.' She squeezed her mother's arms, feeling her eyes smart.

'Aye, you have to find your own . . . touchstone.' She coughed, her voice was harsh, almost. 'And then it . . . floods back. Kate . . .' she cleared her throat . . . 'Kate would like to see Kieran settled down in Wolf House, and I know she'd rather have you there than anyone else. I promised her I would say that, but you follow your own path, Ellie. It's your life.'

'Settling or the thought of it is out of the question just now.' She could say that with truth. Aunt Kate had never worked after she married. Her life had centred round her husband, her children and their children. She was a beautiful woman with her own tranquillity but with an aptness for managing other people's affairs. Mother was not tranquil. She was difficult to deal with, but her long life in McGrath's had made her respect other people's independence. 'I have a job to do first,' she whispered.

She felt the two men's glances on them. 'And Kieran too, if he gets into the Field Ambulance.'

'Here's the train.' Her mother stood up. Mr Cox was beside them with his trolley and his green flag.

'We'll get you a nice empty one, Ellie. Here you are.'

She turned to her mother and they kissed. Both were tearless, and speechless. She got into the compartment with Mr Cox holding open the door, looking impatient. Perhaps his multiplicity of duties was proving too much for him. She arranged her luggage which the stationmaster had thrust in behind her, then turned to the window, lowered it and leaned out. 'This is it, then, Mother.'

'This is it. I'm proud of you, Ellie. Will you take good. . .' The two men who had been sitting beside them pushed in past her, and by the time she got to the window again the train was slowly puffing out of the station. Her mother was standing straight, her hand up to wave. She looked absurdly young, tall, the hesitant hand. The wind had whipped a strand of fair hair across her face. She looks like me, Ellie thought, the other me who might have stayed with her, or the young Maevy who had waved good-bye to her Charlie sixteen years ago.

'Good-bye, good-bye . . .' She stood at the window swallowing her tears, but when she sat down, to her disgust she did make a fool of herself, weeping into her handkerchief for the first five minutes. Nothing mattered. The parting was too much to bear.

'Is it your Ma?' one of the men asked. His face was lengthened into a mask of sympathy.

'Yes, I'm going to France.'

'Ach, nurses are all right! And they have a rare time.' He appealed to his friend, 'So they do, don't they, Gordon?'

'Aye, so I've heard. We're in a reserved occupation. Munitions.' He sang out the last word.

She had been wrong about their occupation as they were about hers. It didn't matter. She was conscious of having left behind, for all time, her girlhood. Well, you had to have a degree of maturity to be a surgeon in the War.

6

La Voie Sacre, as it was known, the road between Bar le Duc and Verdun, was a nightmare of congestion. Kieran, sitting in the long line of American ambulances, had gone through impatience to numbing cold and frustration; now he was in a light-headed state induced by tiredness and hunger, where the constant roar of lorries crawling past him loaded to the gunwales with armour and equipment, the regiments of marching grey-black men, the trundling food carts whose soup kitchens clattered like miniature shell-fire themselves, had become only a background to his thoughts on this June morning. Even the ache in his damaged leg, the result of his cousin Gaylord's shot-gun so long ago that it seemed to be in another world, hardly bothered him.

How many men's thoughts in this chaos of war were elsewhere? In a way it was their only salvation. If one could not mentally transport oneself from this vice-locked situation one would go mad, like those poor NYD cases he had picked up at the station yesterday, wild-eyed and weeping, their trembling hands scarcely able to hold a mug of coffee.

One had to escape from the heavy German guns firing shell after shell into Verdun, the incessant noise which battered one's eardrums, the feeling that the whole countryside was being assaulted, in the air with the busy dogfights between the French and German planes, and on the earth by the constant firing of guns. And one knew that even underground there were thousands of Germans like moles in their deep shelters.

But even more traumatic were the long trails of refugees fleeing southwards from Verdun, more pitiable than the soldiers marching to almost certain death with an eerie false cheerfulness inculcated by the heads of the War machine. Pétain was as good at it as the Crown Prince, '*On les aura!*' One by one the Forts were falling. This time it was Vaux.

A whole family passed them slowly, the parents pushing a handcart laden with a pitiful pile of household goods – pots and pans sticking out between feather beds, chairs, a table, and on top of the pile two frightened children and a terrier which barked incessantly. Somehow the thin, sharp noise of its yapping was more nerve-racking than the heavy roar of the guns.

Kieran's co-driver spoke. Sam Cartney who came from Washington, DC. 'You'd think they would have cleared out last winter, poor devils.'

'People cling to their homes till the last minute, I expect.' He raised a hand to a child of about five, staring curiously at him, smiled and called, '*Bonjour.*' Her timid answering smile stayed in his memory as they drove past them. Would she remember the small incident years later, or would terror blot it from her consciousness?

'They at least can't help it. We walked into this bloody mess deliberately, eh, Hyslop?' Murray-Hyslop took too long to say.

'Yea, we walked right in.' He spoke Yankee, singing the words.

'Wouldn't mind being back in Georgetown. Sunday morning, home from college, visiting the folks. Sitting on the porch reading the papers, swimming in the water-hole with the kids in the afternoon, walking out my best girl at nights. Betsy Mills. Yes, sir, Betsy Mills.' Cartney's voice trailed away, and Kieran, stealing a look at him, knew his thoughts were running on.

As his were. Robert and Edie's wedding – May, a month after his father's death. Mother hadn't been at it. She'd set off for Scotland to stay with Aunt Maevy at Braidholme, and he'd encouraged her because he didn't want her to know how soon he was setting off himself. She'd had enough grieving. Wolf House was a shell without Father. If he felt it, how much more did she?

It was strange, Aunt Maria giving Springhill, her parents' home, to Robert McGrath and Edie Barnes (she had said early on that no one called her Edith), when you remembered that Robert had courted his cousin, Sarah, for so long. It was like getting blood out of a stone to get Robert to talk about it. His quietness was more like Uncle Patrick's than his own father's, that horsy, cheerful man back in Ireland with the fey Irish wife, Honor, who wrote books.

'Your Aunt Maria has got over Sarah not being married,' Edie had said. 'I don't think she agrees with her husband about cousins not marrying, but she's accepted it because Sarah has.' Sarah knew herself better than anyone else. She wasn't the marrying kind. Not like that young sister of hers. Ginny, in her green chiffon bridesmaid's dress which set off her flaming hair, had almost put Edie in the shade.

'But it's still a generous gesture giving Springhill to you and Robert,' he had said.

'It's a way of keeping it in the family, I guess.' Edie was a direct girl. 'When Aunt Maria's mother died, she could have sold Springhill, but I think she still wanted to visit there. It must have a lot of good memories for her.'

'Oh, yes, it was a happy house,' he had agreed. He remembered their visits to Springhill as a boy, and what a treat it had been to go on the ferry across the Hudson, and the joy of a lawn where the river lapped to its edge. Great-uncle Terence's voice came back to him, with its

Irish brogue still strong after years in America. He remembered his mother telling him of Aunt Isobel's twenty-first birthday dance, and how fragile and beautiful the Scottish girl had been beside Aunt Maria's sturdy darkness. And he remembered fluttery Great-aunt Caroline, with her bows and her buttons and her golden ringlets and unsure eyes.

Gaylord had been called after her twin brother. His leg ached, at the thought almost, and at once he was in that dark wood and lunging towards Gaylord to take the shotgun from him. He had never heard such a noise, he remembered thinking, when it went off, confused with the loud clap of birds' wings in his ears. But what about this now, with the whole earth trembling round him?

It had been a fine wedding on that early summer day, with the blue Hudson filling the square window panes, an airy river house. Springhill was made for celebrations, that wide hall and curved staircase rising from it like a stage set. It had been like an indoor flower garden with those splendid gowns, and especially the hats worn by the ladies – Victoria, his step-sister, stately but, he smiled to himself, behind the times as usual in her olive green silk bombazine. She hadn't the style of Emily who always reminded him of those brilliant Audubon kingfishers. Still, he was fond of both stepsisters although they were so much older, and it was grand now to be stationed near Emily and Charles.

Then there had been George's Abigail like a plump pink rose – she favoured pink – and that beautiful wife of Uncle Terence's from Ireland, in her drifting mauve and grey draperies with a great purple hat set on her black hair. 'Sure, instead of being Robert's step-mother,' she had said, touching it. 'I feel like a wee cratur under a toadstool!' Uncle Terence must find it a treat to live with her after Robert's mother, Catherine Murdoch, that unhappy woman who had drowned herself in her bath. Ellie had told him that her mother and Uncle Terence had discovered her

But there was no doubt who was queen of the ball, even including the bride. Dashing about all over the place, her red curls trembling on top of her head where she had pinned them, her green chiffon skirts flying, ordering Victoria's and Abigail's children about, waiting hand and foot on Edie, arranging her train, holding her bouquet . . . It was the life in Ginny, as if it couldn't be contained and she had to run about in order to use up all that energy. And the way she had of laughing so heartily – not at all ladylike, he was sure Aunt Maria thought. She and Uncle Patrick seemed to be in a perpetual state of surprise at what they had produced.

It was strange, he thought, remembering Uncle Patrick's pompous air which had become habitual, and Aunt Maria's solidity, that they should have produced three children who were so different from each other: Sarah so serious and sedate – if she felt sad at having given up Robert, she didn't show it; Gaylord, that tortured soul who had died so tragically; and Ginny, that young, vivid beauty of a girl. Mother said that Grandmother Maeve lived in her all over again. 'That *presence*, Kieran, I don't know how else to describe it. You felt it immediately she came into a room. Ginny has the same.'

Yes, he thought, it was good that Springhill should still be in the family, and maybe when all this was over and he had persuaded Ellie to marry him, there would be coming and going between the two places, Wolf House and Springhill. Ellie would like Edie. They were two of a kind . . .

'God!' Sam said. 'Another bloody hold-up! We've been five hours on this road and only done thirty miles. It's a nightmare.'

'Nightmares come to an end. Smoke?'

'Thanks.' He took out his matches, tossed them to Kieran, and when their cigarettes were lit, he braced himself against the back of the seat, gripping the wheel. 'Say, Bo, you weren't here when the Zepp was hit? No? When was it . . .? End of February. God, that was better than 4th July firecrackers! What a blaze! You could have roasted a ton of potatoes ten yards from it. I got a souvenir, a bit of scrap iron. Keep it for luck . . .' His voice dwindled away.

There was some altercation going on just ahead of them between two drivers. The road was in a pitted, awful state, and a lorry, obviously sinking into a pothole, had revved to get out and bumped into the one in front of it. Some of its equipment had fallen on the road. The two Frenchmen were going at each other hammer and tongs. If he interfered he would probably get his head bashed in. They were an excitable lot.

He glanced at Sam. His eyes were closed. His bony face looked young, looked American. What drives a youngster like him to volunteer for this, he thought. I'm thirty-eight, middle-aged, supposed to know what I'm doing. Time I was married . . . to Ellie . . . He took her letter from his pocket and slowly unfolded it. The Frenchmen were still at it, waving their fists at each other . . .

. . . I'll be arriving in Paris about the 7th July, I expect. You've said your headquarters are at Neuilly, so I wondered if we could meet. I'll go to Monceau Park, to your step-sister's house. I've written to Giselle to tell her and they'll be there too. They have an apartment some distance away, but Terence is due to be called up so they haven't bought a house. Did you know she's expecting another baby, due in September? She said she wanted two quickly since she's a year or two older than Terence, and she's got her wish.

It seems like an age since that day of her wedding, the day of the murder of the Archduke. It's been murder ever since, of the best of our young men, and it's not over yet. I'm glad they're keeping you in Paris. I should be worried sick about you . . .

He lifted his head, feeling again the keen disappointment when he had been told to join this Field Ambulance going to Verdun. He had thought the fighting was tailing off there. It didn't look much like it. He longed to see her, touch her, was tired of living with a phantom . . .

You say we could have had two years of married happiness. But how could anyone possibly lead a normal life with wholesale murder going on all around, and not lift a finger to help? I have to be in on this. I owe it to my father. I couldn't throw away skills which he would have been proud of and become an ordinary housewife like Giselle in France or Robert's wife in far-off America, whom you say you like. Mother understands. I don't think the other aunts do, nor *your* mother.

I think we'll both be glad later that we've been involved in this War, but for the moment I try just to live a day at a time. Do I sound cold-hearted? I don't think I am. I can't tell you how excited I am to be going to France and how lovely it will be to see you if you can get leave.

I love Paris. The comparison between its gaiety and dreich old Scotland is odious, and they say it has retained its gaiety in spite of the War. You said so yourself. I was quite jealous when you told me of all the dances you'd been at . . .

'We're moving,' Sam said. 'Put your *billet doux* away. That's the second time you've produced it. Does it do something for you, eh, Hyslop?' He nudged Kieran in the ribs, leering boyishly. 'Is she a real humdinger?'

'Yes, a real humdinger.' He released the brake, let in the clutch and moved slowly away towards the battle.

7

It was exciting to be travelling through the streets of Paris again. She had been right about the gaiety, Ellie thought: the pedestrians' steps seemed to have a swing about them, the cafes were full and even more colourful than usual with the bright dresses of the women and the foil of the grey uniforms of soldiers and officers.

She had been interviewed at Calais by the chief woman doctor there and given instructions about getting to the Abbey. 'You'll find it exceedingly well run,' she told her. 'People say it is one big happy family. They even have a famous chef who was a patient and stayed on. And a new ward has been opened this year.'

'I'm really looking forward to it,' Ellie assured her.

'You have excellent testimonials. I've told you the bright side first. The work is punishingly hard. We're always short of staff, especially surgeons, and more will be needed soon. You need a strong heart as well as a strong body. Do you think you can cope with the long hours ?'

'My father did the same in the Boer War. I'll try not to let him down.' She smiled.

'I'm sure you won't. But you'll go home a different young woman. It takes its toll.'

But now her heart was light. She had a weekend in Paris before her. She would spend it at Monceau Park where she would also see Terence and Giselle who would be there. The last time she had seen them – and Kieran – had been at their wedding two years ago, just before War broke out. Giselle had written to say how much she was looking forward to seeing her again, and how sorry they were that there wasn't enough room in their small apartment at Passy to put her up.

'But *Maman* would never have allowed it in any case,' she had written, 'her salons are bigger and better than ever now. She tries to hook the big fish like writers and poets. She's even had Colette! To *Maman* the War is an excuse for more entertaining . . .'

Even in the brief time of their acquaintance a rapport had sprung up between them. She had the same *chic* as Kieran's step-sister, but more depth of character, and had not the same desire to lead a public life. Was Emily's compulsion because her private one was unsatisfactory? Charles, her husband, even at Giselle's wedding had seemed withdrawn.

And it would be a pleasure to see Kieran again. She had a moment of doubt as she was driven along the wide streets planned by Baron Haussman. Had she been foolish in choosing a career instead of marrying him and going to live in that fine house in Wanapeake with its mansard windows and wide, welcoming porch? She could have been rearing children . . . But I've been trained as a surgeon – the old argument was there again – and these are exceptional times.

Emily and Charles Barthe had the house full of strangers. Giselle had warned her, but she was momentarily taken aback by the noise and glitter. Emily, scintillating even more in manner and dress than she remembered – she had taken to a curving osprey in her hair – perhaps a shade more brittle, nevertheless gave her a warm welcome. It was difficult to believe she was fifty-four, the same age as Mother; but Ellie thought it conceivable that her mother might look fresher in the mornings. Emily seemed to rely on a lot of make-up.

'My dearest little Ellie – no, I can't call you that when

you're so tall – we're *enchanted* to see you! Aren't we, Charles?' Her husband was by her side, his manner as quiet as hers was extravagant. His pale face, the full black moustache, as sleekly black as his hair, had an age-old look of real, not acquired, sophistication.

'*Ravi*,' he said, a little wearily. Was his love-nest, which was a byword with the McGrath clan, proving too much for him nowadays? How the Scots liked their tittle-tattle with a bit of spice in it, thus assuring them of their own rectitude! But Charles also had his worries. Their twin sons, Marc and Olivier, were both in the French army. Lizzie had said they were charm personified, with a wicked sense of humour.

'Giselle and Terence are already here, and little Clovis is tucked in upstairs. Now you are to go up too and Giselle will show you where you can change into a pretty dress.' The inference was plain. The bright eyes had swept over the grey coat with its tartan facings, the plain shoes and hat, and decided they were not at all *comme il faut*. And certainly not *du monde*. That expression had passed into the family repertoire ever since Emily had used it to describe grandmother.

She herself was in her usual jewel colours, this time garnet-coloured velvet with a low-cut neckline. While she chattered, Charles stood quietly at her side, looking *distrait*. He gave Ellie the impression that he had two worlds to inhabit and had become a little lost in the translation.

'Ellie, you've arrived!' She heard the voice behind her.

'Giselle!' She turned to greet the girl. She was plump because of her pregnancy, but she had the same seductive charm as always, enhanced by the bloom on her cheeks and a loose, flowing dress of silk which looked as light as air. She had developed a sisterly feeling for her step-cousin's daughter in spite of the difference in their ages –

she was eight years Giselle's junior. 'You look beautiful,' she said as they kissed.

'Ah, *chérie*, many thanks.' Her dark eyes flashed with merriment. 'In another month I shall be even more . . .' she blew out her cheeks, 'and waddling about like a duck. Come along. *Maman*'s laid out all kinds of bath salts and perfume for you in your room. You must be *trés fatiguée*.'

'I'd love to see Clovis.'

'You shall later, but he's asleep. Just a baby yet, and here I am again, *enceinte*. But, *c'est fini!*' She gestured with her hands, open-palmed.

'Don't make rash promises.'

'I know, but two is enough, especially in war-time. Terence is . . . but you'll see him soon.'

They had reached the upstairs landing with its soft, pale carpeting. The long corridor had alabaster urns in niches which were softly lit. It seemed extremely elegant to Ellie. 'By the way, I didn't see Kieran downstairs. Hasn't he arrived?'

'Now, there is sadness for you! *Pauvre* Kieran, and you also. At the last moment his Field Ambulance has been directed towards the Vosges. We think it must be Verdun because you must know what a terrible battle that is, and now there is another rout with the town people having to flee from their homes. He left you a letter. Terence has it.'

'What a shame!' She was more disappointed than she would admit. 'Where is Terence?'

'He came upstairs to check on our little Clovis. He adores him. His favourite sitter already! Ah, here he is.'

He was in uniform, and she went to meet him, astonished. As he kissed her on both cheeks – how French he had become – she said, 'Terence! I didn't know you had joined up!' *That* was what Giselle had meant.

He laughed. 'If common-law convicts are able to, I

thought there was no excuse for me!' He was leaner, more assured, but then, he was now a well-known painter, and extremely smart in his grey uniform with shining black boots. So different from his brother, Robert, in America, she thought. He was solid, almost worthy, as befitted a wealthy businessman, but Terence had flair, as befitted a painter.

'Did you *have* to? I thought, not being French . . .'

'Oh, we could have gone back to Ireland and lived with Father and Mother, but my work's here. This is my home now.'

'Did Aunt Honor try and persuade you?'

'No. She doesn't interfere. But Father . . . well, he thinks I'm mad. He wanted me to go back to Woodlea and breed horses until it was all over. No, France has been too good to me.' He put his arm round Giselle. She remembered that cheerful man whom she had grown so fond of when she had stayed at Woodlea with Grandmother. They had talked about War. Now that it was here, it was natural that he should want to protect his son . . .

'Did *you* approve, Giselle?'

'*Naturellement*. France must not be defeated. And I did not want to live with horses in Ireland.' They laughed.

'Did you know there's a big push on the Somme?' Terence asked Ellie. 'I expect that's why you're here.'

'I'm beginning to think so, though I'm going to be stationed quite near Paris. Near Chantilly.'

'Well, you must come and see Giselle when you can. And Kieran, too, when he comes back to Neuilly. Or you can go to the Barthe country residence near Gisors, any time. We'll lay it all on. Oh, I'm stupid! I have a letter for you from Kieran.'

'Yes, Giselle told me.'

He took it out of his pocket and handed it to her. 'Poor

you! What a blow! If it's any consolation I can tell you he looked desolated.'

'I was looking forward to seeing him. Thanks, Terence.'

'Read it while you're in your bath,' Giselle said. 'And *relâche-toi*, but not for too long. *Maman*'s laid on a tremendous buffet. You must be famished.'

She shook her head, smiling. 'No, not really.'

'You'll see Kieran another time. *C'est la guerre. Voyons.* This man is setting off leaving me with this.' She patted her stomach, smiling up at Terence. 'Don't you think that's very thoughtless of him?' Their exchanged glances made her feel excluded.

She peeped in at the sleeping Clovis when she was ready, marvelling at the small curled fists, the look of Terence on the baby features. 'Terence is the most important thing in my life,' she remembered Giselle saying in a letter, 'but then, I'm not a career woman. Perhaps it depends on one's mother.' It could well be true. She thought of Emily, so pleasure-loving, and her own mother, so full of resolution. Ah, well, she said to herself, going down the broad staircase a little shyly, we maun be some way. There was a Scottish saying to fit every situation.

She was helping herself to some delicious-looking *pâté* when an officer in American uniform spoke to her.

'Giselle pointed you out to me. She said you needed someone to cheer you up. Would I do?'

'Giselle is cheeky.' She looked at him, smiling. He was dark-haired, dark-complexioned. She could feel his vitality, see it in his broad shoulders. 'Have you noticed how French people are always pairing off people?'

'That's only logical, and they're a logical race. You're not French, and I know you're not English. Where do you come from?'

'Scotland. How did I give the game away?'

'You said Giselle was "cheeky". The English would have said "naughty".'

'Good for you. I've come out to join a Scottish-run hospital near here.'

'You're a doctor?'

'You're the first man who hasn't assumed I was a nurse. Even worse. I'm a surgeon.'

'They get younger and younger.' She noticed his eyes were dark enough to be called black. 'It's snap, then. I'm a surgeon too, Joe Gould, from Boston.' He held out his hand and his grasp was warm, like the eyes, like Father's eyes . . .

'I'm Ellie McNab. Aggressively Scottish.' She had to laugh.

'I wouldn't say "aggressive".' His glance was still on her. What *would* he say? 'I think this calls for a toast to surgeons. Let me fill a glass for you. Is that all you're eating? You have to *load* your plate. It's probably the last chance you'll get for some decent food.' He talked easily as he helped them to food and drink. 'There are two seats over there by the little table. Grab them while I get a tray for this.'

She passed Giselle chatting with Terence and some other guests. His arm was round her. She leaned against him. Scotswomen never showed their affection like that in public. She turned, saw Ellie and smiled. '*Ça va bien*, Ellie?' Her look was very French, taking in Joe Gould as well.

He was adept at laying the table. 'This is a piece of luck for me,' he said when he sat down. 'A beautiful lady surgeon.' His smile was direct, like a beam. 'You should see the kind I've been working with, rough hairy types. Why didn't *we* think of beautiful ladies!'

'It probably takes a Scotswoman to think of it.' She was lighthearted, teasing.

'She's some lady, I'll say that. You must have worked hard to be chosen.'

She sipped her champagne. It suited her mood. 'Work's endemic with us. My mother's still working. There's a family firm, McGrath's, carters originally. Her father and mother started it. We've a branch in New York. I think Mother joined the company after or during the Boer War – I can't remember. She didn't expect me to waste my time either, so I didn't. We have a dragon of a servant, Susan, one of the family, and she wouldn't have let me off, either. Don't think I wasn't happy. I had a great life. What about you?'

'I don't think the work ethic was as strong in our house. I went into medicine and then surgery because I fancied it. I wouldn't have the patience to sit and listen to people's complaints three times a day. I had a happy childhood. Two brothers and a sister. We kept open house, especially in our place up in Maine. Summers there were fun . . .' He sighed, turned the food on his plate with a fork. 'You can never go back.'

'What made you come here?' she said. 'I mean, volunteer. You didn't have to.'

'Nor did you.'

'It's our War. It isn't yours.'

'Are you pushing me out?' He grinned at her. 'Not yet, but it soon will be. Anyhow, it seemed like a good chance to see the world . . . get away from things. Is your stern Scottish conscience shocked?' She looked at him. He wasn't smiling. He seemed older than she had first thought. He must be over thirty.

'Oh, I'm far from criticizing. I have an American cousin who's here in a Field Ambulance. He'd have gone to Canada to enlist if his father hadn't been dying. I was hoping to see him tonight but he's been sent off. Giselle thinks it may be Verdun.'

'Yea? Where does he come from?'

'Upstate New York. Wanapeake.'

'It's nice there. A good place to live.'

'Yes, I've been.' She sipped her champagne, took another sip to calm her nerves. This wasn't an ordinary social meeting. There was no strangeness, and yet her pulse seemed to have quickened. There was a feeling of ease and yet an undercurrent of excitement . . . 'Our family have spread about the world,' she said. 'Grandmother and Grandfather started it off by coming from Ireland to Scotland. Then their family have spread to America and France and back to Ireland. Giselle's husband comes from County Roscommon in Ireland. He studied art in Dublin.'

'So his mother-in-law told me. She's a vivacious lady. Very hospitable to us Americans, her daughter and son-in-law, too. Have you seen any of his portraits? They're very fine. An Irish dash, maybe.'

'No, not yet. I haven't seen Giselle or Terence since I was at their wedding here two years ago. There's an artistic streak in our family, I think. I have none of it so I can boast. His step-mother, Honor, is a writer, Irish, lovely, and fey. That could have influenced him. His father has a kind of style in living, that's flair too, and so has Lizzie, my cousin. She's a painting in herself. My grandmother had great style, and yet she was very practical. Clever-handed, we call it.'

'Then you must have it too since you chose to become a surgeon.'

'Like father, like daughter,' she smiled at him, 'but, yes, I like it. It gives me pleasure, the "handiness" – what's the proper word?'

'Adroitness?'

'Yes. I think I decided when I discovered I was one of the few medical students who never felt faint in the theatre. But then Mother was a nurse.'

'So in spite of your high moral tone this is an adventure for you?'

'You're convinced about my high moral tone, aren't you?' she laughed at him. 'Oh, yes, it's an adventure all right. I just hope I'm good enough when I get to my hospital.'

'You'll be good enough. Where is it?'

'Beyond Chantilly. An all women's hospital.'

'You mean all the staff?'

'Yes, right down to the burial parties.'

'Hey! Are they all Scottish?'

'Yes, every woman jack of them.'

'Gee whiz!' He got up. 'I'm going to get you some more champagne. You deserve it. Don't run away.'

She looked around, pleasantly excited, and saw that the other guests were in close little groups, as if everyone had found their own level. So had she with Joe Gould. Don't go away, he had said. There was no danger.

She saw Giselle on a sofa having what looked like an intimate discussion with a pretty Frenchwoman. Perhaps they were comparing pregnancies. Terence, distinctive in his French uniform, was with a crowd of older men who seemed to be listening to him respectfully, although, as she looked, she heard a loud guffaw. Two of the men were wearing the same uniform as Joe Gould.

Emily was at the table with a middle-aged man, not Charles. She was talking and gesturing with her usual animation. How had she known that Paris, so different from faraway Wanapeake, was the right setting for her? Her husband was nowhere to be seen. Giselle had told her that her father had the habit of slipping away and going to his study. He was never missed, she said, and that was why he always agreed to Emily giving her large parties so often.

Joe Gould was beside her again, and she felt an immediate warm pleasure, as if she had come into full sunlight again. She took the glass of champagne from him, smiling, and as their fingers touched, she felt it would have been natural to hold up her face to be kissed. She was surprised, overwhelmed at the idea. I'm over-tired, she told herself, or it's a transposition of my feeling for Kieran to him, because of my disappointment at not seeing him.

This time they didn't speak much. 'I'll have to make myself sociable,' she said, but when she turned to look at the groups of people she couldn't envisage breaking into any one of them.

'I came with two other officers,' he said. 'I'll have to do the same. What are you doing tomorrow?' His eyes, his black eyes, were fixed on her.

'Giselle wants me to spend the day with her at Passy where she lives, but I'll only go for dinner. I don't want to intrude on them too long when he'll be going away soon.'

'Would you let me give you lunch, then?' His voice forced her to look at him. There was a tenseness in it. And those eyes were so familiar – like her father's, of course. Was that why she was attracted to him? She'd like to meet him again, talk to him about surgery, find out what books he read, if he liked music . . . no, that was rubbish. She'd just like to see him.

'It might be rude, since I am staying here.'

'The French don't think like that. They're sophisticated. They expect you to lead your own life.'

'Yes, that's true, about Emily, at least. I set off Sunday morning . . .' She made up her mind. 'Yes, thank you.'

'Good. So do I.'

'It would be . . . nice.'

'Only nice?' His eyes teased her.

'Well, interesting.' She felt herself colouring.

'Do you know what I feel?'

'No . . .'

'That if you left Paris without my seeing you again, I'd regret it, like anything.'

She wanted to say, 'So should I,' but it would have been too forward, sound unnecessarily seductive. She should take lessons from Emily or Giselle while she was here. 'That's a bit melodramatic.' Her smile wavered.

'Maybe.' He sipped his champagne, his eyes on her. 'It happens to be true.'

8

Emily said to her at breakfast, 'Did you enjoy yourself last night, *chérie*?'

'Yes, it was a lovely party. You do those things so well. Grandmother often said so.' She had called Emily a brilliant little parakeet, or some such thing.

'I like people and it's good for Charles' practice. This house is suited for entertaining, although I used to say to Grandmother that all that Louis Quatorze is very *demodé*.'

She swept a dismissive glance over the curved mantelpiece, the carved and gilt *fauteuils* arranged symmetrically along the wall, the elegant *buffet*. 'Now at our Normandy farmhouse it's more to my liking. Dear Leezie and Ernest saw it on their honeymoon. *Mon Dieu!* Can it be eleven years already? Yes, I remember, it was May 1905.' And then, with hardly a pause, 'I saw you spent some time with Major Gould. Is he smitten by you?'

'Goodness no, Emily!' She managed not to blush. 'He's a surgeon. We had a lot in common.'

'It looked like that. They're charming, those American boys. They say here that since the Americans arrived prices have shot up, but, *que voulez vous*?' a Gallic shrug. '*La hausse des prix* is nothing compared with the pleasure they give us, wouldn't you agree, Ellie?' Her glance was piercing.

'Perhaps,' she said, and to deflect her, 'but you like Paris all the same?'

'Ah, yes, the culture! So different from back home. I expect that's why there are so many American expatriates in Paris, painters, poets . . . they find something here. Of course some of the American women writers' style of living is not at all . . .' her eyes slanted away. 'I'm afraid they'll come to a sad end. And what about Diaghilev, poor soul?'

'Nijinski?' Ellie said, dragging the name from the recesses of her mind.

She nodded, pleased. 'The pause in the air! Remarkable!' French pronunciation. 'Still, I miss America. It was my home. Ah, well, one can never go back . . .' She bent towards Ellie, her breasts rosy through the fine silk of her negligée, no pyjamas for *her*, 'I have a fitting this morning in the Rue St Honoré. Would you like to come? I daren't cancel an appointment with Pierre. He goes absolutely *fou*!'

'Would you mind if I just stroll about Paris? There are so many things I want to see again. I'm going to Giselle's later for dinner.'

'Yes, we're invited too. You'll enjoy seeing her little *appartement*. She's made it very chic. I adore that child of theirs! Do you think I look like a grandmother, Ellie dear? Sometimes in the morning light . . .?'

'Oh, no!' she said, caught out. Emily would always look like Emily, not even a mother or a wife, just a strange little parakeet, or whatever it was.

'You're a dear, sweet girl, so fresh and lovely and . . . expectant. I thought you'd be despondent because of not seeing Kieran, but Major Gould must have cheered you up. Joe Gould, isn't it? How I miss those American names! I've hinted to Giselle that if she has another boy she might call him James after my father. Oh, I can't think he is no longer with us!' She dabbed at her eyes with a handkerchief. 'How good he was to Victoria and me, always thinking of our welfare, sending us to a finishing school here. Madame Sevigny's. I often wonder where I should be if we hadn't come . . . and poor Kate! They were so happy together. When she was our nurse she was like a big sister to us. I always think of her like that, not a step-mother.'

'Don't grieve too much. I think she's as happy as possible with Mother, and working in Lizzie's hospital helps her, I'm sure.'

'Ah, yes, Leezie will be good for her. Terence should paint her before her beauty fades. Oh dear, look at the time!' The Sèvres clock on the mantelpiece had chimed ten. 'I must fly. Now, promise me, Ellie, if you don't come back here for lunch, go to a really good restaurant. You might be importuned in a cheap one. Oh, it would be much better if you had an escort! He could take you to see *Jude*. It's *le dernier cri*.' She wasn't sure if there had been a 'look' in Emily's eye as she kissed her and hurried off to dress.

She took a taxi to the Pont D'Austerlitz where she had arranged to meet Joe Gould. He was already there, standing at the busy corner of the huge square, and when he helped her out, she was reassured. He was so welcoming, so compact and broad-shouldered in his trim, olive-coloured uniform, his smile white against the darker tone of his face.

'You made it! I'm glad. Was it difficult to get away?'

'Not really.' She laughed. 'Emily was justifying her salon. She thinks you Americans bring variety into the life of Paris.'

'Some think differently.' He was amused. 'We're blamed for all kinds of things – rag-time, blues and, worst of all, bringing the foxtrot along with us!' His laugh was infectious. 'Do you want to have a look at the Seine? I always do.' They stood at the parapet shoulder to shoulder. It was as busy with craft as the streets were with cabs and buses. It was metallic, a French river to match the buildings.

'It's got a steely glitter,' she said.

'Grey and silver, that's Paris.' He turned her away, his hand under her elbow. 'We'll have to watch crossing here.' They stood looking at the crossing streams of traffic.

'What's this square called?'

'Place Valhubert. It's a nightmare. I've driven through it. Right! Here's a space. Shall we go?' He propelled her skilfully through the traffic towards the gates on the other side, stopped her in front of a statue. 'Buffon, Georges-Louis Leclerk. "The style is the man". Pre-Darwin.'

'You've been doing your homework.'

He smiled at her, and she had to lower her eyes because of a rush of emotion. The style is the man. Joe Gould had style, different, particularly appealing, strange . . . They had gone through the gates and ahead of them was a great vista of flower-beds and paths laid out in the formal French pattern.

'That's the Museum of Natural History at the top,' he said. 'Do you want to go round it?'

'Oh, no! I'd much rather stay in the open air and look at the flowers. Look, they're all named.' She bent down to a bed of velvet pansies. '"*Pensées*" I never thought of that. "Pansies for thoughts."' She remembered Jane's collection of French postcards, flowers embroidered on organdie, pansies . . .

'They're pretty. You're pretty.' She wasn't sure if that was what he said. 'Now we've got to find the famous lime trees. I'd give anything to have a good sniff to rid myself of that War smell.' She looked at him. His face was grim.

'Does it stay with you?'

'God, yes! You'll soon know it when you get patients

brought to you straight from the Front – blood, urine, faeces, putrefaction, and that's only the half of it. You can wash and wash and it doesn't go away. And those gas cases vomiting their lungs up . . .' He shook his head. 'Excuse the outburst. I'm putting you off. Sorry.'

'Sometimes it was bad enough in the Infirmary where I worked. I wonder if I'll be able to stand it.'

'You'll stand it. You're surprised at what you can stand. You're only half-awake most of the time, so tired that you have to blink your eyes open to see where to cut.'

'You've been in a long time?'

'Since 1915. I came with a Harvard Medical Unit. The chance came just when I wanted . . . to get away. I started off in London where I was kitted out in British military uniform, and then after learning how to give a full military salute,' he smiled at her, 'you British! . . . I was sent over here. Bailleul, near Ypres. That was terrible. Wards filled with men who'd been gassed, gasping for breath, blue in the face, dying in hordes as their lungs filled up, dying terrified because they were blinded as well. I don't know which was worse, that or the maimed lads you have to further maim to save their lives. Maybe it's the paraplegics who are the worst, impossible to *do* anything, confined to a living death. This is the first decent leave I've had, fattening us up for the next slaughter . . . Hey, I'm sorry, sorry! Here's the lime walk. Just at the right time to stop me. I'm becoming obsessed by the War. Shut up, Gould! Take a good sniff!'

They stood under the hazy yellow of the trees and sniffed, smiling at each other. The sun slanted on his face, making his skin golden. 'What are they called in French?' she said, her eyes on him, the lime smell in her nostrils.

'I don't know. Let's sit down here and I'll look up my dictionary.' They chose a bench, and while he thumbed through the small book he had taken from his pocket, she looked around at the strolling people, the children. One child had a teddy bear which it was trailing by an arm. '*Tilleul*, they're called,' he said.

'*Tilleul*, she repeated, trying to pronounce the word the French way. 'Pretty . . .' This sunlit place, this happiness, and all around them death was stalking. But that was fanciful thinking, not at all like a sensible, well-brought-up girl who had been trained as a surgeon. She spoke in a professional voice. 'I saw some amputees in my cousin's house in Scotland. She has loaned it to the Red Cross as a hospital. They were quite cheerful. Maybe life is precious, even limbless.'

'Yea. Having mine has always meant a lot to me. I like to run, play games, swim, sail. . .' He turned to her, his face lit up. 'I did a lot of sailing when I was young. Great stuff.'

'Was it at that place you told me about last night? Boothbay?'

'Yes, that's it.' He looked into the distance. His arm was along the bench behind her. 'Every summer we went for the whole of our school holidays. Dad travelled up from Boston at weekends. We all ran wild, Irv, Bill, Holly and me. Mom was easy-going and she had a lot of women friends with kids. We talked about "the summer crowd", hers and ours. As soon as you got there you changed into old clothes, canvas shoes, then went down to the boat club and there they all were. The reunions! Catching up with the news! Who was going out with who . . . whom?' he grinned at her, 'who had a new boat, which races we were entering, who was going lobster catching . . . Am I talking too much?' He turned to her with his swift smile, his black eyes full of memories.

'No, I like to hear about it. It's a different kind of America from Wanapeake. But they have the Hudson River. That's lovely, too.'

'You have a lot of family there?'

'Yes. Emily's sister Victoria and her children, and her brother George with his, my mother's brother Patrick and his wife Maria, and their two girls, Sarah and Ginny . . . then there's Kieran.'

'That's Irish enough.'

'Yes, It was my grandfather's name. He's Emily's step-brother. His mother has come to live with mine since her husband died. They're sisters, the eldest and youngest daughter. It's nice for them both. She helps in the Red Cross Hospital I told you about.'

'I'm beginning to get it straight. Has Kieran any children?'

'No, he isn't married.' Now's your chance, she told herself, but didn't take it. 'It's he who's in the Field Ambulance.'

'Good for him. He isn't medical?'

'No, he's in their family business, exporters. He wanted to enlist. Then he has a limp.'

'A birth injury?'

'No.' It seemed easy to tell him. 'He and his cousin, Gaylord, went out shooting together and Gaylord threatened to commit suicide. He was . . . unhappy. Kieran tried to stop him and the gun went off, wounding him in the hip. He lost consciousness and Gaylord was dead beside him when they were found. We think he turned the gun on himself.'

'Families.' She felt his arm slip round her shoulders in sympathy. 'We have dark corners, too. Still, that was a traumatic enough thing to happen to Kieran.'

'It gave him a lot of worry . . . worse than the injury which was bad enough.'

'Maybe that's why he's here.' She looked at him, puzzled. 'Getting rid of the worry, expiating the guilt, perhaps.'

'Well, everyone has a reason. You said you came here for the adventure, to get away . . .'

'Did I? Look, we're getting sad. It won't do. This had to be a happy day, a day to remember. Shall we go and see the teddy-bears and then have lunch?'

'All right.' She returned his smile and got up. She had been charmed by that smile when they had met at Emily's; now it seemed to affect her even more when she saw how it lit up his dark eyes She remembered her father coming into her room to say good-night She would hear the door of the parlour shut, his bounding step on the stairs, and his black, loving, kindly eyes lighting up his tired face. 'No' cooried doon yet?' It was a nightly joke. And then his good-night kiss, his laughing voice, 'Sleep tight, don't let the bugs bite,' the tucking in, the soft closing of her bedroom door. It completed her day.

They wandered about the Zoo, and it pleased Ellie that the animals had plenty of room to wander about in as well. 'They seem as interested in us as we are in them,' she said, when a disdainful giraffe came over to have a closer look.

'They don't often see such a beautiful girl.'

'Only another giraffe would be beautiful to a giraffe,' she reminded him, laughing, but the theory didn't work, he said. The monkeys were too busy examining each other, and the wolves, from the way they limbered round their paddock, seemed to be disturbed by her.

There was a clutch of outsized shaggy donkeys from Afghanistan or the Himalayas, and she loved the apologetic way they turned their backs on them as if they were ashamed to be seen in captivity. But she disliked most of all the lynxes. 'It all fits in with Buffon,' he said, which she didn't understand and was too shy to ask him to explain.

The odour was not of lime trees, nevertheless, and after

a time Joe led her out through the gates to the café in the narrow Rue Geoffroy St Hilaire to sample some Turkish coffee and almond-scented sweetmeats. In the dimly-lit interior they talked animatedly about wolves and where they could still be found and Joe told her about coyotes. Their conversation was easy and pleasant, as if they were laying a foundation to their friendship by finding out how many things they agreed on.

But when the man who sold the newspapers in the corner was beginning to look at them curiously, they got up and found a restaurant for lunch, this time in the Rue Cuvier. She was noting the names in case she was bombarded by Emily for particulars about the Jardin des Plantes and its environs.

Now the friendship, the foundation, was disposed of, and they both knew there was the next step ahead. They sat facing each other over the table and had little to say, or did not know how to say it. Their eyes looked away and then seemed to meet for longer and longer each time.

She became shy and pretended to show interest in the lady violinist who was seated on a gilt chair on a little podium. Her dress was a dusty, floor-length black with tired lace at the elbows, her hair looked like a wig, or a bird's nest. She had bowed graciously to Joe earlier and had gone through a halting repertoire of war choruses, 'Yankee Doodle Dandy', 'John Brown's Body', and having disposed of America to her own satisfaction, had launched herself into a quivering 'Take Me Back to Dear Old Blighty'.

Ellie toyed with her food and made the excuse that she had eaten too much the previous night. Joe ordered coffee. 'It's quiet here today. Perhaps we're later than the regulars.'

'Yes,' she said, 'it's an afternoon quietness. There's only one other couple eating.'

The lady violinist was still playing. 'There's a long, long trail awinding . . .' She seemed surer of this one. She played it with poignancy and sweetness.

'"To the land . . . of my dreams . . ."' Joe sang the words softly. 'Where's the land of your dreams, Ellie?'

'Just home,' she said, 'home sweet home.' She felt the tears start in her eyes.

He put his hand over hers. 'I can see you as a little girl. Did you have plaits?'

'Yes, during the week, but on Sundays Mother curled it with rags. Then she tied it with a butterfly bow at the side, white moiré ribbon. I was allowed to wear my good Sunday coat with its velvet collar, and off we would go, Mother, Father, and I, for our Sunday walk along the Sholtie towpath – that's the name of our burn – a small river.' She had seen his uncomprehending look. 'I was *that* proud. That's how we say it in Scotland, not "*so* proud". And especially proud when patients passed and Father would lift his hat and Mother would nod and smile. Being the doctor's child gave you a particular place in the village.'

'I can see you. Was your hair as fair as it is now?'

'Fairer. Mother is still fair. There's something about the McGrath women. Their hair doesn't go grey. My grandmother was still redhaired at seventy-nine.'

'You should have done research on it, written a thesis on hair pigment. Were you an only child?'

'Yes, much to Mother's sorrow. She dearly wanted a boy, another Charlie. I really think that's why I became a surgeon.'

'It's a more laudable reason than mine. I was luckier than you with two brothers and a sister. We were, still are, a closeknit, loving family. Maybe sometimes people felt . . . shut out. A family can become a kind of citadel.'

'Yes, I know what you mean. It's all right if the family

accept the incomer, but I imagine their combined disapproval is like a kind of . . . bulwark.' She remembered Colin Thomson, and how she had been aware of the criticism of him, barely uttered but strongly felt, nevertheless.

'Yes, it's difficult for the incomer. I saw that: nothing said, just a thousand tiny indications. And the desolation when you find out they have been right, the refusal to accept, for a long time . . . Ah, well, one's personal life fades into insignificance with what's going on.'

'Maybe that's one of the good things of the war. You get your priorities right.'

'Maybe. And yet, if I get over-tired and can't sleep, instead of my thoughts going back to Boston where I worked, it's to those Boothbay summers, and the tarry smell of the tackle shop and the salt smell of the sea, and the rough yet sliding feel of the sheets running through my hands, the wind on my face. And I see the black rocks and the blueness of the sky and water. Why is it always summer when you dream?' Their eyes met. We are, she thought, in perfect accord.

'Because you make it perfect, I suppose. Joe, I'll have to get back. I've to do some shopping and perhaps have tea with Emily and Charles, then change and go to dinner at Giselle's flat. Terence goes off next week.'

'Everybody's going off next week. It's the Big Push on the Somme.'

'Is that where you're going?'

'I expect so. They're putting us all in, but I'm lucky, being noncombatant. It's men like Terence who have the hard part of it. I just deal with the results.'

'Does it make you angry – seeing the results?'

'Sometimes my anger chokes me. Not at the time. I'm an automaton. But afterwards . . .' He shrugged. 'So you have a swig or two of whisky and exchange a few dirty jokes with your fellow officers and fall into bed for a few hours' sleep, and in the morning you get up and do the same thing all over again. In a strange way, you enjoy it.'

'Yes, I know the feeling – practising your skill. Though I won't be as lucky as you, no swigs of whisky and dirty jokes.' His white grin delighted her.

'I have to get used to the idea of you doing the same thing as me.' He looked at her. 'It's incredible. You look strong, yet . . . fragile. Isn't there a Scottish song, "The lass with the delicate air"?'

'Yes, there is. Oh, I'm tough. I've proved it often. And I can do with very little sleep. It's something my father passed on to me.'

'Along with his skill.'

'We'll see.'

They stood once more on the Pont D'Austerlitz, waiting for a taxi. 'Will you give me your address?' he asked her.

'Yes, of course.' She told him, adding, 'near Chantilly.'

'If I get leave may I come and see you?'

'Do you want to?'

'You know I do.'

'To go to the Zoo again?' She tried to laugh, but it didn't work. She felt her mouth twist unbecomingly.

'I don't care where we go. I just want to see you.' He stood close to her so that she couldn't escape his eyes. 'Everything moves faster in war-time. Here today, gone tomorrow. So any subterfuge becomes silly. I want to see you because last night I didn't sleep for thinking about you, and today I've got to know you as if we'd spent years together.' He put his hands on her shoulders. 'Do you feel the same?'

She could not escape his eyes. 'I think it's usual . . . you said it yourself . . .' she was stammering. 'In war . . . you think there may not be much time . . .'

'No subterfuge. I've fallen in love with you, hopelessly, helplessly.'

'Don't say that,' she said. Her heart was pounding against her ribs.

'I shouldn't. I know. It's . . . all wrong. Ellie, could I write to you? I can't let you go like this.'

She looked at him, saw in the brown smoothness of his face a strangeness, as if he came from some ancient stock, unknown in Scotland. Was that part of the attraction? His wing-like eyebrows reminded her of what Kieran had told her of the original settlers in the American continent. His eyes were almond-shaped, his smile charmed her, shook her. 'You could write,' she stammered, 'there's no harm in that.'

'Ellie . . .' His hands were on either side of her face, drawing her towards him. She felt his mouth against hers for a second. 'As long as it's just *au revoir*.' She had an impression of black eyes holding hers for a second, and he was gone.

She watched him walking swiftly through the crowds, purposefully, very American in his gait, head up, the conquering race who had swept into Paris and taken over. Kieran didn't walk like that. Of course he limped, but even so he didn't seem to mow the crowds down on either side of him. He was tentative in his kindness.

The taxi came and she got into it, giving the driver Emily's address. She sat tearless, empty. He had taken her heart with him.

Giselle, Ellie decided later, was more mature than her mother. While Emily made sad mouths about Terence going to fight the Boche, and extravagant remarks about the hardship of war for civilians (she'd forgotten her earlier comment about the gaiety of Paris), Giselle, on the other hand, asked about Scotland, about Lizzie and Kate, Maevy and Isobel.

She had nothing but praise for what she called the *force d'âme* of the aunts, and admired greatly Lizzie and Ernest for giving up Sholton Hall to the Red Cross. 'I should certainly have worked for the War too,' she said, 'had it not been for Clovis and the coming baby.'

'My dearest wife,' Terence said – his talk had become more formal since living in Paris – 'your War work is with the little ones.' The terrible thought struck Ellie that theirs was not a personal choice but Nature's way of making up for the steady depletion of the race due to the War. But how could one say that, even as a joke?

When Terence showed her his paintings later, and she saw the strength in them, she thought how cruel it would be if a talent like his was wiped out. He was only thirty years old and coming to the height of his powers. Even as a young man he'd shown a great gift for portraiture. She remembered the one he had done of Grandmother and how he had captured her essential quality, 'an approachable and irreproachable dignity', Ernest had commented.

'Are you afraid, Terence?' she said. 'I mean about the actual fighting?'

'Strangely enough not.' He smiled at her. 'You'd think a bloke like me would have super-sensitive feelings, that it's the sturdy no-nonsense types who are the most use, but it's not always the case. We react quicker, our adrenalin flows more freely, perhaps. The only thing I'm afraid of is of dying and never seeing Giselle again. That's what marriage has meant to me, to us. But I have to go. My work would be worthless if I hid in my studio and painted with all this going on. It would have no meaning.'

'Yes, I see that. Maybe this is the last war when men are going to feel like that.'

'Perhaps so. I hope you and Kieran know the same

happiness. He was broken-hearted at not seeing you. We had a long talk, or he had, mostly singing your praises.'

'Oh, I'm not worth anything.' She was suddenly full of guilt. 'But when I see you and Giselle together I wonder if I'm being selfish. If we'd married we could have forgotten all about the War in America.'

'No, you couldn't. It's nothing to do with place. Neither of you could.'

She sighed. 'I wonder if, when all this is over, women are going to feel content with a life devoted entirely to the home. I've never heard a lecture on *that* from the Suffragistes!'

'That's a point.' He couldn't understand.

She smiled at him. 'I'll write and tell your father how well you're looking. Mother says he's anxious about you.'

'Yes, I know, but Honor's like Giselle, strong. She'll cheer him up.'

When they went back to the salon Charles was on his feet. 'I'm sorry, Ellie, but we have to go. I have just remembered I've left some papers in my office and I must pick them up tonight. I have to study them before tomorrow.'

'Of course,' she said. Was it subterfuge for a midnight visit to the love-nest, she wondered. If there was one. Really, Paris made one think quite differently.

She went with Giselle to have a last look at the sleeping baby before they left. 'He's cuddling his "Martin",' Giselle said, 'his teddy-bear.'

She hesitated, and then thought, I'm twenty-four for goodness sake, a grown woman. 'I saw some big ones today at the *Jardin des Plantes*. Major Gould took me there and then gave me lunch.'

'How nice! Is he married?'

'I didn't ask.' She went to the mirror and touched her hair, bent forward pretending to examine a spot on her chin. Joe Gould's voice was in her ear, '. . . nothing said, just a thousand tiny indications . . .' She fluffed some powder on her cheeks. They were burning. '. . . And the desolation when you find out they have been right . . .'

'He seemed *charmant*. They don't waste much time, the Americans.'

'What about me?' She managed to laugh. 'It was a perfectly innocent outing. Don't let your imagination run riot! Now, I'm going to keep an eye on you for Terence. I'll come and see you whenever I can, and will you promise to let me know if there is anything I can do to help?'

'You're so kind, Ellie. Truly kind.'

'Rubbish.' She put her arms round the girl. It was a strange gesture for her who was usually undemonstrative. 'I'm very fond of you and Terence, and we're a close family. That's how it should be. I hope Terence will be home soon and that the baby arrives without much difficulty . . . Oh, and that this old War's over much sooner than we expect!' She felt Giselle's swollen stomach between them, and thought, she knows more about life than I do.

'I'll be all right.' She hugged Ellie. 'It's you who are the brave one.' She released herself and went to the dressing-table where she opened one of the small drawers. She came back to her with a key in her hand. 'This is the key to our farmhouse near Gisors. It's in a little village called Chateau-sur-Epte. Anyone would direct you. Have this. You might like to spend a weekend there. You could take someone with you.'

She felt her face grow red and turned to the cot to hide it. 'Take someone?' She heard her voice, strangled in her throat with embarrassment.

'Kieran, for instance. Anyone. What's that old proverb about catching time by the forelock?'

'Oh, yes.' She'd been mad, jumping to conclusions . . . 'Well, if Kieran gets leave again . . .' She turned back, managing a smile, 'Although we don't do things like that in Scotland. My mother would have ten fits.'

'Ah, but you're in France now! Besides I wasn't suggesting . . .'

'Are you ready, Ellie?' Emily had appeared at the door. 'Charles, I'm afraid, is getting a little impatient.'

'Yes, of course. We were chatting . . .'

'My father is always forgetting to bring his important papers home, you know.' There was a smile hidden in Giselle's eyes as they met Ellie's.

Emily shrugged her shoulders. '*Tant pis*. One excuse is as good as another.' She didn't seem unduly perturbed.

9

There was no time to think of home and Mother, of Lizzie, Ernest and the aunts, no time to think of the brief time she had spent in Paris, no time to think of Kieran; above all, no time to think of Joe Gould, and she was glad of that.

The worst of the fighting was over at Verdun for the time being, but with terrible slaughter. The 'mincing machine', it was called, and even the Butcher Mangin had not been able to keep back the Germans. But men were needed for the next offensive on the Somme, which in the event was going to prove just as costly in lives. However, the doctors at the Abbey were thankful for small mercies. There was a limit to the numbers they could cope with.

All the new offensive seemed to be yielding was an unending procession of wounded and dying men, not the success which everyone had hoped for. Indeed, the more optimistic of the doctors had even believed that the Allied onslaught was going to end the War. The ambulances worked day and night ferrying the wounded men on the last lap of their journey from the Field Dressing Stations to the hospital. Ellie often marvelled at the cheerfulness and stamina of the drivers, some of them quite young girls.

She had been used to stress and long hours at the Royal Infirmary in Glasgow, but not to being so tired that she found she could go to sleep standing up, or while eating. The tiredness at times was so overpowering that she was afraid to go to bed in case she could never be roused again. All fears about her competency had gone. In the theatre she obeyed orders for the first week and only assisted the other women surgeons; then, as the list of men due for operation lengthened daily, she was left to her own resources

The first time she found herself amputating a young boy's leg she was amazed at her calmness as she set about it, as calmly as if she had the book of instructions propped up in front of her. 'At the beginning of the operation care must be taken to ensure that the flaps of muscle and skin will be adequate to cover the bone without tension . . . The bone is then divided with long sweeps of a sharp, fine-toothed saw. . .'

It was only late at night, when she was having a brief rest, that a violent shivering took hold of her and her sleep became more of a nightmare, compounded of the rasping sound of the saw on bone, the gangrenous smell, the pus and blood, the boy's face.

She was back again at the theatre in a few hours, quietly giving directions to the orderlies as another patient was brought in. This time she didn't look at the face.

She had little time to admire the lofty wards – the Canada ward had just been opened – she only knew that all of them were light and airy, the stone walls relieved by the white sheets and scarlet bedcovers, most of all by the flowers brought in from the Abbey gardens. The heating might be a problem in winter with only the stoves, but that was a long way off yet.

For the time being its medieval grandeur and coolness were restful, and a brief walk outside in the spacious grounds did more to restore her than stretching out in her monk's cell of a room. Sometimes during the night, if there was a hiatus in the work, she would steal out in the misty darkness – they were on the banks of the Oise – and walking down the gravelled drive she would realize that, subconsciously, Joe Gould had been with her all along. Not Kieran. His quiet gentleness had been eclipsed by the immediacy of the American, and her memory of Colin Thomson she dismissed as a mere adolescent infatuation.

Joe hadn't written, but if he was stationed in a hospital near the fighting there would be no time for that. Kieran, on the other hand, had written to tell her he was back in Paris. With the lessening of the ferocity of the fighting at Verdun they had been instructed to report back to Neuilly. For the moment they were kept busy at the Railway Station picking up the severely wounded cases who had been despatched for long term treatment.

Promise me (he wrote), that if you get time off you'll come to Paris. I think of you constantly, and have even dreamt that I might persuade you to marry me in France and carry on with our work. Just to know that you were my wife would mean everything to me.

The old idea of settling down in our own home is like an impossible dream in the midst of this terrible, never-ending destruction. Nothing would make me give up what I'm doing to help, and that's little or nothing compared with you. We'd never be at peace with ourselves – you were right – and, in fact, if America comes in I'll have a shot at enlisting. They're taking all they can get now in the French and British armies. I've come across men as old as sixty who've fought in the Boer War, and some of the young ones I'm sure haven't had their seventeenth birthday. The hungry maw of the War devours all ages.

But I dream, Ellie, of our life together when all this is ended and we have 'our place in the sun' – that's how I think of it – at Wolf House. That's what drove on the Germans, I've read, a wish for a place in the sun.

I shouldn't expect you to settle down as a housewife unless you wanted to. If you wanted to continue with your work in an American hospital, believe me, I'd understand. This War has altered many things, not least my way of thinking. All I want is that we should be together . . .

She wept as she read his words, and she wrote in her brief notes home, 'Tell Aunt Kate that Kieran is in Paris again and quite safe. I hear from him regularly and he always asks me to send on to all of you his dearest love.' She was amazed at the appreciation she had of all his fine qualities, his care for others, his gentleness, and how it left her unmoved. Her mind and heart were full of Joe.

But she at least had her work. It was worse for those at home. And then she would be comforted by the thought that those three indomitable sisters would also have little time for worry. Isobel and Kate would be in Lizzie's hospital daily, her mother, as well as going daily to McGrath's office, would be spending the weekend at the hospital and sometimes as relief during the nights.

In the early days of August she had a letter from Maevy which made her open her eyes in surprise.

Well, it's happened as I thought it would. Ernest left last Saturday for London to take up his duties as an Intelligence Officer. He will probably be going to France.

I spent the weekend with Lizzie to keep her company. This is the second time she's had to bear this kind of parting, and Nigel never came back. She took Ernest's going well, as you'd expect from her, but that's a rare love between them and you could tell her heart was sore by one look at her.

She kept on with her usual work, organizing the whole place and everybody in it with that bright, lovely smile of hers, but at night she broke down and cried in my arms. 'You understand, Aunt Maevy,' she said, 'you know what it's like.' I tried to cheer her up, said that at least he wouldn't be fighting and she'd find that as great a comfort as I had when Charlie was away in South Africa. There's only one way to cure a heartache or make you thole it, and that's work, and I know, my dear lass, you've found that out many a time . . . although I'm hoping in your case there are no heartaches and that you're looking forward to a good life with Kieran . . .

Do you ever hear from your Uncle Patrick or Aunt Maria? If not you're going to get the shock of your life. Ginny, their Ginny, is here working as a Red Cross nurse! Apparently nothing would do, Maria says, but that she must attend a course in nursing in Wanapeake and after that in New York, then she dropped the bombshell that she'd applied to come here. She got round the authorities (you have to be twenty-three to be accepted by the Red Cross), by saying she would be helping the other nurses under her cousin's supervision.

She's headstrong, all right. I used to think she was like my mother, but she was level-headed. I have my doubts about Ginny. Mother thought out things thoroughly, did nothing by impulse. Look at how she started McGrath's. A lot of careful thought and planning went into that . . .

Oh, but she's like your grandmother in appearance, those eyes which convince you you've never seen bluer, and the same carriage. Lizzie has always had a look of her, but her hair is darker and she's of a smaller build.

She's won over the patients already with her back-chat and that devil-may-care way she has of walking down the ward. 'Hi-ya, fellas!' she said to them the first day, and they roared back, 'Hi-ya!' At least they did till I stopped them and suggested to Ginny a quiet 'Good morning' would do. She doesn't take offence. She has a sunny temperament.

One of the lads said to me the other day, 'By Jove, Mrs McNab, this is the place to come to for a tonic!' 'I hope you're including me,' I said, just to pull his leg, and he said, 'Och aye, you're all different and yet all the same. There's a somethin' there a canna quite describe. It must be in the blood . . .' I was pleased about that, though I'm nothing compared with the others . . .

So you see, even in a quiet place like Sholton there's always something happening, but when you come to think of it there aren't many families who haven't had their lives disrupted in one way or another. I pray every night, like millions of other mothers, for it to be over soon.

Everybody I meet is always asking for you, and Susan never lets a day go past without your name on her lips. She's looking her age these days. I'm glad we're all about to help with the chores, because many a time she doesn't look up to much. Can you imagine that kitchen at Braidholme without Susan . . .?

August, 1916, was like no other August she had ever known. If it hadn't been for the carefully-planned system at the Abbey, no one could have carried on. Night and day the wounded, dying and dead were carried in. The smell of ether and chloroform was constantly in her nostrils, only partially subduing the smell of putrefying flesh.

She could not look at food although it was always excellent, as befitted the famous Parisian chef and one-time patient. It was only when it was sharply pointed out to her by a senior surgeon that if she did not eat she would become a liability, that she forced the food down.

The strange thing was that while all her intellect revolted against the sickening ruination of young, healthy bodies, her fingers became more adroit. Too much intensity in any field of endeavour, she had discovered through experience, did not promote excellence. A slight 'shift' of concentration, almost like that of a somnambulist, was the state of mind to aim for. That was not difficult. She was lucky if she got three hours of undisturbed sleep each night.

She was swift, she was reaching the peak of her development as a woman and a surgeon. Sometimes she was doing two operations at once, giving instructions to the anaesthetist, going from one supine body to another. What was uppermost in her mind was that the agony which the men had sustained on the field and then on their journey to the Abbey had to be stopped.

High Wood supplied almost more casualties than they could deal with. From time to time the men in urgent need of operations arrived on the table direct from the Front, and, to begin with, impatience made her strip them of their tattered uniforms herself, but she quickly learned that a surgeon's undamaged fingers were her most precious asset. One couldn't sew those interminable seams in damaged flesh with bleeding, raw hands.

In early September the surgeon in charge asked to see Ellie. 'How are you standing up to it, Miss McNab?' she asked. 'There's been no time to have a word with you.'

She smiled at her, a woman of fifty who might well have left husband and family to be here. 'You're very young.'

'Fine,' she said, 'no bother.' She was dizzy with fatigue. 'But I'm lucky. My father was a surgeon in the South African War and sometimes I felt . . .' she hesitated.

' . . . that he was at your elbow telling you what to do?'

'Yes. How did you know that?'

'I think because we all take strength from whatever quarter we find it. And there's no doubt we get fanciful notions when we're over-tired. We're living in extraordinary times. Have you ever heard that the soldiers were convinced there were angels at Mons?'

'No, I hadn't.'

'Many say they saw them, and that they guided them to safety. Ah, well,' she sighed, 'there's more in heaven and earth . . . I called you in to tell you I'm well pleased with your work, and since the list is a little less long this coming weekend, you could go off on leave. Have you anywhere to go?' Joe Gould, her heart said, but where was he? Still, there was Paris.

'Oh, yes, Ma'am! To Paris!' She was suddenly happy. 'I've relations who live there, and a cousin stationed at the American Hospital at Neuilly. He's in a Field Ambulance.'

'That's fine. Well, off you go and see them, but be back by Sunday night. I'll arrange transport for you.'

'Oh, thank you,' she said, 'thank you!' She had difficulty in hiding her tearfulness. She must be in need of a break.

She was like a girl out of school when she set off the following morning in an ambulance which was taking two patients in urgent need of orthopaedic treatment to Paris, driven by a young girl who, while maintaining a correct demeanour, had seemed 'distant', as Mother would say. When she spoke Ellie recognized the accent. 'It's a far cry from Edinburgh, this,' she said. 'I'm from Glasgow.' She saw the girl's profile freeze.

'Glasgow!' she said, horrified, and didn't speak for about ten minutes.

But her disapproval and the disappointment about not seeing Joe Gould – she must be mad even to think of him since he had not written to her – did not prevent Ellie from feeling light-hearted as they drove through the benign countryside of the Île de France. The switchback road took them through rolling fields and flat plains, through dark forests partly concealing great houses of pale stone turreted and balconied. At Argenteuil they began to see the encroachment of the city and Ellie tried once more with her driver. The patients were giving no trouble. They had been sedated for the ride.

Once she had praised the magnificence of Princes Street the girl became quite human, and soon she was singing along with Lily, as she was called, who said she did it often to pass the time. She was happy. She thought of Giselle and the coming baby – it might already have arrived – of Kieran whom she had managed to forewarn, and that soon she would be in Paris again.

But when they had gone through the Porte St Denis and Lily was threading her way carefully along the busy streets, her thoughts were again with Joe Gould, not Kieran. What a strange interlude that had been, but why hadn't he written? Had he regretted saying he'd fallen in love with her, 'hopelessly', as he'd put it?

But it had been there, the feeling between them, strong, asking to be acknowledged. In any other circumstances it would have had to be acknowledged. Only her natural cautiousness had prevented her from saying, 'I feel the same.'

The strange thing was that at this moment she could see him clearly, feel the strength and vitality which had come from him, imagine the line of his jaw, the high cheekbones, the black eyes, that American-Indian look, was strongly aware of that particular subtle appeal he had for her.

She discovered something about herself, sitting beside her driver from Scotland's Capital City. She was like her grandmother, that unique woman, so capable, so beautiful, and also a woman of strong passions. *She* had had an extra-marital affair with Jonty's grandfather, hadn't she? Of course, she had married him when her first husband, Kieran, had died so tragically, but at one time passion had meant more to her than fidelity.

But it isn't the same situation at all, she told herself. *You're* not married, nor is Joe. 'Isn't he?' a voice inside her said. 'And the desolation you feel when you find out they've been right.' His words came back to her. Didn't that indicate there was someone else in his life? 'But he would have said, wouldn't he?' The inner voice didn't hesitate. Did you tell him that you had some kind of understanding with Kieran?

Had their secrecy been because neither of them wanted to spoil their relationship, tenuous though it was? That had been *her* reason, but surely if he had wanted to see her again he could have written? Was he ill, wounded or killed? Any of these was possible. Or had he had second thoughts? Had he thought it wiser to stop the relationship altogether? Kinder? What would you do if he *told* you he was married?

'Take me back to dear old tiddley-pom-pom-pom . . .' sang Miss Auld Reekie. What had Grandmother done when she met Lord Crawford? There were times when passion was stronger than convention. She felt her mouth twist at that penny-novelettish, *Peg's Paper* kind of thinking. She wasn't like that. She was a young professional woman doing valuable work behind the Front Line, as valuable as any man. Ah, but I'm a woman, she thought . . .

'This is the American Hospital,' the lass from the Royal Mile said, and with a smirk, 'Are you sure it's your *cousin* you're meeting?'

'Would it matter?' she said in her best Miss McNab voice. 'Will you wait here, please, till I see about the patients' admissions?' She got out, then leaned into the cab. 'You're a good soul to give me a lift here. I'll forgive you for coming from Edinburgh.' They laughed at each other, comrades in arms.

10

They had lunch together in a Brasserie near the Auteuil Racecourse. She was genuinely glad to see Kieran. The feeling of ease and 'rightness' with him was strong, and his evident love was flattering as well as reassuring in a world which seemed to have gone mad.

'You look thinner,' she said. 'I bet you're working twice as hard as you need to. Are you getting enough sleep?'

He grinned at her. 'Hark at the doctor! I might well ask you the same. Your face is . . . fine-drawn. I get the feeling that you're having to make decisions every day which "take it out of you", as the mothers would say. You're being asked to give too much.'

'Shut up about me,' she laughed, 'I'm fine. Why don't you tell me I'm looking pretty instead? That's what every girl wants to hear.'

'I don't think you're pretty,' he said seriously, and when she looked at him, 'I think you're beautiful. But then I've thought that for ages. Beautiful inside and out.'

'You wouldn't think that if you could X-ray me. I have all kinds of wicked thoughts.' Joe Gould . . . her heart stabbed. Was it always there, the thought of him?

He shook his head. 'You'd be surprised at what's inside *me*. Verdun taught me compassion, but also hate. I've wept with hate when I've seen some of these men mangled beyond recognition. I could murder with my bare hands the powers-that-be. The Somme is developing now in the same way, and when the slaughter gets less we'll be into a long war of attrition. There aren't many men joining up now with visions of glory in their heads.'

'Except the very young ones, perhaps.'

'Not for long, because their lives are short. They see through it on their deathbeds. And the refugees! You can even get to hate *them* for clogging up the roads, wretched people who're pushing their entire homes on a wheelbarrow. Fancy hating them!'

'Don't be hard on yourself.'

'Oh, I've nothing to complain about compared with the *poilus*. They're as good as dead when they're wounded. Their medical services aren't geared to long-drawn-out affairs like Verdun.'

'They learn. They have to.'

He nodded. 'There was a château four miles south of Verdun where we had to go . . . well, that was indescribable. Everybody, doctors included, in a flaming temper because they couldn't cope with the rush of casualties day after day. We had to pick them up and drive them to the nearest railhead. Because the roads were choked it could take up to five hours to go ten miles. As often as not the wounded we were carrying were dead before we got them there. There was a certain relief that the screaming had stopped . . . they screamed in agony when the ambulance jolted. Somehow it's worse in French. Cursing the Boche. These *poilus* are trained never to give up. They're fanatical about defending their soil . . .'

'But you won't give up?'

'Give up?' He looked at her. 'What a hope! I'm just pouring out my heart to you because you're Ellie and I love you very much.' He grinned at her. 'If you really want to know, I'm enjoying myself! I bet you are too, in a strange kind of way.'

She laughed at him. 'We both must be mad. I went through what you felt the first week, but I'm luckier than you. The immediacy of my work doesn't give me much time for speculation. Not that I'm important – I'm not saying that – just one cog in a system which runs on oiled wheels, and I know if I let them down I throw a spanner in the works. What an organizer Dr Inglis is ! It permeates right down the line to the drivers, the stretcher bearers. Everybody helps everybody else. No job is sacrosanct.'

'Maybe it takes women to organize things better.'

'Isn't that what the suffragettes are trying to prove? No, not better, as good as. Look,' she pointed with her coffee spoon, 'this is how it goes. When the men arrive after a long drive in our ambulances they get hot soup and cigarettes. And a welcome. Of course there are some who have to go straight to theatre where we're waiting. Then their baggage is whisked from them, labelled, they are bathed and put to bed, and their uniforms and underclothes are hauled upstairs on a block pulley to a gigantic attic where they are fumigated. There everything is sorted out, washed and mended. We have a local woman who sees to that. Downstairs in the wards the medical staff are seeing to the men's bodily complaints, getting them well as quickly as possible, and sending them away when they're fit in clean, mended clothes, which is just as important as a stitched-up wound.' She took a breath. 'I'm sorry, I got wound up, but it *is* efficient.'

'I'm lost in admiration. Go on.'

'No, you've heard enough. I've enjoyed this.' She gestured to her plate. 'What was it?'

'*Moules Marinières*.'

'Well, it was nice. I'm so used to eating for fuel that I forget to savour, even though our chef is one of the best.'

'Why don't they sack Asquith and Wilson and put some of your women in their place? We could do with some practical common sense and planning . . .'

They walked in the Bois arm in arm. Under their feet the ground was thick with last year's leaves and already some of this year's, a brown drift. They passed a boy sitting alone playing a flute, and the sad, reedy sound followed them, emphasizing the quietness.

'Do you think he's Pan?' Kieran said.

'No,' she smiled, 'nothing so romantic. His mother probably got sick of the sound and sent him outside to practise. But it adds . . . atmosphere.'

They sat on a tree stump and watched the people strolling past. 'Grandmother drove through here in a carriage with your sister,' Ellie said. 'Can you imagine them, dressed to kill, with their parasols. Another world. The War seems far away, like a bad dream.'

'What about my idea of getting married? You didn't reply to my letter.' He drew her closely against his side.

'Because I didn't know what to say.' She didn't now, and prevaricated. 'Besides, it wouldn't be a proper marriage, you in one place and I in another.'

'Half a loaf's better than no bread.' She turned to look at him and saw the longing in his eyes. He was pale, he looked tired and undernourished. He needs looking after, she thought, but, then, pity shouldn't be a component of love.

They walked on without speaking. If he asked me at this moment to spend the night with him, would I consider it? Everybody's doing it, more or less, since no one can count on being alive tomorrow. But both their upbringings were against it. Love had to be of the kind which would sweep away moral scruples. His might, but not hers for him.

'You look sad, Ellie,' she heard him say. 'Wouldn't you consider it?'

'I'm too busy to think about anything like that. It's not the time . . .' She felt miserable, saying that. She wasn't too busy to think about Joe Gould.

They decided to go to Monceau Park and see Emily who would be able to give them the latest news of Giselle.

She would ask them to stay, of course, but if Kieran refused, would she go to an hotel with him? All thoughts of that nature were wiped out of her mind when the maid told them that Madame 'McGratt' had been taken to the nursing home yesterday and the baby had arrived. They looked at each other and decided they must go to see her. They would probably find Emily there too.

The matron showed them up to Giselle's room, saying Madame was very well and so was her little son. They found Giselle sitting up in bed. The baby was in a cot beside her. Emily, on a chair near the window, in a violet costume and tiny hat crowned with a bird in full flight, was dignified, as befitted the role of grandmother.

'Oh, what a lovely surprise!' the girl said, holding out her hands. 'Kieran and Ellie! *Maman!* How did you track me down?'

'We went to Monceau Park,' Kieran said. 'Don't you look proud!' He kissed his half-sister, then Giselle.

'Come and see this lovely little chap, Kieran.' Ellie was crooning over the baby.

He put the roses they had brought in Giselle's arms and bent over the cot. 'He looks pretty all right to me,' he said. They laughed.

'Why didn't you let us know you were in Paris?' Emily said. She looked wan, Ellie thought.

'We didn't get any warning.' She was still bent over the baby, enchanted, slightly wistful. 'This is the only kind of patient I don't see in my hospital.' Men dying, babies arriving, Nature's way . . .

'What lovely roses!' Giselle said. 'Thank you both.'

'They're not half as beautiful as you.' Ellie came over to stroke the girl's hair. 'I've thought of you often, knowing the baby was due. Weren't we lucky to be in Paris?'

'Yes, he only came yesterday. *Maman* would like me to

call him James after Grandfather, so we've decided to compromise and call him Jaime. It's easier for us to say.'

'Jaime.' Ellie tried out the French pronunciation. 'Has Clovis seen him?'

'Not yet. Tomorrow, my friend Madeleine, who is taking care of him, will bring him in.'

'And Terence? What's the news of him?'

Giselle's bright face saddened. 'None, unfortunately. But Father sent him a telegram.'

They chatted for a little time, but when Emily got up to go, Ellie said they would leave with her. 'We don't want to tire you,' she said, 'doctor's orders. If I have time before I go back to Chantilly I'll come again.'

'But I haven't heard anything about your work! Or Kieran's ambulance, for that matter.'

'He's bringing them in and I'm patching them up. That's all there is to it.'

'Ah, Ellie, you're so *pratique*. So Scottish. My Terence is the same. "It is nothing to go and fight Germans," he says. Nothing at all. I worry so much. Tell me, is it terrible?'

She compromised. 'Not for me. And truthfully, even when they're wounded I never cease to be surprised at how quickly they get better . . .' She stopped herself from saying, 'of the most terrible wounds.'

In the street outside Emily said, 'Charles has our motor car and chauffeur. He has had to go away on Court work for a few days. I'm going to get a cab. Will you come back with me?'

'Well . . .' Kieran hesitated, 'we had plans . . .'

'Only for the four o'clock, please. Do come.' Ellie noticed now in the daylight how pale and drawn her face was. 'Then you can go where you like. I know you want to be alone. But you must promise to stay overnight with me, won't you, Ellie?' She appealed to both of them, 'I need your company . . . very much.'

'Of course we will.' Perhaps it would be a solution as well as helping Emily, whatever her reason was.

Later, when she was sitting on the plump sofa while Emily poured tea, to her surprise her cousin burst into tears.

She exchanged a glance with Kieran. 'Oh, Emily, dear,' she took the cup from her, which was trembling in its saucer, 'I knew there was something wrong. Tell us what it is. If there's anything we can do to help we will, won't we, Kieran?'

'Of course, anything in the world. Come on, old girl.' He got up and knelt beside her, 'Tell us. We're family.'

'The thing is, I couldn't tell Giselle, not right away. She's so happy. And just when I need Charles he's not here. It's so typical. The telegram came yesterday addressed to Giselle. After she'd gone to hospital. I had insisted on her staying here for the last few days. I didn't want her going into labour in her apartment with no one there to help her. She only has a daily woman. I opened it. I didn't hesitate. It's in my handbag.' She looked round. 'Where did I put it? Oh, my mind's so confused!'

'Never mind,' Kieran said, 'telegrams are short. Tell us what it said.'

'I can remember every word.' Her face was tragic. '"Regret inform you Lieutenant Terence McGrath injured in battle. Can be visited at the Condé Hospital . . ."'

'Oh, God,' Kieran said. 'I wonder how badly?'

'I can tell you that. That's the terrible thing. I went to see our doctor, a very old friend, and he found out for me. His right arm and hand have been badly injured, but worse than that, he's been gassed.'

'Have you let Uncle Terence know?'

'Oh, yes, I've had to do everything. Armand, Doctor

Duval, such a dear man and an absolute *tower* of strength to me' – she looked ridiculously coy for a moment – 'sent a telegram to them and we had a reply today. He and Aunt Honor are on their way from Ireland.'

'What a shock it will be for them!' Ellie was stunned, and yet, why should I be, she thought. Verdun equalled death. Why should she have imagined that Terence would escape? 'Perhaps I could see him at Condé . . .' 'Right arm and hand . . .' It could mean anything – broken, mangled, gas-infected. She had seen some terrible cases where amputation was the only solution, but even that was nothing compared with the effect of chlorine or phosgene gas on the lungs, the acute bronchitis and oedema, the terrible struggling for breath, sometimes asphyxiation and death. Now her mind jumped to another terrifying thought. He was a painter. Was he right-handed? 'Would you like us to tell Giselle?' She tried to keep the anxiety from her voice.

'Does she need to know yet?' Emily said. 'It will break her heart.'

'No it won't,' she put an arm round her shoulders, 'not Giselle. She's brave. And she has to know, Emily. The telegram was addressed to her. She might hear it in another way and that would be too terrible.'

'And maybe his poor face is affected too!' She looked pitifully at Ellie. Her cheeks were streaked with black from the kohl she used on her eyes. 'Such a fine-looking young man! Together they were such a handsome couple, my Giselle and Terence. Everybody said so. Give her another day, please. She's so happy with little Jaime.'

'Perhaps you'll feel up to it tomorrow.' She wanted to say, 'You're her mother.'

'No, I simply couldn't. Much better coming from you. You're a professional, you can be dispassionate, a mother's love . . .' she dabbed at her eyes, 'there's nothing like family, is there, in a crisis? You go tomorrow. When do you have to go back?'

'Some time in the afternoon.'

'Well, that will give you time. I think I'll go up and lie down for half-an-hour, and then the three of us will go out to dine at the *Café de la Paix*. It's *très gai* these days, all those *lovely* uniforms. And it's my treat, Kieran,' she said firmly, 'I won't hear of you paying. And knowing you're in the house with me during the night will help me so much. Oh, I'm so glad you're here to support me.'

When she'd gone Kieran looked at Ellie. 'Terrible about Terence. I really thought he was getting away with it. I kept thinking I would be detailed to pick him up.'

'Yes, poor Giselle. Should we go tomorrow morning?'

'I think you should go alone. You'd be better at it.'

'It might be easier for Giselle, that's true.' He looked sad, she thought, not only for Giselle. She supposed it was because their time together was being swallowed up. But as Emily had said, they were family.

She was slightly amused later, however, when she saw how well Emily could put her anxieties behind her. She came downstairs at seven o'clock dressed to kill in her favourite purple with an osprey in her hair, saying that '*le docteur*' would be joining them to make up a foursome. 'Dear Armand,' she said, 'I don't know what I'd do without him.'

11

It was the most difficult thing she had had to do since she had come to France, she thought, as once again she mounted the stairs of the nursing home. The matron had told her Giselle was resting and the baby had been taken to the nursery so that she wouldn't be disturbed. 'He has strong lungs, that one,' she said, 'a vigorous child.'

'They're both well?' she asked.

'Yes, there are no complications. An easy birth and a beautiful baby – a good thing in this terrible world we are living in.'

'I ask because I have bad news about her husband. I'm a doctor, a surgeon.'

'Oh, *mon Dieu*! Yes, Madame told me about her clever cousin. He is not . . .?' Her hand went to her mouth.

'No, not that. He's been wounded. And gassed. He's in a hospital at Condé. She has to know, of course – if she's strong enough.'

'Is one ever strong enough for these blows? But, yes, the strength comes. I agree with you she must be told.'

She wasn't sleeping. In a cowardly fashion Ellie had told herself that if she were, she wouldn't disturb her. But Giselle sat up when she saw Ellie, fully awake, her dark eyes lively. 'Oh, *comme je suis heureuse!*' She held out her hands. 'You were able to come after all! I was just lying thinking of . . . Terence.' She laughed. 'Sit down. I'll ring for some tea.'

'No, thank you.' She kissed her and sat down. 'You look grand. No aches or pains?'

'Absolutely not. I'm going to get up for a little while later.'

'Don't overdo it.' In at the deep end, she thought. She had developed the habit of repeating the words when she had to convey bad news at the hospital. 'Giselle, I have to tell you,' she leaned forward and took the girl's hands, 'Terence has been . . . wounded. I'm so sorry.' Giselle's eyes flew open as if she had been struck.

'Wounded? You don't mean . . .? Is he . . . *dead*?'

'No, no! You know I wouldn't lie to you. He's in a hospital near mine. I'll go and see him as soon as I get back. You're not to worry.'

'Is he . . . badly . . . wounded?'

'I don't think so. It's his arm. Dr Duval got in touch with the hospital, but I must tell you, he's also been gassed.'

'Oh, no!'

'It mightn't be so bad. They wear masks sometimes . . . but I promised to let you know right away.'

'It can't be true. Gassed! Oh, that's terrible! The worst possible . . .'

'Take it easy.' She got up and put her arms round the girl, held her close. 'You must be strong. That's how Terence thinks of you . . .'

'How do you know all this?' Her voice was shrill with the effort to control herself.

'A telegram came. Your mother wanted you to be stronger before you got the news. But I know you. You're strong, as Terence is. Dr Duval says he's in good heart.' A white lie in such circumstances was always permissible. She sat down and smiled, or tried to smile. Giselle's face was as white as the pillows. She sat stiffly against them, her eyes unfocused, tearless. 'Giselle!' She spoke sharply. How often she had spoken like this to shocked patients. 'Look on the bright side. He's out of the firing line at least. You'll see him soon and you'll be able to tell him about little Jaime. In Scotland we say "Jamie" for a wee one. Oh, cry if you can! Think. It could be much worse.'

'I can't. Not yet. I have to know. Gassed. That's . . . bad, isn't it.'

'Yes, of course it's bad, but not fatal. He'll have trouble with his lungs but he's healthy and young. He'll get over it.'

'I never thought . . . of anything happening to him. When he went away in July I was optimistic, we both were. I thought it couldn't happen to us, that he'd missed the worst of it, that terrible *débâcle* at Fort Douaumont. I don't think anyone in Britain has any idea how we French are affected by Verdun, how we've agonized . . .'

'We realized, even if we couldn't feel it as badly . . .'

'It's been our crucifixion. If you'd been in Paris last winter and spring you'd have seen. It was like a morgue. People reeled with the shock. One hundred thousand Frenchmen killed! But at least Terence wasn't one of them. I was glad! Glad! Does that sound cruel?'

'You were thinking only of Terence. I don't blame you for that.'

'Then Monsieur Pétain took command. He restored our morale. We read that the German attack was beginning to falter. Terence and I joked together. We said perhaps there would be no need for him to go at all . . .' She paused, twisting her hands. 'How stupid and childish that was! Then came *Mort Homme* . . . men dying from the long range artillery, who hadn't even seen the enemy. Ask me if there is anything you want to know about Verdun, Ellie. I *spoke* Verdun, *thought* Verdun. I became superstitious. I kept crossed the fingers. "It will be over," I kept saying, "he won't be needed . . ." Every time I read about the land round Verdun being like a charnel house, protruding stumps of trees which weren't stumps of trees but human limbs, men drinking their own urine, I would think, "Ah, but *he* isn't there." Wasn't it selfish, Ellie? Did I not deserve to be punished?'

'Any woman would do the same. they want to protect . . .'

'Would they? When you arrived, and I knew it was because of the offensive on the Somme, I was glad. Verdun was virtually over – for the time being, at least. I didn't mind Terence going. I saw him off cheerfully. It was Verdun at its height which had seemed to me like a beast ready to devour him. Verdun had only spelled one word to me: "Death".' She looked at Ellie, her eyes wide and staring, her face white.

'Well, he isn't dead.' She wanted her to stop about Verdun now. 'Far from it. He'll get good treatment where he is. I'll be able to report to you how he's doing, how his arm is healing . . .' Could she ask if he was right-handed?

'And I'll go and see him. That's it. I'll get up and go and see him. Right away.' She was still tearless, but now shivering violently. Ellie looked at her and abruptly got up. 'I'm going to get Jaime.'

She followed the sound of crying infants and found the nursery on the same floor. She had to summon up her halting French to explain to the nurse in charge. '*Le bébé de* Madame McGrath . . . Jaime . . . She . . . desires him . . . *mauvaises nouvelles* . . .'

'*Son mari?*' Ellie nodded. '*A, la guerre! Merde!*' The nurse walked to a cot, bent over and lifted the baby in it. She came back and handed the white bundle to Ellie. '*C'est la meilleure consolation*.' The child was like a peace offering.

Giselle was sitting as she had left her, her face still ashen, her eyes sunken. 'Here's little Jaime,' she said, putting him into her arms.

She watched them, the sleeping baby against his mother's breast, the gradual dissolving of Giselle's face from its stoniness into tears. 'That's it. Cry away. Now, you're a brave girl. You know what you have to do. Get well quickly and visit Terence. He needs you.'

She raised a streaming face. 'You understand, Ellie. I'm all right now. I'm sorry. I am perhaps a little weak yet. Do his parents know?'

'Yes, they're on their way. Think of them, and the blow, particularly to his father. They'll need your support. You'll support each other. That's how it goes . . . in a family. And don't worry about Terence's arm. I'm sure he'll still be able to paint.' Giselle nodded and bent her head to the child. She slipped out.

Kieran saw her off at Neuilly again. Lily was waiting, her pug-nosed face like a slab of Scottish granite, but it broke up when she saw Ellie. 'Well, doctor, did you have a good time?'

'Interesting.' She laughed. 'This is my cousin, Kieran.'

'Been painting the town red, have you?' She was comradely, one uniform to another. 'They tell me the Place Pigalle is where to go, but I don't have a cousin.' Her look was sceptical.

Kieran laughed at her. 'I'll lay on an escort for you next time you come to Paris. Let me know.'

'Would you really? Well, at least that's something to look forward to . . .'

They had kissed when they'd walked in the Bois again after their lunch, but they were both saddened by the news of Terence, and the kiss was more one of compassion shared. It wasn't the time. She couldn't rid herself of the image of Terence with a mangled arm hanging at his side, his face contorted with coughing. That was even worse.

And they had had a lot to discuss. Kieran would make himself available as much as he could to his uncle and aunt when they arrived from Ireland. She on her part would write and tell him what she thought of Terence's condition when she visited him. There would be a lot of work waiting for her, but she would go as soon as she could.

'I thought it might be calming down a bit, since High Wood.'

She shrugged. She could Still hardly speak about the last two months. Once, to her shame, she could remember stripping off her rubber gloves and saying to the surgeon who was operating with her that she might as well be working in a butcher's shop. 'If you mean, has the fervour gone? well, it has. The men coming in are disgruntled as well as wounded. "It's murder out there," is their usual comment, "bloody murder." The spark's gone. Futile attacks, another hundred or two casualties. The terrible thing, Kieran, is that for all that slaughter we've only gained a strip of land about a mile across.'

'How many wars have we to fight before we realize the pointlessness of it all?' he said.

He helped her into the ambulance and stood on the pavement while Lily revved up. 'It was good all the same.' His eyes were loving.

'Yes, good.'

'Next time it will be better . . .'

'Next time. . .' Anything else she might have said was drowned by the rattling engine.

'Back to Purgatory,' Lily said cheerfully. And as she steered her way along Rue St Denis, 'Well, at least you saw a bit of life in Gay Paree, doctor.'

'Oh, yes, I saw a bit of life.' She encouraged Lily to go through her Scottish repertoire of songs so that she would be alone with her thoughts. And as if as a panacea, they turned to Joe Gould.

12

It was Honor McGrath's greatest wish to visit Paris, not under these circumstances, she assured her husband, but she couldn't keep down a thrill of excitement as they drove along the Champs Elysées *en route* for Emily's sumptuous house in the Monceau Park. 'If we hadn't been coming here to see that poor lad of yours, Terence,' she said, 'you and I could have had a devil of a time.'

'Aye, sure enough. I looked the Barthes up. They're not too far from Auteuil and all those darling horses.' Terence's life with Honor had given him a rich brogue, all the stronger because of its late adoption. Over the years the high-spirited lad from Glasgow had become expansive, his figure had filled out and become rotund, but his shock of red curls were still without a trace of grey in them, as his mother Maeve's had been when she died.

'And I should have been rooting amongst the old buildings and seeing if I could have found some old books and maps on the *Rive Gauche*, as they call it. There's been a deal of change here what with the Romans and the English – *they're* always there when there's any annexing to be done. Did you know that the two great restorers were Napoleon and Baron Haussman? The others were forever pulling it down.'

'Well, when you've exhausted owld Ireland you can come here and write a book about Paris. Giselle and Terence would be glad to see you . . . ah, that poor boyo!' His face saddened. 'I wonder if they'll have more news of him.'

'They won't have been standing still, you may be sure

of that. And you and me will just set off as soon as we can to the hospital. They wouldn't try to stop his own father from seeing him, would they?'

Emily and Giselle were waiting to greet them. Charles hovered in the background, a phantom-like host who in his own way put everything he had at their disposal. His bemused expression Honor put down to the fact that it had been bad enough coping with an American wife without complicating it with her Irish relations.

'Our home is yours,' he said. It certainly isn't, Honor thought, taking in the large gilt mirror above the Louis Quatorze Boule table – she knew her periods – the paintings, the Aubusson carpet . . . Woodlea couldn't hold a candle to this elegance. His lips on her hand had been cold, but she had thought maybe he kept his ardour for the mistress Terence's mother had told her about. Surely if he were so cold at home he must be hot somewhere else. It was the law of averages.

Giselle was thinner but with more vitality than her father in spite of her anxiety. 'You are so kind to come. Together we will go to see Terence tomorrow.' Her pale cheeks were washed by a sudden wave of colour, perhaps because she had just been enveloped in a bear hug by her father-in-law.

'Have you news of him?' Terence asked.

'Yes, a letter, but not written by him, from a *copain* at the hospital. "I progress admirably. I love you very much." *C'est tout.*'

'What more could you want?' Honor said. 'Now, then, are you going to take me up to see those two darlings of yours? I have to tell my girls all about them. Clare says to tell you that you look like beating her record.'

'How many babies has she?'

'Two now, but she and Aidan won't be happy till they get themselves a girl.'

'I, on the other hand, am content.' Honor, looking at the restrained elegance of her dress, thought she wouldn't want to be tied to a nursery for long.

In the bedroom upstairs, when the new baby had been duly admired and dandled, Honor came to the point. Like many artistic people she had a surprisingly practical side to her nature. Indeed, Terence said her fey demeanour was a ploy to steer people away when she was engrossed in a book, and if there was anything to be settled she was more direct than he was. 'You won't know how badly Terence is affected, Giselle?'

'It's his lungs chiefly which are giving most anxiety, but with Terence it will be his useless arm. I know.' She was calm. '*Maman*'s friend, who is also a doctor, has been in touch with the Condé Hospital. You know Terence. What would he do if he couldn't paint again? It would be his whole life ruined.'

'It's never your whole life, as you put it, and don't get yourself into a lather. That's one of your father-in-law's remarks.' She smiled. 'He gets mad when one of the stable boys rides a horse too hard. He's nearly bursting with rage if he sees one of his darlings with its flanks spattered with foam. It's marching orders for the lad the next day. Has your Terence ever told you of his grandfather, Kieran?'

'The gentle one?'

'That sums him up. With gentle hands on a horse. Maybe your Terence has them too, except he's painted with them instead. Now you take it easy and tell your lad to do the same. Don't let your thoughts run ahead of you. That's what I do when I'm writing, but it doesn't do in real life.'

'Ellie has the good hands also?'

'Yes, the best heirloom you could have, though I think

it came from her father as well. Now, Ellie's the one to tell you straight. have you heard from her?'

'Just the briefest of notes. She's working so hard. She told me she only manages a few hours' sleep each night. But she's explained to me the different kinds of gas and what to expect from phosgene. Mustard is the worst. It burns and blisters the skin. With phosgene it is one's lungs, but with chlorine one goes blue and drowns in the water from them.' She was poker-faced, like her father.

'It's crazy, gassing folks! Whatever will they think of next?' Honor was horrified.

'She says the worst effect can be the shell shock. The whole nervous system is affected, you see.' She was like a child repeating a lesson.

Honor shook her head. 'There's no sense in it. But if there's any winning to be done, in the end it will be the English. I don't know why their emblem is a bulldog. I always think of them as terriers. Have you ever seen them chasing rats?' She saw incomprehension in Giselle's face, a city-bred girl. And yet she didn't find Giselle as strange as some of the English with their loud, braying tongues, more foreign to her than real foreigners, like this poor lass. 'I wonder why we women go on bearing sons for them to slaughter? At least I had the sense to have three girls.'

'But *they* have sons.'

'Yes.' She'd used up her platitudes. 'Now, you and Terence and I will visit your Terence tomorrow. Do you feel up to it?'

'*Comment?*'

'Are you well enough to go?' She must learn not to speak idiomatically here.

'Yes, oh, yes. I'm glad you want us to visit right away. Maman wishes me to wait. She's afraid . . .'

'No, you have to go. He needs you. We'll see what he's

like and we thought that – once he's ready to travel, of course – you might like to come to us with your babies. Everything's quietened down now in Dublin after that terrible Easter Monday. That old house, Woodlea, *reeks* peace, where Terence's grandmother was born, and buried. Her fragrance is still there.'

'I'd like that. Maman wants me to give up the apartment and come here, but, no, she would grow tired of Clovis and Jaime. There's our farmhouse, of course, in Haute Normande, but it would remind Terence of the fighting. The Somme isn't far away. I gave the keys to Ellie in case she got a chance to go with Kieran.' *That's* French enough, Honor thought.

'Well, no one would interfere with you at Woodlea. There am I shut up in my study spinning stories out of Ireland's history, Terence doting on his horses from morning till night – you'd have the run of the place. You could re-create yourselves sure enough and Terence could paint again . . .' That had been a mistake.

'If he can.' The poker-face. Her girls would have been flinging themselves into her arms.

'If he can't he'll find something else. Terence isn't the kind to feel sorry for himself. He's a McGrath.'

They set off the following morning in Charles' Continental Rolls, driven by his chauffeur. Although Emily was always full of extravagant notions, it was Charles who came down to earth and arranged the journey. 'Emily will take care of the children. There's still a nurse here so she will not be entirely responsible for them.' And as he saw them off, 'I am sorry it is not my old Delaunay-Belleville. Leezie and Ernest had the pleasure of riding in it on their honeymoon. That would be . . . nineteen hundred and five. *Oui, c'est exact.*' He was. 'I prefer a Mercedes to this, but that would be asking for trouble nowadays. Do you agree, Terence?' Terence said that he did.

He and Terence, strangely enough, got on well together, one so citified and pale, the other growing slightly bucolic and even more countrified in his late middle-age. They showed a more than polite interest in each other's passion, motor cars and horses. 'After all,' Terence commented, 'weren't they both built for speed?'

'We appreciate all you've done, Charles,' he said, 'and never a word from you about your own two sons in Serbia.'

'Ah, they are not an anxiety to me,' Charles assured him. 'With my influence and their *savoir faire* they are both Staff Officers. I could have arranged a similar post for Terence, but, no, he wished to enlist and fight for France, his adopted country. Brave, but foolhardy. The romantic ideal, you understand, but how much easier it would have been for everyone if he had taken my offer.'

'He never told me that,' Terence said.

'Well, he's a man now, isn't he?' Honor had said that too. 'He doesn't have to come running to his Papa about everything.'

The journey through the outskirts of Paris was smooth in such a car. Honor, delighting in new impressions, almost forgot the purpose of their visit. How quickly the opulence of the Right Bank disintegrated into those working-class suburbs, but how different the people here looked from similar Irish, more bustling, and more shopping done in the open at laden stalls of fruit and vegetables. And what a lot of talking they seemed to indulge in! Anything to do with food seemed to make the French garrulous, she thought, either the purchase or the consumption of it.

In Ireland a bell fixed to the shop door warned the

owner of your arrival, and in the semi-darkness – they still treated gaslight as coming from the devil himself – your purchases were made and gossip exchanged in a confidential manner, almost like seeing the doctor or attending Mass.

But once through St Denis they were into the country again, great oaks lining the roads, the glimpses of turreted mansions at the end of pencil-straight avenues. They were like the shoppers, open to the eye, not concealed like Woodlea by a twisted drive, a thick belt of trees and shrubs. Maybe it was the rain in Ireland that made them grow so thick.

The matron received them and Giselle took over the interview as the woman appeared to speak only in French. Honor heard the word '*médecin*' several times, but had to wait until they were alone again to know what had been said.

'She says the doctor will see us before we go up.' Giselle's face was very white, her expression reminding Honor of Rusty, a favourite hound at Woodlea, a suffering, essentially female expression, and sometimes, after her latest litter, a slightly bedraggled look. Not that you could ever call Giselle bedraggled – she had the same Parisian smartness as her mother although less flamboyance in dress – but the 'look' was there. She'd seen it on herself in the mirror after birth, as if nature had taken its toll, made the hair limper, the muscles slacker. And added to this condition, Giselle had the trauma of a wounded husband.

The doctor spoke English fluently but with a thick Parisian accent. He waved away Giselle's offer to translate. He was obviously proud of his accomplishment. 'I have studied in America,' he informed them. 'Now, about Second-lieutenant McGratt, your husband, Madame . . .'

'This is his father and step-mother,' she said.

'*Enchanté*.' He shook hands briefly. 'I have to tell you that the lungs are still badly affected. One fears, but hopes . . . as we hope to save the arm.' Honor didn't look at the other two.

'*Save* it?' Terence said. His red cheeks had drained of colour, leaving little worms of purple on the whiteness.

'Yes, at one time I should not have said so. A gas-infected wound is difficult to deal with. Sometimes there is no alternative but to . . .' he looked into the distance. Honor had her arm round Giselle's shoulders. The girl was brave. She hadn't broken down.

'What . . . about his general condition, doctor?' Her voice was clear. 'Is he shocked?'

He nodded slowly. 'I hope not severely. He has the natural reaction of any man who has been through such an experience. Ah, *mon Dieu*, those long-range shells! Sometimes if the psychological effect is serious, it is necessary for the patient to enter a hospital devoted to the treatment of neurasthenia. But your husband has a sound physique. What is his *métier* in peace-time?'

'He's a painter.'

'The artistic temperament?' He drew in his breath between his teeth.

'Since he has a sound physique there are hopes of a complete recovery?' Those ifs and ans and buts of the medical profession, Honor thought, making her speak sharply. She supposed they had to cover themselves.

'Yes, there are hopes. I will commit myself no further. Now,' he was brisk as he spoke to Giselle, 'I advise you to see him one at a time but only for five minutes. By the way,' he brightened, 'your relative is here today, also by chance, Mademoiselle McNab, a surgeon from a hospital nearby.'

'Ellie!' Giselle turned to Terence and Honor with pleasure on her face.

The doctor was smiling. 'That is good for you? A capable young lady. She has visited and kept in touch with me when the patient's condition gave cause for anxiety, but her workload in the Abbey . . .' His English failed him. '*C'est incroyable!* Will you come with me Madame McGratt? And you will also see your relative. Now, is that not a stroke of luck?' He repeated the phrase, 'a stroke of luck, *hein*?' looking pleased with himself.

'On you go, Giselle,' Honor said, 'we'll wait here.'

She turned to Terence when they had gone. 'Your poor lad. One minute we're living the life of Riley in Ireland and then we come here and see the tragedy of this War. It's as if we've been hiding our heads under a blanket, and here I am writing about bygone battles when this is going on every day. It makes me feel downright guilty.'

'I'm too old to feel guilty,' he said. 'I'm just glad we have a refuge for them to come to well away from it. Terence has paid his dues.'

'That's true.' She put a hand on his arm. And I just hope it's not a lifelong payment, she thought. 'At least you have Robert safe in America.'

'Yes, but they'll be in next.'

'But he's not an artist. He'll put McGrath's first, not the War.'

He nodded and smiled round at her. 'How clear-headed you are in an emergency, my darling.'

'And how woolly-headed at other times?' She kissed him on the mouth. 'I'm with you in your pain, Terence.'

Giselle came back, accompanied by Ellie, one so dark, the other so fair, Honor thought. Giselle's smile was wavering, Ellie's beautiful as she came forward eagerly to greet them. 'I could hardly believe Dr Reynaud when he told me you were here!' She kissed them both.

'A coincidence and a half.' Terence was ebullient.

'Someone up there's taking care of us. We were hoping to see you sometime, but not so soon.' He turned to Giselle, his voice tender. 'Was he not as bad as you feared, lass?' Honor had put an arm round her.

'He is weak, terribly weak. The coughing, you see.' Her eyes suddenly swam in tears. 'There is pain in his arm but he says he doesn't worry about that.'

'The treatment is excellent here,' Ellie said. 'It's one of the American hospitals. The latest equipment. I . . . know one of the doctors . . . as it happens.' Honor saw the hesitation, even a slight colour in the girl's pale cheeks. Her eyes were dark-ringed, she looked fatigued, but that seemed only to add to her beauty. No one looking like her was going to escape admiration in spite of Kieran, though why the devil she couldn't marry him and set his mind at rest was a mystery. Terence had told her that Maevy had been the same, putting off that fine man, Charlie, for ages because of her career or some such. Didn't they know they could have their cake and eat it too, and hadn't she herself trained Terence not to get in her way when she was writing? It worked beautifully, she at her desk and he with his horses. It was all just a matter of organization.

'Well, that's useful,' she said.

'Yes . . .' Again the hesitation, then, quickly, 'I only found out when I came to see Terence for the first time. The improvement is tremendous . . . now.' And it was obvious she had kept Giselle in the dark at the beginning. Well, the McGraths were no fools, the women especially. This one could well be their flower. 'I'll stay with Giselle until you and Uncle Terence come back. Go to the reception desk and they'll send someone with you to show you the ward.'

* * *

When Honor saw Terence, she could have wept for his father and the shock it gave him to see the poor, pale, choking lad with the blue lips and the heaving chest. 'Oh, son!' he said.

'Father!' The two men gripped each other's hands as if they would never let go.

Honor kissed his cheek. 'I have to take my chance, Terence,' she said, 'in between your poor coughing.' She saw the tears well up in his eyes. 'But, sure, I'm not going to come all the way from Ireland without doing it.'

'Will you look at me?' he said. 'Crying like a baby. It's seeing you all . . . especially Giselle.'

'I hope you remembered to congratulate her on giving you a fine new son. Oh, he's a beauty! A look of your father, I thought, nothing of your father-in-law, unlike little Clovis.'

'Charles is one of the best. We . . . overpower him, all us strapping McGraths.' Terence's voice was cheerful to hide his emotion. She knew her Terence.

'He's been very helpful to me ever since Giselle and I married. You're right, Father. And he's got me some good commissions.'

'He's proud of you, that's why.'

'We saw Ellie,' Honor told him. 'She says you're greatly improved.' Her voice was drowned by his coughing.

'I owe . . . a lot . . . to Ellie. She supported me . . . in the . . . oh, blast! . . . dark days. But I'm fine now. This sounds . . . worse than it is. I'd be up . . .' his voice became stronger, ' . . . if it weren't for a stupid gash in my leg. Self-inflicted. I must have tripped over some wire. They're still watching it.'

'That'll mend,' Terence said, 'and the coughing will get easier. Are you worried about your arm being weak for the painting?' That was clever of him, Honor thought. Out in the open with it.

Now they saw the effect of the shelling. He shuddered suddenly and violently, his eyes flickered like a frightened horse. He turned his head away from them.

'Take it easy, son,' Terence said. He put a hand on his shoulder. 'We're here to help. Spit it out.'

His voice was low. 'I'm . . . worried all right. It's my livelihood. My family's livelihood.' She thought of saying Pisarro had painted with sticks but you could push jokiness too far. She spoke firmly.

'As you get better yourself your arm and hand will get better. Mark my words. I'm Irish. I'm a great believer in mind over matter. I've seen things . . .'

'You're not going to suggest I rub henbane into it or some other devilish potion?'

'I know *I*'ve never been the same since she scattered the fairy dust in *my* eyes,' his father said.

Terence turned round again, his eyes steady, his mouth curved in a smile. 'And I suppose she tells you which horse is going to win at the Curragh?'

'Sure enough,' Honor said. 'If you come and stay with us for a while you'll win so much money you'll never have to do a hand's turn again. Seriously, Terence,' she leaned towards him, putting her hand on his good arm, 'when you've finished your treatment, would you like to come and stay at Woodlea with Giselle and the babies? I've spoken to her and she fancies it. You'll be given a good long leave.' She wouldn't even *hint* that he would be invalided out. 'The soft Irish air, if nothing else, will finish the cure.'

'And would it take the sound of the shelling from my ears? It's there day and night.' The eyes were flickering again but he managed to control the shaking.

'I tell you son,' Terence said, 'the birds kick up such a racket in those tall trees that it's difficult to hear anything else. Or it's Honor yelling her head off at old Edna in the kitchen.'

'Is she still there?'

'Aye, and all the familiar things. Especially the peace. You think of it.' He got up. 'We'll go now. The doctor said five minutes. But you won't be able to keep us away from here. We'll be back soon.' He laid a hand on Terence's shoulder and turned his head away, his mouth working. Honor bent and kissed her stepson again. What a performance, she thought, the tears choking her.

On the way downstairs she said to her husband, 'Wipe your eyes, mavourneen. You might upset Giselle.'

When they went into the room there was a man with Ellie and Giselle. He rose to his feet, broad-shouldered but slim and with a foreign kind of charm, not French, in his dark-skinned face.

'This is Major Gould,' Ellie said. 'Terence's father and stepmother, Joe.' She knew instantly that they were in love – not a steady affection such as she and Terence had achieved, but an urgent passion. They would have to do something about it.

13

They were sitting in a Chantilly café opposite each other. She had refused any food, saying that the coffee was welcome. 'I have such a thirst these days,' she told him, 'but not hunger. We're all the same in the Abbey.' She smiled at him. 'Maybe we live on our nerves.'

'You should eat.' His concern was in his eyes. 'You're much thinner since I saw you last.'

'Oh, rubbish!' she said, pleased. She shared with her mother a pleasure in any comment about loss of weight. 'I can't have altered much in such a short time.' But it wasn't a short time. It was two months and he had scarcely ever been out of her mind. 'Why didn't you write?' she wanted to say. The sight of him was like food and drink to her. She lowered her eyes, sipped her coffee. 'It was a surprise you being posted to Condé. A coincidence. Have you been here long? I've visited my cousin a few times.'

'Only a week. I was in a hospital at Amiens, miles away. I was overjoyed when I realized how near I'd be to you.'

She blurted out, 'You could have written. Two months. I gave you my address.' Too late she tried to adopt a light tone.

He took her hands across the table. 'I wanted to. Day and night I wanted to.'

She raised her eyes to meet his, and felt faint. 'Two months,' she repeated stupidly.

'What I said to you that day we went to the *Jardin des Plantes* still holds, only more so. I fell in love with you. I'm in a state of love.'

'Funny way of showing it,' she said like a child.

'I thought it best. You told me about your cousin, and about him being in Paris. I saw affection in your eyes. I knew only a damn fool wouldn't love you. I thought it best . . . to stay out of the way.'

She was suddenly fiercely, irrationally angry. She was surprised at the physical effect. Her cheeks flooded with colour, there was a pounding sensation between her eyes, she felt sweat in her armpits. 'That wasn't it, I know! Kieran could simply have been a good friend, which he is. All right, yes, he wants me to marry him! You're clever if you knew that. But I wanted to go to France. Oh yes, I thought, I more or less said, that I *might* marry him when the War was over. At least I'd see . . . We think the same, we're suited, both conscience-stricken about it, although neither of us *needs* to be here. But there are other things we have in common. He's gentle and kind. The family would like it. Kieran wants it . . . But that wasn't it, was it?'

'Go on,' he said harshly, 'you first.'

'The strange thing is that he was in love with my cousin, Lizzie, first. I think it rankles a bit with me still. How can I expect a man fourteen years older than me not to have had experience of love? *I* have. But she's happily married now, and perhaps he saw in me to begin with something of Lizzie. Perhaps he only sees what he likes in women within his own family. Who knows? Anyhow, we have a good basis of love. It's there if I want it.'

'But you aren't in love with him. You wouldn't be so analytical if you were.'

'It would come.' Her anger flared again. 'You're side-tracking me. I've lost my naïvété since I came here. You have to grow up quickly, chopping, stitching . . . you're trying to make me give you up because of Kieran, to put the blame on me. It isn't the real reason, is it?'

'No,' he said. He let go of her hands. 'I'm married.'

She sipped her coffee. *Act* grown-up then, she told herself fiercely. The liquid had an acrid taste under the cloying sweetness of condensed milk. If I were asked what I remember from this War, she thought, I'd say the sound of my saw in the theatre, and the taste of condensed milk. 'I see,' she said. Well, of course she had known it from the little he'd said, from the lot he'd left unsaid. 'She isn't right for you,' his family had told him. But were families always right? She felt a stab of sympathy for the unknown wife at the place he'd talked about, Boothbay, wasn't it, surrounded by his family, his 'crowd', an alien. She drained her coffee to the dregs and got up. 'I'm glad,' she said, 'you've had the courage to tell me,' began to walk towards the door. She was aware he was on his feet too, heard the small noise of some francs being thrown on the table. He was at her side.

'Let's walk.' He opened the door for her, and outside adjusted his officer's cap. He looked rakish, except for his eyes. 'You wouldn't be silly enough or cruel enough to leave it like this?'

'No.' She buttoned her coat, adjusted the tartan collar. It gave her dignity, which she needed. 'But you should have said at the beginning.' She smiled at him, almost gaily. 'Then I shouldn't have gone on thinking about you.' They were in the middle of the street, suddenly separated by a noisy bunch of soldiers, were together again. 'I've to get back in any case. They've been more than kind to give me time off to see Terence.'

'That's your young cousin?' Their conversation had to be casual in this public place.

'Yes. You met his wife, Giselle. French. Do you think he'll recover completely?'

He shrugged. 'Too early to say. Those gas cases are difficult. I'm keeping a special eye on him.'

'The arm is an especial worry. He's a painter. Considered good.'

'Then he needs his hands. It's the psychological effect of the gas. Still, it could have been worse. Mustard. When they've no upper lip, or their noses have been sliced off or they've lost half a cheek, it's worse.'

'I don't know what's worse. I don't know anything any more. I hope he's a fighter. I had a grandmother, Maeve, the queen of fighters. Some of our family have a bit of the same.'

'If he has, he'll make it.' They had been walking as they spoke and now he steered her into a quiet side street. There were only a few children playing, and they were immersed in their game. 'How are you getting back?'

'The same way as I came. There's an ambulance leaving your place at five.'

'Let me take you. I'm off until six. Ellie, please. I want to talk to you.'

'What's the use? You're married.'

'I'm not a leper because of it.' He smiled round at her. The rakish tilt of the cap made her go sick with desire for him. Nobody bothered about marriage in the War. 'Whose name did I call out?' some of the men asked her when they recovered consciousness. And when she told them, 'Bloody hell, did I? Don't tell the wife . . .'

'But you might be branded on the forehead.' She was able to laugh. Who ever heard of a moral principle in a slaughterhouse like this?

He began talking as they walked through the narrow streets. 'Her name's Gilda. It's been a failed marriage for some time.'

'Do you still live together?' she asked. It seemed important.

'Not much. She goes off for long stretches. She's a

dancer, you see. Her parents hoped that when she married me she would give it up. The stage, I mean.' He paused, said, 'I used to think she was amazingly beautiful. I don't any longer. It's finished. Has been for some time.'

'That's sad.'

'Not for her. There have been others. I asked her for a divorce before I came here, but she doesn't believe in it. She's a Catholic. Several times I asked . . . Oh, hell! I'm listening to my voice, watching out for the whining note creeping into it. And here's my car.' He stopped her with his hand on her elbow. They were in a small square near the hospital. They had walked in a circle. 'May I take you back?' She met his eyes under the rakish tilt of the cap. They were suffering.

She shrugged, nodded. It was a trifle compared with the other things, that he was married, that his wife wouldn't give him a divorce, and yet not a trifle since he would still be with her.

'It was my mistake.' He was driving carefully, reading street names. 'Choosing someone who wasn't . . . constant, who didn't want children. Maybe it was as well, from a child's point of view.'

'It doesn't always follow. Lizzie, the cousin I told you about, is the most beautiful and well-balanced person I know. She's really Terence's father's illegitimate child conceived when he was married to a woman who committed suicide when she heard of the baby.'

'Not a good start,' he said, his mouth turning up.

'My grandmother took her, made her what she is today. Even when she gave her to another daughter who was childless, it didn't matter. She was as she is today. Then a village woman spilled the beans to her, but she got over that and married Nigel who died in the Boer War – my father took off his leg, gangrene – and now she's happily married to Ernest and her house is a Red Cross hospital.'

'Wow! Quite a history! You sound as if you admired her.'

'I do, oh I do.'

'Turn the limelight on yourself, honey. There's just as much there.' 'Honey'. The last thing I am is a honey, she thought, but it was nice to be called it. 'Lizzie couldn't do what you're doing.'

'Rubbish. She could if she'd been trained. Who's talking? You're another one who doesn't *have* to be here.'

'I'm using the War selfishly, to get away from my problems. I wanted to be so tired that I wouldn't think. Besides, it's damned good experience. I'm loving it, and the company. I'm a gregarious kind of guy. And if I hadn't come I shouldn't have met you. And fallen in love. Even just to see you when you visit your cousin is something.'

'Is that enough? Just to see me?' Her heart ached. She could see the ruined tower of the Abbey in the distance, a grey-gold pencil against the September sky. It would soon be over. They'd meet briefly at Terence's bedside, perhaps she might have another coffee with him. She might one day find he had been transferred. How would she get through the next hours, operating all night, with such an aching heart? If she could cut it out the way she chopped off limbs . . . Often they told her they felt pain in the missing leg. There was no cure for cut-out hearts. It would bleed and bleed. The soil of France would be rich for years . . .

He had stopped the car in a little lane without her noticing. Colin Thomson used to do that and she would know what to expect. Was life a constant repetition? It was really a clearing in the forest. Those tall Île de France trees, she thought, so many forests in this part of France, relics of the time when the nobility had their houses here. Pleasant glades . . . *les très riches heures* . . .

He had one arm along the back of her seat and with the other he turned her face by the chin to meet his eyes. 'What age are you, Ellie?'

'Twenty-four going on for twenty-five.'

'I'm thirty. Are you a virgin?' If they hadn't both been doctors she would have blushed.

'Yes. I haven't had much time to be anything else. I've worked like a Trojan passing exams. An infant prodigy, me. I've had one boyfriend lusting after me. Not Kieran.'

'I like case histories,' he said, laughing.

'Do you? I think it's a case of history repeating itself. My mother would have been older than me when she married, and I've always gathered that was the first time she dipped her toe in the water.'

'I'm no saint,' he said, 'or rather moralist. Love is meant to be expressed, even outside marriage if marriage isn't possible.'

'No,' she said, 'I'm not in the market for illicit weekends.'

'That's what I wanted to know.' He released her and turned on the engine. 'I respect you for your principles. And I'll always love you.' He reversed the car slowly into the road, concentrating because of the tall forest trees. 'This is not a flash in the pan. It is the best and truest love I'm capable of, will ever be capable of. I just wanted you to know.'

'Thank you very much,' she said. She felt her insides shrivelling up. This must be how a dried-up spinster felt, all the juices solidified.

He drove between the tall roofed gatehouses and up the drive towards the Abbey. Through the poplars at her side she could see the silver line of the Thève which had been there even longer than the golden-stoned old building ahead of them. He jumped out at the huge door, went round the motor and helped her out. His hand went to his cap in a salute.

'My French cousin, Giselle,' she said, 'gave me the keys of their summer house near Gisors. Do you know it?'

'Gisors? I think so. Yes, it's on the border of Île de France and Normandy. It's escaped the worst of the War.'

'I've been planning a weekend there for a long time. I'm due one at the end of the month. I truly need to get away on my own. I'll never collapse – I'm a strong Scottish lass – but some days I think I'm not far from it.' She laughed. 'I'm ashamed to hear myself saying that. My father would be ashamed of me.'

'We all feel it. You *look* as if you felt it. When I first saw you at your cousin's bedside I thought you looked like a ghost of the girl at the Zoo.'

She laughed. 'Anyhow, I'll be there, at this little village, Château-sur-Epte, it's called, Giselle says. It's on the west side of the river. Walking, resting, living like an ordinary person again. No smells, except maybe woodsmoke. If you happened to be off that same weekend, or even for a day, I'd cook you a dinner, or a lunch, of sorts. I go crazy with joy at the thought of just cutting up *vegetables*!'

His smile was brilliant on her. 'Château-sur-Epte, on the west side of the river. What's the name of the house?'

'La Hirondelle.'

'One doesn't make a summer.'

'Come again?'

'*La Hirondelle*. Swallow.'

'Oh, yes.' She laughed. She was so happy that she'd taken the plunge. More or less invited him. In at the deep end. Regret was for things *undone*.

'Right. Unless we get shelled or I drop down dead, I think it's more than likely I'll be passing in that direction. Look out for me, will you?' His eyes were deeply on her. She had to make herself turn and go up the steps.

There is no commitment, she told herself, running upstairs to her cell to change into whites. I've only told him I'll be there . . .

14

Maevy was at her desk that morning at eight-thirty, the day of Jonty's birthday party which, fortunately, had fallen before he went back to Eton for the Michaelmas term. There was no diminution in the work at McGrath's, in spite of the merger and the corporate umbrella of Globe Express Deliveries.

She had slipped easily into Ernest's organizing chair. Dan was too busy with the heavy side of the business, which had developed and increased with every year of this never-ending War. He took charge of the buying of the vehicles required. The War Office contracts, as well as being lucrative, gave privileged petrol and exemption badges for the fitters and drivers.

The same couldn't be said of the lighter commercial work, but she wasn't sorry they had had to drop that. She had never liked the idea of McGrath's vans or carts bearing their customers' names. Credit where credit was due, she had said. Besides, there was a constant obsolescence with the lighter type of vehicle. That was the only good thing she could say about this War, that it stepped up innovation and production.

There was still the vexed question of the horses. Their fleet had declined considerably, so much so that this year they had sold off their old stables at Bridgeton and were now sharing with Bannister and Craig, and Naylors, their complex of garage and stabling at Cannongate, where they could pool resources, veterinary services and hay and straw supplies which were becoming more and more difficult to obtain.

She thought sadly of her father. There was no doubt about it, the halycon days of the horse were past. How he would have grieved! Still, he would have been pleased to know that the tradition was being carried on by Terence in Ireland. He would give them all a winner one of these days.

And Father might have been amused, or amazed, at the women carters they employed, often the wives of the men on active service. They had good hands on a horse, and there they were, sitting up on those open carts, a canvas bag over their knees and another one over their heads, as happy as Larry. There was no doubt about it, women were proving the equal of men. It was a pity it needed a War to convince people.

She examined the papers on her desk, carefully checking the accounts. She was nearly as good as Isobel at adding up. There was no doubt that the biggest revenue was from removals – that and storage. She permitted herself a quiet pat on the back there. Often, sadly, through death or the dissolution of a marriage – the women as well as the men were not all faithful and had proved their versatility in other fields as well as carting – quantities of furniture were left on their hands. Because they had instructions to realize its value she had instituted monthly auctions.As well as a lot of rubbish there were some choice pieces and Lizzie had been early on the scene, earmarking the best antiques for her Great Plan.

She wouldn't say what it was, and why shouldn't she have her secrets? How like Mother she was, she thought. She remembered how carefully Maeve had planned this very firm from which they all reaped so much benefit, the careful laying of her schemes, the seduction – verbal, of course – of that poor cousin of hers, Duncan, the humble beginnings. She still had that little bureau Father had been given for his first order, a removal of a widow's bits and pieces for which he had been paid the princely sum of five shillings. If he could see what they charged now! Not profiteering – she wouldn't have permitted that – but the rate for the job.

And now McGrath's, incorporated to be sure, but their name still well known, was one of the best firms in the country, with infinite possibility of expansion along different routes.

The auctions would continue without a doubt. There was the possibility of refrigerated stores, and even refrigerated lorries. Dan and Jack were looking into the figures now. Shipping was thriving in Patrick's and Robert's careful hands, and from that there was the possibility of a travel agency. That had been Lizzie's idea. Something like that would suit Jonty down to the ground when he had finished his schooling, or perhaps he would become interested in old furniture. They had plenty of it abandoned in their repositories.

He had his mother's and his great-grandmother's love of fine things, a sensitive boy, a difficult boy to fathom. Lizzie had confided to her that he wrote poems, although he hadn't let her see them. He was secretive, like his paternal great-grandmother, Annabel, Mother's one woman friend, 'a creature of the woods', she'd called her.

She pondered the phrase, thinking of the Sholtie Woods bordering the estate, and how walking by the high stone wall they had scuffed the leaves with their feet on their way to school. An abiding childish memory. As was that of Lady Crawford climbing their fence when she was taking a short cut through their vegetable garden at Colliers Row. And showing her petticoat as Terence had commented. Terence would. But she and Mother had got to know each other on that bench at the back door – a friendship until death.

Ah, well, she had better get on with the work and stop

dreaming. First of all she must get those figures from Accountancy. Ernest might just be home for Jonty's birthday and he would like to see them. He had been in France three months now, interrogating prisoners of war, and he must be due leave. Knowing Ernest, he would manage it, just as he seemed to manage everything else in his life. Lizzie was a lucky woman. She wasn't likely to lose Ernest in this War as she had lost Jonty's father in the last.

She lifted the telephone on her desk and said to her secretary, 'Ask Mr Richardson to come in, please. And bring the folder for Parkhead.'

Ginny had come upstairs at five o'clock, ostensibly to help Lizzie with the preparations for the birthday party. She loved it here. In the short time she had been at the Hall she had grown very fond of Jonty, indeed of the whole household. There was a warmth and a lightness which she had never known at home, and the source of it was Lizzie, there was no doubt about that.

Mother was Mother, but her lack of humour was the trouble. Lizzie never said, 'Oh, Ginny . . .!' in that *reproachful* way, and even Aunt Maevy's discipline was more acceptable. You knew where you were with her. She told you straight, and it didn't colour your relationship afterwards. And she gave praise where it was due.

Ernest was a charmer, that was her secret word for him, and if Lizzie was unlike Mother, Ernest was miles removed from Father! If she ever married she hoped it would be someone like Ernest, suave, sophisticated . . . those callow boys back home had a lot to learn.

'I've come up to help your mother,' she said to Jonty who was sitting reading in front of the fire. She plumped down on the sofa opposite him. Mother would have said, 'Ginny!' and to please her she would have had to sit upright like a lady, knees together. 'Did you hear me, birthday boy?'

'It's all done.' Jonty flicked his eyes at her from his book. 'She's luxuriating in her bath.'

'Lovely word, "luxuriating".' She stretched out her full length amongst the cushions. 'A real old Etonian word.'

He looked up at her, 'Back where you come from I expect they'd say, "wallowing", but then they don't know any better.' His swift smile disarmed her. He was a charmer, too. 'She's hoping Ernest will make it for tonight.' He put down his book and stirred the glowing logs. Lizzie liked a fire summer and winter except in the rare event of a heatwave.

'So she's making herself nice for him?'

'She's always "nice", as you put it.' His upper-class English voice struck her as strange after the rough Scottish ones of most of the patients downstairs. Especially the two Bantams. 'You can't say two words without blaspheming,' she had said to one of them, his five feet two further depleted by the loss of a limb. 'Aye, guid gear gaes inty sma' buik,' he'd said, his cheeky face raised to her. They said they were grand fighters. 'She gets her bath salts and perfume from France always,' Jonty was saying. 'Ernest really indulges her. They're a couple of lovebirds. Makes me sick, sometimes.'

'Are you jealous, little boy?' she said, stretching out on the sofa so that her body looked slimmer than ever, long torso, long, slender legs. 'So why don't you get a girlfriend for yourself? You must be the age for it now.'

'Oh, there are plenty around.' He spoke loftily. 'Some of the chaps creep out at night and meet the Windsor shop-girls. I call it puerile. I've better things to do.'

'Such as?'

'Studying. I have to get my final OTC exam this year. And there's . . . writing.'

'There, I told you, didn't I?' she said. 'Love letters. Now I know.' She clapped her hands, sitting up and looking at him. 'Little Jonty writes love letters,' she sang.

'You're an ass, Ginny. It must be because you were brought up in that rough place, America. Hoodlums. Why would I waste my time writing love letters to snotty-nosed little shop-girls, or maids, for that matter?'

'Oh, listen to the snobbery!' She was enjoying teasing him, her favourite pastime. 'You wouldn't get *that* in America, that's one thing! There all men are equal. And here they continue to perpetuate the snobbery by sending you to those awful public schools. "I say, you chaps!" She threw back her head and laughed. 'I thought Lizzie and Ernest had more sense.'

'It was nothing to do with Lizzie and Ernest. It was my father's wish. The sons of Sholton Hall have always gone to Eton.'

'Oh, listen to it!' She lay back again on the sofa, stretched still further. It was good to feel that taut feeling in one's waist after all the back-bending downstairs. 'That's what's going to be the downfall of Britain. Class! You're all *obsessed* with class. That and seducing little shop-girls and maids and waitresses because the daughters of the gentry won't let you near them unless you put a ring on their finger . . .'

'You're uncouth, Ginny,' he said, 'really uncouth. I've told you I'm not interested in that sort of thing and I wouldn't waste paper writing that kind of drivel. Poems are different . . .'

She seized upon the remark with glee. She'd known he was up to something during these holidays with his incessant scribbling. 'Ah, now the cat's out of the bag! You're writing poetry! Is it love poetry? All about flowers and sunsets and walking down the lane hand in hand?'

'You make me sick!' He threw himself away from her.

'It's war poetry! What else could I write about when there's a war on!' He was shouting now. She'd made him angry. It was fun baiting him. He was so vulnerable and so handsome when he got angry. That lofty look which must come from his father, the high forehead, the air of elegance. Even at sixteen he was elegant, with narrow feet and hands, a patrician air.

'War poetry?' She'd risk going a little further. 'How can *you* write about the War? You've never been there!'

'Not yet,' he said, suddenly quiet again. 'Now, shut up. I know you tease me because you're bored.' He was maddeningly cool. 'Go and dress yourself like Mother. Try and make yourself as beautiful . . . if you can.'

Lizzie came into the room wearing a cream lace dress with a broad cummerbund of tangerine velvet. Her yellow opal earrings complemented it and her burnished copper hair dressed high on her head. Her blue eyes seemed even deeper in colour because of the creamy paleness of her face. 'Oh, you've come up, Ginny?'

'What a relief!' Jonty said, 'someone decent at last!' Ginny saw the pride in his eyes. 'You smell nice, Mother. This room stinks because of Ginny.'

'That's a terrible thing to say.' Lizzie laughed at him. 'You'll have to apologize to your cousin.'

'Oh, he's just a little schoolboy.' Ginny got up. 'Still, I will have a bath to get rid of the *hospital* smell. I love your cummerbund, Lizzie. Makes your waist look smaller . . .' She should have added, 'if anything. . .'

'I can't tell you the difficulty I had getting it hooked.' Lizzie was too equable. She didn't readily take offence. She was so sure of herself . . . 'But Ernest might manage to come home and this dress is his particular favourite.' Her eyes were glowing like jewels, not only from the reflection of the fire. She spoke affectionately. 'You've had a gruelling day, I know, with those new intakes. Have a sherry before you go. And don't wear anything too fetching. I don't want to be eclipsed.'

'Fat chance,' Jonty said, glowering at Ginny.

Lizzie laughed. 'She's been teasing you again. Never mind. You pour the sherry for us, darling, and take one for yourself. After all, it's your birthday. Your sixteenth birthday, I can hardly believe it. Born in the Boer War and nearly old enough for this one. Thank goodness you're not. I couldn't bear it.' She's beautiful, Ginny thought, looking at her with her arm round her son, now taller than she was, now probably more beautiful than she had been sixteen years ago. It would be difficult to outshine her, no matter what she wore.

The party was a cheerful, riotous affair by the time dinner was over and they had returned to the drawing-room which had been cleared of most of the furniture and the carpet rolled up for dancing.

Lizzie had invited any of the patients who were able to walk to come upstairs, and even two or three of the amputees who had said they wouldn't mind a bit of fun. There were plenty of willing ladies to take care of them, as well as nurses to wheel their chairs and feed them, if necessary. Kate, Isobel and Maevy vied with each other in their attentiveness, and Belle Geddes was there if the excitement proved too much for anyone.

If Lizzie was disappointed that Ernest hadn't made an appearance she didn't show it. Earlier, in the dining-room, she had put Jonty at the top of the table and taken her place at the bottom, after having arranged the thirty or more people nearest those whom they knew or felt comfortable with.

She was an expert hostess, Ginny had thought watching her, now standing at a small table with Jonty ready to cut the birthday cake. Her natural charm and beauty, her outgoing nature and sense of fun, added to years of experience, had produced someone who could take charge without appearing to do so, who could find the right word for everyone, create the right atmosphere.

The aunts helped too, and she had to admit they were an asset to any gathering – Aunt Maevy stately in her brown velvet; Aunt Isobel fragile with her thin, clever hands, her quick movements; Kieran's mother, different from the Aunt Kate she had known all her life at Wanapeake, quieter, with a sad sweetness. A part of her had been buried with Uncle James. If I had to confide in anyone I'd choose Aunt Kate, she thought, but what would she want to confide? Her feelings were too confused, too indeterminate, she hadn't found her right niche here after all. I suffer from a complaint which is unnameable, she thought. When I'm in one place I always want to be somewhere else.

Aunt Kate knew her background, of course, of the difficult circumstances at home, that beautiful stone house which never had the warmth of this one. Sarah, kind and distant, with her never-ending good works, Father obsessed by McGrath's and little else, Mother always concerned about his welfare above anyone else's. Are they right and am I wrong? she wondered. She remembered a Scottish saying of her father's, 'Everybody's out of step but oor Jock.' Was she like Jock, always blaming her family, never herself?

'I don't understand you wanting to go to Scotland to help Lizzie,' Mother had said. 'Surely there's enough to do here. You could help Sarah in her War charities. But you're quite right, Father wouldn't hear of you going to work in New York and living away from home in these times. When you're twenty-one, perhaps.'

What magic was there in that number? What mantle of commonsense was going to fall on her then? Gaylord had been twenty-six when he had shot himself, although you were never allowed to put it that way. It had been an accident . . .

'It's dull here,' she had said, 'I want to be where there's life, where I'm doing something *definite* for the War.' Mama had said she was an ungrateful girl. But you had to feel sorry for her. Gaylord's death had withered her in some way.

It was Aunt Kate who had put the idea of coming here into her head when she had been talking to her about how frustrated she felt. 'I don't think your mother would mind if it were Lizzie's hospital, and your father thinks the sun rises and sets on Scotland, although he'd never go back there.'

'Why is that?' she had asked her, and Aunt Kate had told her of his first marriage to a girl called Bessie Haddow, his childhood sweetheart, because she was having a child – Lizzie, in fact – by Uncle Terence, who was already married. 'The things that go on in Scotland!' she had said, having to joke although she was astonished. Two brothers, loving the same girl, and then Father, of all people, marrying her to give the child a name.

'A penny for your thoughts.' Magnus Muir was standing beside her. He was an officer in the HLI, wounded on the Somme in the first push in early July, and still not wholly recovered. As well as being wounded, although not seriously, his right eye had caught a sliver of shell and he was still under treatment from the ophthalmologist who called at the Hall. He considered himself lucky and was hoping to get back before it was all over. His rakish white bandage over the damaged eye had a certain charm.

'I suddenly felt homesick,' she said, not strictly truthful, 'not like me.'

'I know the feeling.' He had a whimsical moustache on his upper lip in which he took great pride. 'I get the same for the mountains. Tramping over the moors on a shoot

. . . God, if I couldn't do that again, that would be the end! But first I've got to have another pot at those damned Huns. Then it's me for the Heilans.' His moustache moved in a smile.

'And Flora?' A fair-haired florid girl in tweeds had been twice to see him.

He shrugged. 'I don't know about Flora. Not with so much damned competition about, eh?'

'What can the man mean?' she said, deliberately vague.

'She's really Rhona's friend, my married sister. She just happened to be in Glasgow. An emissary of the family, don't you know?' He spoke like Jonty. Why did they go on about Scotland being the best place in the world and yet send their sons to be educated in England? 'Did I ever tell you you look good enough to eat in that nursing outfit?'

'I can't remember.' She pouted her lips.

'But this! Full dress kit!' He surveyed her from top to toe, 'Gee whiz! Leaves me speechless!'

'Just a rag, Magnus.' She felt glad she had bought the lime green chiffon. Lizzie had been with her and wouldn't hear of her having anything else. She had thought it far too expensive but Lizzie had been adamant. 'Never grudge money on good clothes,' she had said, 'Grandma taught me that. It's not only the cut and the material, it's the dye. You get what you pay for.' She had been right. She had received compliments from everyone she had spoken to tonight, even Belle Geddes who was inclined to be rather sparing in that direction. 'You're a picture, Ginny,' she had said, 'good enough to frame.'

Now, looking at Lizzie with Jonty as they both held the knife to cut the cake, she thought that perhaps she was outshining her for once. What was missing in her was that sophistication, but against that she was nineteen to Lizzie's thirty-eight. You couldn't have three children –

Annabel and Kit were sitting on the floor, their eyes avid with greed – without losing some of your bloom. Hadn't she admitted she had had difficulty in fastening her cummerbund, while *her* waist could be spanned with her own two hands?

The two maids were handing round glasses of champagne on silver trays. Lizzie had told her that Cathy and Jessie were the only two of the Hall staff she had kept on. Thomas, the coachman, had died – 'he hated motor-cars,' she had said as if that were the reason – and the butler, Redfern, had been set up by Ernest in a cottage in the village although he was allowed to potter about in the Hall when he liked.

Annabel and Kit had jumped up at their mother's bidding and were handing round the cake. 'A tip-top family,' Magnus Muir said in her ear. 'The Honourable Mrs Murray-Hyslop is one in a million. The chaps downstairs all adore her.'

'Yes, I know.' Youth didn't score against maturity after all.

Lizzie had her glass raised. 'Let's all drink to our birthday boy, Nigel Jonathan, Lord Crawford, better known as Jonty, who came into our lives sixteen years ago today!'

'Jonty!' they all said, raising their glasses, 'Jonty . . .!' Ginny saw the aunts helping the amputees. Aunt Isobel, in lemon voile as pale as her hair, was holding Brown's cake for him while he took a great slurp from the glass which he held with his one hand. He'd been told off about drinking on the sly before. They weren't all angels because they were disabled. People were as they were. This man standing beside her, for instance, had always been the same. Always ready for a bit of 'slap and tickle' – that was how the patients talked – but when it came to marrying he would settle for one of his own kidney, like florid Flora. *She* would like to marry someone who would sweep her off her feet, black, white or yellow, it wouldn't matter a scrap, nor if he was of high or low degree, just as long as their love was strong and she liked him for what he was.

She watched the care with which Aunt Isobel was feeding Brown, and the sycophantic smile on his face. All her geese were swans, especially Ellie. She was getting tired of hearing about Ellie McNab, surgeon at the Somme, battling against terrible odds with a brave smile and a knife in her hand . . .

'Now I'm going to ask Sir Edward Hamilton, an old friend of the family, to propose a toast to all our friends who have fought or are still fighting in the War. Sir Edward Hamilton.' Lizzie clapped, smiled at the man and sat down.

Ginny had been introduced to the Hamiltons earlier in the evening, he stiff, square and grizzled, she like a doll, a rather cheap doll with her painted face and yellow hair. He was on the board of the Crawford's firm, Lizzie had told her, but not that he had managed to appropriate the lion's share of its assets, ousting Jonty. Aunt Kate had given her that piece of information. 'But Maevy will see Jonty all right in McGrath's,' she had said. She had noticed that Lizzie seemed rather cool towards him.

He was a good speaker, there was no doubt. He paid due homage to 'the boys at the Front', and had made it his business to find out telling little details of the men in the hospital. She saw Magnus's moustache move when he mentioned his MC. He commended them all on their bravery and hoped they would soon be well enough to go home or back to fight again.

'This is a family which has given a great deal to its country,' he said. 'The Honourable Mrs Murray-Hyslop's first husband was killed in the Boer War, her present husband, Chairman of Globe Express Deliveries, is serving as an Intelligence Officer in the current conflict. We had hoped he would be with us tonight, but the evening isn't finished.

'And there's Elspeth McNab, cousin of young Lord Crawford whom we're honouring today, who is at present acting as surgeon in a hospital near Paris, run entirely by women. Her mother has asked me to say that.' He smiled at Maevy, who nodded, satisfied.

'She's been there since the Big Push on the Somme at the beginning of July. She has toiled valiantly through the thick of the battle and also the *guerre d'usure*, as it is called there, the interval, the period of attrition. This month, her mother tells me, she's been working day and night since General Haig mounted his fresh assault along the line from Combles to beyond Thiepval, where he has put in tanks for the first time. I'm sure many of you, like me, will check the progress of the War on a map. She has been on duty through the Battle of Flers-Courcelette, and seen Thiepval fall a few days ago. What a record for a young girl of twenty-five!' There was an outburst of clapping. The armless men kicked their chairs, those who had legs. 'Whoever said women weren't the equal of men?' He held up his hand to stop the applause.

'And there are other members of the family doing their bit in France: Mrs Murray-Hyslop Senior's son, Kieran, in a Field Ambulance in France, Terence McGrath's son, "young Terence" as he's called, at present in a French hospital after having been wounded and gassed at Verdun.

'And words fail me,' he smiled round at Lizzie, 'when I come to our hostess, who by her charm, beauty and organizational ability has made a hospital out of her own home, which is the best run in Scotland.' Lizzie beckoned him, and he bent down to hear her. 'She says,' he said, straightening, 'that she couldn't have done it without the help of all the nurses here, and the valiant support of her three aunts, and she thanks them all.'

Magnus Muir gave Ginny's waist a squeeze. 'He forgot to mention the nurse we're all madly in love with,' he whispered in her ear.

'And now we have Lord Crawford, the young scion of the family here, at the beginning of his adult life, at a famous public school, doing his best in his own way to be a credit to his father and mother . . .' Not step-father, Ginny noticed. She saw Jonty avert his head in embarrassment. 'The Crawfords are a respected family in Sholton – one might say they *made* it with their Ironworks, which I can say in all humility have been furthered in their success by my own poor efforts . . .' What a nerve! Ginny said to herself, if what Aunt Kate had told her was true . . . 'I think you will all echo my fervent wish that this terrible War will be over before he's old enough to add lustre to it . . .'

'The young scion looks as if he'd like to buckle on his sword right away,' Magnus Muir said.

'I thought he looked disgusted a minute ago with all that claptrap.' Ginny looked again. Jonty's cheeks were flushed, unusual for him. She saw her mother whisper to him, and he nodded, it seemed, reluctantly. When the apprause for Sir Edward Hamilton had died down he got to his feet, then straightened himself, looking around the room with his head high.

'I thank everybody here for their good wishes,' he said. 'It seems terrible to be having a birthday and enjoying myself when other people are fighting for us. Rest assured I'll do my duty . . . when the time comes, and try to be a credit to . . . my father.' He sat down to an outburst of genuine applause.

'I've seen boys not much older than he,' Magnus said, 'being mowed down by the thousand. Mere babes. Screaming to be shot to put them out of their agony. Sorry,' he said . . .

She looked at him. He wasn't so old, maybe twenty-two, but there were lines round his mouth, and a weariness, a bone weariness of the spirit as much as the body. Had he been made old before his time?

'Champers,' he said, 'goes to the head, don't you know?'

'And yet you'd go back?'

'It's a job, like everything else, even breeding pheasants which I grant you is much more fun. The difference now is that the heart's out of the men. They're sick to death of it, sick . . . maybe one day somebody'll write a book about it, about the blunders, about Haig's obstinacy, about the tanks put in too soon, about the rats that eat your food, of frostbitten feet and the stink in the trenches, of being too close to your fellow-men, about the mud and the slime . . . Hey, that's strong stuff, eh?' He shook his head violently. 'The only one I wouldn't mind being close to is you, gorgeous Ginny.' He put down his glass. 'Come on, Mrs M-H wants us to dance. There she is, with her son, putting on the phonograph . . .'

'Forget what I said, eh, Ginny?' he said when they were waltzing in time to the music. 'Not pukka, especially for an officer.'

'And a gentleman? Did you mean what you said about the War? Why shouldn't you say it if it's true? *You* should write a book about it. Or what about poems?' She had thought of Jonty.

'Haven't that kind of talent. Only for spotting gorgeous girls, like you.'

She laughed. 'Do you really think I'm gorgeous?'

'You don't need me to tell you that. Don't you ever look in your mirror? You're ravishing, completely ravishing. Only thing,' he glanced down at her as they swung, 'you haven't learnt all the tricks.'

'What tricks?'

'Your face gives you away. You haven't learnt to

conceal what you're thinking. I was watching you listening to the speechifying. You should take a leaf out of your cousin's book. She could teach you a thing or two.'

'Thank you very much,' she said, 'for nothing.'

He was a good dancer, light on his feet, with a strong arm. He whirled her until the chiffon panels of her dress stood out horizontally from her body, making her feel like the green stalk of a flower. She saw admiring glances. The amputees were being pushed round the room in time to the music by Annabel and Kit. There was a lot of laughter. Sir Edward's doll wife was dancing with Jonty, whose face was a mixture of expressions, chiefly embarrassment. Lady Hamilton was pressing herself close to him. He seemed to have to extricate his legs from her flowing gown with every backward step.

'Lady Hamilton's making up to our birthday boy,' she said in Magnus's right ear.

'Is she?' He glanced round in the middle of one of his loping strides. 'Oh, yes! By Jove, he's going to get more than he bargained for.' He looked lewdly down at her. 'Ah, well, we all have to make our own discoveries.'

She saw Ernest come into the room dressed to perfection in his officer's uniform, his Sam Brown belt gleaming round his slim waist. He made straight for Lizzie, who was sitting beside Gregson whose leg was still in plaster. Without a moment of hesitation she rose and went into his arms. They parted immediately but her face raised to his was radiant, ten times more beautiful.

Later, when she was walking with Magnus Muir in the garden and they stopped under the shelter of some rowan trees, she let him kiss her. She thought of Jonty and the doll wife pressing her body close to his. Now she was doing the same with Magnus, and it was heady and exciting and she didn't care if it was silly and too forward for a girl of nineteen. There was a War on.

15

Ellie was in the Barthe farmhouse. She had tried to telephone Joe but had been told he was operating. She left a message but doubted if he would get it if the Condé Hospital was in the same state of activity as hers.

It had been a terrible time. They could always tell when there would be a new influx of patients by the intensity of the bombardment. In a way the gradual crescendo of noise reminded her of births she had often attended, how at the peak of the pain, when it was not to be borne any longer, the baby would emerge and she would be able to take it from the woman, show it to her and put it to her breast. Once she remembered thinking that she wouldn't like to die without having had the same experience.

But that had been constructive. What about guddling inside a body in an effort to repair damaged organs and not succeeding? Or searching for shrapnel? Or sawing off limbs which were too far gone to save? Every ward was packed out. The chaplain had told her they were burying a hundred bodies a day.

When Thiepval fell and the anxiety was over, she had been given this weekend off. She had felt badly about it, looking around the white faces of her fellow surgeons, but they had urged her to go. They talked of her as the baby of the outfit. She was certainly the youngest there. She had given in because she had reached the stage when she wasn't much use to them. Her hands shook between one batch and the next, and when she should have been resting, she found it impossible to sleep. Terrible images filled her mind – broken, bleeding bodies, an endless procession.

She had taken to walking in the grounds of the Abbey rather than resting. To walk by the banks of the little Thève and hear the purling water made her think of the Sholtie Burn. She would think of the garden at Braidholme which her grandmother had sown so thickly with flowers and which her mother had kept in the same way, a cottage garden. And the summer-house where they had tea and which Mother had often said had been Grandfather's and Grandmother's favourite place.

But even that peace was changing because of the War. Maevy talked about munitions factories being built along the main Glasgow road and the settling of new people in the village, who were looked at askance by the old inhabitants. 'But, then, they're dying off one by one,' she said. 'When your father was alive I could walk down the street and everyone was a "kent face". Never mind, we'll keep Braidholme as a fortress for the three of us, Kate, Isobel and me, and there will be plenty of room, if and when you come from America with Kieran, and maybe a family . . .'

Kieran was a faithful writer. She had seen him once briefly when he had brought some patients, but they were both too busy and involved to do more than speak for a few minutes. His letters, however, were a joy in that he kept her fully informed of all the family both in Scotland and America.

He was able to tell her that Terence was now in a Paris hospital where he was having plastic surgery. 'Whether he'll ever be able to paint again is another matter,' he had said. 'His mother and father have gone back again to Woodlea to get it ready for their coming. Clovis and Jaime are lovely. I dare hope that one day . . .'

What would he say if he could see her in this house of

the Barthes, pretending to be an ordinary housewife and hoping against hope that Joe Gould would turn up?

When she had arrived, she had called at the caretaker's house in the village, as Giselle had told her, and Madame Jacques had taken off her apron, rolled it up, and accompanied her to La Hirondelle where she had set to with a will to light fires. She had kept it aired. She had brought some provisions from her own home to start Ellie off, and later perhaps Madame would like to make some purchases herself.

Was she expecting guests? Ah, only one? A husband, perhaps? 'Perhaps,' she had said enigmatically. If Madame Jacques carried tales she did not know whose name she would like bandied about, Kieran's or Joe's.

Who she would like to spend the weekend with was not at issue. Kieran, of course, would be a dear, affectionate companion, but Joe obsessed her. It was as simple as that. He was married but he obsessed her, how he looked, how he spoke, how he thought.

Of course if he did manage to come it would only be for a short visit. She would give him a meal, some good French wine and see him off again. There could be nothing else since he was married, and what was worse, married to a wife who would never give him his freedom.

She was not impatient. The joy of doing simple, housewifely things was a new experience – preparing food, stoking fires with the wood she had brought in from the shed outside, washing her own clothing, her hair, her body, sitting by the fire, reading.

Time slipped past. This was the beginning of her second day. She was due to go off tomorrow morning. Where had yesterday gone? She had spent part of it climbing the steep road from the village to see the ruined castle, and had walked along the ramparts above the moat. The view was French, peaceful. At the foot of the village she could pick out the elaborate gates and the steel-grey slated roof of the turret on Emily's 'simple' farmhouse. Beyond that was the unravished countryside, the trees now tawny with approaching autumn. Yesterday she had picked a basket of pine cones and burned them on the fire.

When she walked down again, her feet slipping on the steep slope, she sat outside the cafe near the church. The men at the other tables seemed to be locals, all old men, with the lack of curiosity of the aged. '*De Paris?*' they said. And when she said, no, but that her relatives were, the Barthes, they nodded. '*Le même.*' Enough said. Parisians were *tout à fait different* from the Normandois. One accepted them, *c'est tout*.

They didn't talk much about the War. Although comparatively near, it was still remote to the Vexin. The Boche would go away as they had come. Here they could play a waiting game. They were used to waiting for the seasons to come. She thought of them secretly as turnip heads, peasants in the real sense of the word. The average Scottish villager was quick-witted in comparison.

Her chief delight was the river which ran through the orchard at the back of the farmhouse. The Epte was slower moving than the Sholtie, but in places it purled over stones in the same way. She sat for hours on its banks, reading, dreaming; on the late afternoon of the second day she took off her clothes and slid into the cool water. The silkiness of it did more to wash away the hurt and soreness of the War than anything else. She felt cleansed.

She had a glass of wine in the evening before she started to prepare dinner. Broccoli soup first because there was a fine kitchen garden full of it. Chicken with cream, a roast farm chicken which she basted and stuck with rosemary. '*Mettez un citron dedans*,' the farmer's wife had told her. 'A young one like that needs a delicate flavour.' She had found some late strawberries hidden under their leaves, and had bought some Kirsch to pour over them in the village shop.

The chicken was in the fire oven, the soup was made, ready to be thickened, she had hulled the strawberries and put them to marinade in the Kirsch. She had been upstairs and changed into a light blue cotton dress, her only mufti, but she had washed and ironed it carefully and bought a new piece of velvet ribbon for the collar. Her hair was lemon fresh. She had been given a bag of them in the *épicerie*.

She sat down at the crackling fire and tried to read. It was no use. She was restless, excited, consumed with longing, and fear that he would not come. The pleasure of the day-and-a-half faded, the tranquillity, the lack of pressure. It was all of no account if he did not come.

At first she thought it was the distant noise of an aeroplane's engines, but as it came nearer and nearer and became without doubt the noise of a motor car, she started out of her seat and stood listening until she heard the engine stop. Then she ran to the door and flung it open. When he got out of the motor he took her in his arms without speaking.

After a time she said, 'You got my message after all?' She was trembling with happiness, trying to control it.

'Yes. As it happened I was in the same boat as you. No time to think. And then, your message, manna from heaven, work had slackened off, and here I am.' His eyes were full, moist, on her. She could hardly bear it.

'Come in, come in!' she said gaily, skittish even, taking his hand and leading him into the beamed sitting-room.

It was bright with the fire and shaded lamps. Even though Emily always talked about 'the farmhouse', the room had some of her own Parisian elegance in its too-elaborately draped hangings, but fortunately they and the chair covers were made of an old French floral print, *a toile de Jouy*. There were Persian rugs scattered on the bare floor, and Ellie had massed flowers from the garden into the porcelain jardinières which stood in corners – tawny chrysanthemums, dahlias, petunias, autumn berries. The pleasure of that simple operation had been so great that she had lingered over it.

'Pleasant place,' Joe said, looking around. 'Faint touch of Madame Barthe.'

'She calls it a farmhouse, but there are no animals, not even a humble goat.' She was dizzy looking at him.

'I like the paintings.' He made a tour of the walls with his arm round her. 'That's exquisite.' He pointed to a small seascape. 'I'd call this a rest home for war-weary veterans. And I can see your hand too.' He waved at the flowers. 'Lovely.'

'I was hoping someone would pass by,' she joked. Their eyes held. She felt dizzy again. She hadn't eaten all day, forgetful, obsessed. 'I'd even roasted a chicken in the hope that the smell would drift out and entice . . . someone.'

'I wouldn't compare you with a roast chicken if we're talking of enticement,' he said. How dark he was, and yet how fatigued. She had always associated paleness with weariness, now she saw it could be conveyed by drawn features, tired, sunken eyes. She had seen the same in herself in the mirror when she had arrived here, and yet how quickly it had disappeared. It was mostly lack of sleep.

'You look as I did when I came,' she said. 'The treatment here is very beneficial.'

'I hear there's a good doctor on the premises.' His voice was husky, his eyes never leaving her.

'Yes, but she only takes very special patients.' She had a great desire to put her arms round his neck, to pull him towards her, to say that this was part of the treatment. She saw herself doing it, her abandoned, obsessed self, not the strictly-brought-up, hard-working Ellie with the strong conscience. Did he see all that in her eyes?

'How does the cure begin?' Did he feel like her? His mouth was still smiling, and she thought, don't rush it, you've always been too intense . . .

> She bid me take love easy, as the leaves grow on the tree;
> But I, being young and foolish, with her would not agree.

One of Charlie's books of poetry?

'How does the cure begin?' She saw Charlie with a book in his hand at their fire at Braidholme, she sitting pressed against his knee, Mother sewing . . .

'With a good dinner. Would you like to go upstairs and have a wash, and I'll dish up the chicken. It's clamouring to come out of the oven, and I've got to thicken the soup with cream . . .' She became housewifely. 'I'm very nervous about this dinner,' she laughed, 'I'd much rather do a gastroscopy.'

'It's probably more difficult. Gastroscopies are ten a penny, good dinners aren't. Give me a call if you need any help.' He released her without kissing her as she had hoped and strode towards the door, sure of his bearings already, she thought, a house-trained man, a married man. Had *she* trained him?

He had taken off his jacket when he came down again, and loosened his tie. It made him look younger. He looked freshly shaved. He would be the type who had to shave twice a day. 'Permission to appear in a state of undress?' He found her in the kitchen and saluted smartly.

'Well, look at me,' she said, indicating her blue cotton. 'Isn't it great to be out of whites? I've never felt so good.' She felt about nineteen. 'Two days of this have made a new woman out of me. Could you carry the chicken into the dining-room?' She wanted to use his name but couldn't. 'I'll bring the plates. The soup's already in. The dining-room's at the end of the corridor. Look, I'll go first.' She had the vegetable dishes on a tray and she chattered out of nervousness as she walked along the stone-flagged hall. 'Running on like the Sholtie Burn'. That was what Father had said of some of his patients.

'Are you sure that's not too heavy for you?'

'Me? I've handled twelve-stone men and more in my time. Sometimes if it was a new orderly and she was squeamish, she couldn't touch . . . the dead.' They were in the dining-room now. 'Yes, that's right. On that serving table beside the sideboard. I hope you're a good carver.'

'You must be joking.' They laughed together. 'Shall I light the candles?'

'Please. That's everything. Now we shan't have to jump up and down after every course. We had a faithful Susan, still have, at home. We all love her very much. She's getting old . . .' Facile tears sprang to her eyes. Susan, who had taken care of her for so long. 'An' whit in the name o' aw that's wonderful are ye up tae?' She heard her voice. 'Of course, a'm jist a simple soul, a never went to no university like some, but a ken fine richt frae wrang . . .' 'Oh, thank you, Joe.' The name had come. He had put down the chicken, lit the hot plate under the vegetables at the same time as the candles (yes, house-trained), now he was holding her chair for her. Such attention. His face, opposite hers now, was mysterious as well as dark, that American-Indian look intensified by the shadows, showing the high cheekbones and the hollows underneath them, the fine, smiling mouth. This was her love, married or unmarried, for one evening, for eternity.

'*Bon appetit*,' he said, raising his glass to her.

'Do you have a favourite servant in *your* family?' she

asked, passing the rolls she had heated in the little oven beneath the chicken. He shook out a crackling white napkin she had found in the sideboard drawer.

'Yes, black, strangely enough for Boston. Too far north. Susannah, wouldn't you know, fat, smiling. We used to say, Irv, Bill, Holly and me, "Laugh some more, Susannah." She had the bestest laugh you ever did hear,' he mimicked a Southern accent, 'rich, chuckling, her whole body shook with it. And I had a secret as a small boy. I loved to be hugged by her! Well, three eiderdowns wouldn't have been so soft.' His smile was wicked. 'This chicken is dee-licious. Where did you get your recipe, ma'am?'

She tapped her temple. 'Well, sir, I guess I just made it up out of ma own head.'

'Allow me to tell you you couldn't have put it to better use.' He chewed, watching her splutter into her napkin. It would be all right if they went on like this, light-hearted, Silly. She didn't want to tell him how she felt, which she might blurt out if she became too intense. There was the other woman. She was called Gilda. She would think of *her* as the other woman.

'My grandmother, Maeve, bought our house,' she said, 'then my mother, father and I lived in it. Oh, we were so happy together! He was an exceptional man. Even when he was away at the War we didn't worry because he was non-combatant.'

'Just like us.'

'But quite a lot have died . . . in one way or another.'

'Comparatively few. More chaplains, statistically speaking.' They were on a safe, conversational plane. 'Particularly Roman Catholic chaplains. They're always at the Front, giving extreme unction. I've seen them take up arms, and we've certainly had one in the theatre from time to time, giving anaesthetics. The Anglicans most of the time want it as cosy as they have it back home. Have you noticed?'

'We have some who visit. They seem . . . *quite* nice, but then I'm prejudiced. But I'll admit, the RCs have a certain kind of authority.' She screwed up her forehead. 'I'd have to think about that. We have had a lot of French soldiers, and sometimes if they're seriously wounded they'd rather have the priest than us.'

'Do you like the French?'

'I know some don't, but I'll say this about them. They were the first to use us at the Abbey. Back in Scotland, oh, they were suspicious! "Wummen! A never heard the like! Oh, my, it's fair scandalarious!"'

He laughed. 'Is that how they speak in your land?' 'Land', she thought. American was a different language. 'I'd love to visit there. All that lovely heather, and mountains, and leaping waterfalls . . .'

'And a deer on every crag and hairy cattle. I tell you, Landseer has a lot to answer for.' Oh, it was going fine, safe conversational topics. 'Our village is a little pocket of rusticity in the middle of steel works and coal bings and now munitions factories.'

'You don't say! Well, we're in the city, of course, but we have the Boothbay house on the ocean.' The 'ocean'. The *sea*, man, the sea . . . 'You can never get too overcrowded on the ocean . . . unless they push you into it.'

'That's a point. Well, when we get married . . .' She stopped short, horrified, knew her cheeks were on fire. She looked stupidly at her wine glass. It was empty. She vaguely remembered Joe refilling it. Had she been slurping it down all the time she was having that safe, conversational conversation?

'When we get married . . .' he said calmly. 'Were you thinking of your Kieran when you said that?'

'Yes . . .' She looked at her plate fixedly, willing the colour to drain out of her face. She felt sick. She played with her knife and fork. 'No . . .' she fought back the sickness. 'It was beginning to be a dream. You and me, at dinner, talking and laughing . . . in the candlelight . . . and I was telling myself it was any night in our lives . . . one of many . . . I forgot . . .' She raised her head to look at him and his face swam in front of her, two faces, two sets of ears, the second set starting from his nose, two loosely tied ties, 'Oh, God,' she said, putting her head in her hands, 'I feel so . . . sick . . .'

He was round the table in an instant, bending over her, his hand pressing on the base of her neck. 'Take it easy. It's all your preparation and the work you've been doing, more than any able-bodied man could tackle and you so fragile, "just a wumman" – ' he'd remembered – 'it's all been too much for you . . .'

'No,' she said, 'it was the wine. You filled my glass twice. We only drink ginger at home. Wine is for special occasions.'

He laughed, 'My poor darling. But this was a special occasion.'

'Oh, yes, I wanted it to be, so much.' His hand at the base of her skull, steady, reassuring, was helping. The waves of sickness were lessening. Maybe she would be able to get up soon without making a fool of herself. Was that how soldiers felt when they were given a tot of rum before they went over the top? Dead drunk? Who in their senses would go cold sober into battle? But this wasn't a battle. She had been vanquished before it started, a willing victim.

'Do you feel well enough to come and lie down next door?' he said, 'or must you get rid of that lovely dinner?'

'You're laughing at me.' She had heard it in his voice.

'Laughing at you! What an idea! Let me help you.

That's right. Lean on me. We can finish it later. I could make chicken sandwiches and there are the strawberries . . .'

'Don't mention food,' she groaned. She was moving shakily, he was supporting her along the stone-flagged hall, she was in the warm sitting-room, the sofa looked inviting, she sank on to it, felt a little better because she had reached it safely. 'Oh, I feel such a fool!'

He was bending over her, covering her with a soft rug which had been draped over the back. 'You may feel a fool but you look very beautiful. You . . . tear at my heart. Relax, close your eyes.' He expertly propped her head with cushions, tucked her in. 'There, there. . .' His hand swept over her eyes, closing them. There was black darkness, nothing . . .

Flames, flickering and dancing on her eyeballs, red, yellow and black. The Braidholme fire. She could see Charlie sitting in his high-backed chair with a book in his hand. His black eyes looked with love on her, he was reading from the book. 'She bade me take things easy . . .'

She slowly opened her eyes and saw the log fire in a strange fireplace, different from the Scottish one with its blue Dutch tiles and its cast iron hood. This was a generous hearth, a yawning hole with a great basket holding the burning logs. The chair was empty where her father would have sat, and besides, it was different, richly carved, tapestried. She trailed her hand and it drew across someone's face.

'Hey!' Joe said. 'Are you trying to put my eye out?'

She rolled to the edge of the low sofa and looked down. He was lying stretched out on the hearthrug, his head pillowed on his folded arms. She could see the fire dancing on his polished belt, the silver buckle. 'Oh, it's you down there,' she said.

'Who else? I've been keeping watch at your feet like a faithful dog. How do you feel?'

'Fine.' She shook her head to test it. It was heavy, a typical hangover probably – she had no experience of one. 'Just fine.' She looked down at him and he held out his arms. 'Come and join me. It's cosy here.'

It was easy to roll, to be received into his arms. His body was warm from the fire. She felt it through his shirt, the hard, muscular chest. His arms held her, comfortingly, closely, and she didn't meet his eyes because she was shy. She should have sprung up and got busy with the dishes. The place must be in an awful mess. 'The dishes . . .' She struggled, not a great deal.

'All done. And I've sliced up the chicken and made sandwiches for after. . .'

'After?' she said faintly. It was a mistake to ask.

'After . . . whatever. Don't let your conscience keep nagging at you, my darling. You owe yourself . . . this. Be still in my arms. It will be something to take back with us.'

Well, of course, that was sensible, grown-up talk. 'Be still in my arms.' Recreate yourself for what lies ahead. His wife didn't want him anyhow, although she wouldn't let him go. But it wasn't easy. The comfort turned to longing, and she moved restlessly. She met his eyes and did what she had wanted to do since she saw him, raised her arms and put them round his neck, and he kissed her.

'She wouldn't mind, would she?' she said. 'I need comfort. It's been hard for me pretending all the time it was easy, seeing those terrible injuries, dealing with them as if it was nothing at all. It's rightly named a theatre. You're performing all the time. The orderlies think you don't feel a thing when they lay those mangled bodies in front of you, and you see the smashed and broken limbs, the ruined faces, the despair and fear in them, sometimes the sightless eyes. You want to cradle them in your arms, like this, but you have to be cool and resourceful and in charge of the situation and not show that your heart is bleeding . . .' He stopped her by drawing her to him, kissing her, again kissing her.

'It's too much to ask of you, just a girl.'

'But they *didn't* ask! I wanted to do it, couldn't get here quickly enough. Charlie did it. Mother would have nursed if she could have left me. We are . . . a family devoted to service . . .'

He released her for a moment, and his eyes were Charlie's eyes, deep, black, full, moist. 'Why don't you devote yourself . . . to yourself? For a change. To love?'

'But you know why. There's . . .'

'I've written, pleaded with her to give me my freedom. I've told her there's someone else, you, that she can't be so cruel as to keep us apart.'

'Do you think she will be . . . so cruel?'

'I don't know, oh, I don't know. But I've never pleaded like that before . . .'

'Maybe she'll agree, because of the War.' She was pleading too. 'We're not doing her any hurt. We just want to love each other.' He caught her to him, and the word seemed to be burning inside her, 'love', 'love', 'love' . . . Surely no one with any heart could grudge you love when there was a War on. 'Yes, please,' she heard herself pleading, 'Yes . . . please . . .' She was helping him with the buttons on the blue cotton dress, gave up, tried to untie his tie, there was drumming in her ears. 'I've never . . . this is the first time . . .'

'Yes, you told me in Paris. I just want to hold you, see you without your dress, that's all, that's all . . .' But after a time it was she who pleaded again. You might as well be hung for a sheep as a lamb when it got to this stage, and how could she turn back now when she was so eager to experience this wonderful thing which had existed between Maevy and Charlie? So much happiness. She had vaguely glimpsed it with Colin Thomson. Kieran? Could she . . . with him? He was too gentle, not sure and direct and strong and forceful like Joe, now in complete charge of the situation.

She shouted out at the moment of climax and then lay quietly in his arms until their breathing slowed. And she sighed, a long, quivering sigh. You pleaded, she reminded herself. It was you. Well, there would be no recriminations. If she died now she would die happy. The words sounded familiar. Was it a poem, or had countless lovers said it down the ages?

Later they ate the chicken sandwiches – she was famished – and then they went to bed and slept dreamlessly. But towards morning she wanted to die all over again, and apparently so did he, for this time it was he who pleaded.

16

By a strange coincidence both Kieran and Joe were sent up to the Ancre where there was a last desperate push on in spite of the miserable weather. It had broken after Ellie came back, and there was incessant rain with great glowering skies pressing down on the Abbey which seemed to fit her mood. The news was bad. 'Desperate nibbles', someone called each side's advances and retractions. Joffre was as adamant as Haig. And the eternal fighting was made worse by the mud and slime.

She felt as depressed as she had been joyous, not through any feeling of regret, but simply because of the lack of any future. She had found the love of her life in Joe, but leaving aside the uncertainty of War, there was still the one insuperable obstacle to their being together. His wife was unwilling to release him from their marriage.

At night, despite her tiredness, she would lie awake. What was she like, this unknown woman? Gilda. She had formed the impression of someone pretty but flighty, too loudly dressed. Was she bitter and spiteful as well? Or was it that she truly loved him and hoped he would come back to her? Why shouldn't she? she reminded herself. She herself must try and not be bitter and remember instead the time they spent together. It had been the high point of her life. She had that at least.

During the day she had no time to ruminate. She was kept busy with the examination and clearing out of patients who could be discharged. Beds had to be kept ready for the overflow of patients who needed longer care than they could get nearer the Front Line.

The men were bitter, too. It had all gone on for too long. What were those generals thinking of who played chess with their lives? Once, going into a ward, she heard a low singing, and stood listening at the entrance. There was a new patient, an Ulsterman, seriously wounded in the abdomen and brought from the Somme yesterday, and she saw his arm waving weakly. He appeared to be leading the song.

'If you want the old battalion,
I know where it is . . .'

His arm wavered as he tried to beat out the rhythm. She heard the ragged chorus.

Hanging on the old barbed wire,
I saw them, I saw them,
Hanging on the old barbed wire . . .

She had to turn away to wipe her eyes which had filled with a rush of scalding tears. *Come on, Miss McNab, pull yourself together* . . . She had letters from Kieran and Joe, one long, obviously written with a stump of pencil, the other brief. 'Working flat out here. Billeted in a disused school near a village called Beaumont Hamel. Bitter fighting. I'll never forget . . .'

Kieran's was discursive, a release of the spirit.

This is the worst place yet, probably because of the weather. Even the burial parties are sick of it . . . bodies too far gone. You walk on them, carrying the stretchers . . . Oh, to breathe the sweet air at Wanapeake! Once long ago I took Lizzie fishing on the upper stretches of the river. It was paradise compared with this, sheer paradise . . . When you visited us I was *hors de combat*, worse luck, because of that business with Gaylord. The pain here has blotted that out. RIP, Gaylord. Maybe you and I will go on the river sometime soon. If I close my eyes I can see it, the brilliant flash of the old kingfisher, the wagtails bobbing on the stones. That picture, especially those jaunty little wagtails, keeps me going, makes me forget this terrible debris round me.

I think I'll give up this stretcher business and get a nice cosy job going round the beds enquiring about missing men on behalf of their relatives. On second thoughts, no, it's ghoulish and makes the men relive it all over again. When we come into the War as we must surely do soon, I'd rather join up and be in on the action instead of clearing up the mess afterwards.

But maybe it'll be over before I know it and I'll be showing you those lovely walks and I'll teach you to fish and we'll listen to the silence . . . I love you.

She remembered Joe saying how lovely it was to see the undecimated countryside around La Hirondelle. 'There's something completely idiotic about it,' he had said, 'slaughtering thousands of men for, say, one broken-down old farmhouse. It had to be wrong.'

'Will you give it up?' she had asked him, and he had smiled and said, 'No, will you? Mine's not to reason why. I don't see beyond the next shattered body.' 'Have you noticed,' she had said, 'sometimes how even the worst wounded, the ones for whom there's no hope, are smiling?' He had agreed, and they had sat silent, staring at the flames.

'One thing,' she had heard his voice, 'we'll never be the same again. The men who march away aren't the same when they come back, nor,' his arm drawing her closely to him, 'the women . . .' No, she wasn't the same girl as the young, untried one who had left Braidholme. Mother would not recognize her. She would never be that young again.

Terence and Giselle came to see her, and she was able to spend ten minutes with them in a small waiting room off the cloisters. It was dark, cold and uninviting, and she apologized. 'I've forgotten what it's like to see a fire,' and then her innate honesty made her say, 'No, that's not true. I spent a weekend at La Hirondelle. It was lovely, Giselle. I burned nearly all your wood.' And my boats.

Giselle's eyes were on her, intelligent, too intelligent to ask questions. 'Keep the key. Any time you can manage it, go again.'

Some day I'll tell her, she thought. 'And how are you, Terence?' She smiled at him. 'You look fine.' He didn't. He was thin and pale, and she noticed how his chest heaved, and how his arm hung. And he's saddled with bronchitis, she thought. It'll get worse as he grows older. A legacy could be as bad as death.

'Couldn't be better.' He had a febrile brightness. 'The arm and hand's coming along nicely. I'm on leave. They say I can go to Ireland provided I report at the end of three months. The trouble is – I didn't remember this – I had a lung infection when I was a child.' He laughed. 'I must have got it in sooty old Glasgow, so it looks as if Giselle will have to put up with a hacking old bore for good. I don't know how she'll stand it.' Nor you, she thought. Gas was the worst thing. It sapped energy and spirit, even the wish to survive.

'She'll stand you all right. When are you off?'

'Just as soon as we pack our bags and get the children ready. Jaime's thrilled to bits at the thought of it. Isn't he, Giselle?'

She smiled at him. 'Yes. He gurgled and blew bubbles when I told him. And Clovis is practising saying "boat".'

'He'll come back with a fine Irish brogue if his grandfather and grandmother have anything to do with it. And all those little cousins.'

'Any news of you getting some decent leave and coming there, too?' Terence asked.

'No.' She shook her head. 'We're up to the eyes.

There's this latest push on the Ancre. I suppose you know Kieran's there. But I was promised Christmas.'

'You deserve it,' Giselle said. Her eyes seemed to be searching her face. 'Kieran called in to see us in Paris before he left Neuilly for the Somme. Talked about you all the time.'

'It's lovely to have seen you both.' She got up. 'But there are patients being prepared for theatre. I shouldn't be here.' She put her arms round Giselle. 'Take care of this man of yours,' and to Terence as she kissed him, 'I hope you feel strong enough to paint soon.'

'At least my eyes are all right.' His smile was bright. 'And Father has his latest thoroughbred lined up for me. He wants it done before it romps home to victory.'

She walked with them along the cloisters, and stood waving to them as they went down the drive with the Theve running alongside it. 'Take care of yourself, Ellie,' Giselle said. 'We all love you very much.' Why had her eyes filled with tears? Really, it was daft. She hurried back towards the theatre.

That night the talk in the mess was more cheerful. The news was that the fighting at Transloy Ridge and Ancre Heights was over and that the field fortress of Beaumont Hamel would soon be captured. 'I have a friend there,' she said, 'one of the surgeons.'

'Ah, it's not over for him, then. There's the aftermath.'

She was on duty. That's what I deal in, she thought, getting up, the aftermath, the putting together of pieces . . .

17

Her mother's letter had been lying in her drawer for about a week.

It's coming near Christmas and we're all looking forward to you coming home. You did say a long time ago that it was likely. Lizzie is already planning lots of parties, but I'd like you and the aunts to have a quiet Christmas dinner here. You need to relax first and not be swept into a hive of activity right away.

Aunt Kate, of course, would love it if Kieran could come with you. He has a special place in her heart and the thought of seeing him cheers her up. That and working hard in the hospital has helped to get her through the hard time since James died. I know what it's like. Is it possible, do you think?

And when you're rested it will be fun for you at the hospital as well. Ginny is organizing all kinds of things. She's full of energy, almost too much at times. Although she's so like my mother, she never had that restless quality, but I must remember it's a different generation, and she's only nineteen.

Magnus Muir, a patient who was here all summer, is coming from Inverness. He got a piece of shrapnel in one of his eyes and is still on leave. He's bringing with him any of his friends who happen to be on leave as well. I think he's quite keen on her, but Lizzie tells me Ginny doesn't want to settle down yet.

I think she has a notion to nurse in France, and I know she works hard at her classes and already she's quite efficient. Of course she's too young to go overseas, but she says they can't stop her working in a French café serving teas and coffees to the soldiers! I don't know what your Uncle Patrick would say. My opinion is that she and Jonty egg each other on.

Jonty gives Lizzie a little worry. I don't know if it's because of Ernest being away, but Lizzie says his school reports aren't as good as they used to be. 'Lacks concentration' is the usual comment. Of course he's at a difficult age. I told Lizzie that. I never had any trouble with you (oh, yes, you did, Mother. Have you forgotten Colin Thomson?), but I know a boy's different. This War is unsettling for every age, a disruption of all our lives. Even at McGrath's (I still call it that), there's constant trouble with finding workmen and then keeping them. There isn't the same feeling of loyalty. They go where the money is highest, and who can blame them?

But any little complaint we might have pales into insignificance beside what you and others like you are putting up with. I'm *that* proud of you. Maybe I show it too much. Once when I was telling Lizzie about your latest letter, Ginny, who was listening, looked up and said, 'I expect she's Haig's righthand man by this time!' So I'd better watch that I don't become a *sprowser*!

Isobel runs the business side of the hospital like clockwork. Never spares herself, and has become Lizzie's righthand man, since we're talking about that! Oh, I'm lucky to have two dear sisters beside me, and how lucky Kate and I will consider ourselves if you and Kieran come home for Christmas.

Your loving mother . . .

She had looked at the letter each day and wondered how to answer it. She worked harder than ever, her long hours in the theatre leaving little time for sleep. Once she felt faint but managed to cover it up. Masks were a godsend. She must remember not to skip meals.

That evening Mrs Gregson, her chief, sent for her. She looked up as Ellie came in, a tired, middle-aged woman like her mother in many ways, she thought, using her talent when no doubt she would prefer to be back in Edinburgh with her family. 'Sit down, Miss McNab. I thought I'd remind you that your leave's due soon. You may go on the twentieth December for two weeks.'

'I was thinking, ma'am . . . some of the patients tell me there's still quite a lot of activity on the Somme. Aerial bombardments. Maybe since the weather's so bad I should wait . . .' She saw the woman's face and stopped. Oh, she had been stupid, stupid . . .

'Yes, I've heard a few stories. All the more reason for

getting out of the place. And I must keep to our leave rota, Miss McNab. I should be obliged if you would make all necessary arrangements.'

Very well, ma'am.'

Her face softened as she gathered together the papers on her desk. 'You get away and have a rest. Maybe you'll get snow in Scotland, nice clean, white snow.'

'Not in Glasgow.' She made herself smile.

'But you don't live in Glasgow? It's Lanarkshire, isn't it?'

'Yes, Sholton.'

'Anyhow, it couldn't be whiter than your face. Have you taken a look at yourself lately?'

'Me?' She put a hand up to hide the rush of colour. 'I feel fine.'

'You look thoroughly worn out. There's nothing worrying you, is there?' Her look was professional.

'Not a thing.' She was flustered, felt the tears at the back of her throat. She got up quickly. 'Thank you very much, ma'am. I'll go off on the twentieth December.' In an effort to cover her confusion, she added, 'How about you? Will you get home?'

'No. I'm staying to organize the Christmas parties. And believe it or not, I'm Santa Claus. It's an all-women hospital, Miss McNab. Have you forgotten?'

She tossed and turned that night in the worst agony she had ever known. When her alarm went off in the chilly hours of early morning she got up and started wearily to dress. Her white blouse rasped against her breasts as she tucked it into her skirt, and they were sore, tender. She moaned, turning her head each way, biting her lip to prevent the sound.

'What am I to do?' She whispered the words to her reflection in the mirror as she ran a comb through her hair which seemed dull, lank, no life in it. 'Love hurts,' she said to the white face, the snow-white face. 'Oh, love hurts . . .'

The letter lay in her place when she went down to breakfast. She saw the handwriting and tore it open, feeling her heart leap crazily about in her chest. 'Dearest, darling Ellie . . .' Her eyes ate the words.

I've the most wonderful news. I can hardly write it, my hand trembles so much. Gilda has written to say she'll give me my freedom. I don't think it's through a change of heart. She's met someone who's a better bet than me who wants to marry her. Good luck to both of them. Whoopee! As soon as I get someone to stand in for me I'll drive over and see you and we'll make plans. Could we get married in Paris, do you think? In haste and with all my love, Joe.

The joy which flooded through her was so great that she had to bend her head to conceal it from the other women. She made some excuse and, leaving her breakfast untouched, she got up and left the room. It was unbelievable, a miracle, she didn't deserve it. She would write right away, no, she wouldn't, he was coming to see her. But she'd send a note to Mother and say that it was difficult at the moment to get home. She would write explaining soon. What would she and the aunts say, think? They wouldn't be pleased. And there was Kieran. She had been unfair, terribly unfair to Kieran. He didn't deserve it.

But, oh, the joy of seeing Joe, of being able to tell him . . . she went straight to the wards. She must calm herself. Work, that was the answer, it had always been the answer. She saw one or two patients looking at her as she did her round. One, a Bantam – they'd cheek for anything – said, 'My goodness, there's a big change the day, sure there is?

Ye've been gawn roon this place as if somebody had stole your scoan. Hae ye come inty a fortune, Miss McNab?'

'Jimmy,' she said, 'God's been very good to me.' No wonder he looked flabbergasted. It wasn't the professional Miss McNab speaking.

'Goad?' he said, 'Goad? Him up there above the blue wally clouds? Well, mebbe he's been good to you but it must hae been yin o' his aff days when a got this bluidy shrapnel in ma bluidy leg.' The nurse with her tut-tutted.

When she was having a cup of tea in the mess an orderly came in and said there was an officer in the waiting-room to see her.

'Is he wearing an American uniform?' she asked her when they were walking along the corridor.

'Yes. Nice looking chap. They always look twice as tall and twice as handsome as our lot.'

'I'm inclined to agree with you,' she said, her mouth working.

When she opened the door it was a stranger in the room. Her smile died, then revived. He'd offered to look in and tell her Joe would be here soon. But he looked grave. She recognized the downward, tell-tale lines on the face. He was a bearer of bad news. She had seen that look too often. But it would only be that Joe had been delayed. 'What is it?' she said. Harshly.

'I'm Jacob Cohen.' He held out his hand. There was no pressure in his fingers. He was thinking of what he had to say. 'God, I don't know how I'm going to tell you this, Miss McNab. Will you sit down?'

'How do you know my name?' Harshly, again. It was the only way she could stop herself from screaming.

'He told me. Joe told me. He asked me to come and see you. Will you please sit down, *please*, Miss. Just sit down?'

'No,' she said, staring at him, 'I have to . . .'

'It'll be better, I'm telling you. Please sit.' His voice was suddenly one of command. She sank down on a chair. Perhaps it would be better.

'A terrible thing happened.' He sat down too, leaned forward and took her hands. He was a pleasant-looking young man, dark, Jewish, of course. Why 'of course'? Oh, yes, his name . . . 'Our CCS was tented. You'll know that. And that those darned Boche planes have been doing a lot of damage with their bombs. You'd think they had never heard of the Geneva Convention. Well . . .' his sigh was audible, seemingly drawn from the depths of him, '. . . I was in a billet with Joe in the village, and I strolled over at night to see how he was getting on. I wasn't on duty, but sometimes I'd just do that for a chat. We kept each other going that way, even when we were operating. Chatting and joking. . .'

'Is that allowed?' She was polite.

'Oh, yes. We're easy as long as the work gets done. Maybe we're not as formal as you. Well . . . you have to brace yourself, Miss McNab . . .' She saw the sweat on his brow, even felt the rapid flicker of his pulse against her wrist, '. . . when I was twenty yards away from one of the tents I saw it get hit, saw the flames, the dust, the smoke, heard . . .' she saw his swallowing, 'saw everything. I'll never forget it. Everything . . . went up.'

'Were there many patients?'

'Around fifty. Joe was in it.'

'You got him out, of course.' Love hurts, oh, love hurts . . . was there ever a hurt like this? In her heart, in her throat, in the hollow of her elbows, behind her knees . . .

'Yes, we got him out along with the others. There were a lot done for. Patients.' Ah, *patients*, not Joe . . . 'I was with him when he died.'

'What did he say?' there was that harsh voice again. It

couldn't be her. People, patients, had said what a soft Scottish voice she had.

'He said to tell you he was sorry, so sorry, and that he loved you. You were the only one . . .'

Jacob Cohen's eyes were close to each other, separated by the cliff of his nose. She swayed away from him, but he still held her hands and now his grip was firm. He wasn't going to let her go, to die, like Joe . . .

The hurt was so great that she swayed, backwards and forwards, backwards and forwards, anchored by his hands. He let go quickly and pushed her head down between her knees, stroked the nape of her neck. 'Let go,' she thought he was saying, 'let go . . .'

'I'm dying, dying . . .'

'No, you're not.' He stood up, pulling her with him, and took her in his arms. He was smaller than her. His arms weren't Joe's, but she knew he was doing his best in a difficult situation. She would have to help him, but clinically, she had a moment of cold reason, she wondered why this terrible hurt didn't burst open her heart, dash itself through the wall of her ribs in flying pieces like shrapnel . . .

'Thank you,' she said. She pushed this strange man away from her. 'We were going to be married. Did he tell you? I had a letter from him this morning. Look, it's in my pocket.' She fumbled. 'I'd like you to see it.'

'Later,' he said. 'Let me get someone. A woman. It's too much for you to take in right away. God,' his face was suddenly very young, 'it's terrible, a great pal like Joe. He told me . . . everything. How things were going to be fine for you.'

'No,' she said, 'not any more. Never any more.' She put her hands on either side of his face. Now the hurt was back, worse than ever. She wasn't going to be able to stand it. 'You're a doctor. Could you give me something, anything, just for the first bit . . . please . . .'

18

The boat Kieran and Ellie travelled home in was packed to the gunwales with soldiers and other personnel on leave, a raucous, singing band of men with some nurses amongst them who were never silent.

She was only half-aware of the noise and movement around her. The socially developed side of her made her go through the motions of politeness, the other half was dead, not dead-dead, worse luck, she thought, the stunning ache was with her night and day, even preventing her from being sea-sick like so many others who had boarded the old ship so jauntily at Dieppe and were now forced to stagger down below.

The crossing was stormy, rain-lashed like the battlefields they had left. No white, white snow . . . She and Kieran sat together in any corner they could find, speaking little until her terrible restlessness would force her to rise abruptly and leave him, to walk endlessly round and round the decks, welcoming the buffeting as the ship lurched, the crowds of men she had sometimes to force her way through, anything which would relieve the hurt.

Kieran was worried sick about her. That she was aware of at least. To begin with he had been solicitous, managing to find a rug to wrap round her, indulging in small talk, trying to make her eat, but he had given up. 'I don't know what to do, Ellie,' he said. 'I've never seen you like this before. You've been *my* prop always, so calm, so resourceful. Is it that I've been expecting too much of you? Has everyone?'

'That's it, Kieran,' she said. 'I'm not what you thought

I was. If you're disappointed in me, it's nothing to how I feel. I'm . . . ashamed, ashamed to inflict myself on you in this state.'

'Don't feel that.' He put his arm round her. 'You're worn out. You'll be different when you get home.'

'The truth of the matter is,' she said, 'my life is over. I want to die . . . die . . .' She had to get up and walk away from him again.

In a dream she knew they disembarked at Newhaven and began the slow train journey to London and then Glasgow. She got through it somehow by huddling in a corner in the swaying, packed trains and sleeping from sheer exhaustion. In a dream she managed to greet her mother fondly in Central Station and after that couldn't utter a word. She was aware of the meaning glances between her mother and Kieran, the businesslike transaction of luggage into the large motor car which was waiting for them at the entrance.

'Lizzie got her chauffeur to pick me up at York Street and then come here to meet you.'

'That was nice,' she said. She didn't recognize the man who was driving. A new one. Not Coates. The last one must have joined up and got killed . . . killed . . .

She was spared any greetings with the aunts. Her mother must have had a quick word with them. She heard their voices in the hall, perturbed, saw Susan's concerned face – how lined it was – and was then taken straight up to her old room where her mother helped her to undress.

'Don't say a word,' she said. She was Sister McGrath again. 'I'll see to everything.' She slipped the nightgown over her head before she was fully undressed. That was tactful. But she knew her mother. She had sharp eyes. 'You've had more than you can stand. Whatever it is.' She waited as if for an answer. 'Sit on the bed. I'll pull off your stockings. Kieran's gone for Belle Geddes.'

'You shouldn't have bothered, Mother.' She was past caring.

Oh, the comfort of her own bed in her own room, the snow-white crispness yet softness of the sheets, heated by Susan's stone 'pigs', the faint lavender smell, the air which even on a December day had a steely freshness in her nostrils, yet warmed by the glow from the leaping fire in the black grate under the white mantelpiece. The sprigged curtains on the sash windows, the virginal freshness of everything was so beautiful, so unsuitable.

She knew Aunt Kate tiptoed in and looked at her, dark, sorrowing eyes, then Aunt Isobel, a wisp of a woman with dry soft fingers stroking her brow, then they faded away and Belle Geddes was there, expert, crisper than the sheets, completely professional as if she hadn't known her since she was a child, as if the love of her life hadn't been Charlie, her father, a confirmed spinster now because of that. No one would ever do after Charlie.

She didn't examine her. She stood and looked at her for a long minute, and then said, 'We'll call it nervous exhaustion for the time being, battle exhaustion. I'm going to give you something to make you sleep some of it away. You can tell me when you're ready to talk. How's that?'

She nodded. It was a fraction better already. Nothing would ever get rid of the ache, but to be with her own folk helped. She held out her hand and Belle took it in her own. 'If you can just give me a chance to get a grip of myself . . .'

'I'll do that.' The pressure of her fingers was there. The eyes were intelligent, and patient. She could wait.

It was hunger which drove her to struggle up on the third day, something as ordinary as hunger. She had been hovering between sleeping and waking, not even knowing why she was here, when the smell crept upstairs. Susan's roast leg of pork.

There was no one who could cook roast pork like Susan, with the crackling brown and crisp and the whole joint shining and golden-brown, the accompanying apple sauce at the right degree of tartness . . . even that was in her nostrils . . . their own apples from the orchard gathered by Susan in her white apron, stored in the attic to the right degree of ripeness, stuck with cloves and baked, then sieved and potted in neat glass pots.

When her mother brought up her dainty tray of poached egg on toast, the glass of milk, she said, 'Are you having roast pork?'

'Yes,' Maevy said. 'Can you smell it?' She saw her clearly for the first time since she had arrived, a woman in late middle-age, worn, worried, but still with her crown of fair hair and her erect carriage. 'It's part of the Christmas fare. Boxing Day. Isn't that what they call it? I'm not used to those new-fangled notions.'

'Christmas?' she echoed stupidly, 'I haven't missed Christmas?'

'You slept through it.'

'Oh, Mother . . .'

'Never mind. You didn't miss much. As long as you're sitting up and taking notice. Do you fancy some of what we're having?'

'Could I have a taste?' The radiance of her mother's smile made her want to weep.

'Aye, you could that! There are stovies as well.' Potatoes, roasted in the pork fat with shallots peppering them with green, and glistening with the coarse salt sprinkled on their plump sides.

'Maybe one.' She was suddenly ashamed of herself being waited upon by this tired woman who had the cares of a business on her shoulders as well. 'I'll get up and have it, Mother.'

'Oh, you couldn't come downstairs yet! You haven't got your sea legs.'

'No, I don't mean that. But that wee table by the window. I'll put on my dressing-gown.'

'There's a new one here that your Aunt Kate went into Wilson's and bought for you.' She got up and fetched it from the wardrobe. 'I've never seen anything like it.' She showed it proudly, soft white padded material with lace and pink ribbon at the throat and wrists. When she helped Ellie into it the inside was as soft as a duck's breast, and as warm. There were slippers to match. She was deeply ashamed at the evidence of this unquestioning love around her. 'And your presents are in the foot of the wardrobe.'

'Presents . . .?'

'Christmas presents.'

'Mother, I'd like to tell . . .'

'Shoosh!' Maevy held up her hand. 'Belle says there's to be no baring of souls yet. You get yourself over to that table while I'm downstairs getting your pork and stovies.' Her eyes were glistening with tears. It was as if she'd been given a crock of gold.

'When you come up, I'll . . .' she said to her mother's retreating back.

It was Susan who came with the tray. That was clever. An old woman, now, thin, bent, older looking than her seventy-two years. Her hair was steel grey, screwed up in the usual tight bun, pepper-and-salt hair, the same colour as her pepper-and-salt house dress. They had stopped her wearing a pinny long ago. 'My goodness, Ellie,' she said, 'it's a treat to see you up. You've had them all worried out of their skins downstairs and it Christmas.'

'I'm sorry about that. How are you keeping, Susan?'

'Oh, I'm getting by.' She sniffed as she put down the tempting plateful. 'If I can keep them oot o' ma kitchen. If it's not your Aunt Isobel it's your Aunt Kate, forever meddling with what doesn't concern them. Now, there you are. Eat it up afore it's cold. The nicest leg of pork I've seen for a long time, and done to perfection if a say so masel. Maybe it's the last we'll see with aw this talk about food rationing noo. Dae ye ken,' the familiar stance, arms akimbo, 'they want me to get rid o' ma awl grate! Did you ever hear such a pack o' nonsense?'

'You stick to your old grate, Susan, if it gives results like this.' Her appetite was waning already.

'Aye, you're right there.' She went to the door, turned before going out, her eyes wondering, her brows furrowed. There was no malice, just puzzlement. 'Battle exhaustion, that Belle Geddes says. A thocht that was just for the men?'

She shook her head. 'No, women get it too.' She was glad when she heard the soft click of the door. The ache was back again. There had only been a little respite. She turned over a slice of pork with her fork, over and over, in an agony of spirit.

She was sitting at the window later that day, staring out at the sodden garden, when Belle came to see her.

'I heard you were up. How do you feel?' She sat down beside her.

'I feel . . .' she shrugged, 'I feel . . . I've been in bed long enough. I can't have them waiting on me hand and foot. It's selfish, to say the least of it.'

'It's the only way they can show they're worried about you. But you're a strong girl, Ellie. I never knew anyone who ailed less.'

'And I'm not ill now.'

'Grief's an illness. I should know. You have to talk to someone about it. Your mother is the one.'

'I can't, not yet. There's . . . the shame.'

'Well, try me, as one doctor to another. Would that be better?'

'Maybe.' She looked out of the window, at the trees lashed by the rain, the lowering sky. Let it go, she told herself, let it go . . . 'I loved a man.' How sad a winter garden was. 'We were going to be married. Then he was killed. He sent . . . Jacob Cohen. He'd been with him . . . at the end. I thought at first he was . . . an emissary of love . . .' What a stupid kind of thing to say about that kindly Jew who had held her in his arms. 'Come unto me all ye who are heavy laden . . .'

'When did you first realize you were pregnant?' It was a doctor's question and she answered in the same way, almost automatically.

'I missed my first period in the middle of October but thought nothing of it. I'd been irregular. Most of us were – tension, lack of sleep, a bit anaemic, everybody is affected in some way by the War. But then again in November, and this time I knew it wasn't just anaemia. There were the usual signs. And the knowledge. The knowledge . . .'

'So you're two months' pregnant, you'd say?'

'Yes. And Joe's dead.' She didn't know how she could speak so calmly. Her mind had lost its ability to feel, to react. She was numbed by grief. She was glad of it, this new state. Anything was better than the hurt, the *suicidal* hurt. She'd gone through in her mind all the obvious avenues of escape, but Belle was careful. As careful as she would be in the same circumstances. All medicines were kept out of reach.

'You've luck anyhow on your side.'

'Luck?' She looked at Belle. Her lids felt heavy. It was an effort to keep them open.

'You're surrounded by people dying to help you, console you. When your father died they were all too busy consoling your mother. If *I* could live through that, so can you. And you have Joe's baby inside you. Something of him.'

'He was married.'

'Yes?' Belle's voice was level.

'I knew when we . . . and then his wife wrote to him, agreeing to give him a divorce. He wrote to me, a short, happy letter, that it was all right. It seemed like a miracle. I really believed in God for the first time, not old Murdoch's God. Do you remember him? Catherine's father? Everything was . . . golden. And then along comes Jacob Cohen and tells me . . . and tells me . . .' She fixed her eye on the willow which was being lashed cantankerously by the wind.

'How did it happen?'

'The tented hospital he was in was bombed.' She shook her head from side to side to clear it. 'It's the *randomness* of it. He was doing his rounds after operating, probably so happy, like me, that Gilda – that was her name – had promised him his freedom. His happiness would be showing on his face, as it was on mine . . .'

'Cruel,' Belle said, 'cruel. I'll give you that. Random. There's no pattern. That's what's so disappointing when you discover there's no pattern, that it's *all* just random. The only reality. It took me a long time to accept it. But there's life left – after death.' She smiled. 'And *you* can make a pattern. There's still pleasure to be had. A walk by the Sholtie. Or that wind in the trees.' She'd noticed, too.

She couldn't be doing with that moralizing. She was

empty. That was all. She looked at the whippy willow. It was certainly resisting. It was hanged if it would give in.

'You'll have to tell your mother, Ellie. About Joe. She knows you're pregnant. She's having her own private agony.'

'She knows!' She was surprised for a minute and then wasn't. Of course she'd know. She was an intelligent woman and a nurse, and her mother. Mothers were born intuitive. 'It's . . . the telling. She's always thought *that* highly of me.'

'Well, you have to come off your pedestal sooner or later. You're run of the mill now, ten a penny. Thousands of girls are in the same boat as you, carrying the child of a dead man.'

'That's crude.' She suddenly began to weep, looser, freer tears, as if the ice in her breast had melted. 'Oh, love hurts, Belle, love hurts . . .! It's Joe all the time. I hardly think of the baby, it's Joe, night and day I see him. He had a . . . peculiar quality, a special quality for me. I felt it right away. As if I'd been waiting for him all my life. I'd like to die . . .'

'Dying's easy.' She produced a large white man's handkerchief and gave it to her. 'They're more useful than the lace-trimmed variety in our work.' She was smiling, wryly. 'It's living that's the difficult thing. Now, see here,' she bent forward, 'you have to decide who you want to know first. They're all distressed about you, but there's not one shockable one amongst them. By God, you're lucky! If you'd known *my* mother! Think of Lizzie who would have been a bastard if Patrick hadn't married her mother. Holy Joe's daughter, Catherine Murdoch, your Uncle Terence's wife, would never have adopted her husband's byblow in a hundred years. Ernest, he's a man of the world. You'll never shock Ernest. Your mother's and your aunts' love is greater, far greater than any feeling of dismay they might have. They've all suffered in their own way, Kate maybe the least, but she's practical. I've seen plenty of signs of it. Don't forget she coped with four stepchildren and now she's running this house while your mother works. And helping in Lizzie's hospital.'

'Who do you think I should tell first?'

'Kieran.'

'Kieran!' She had almost forgotten him, or had wanted to forget him. She'd done him a great injury.

'He's been to see me. He's nearly out of his mind, as ill as you are with anxious love.'

'Kieran,' she said, 'I'll break his heart.'

'No, he's tougher than you think. Then tell your mother. Tell her how you loved Joe. She understands love. That was a rare thing between her and Charlie. How I envied them! Take it in easy stages. It will spread without you hardly having to say a thing. But it will stop with the McGraths. They're a close family. I'll write to your chief in France and tell her you've been ill. Explanations to follow.'

'I won't be able to go back.'

'No, that's finished. But you've done your bit. Take it day by day. And remember you're blessed. You're going to have a child.' She got up, spare, elegant, hardly any of the old Belle left except for those strange silver-grey eyes, all the seductive curves gone. 'Do you know,' she said, 'it's the one regret in my life, that I never had a child. A barren womb makes a barren soul, but, there, I know by your face you don't like my philosophizing.' She bent and patted her hand. She had never been one for womanly exchanges of affection, Belle.

19

The aunts were at the hospital, Maevy at McGrath's, when Kieran called. It was a bright cold day after all the rain, and when he came in he kissed her and said, 'You need some fresh air.' She saw he was nervous. 'Would you like to come for a walk?'

'I'd thought . . .'

'Come along. It'll do you good.'

'I hope you're not going to be hearty,' she said, getting up. She sounded like her mother to herself. Still, it was a good idea. Sitting opposite him at the fireside would have been too painful.

They set off with Susan admonishing her at the door as if she was still a child. 'Put your galoshes over your shoes, for goodness sake! Oh, no, you know best,' sarcastic smile, 'you always did. A'll keep ma mooth shut. Well, whit aboot a gravat for your neck? Here's yin o' your faither's. Your mither wouldny let me put it away.' She took down a long grey scarf from a hook in the hall, which she wrapped round Ellie's neck. 'There, now. Off ye go, and don't tire her oot, Kieran. The lassie's no' right mended yet.' Does she know, I wonder? she thought as they walked briskly along the road.

'Where are we going?'

'Down the Sholtie Brae, I thought, to the river. I think the towpath will be fairly dry.'

'All right.' It was better than running the gamut of welcomes she would get if they walked along the village street . . . 'My, you look fine! When d'you have to go back, Ellie?' And she a fallen woman.

The trees lining the bank were taller than she remembered, but with their dark, leafless branches weren't oppressive. The winter sun danced through them, making the puddles iridescent and the river gleam.

'You've lost weight,' Kieran said as they walked carefully, skirting the puddles. Susan was right. She should have worn galoshes. The river, she noticed, was swollen, heavy-looking – why did she think of similes which could also apply to herself? Except barren, like the trees.

She took her courage in both hands. The War has helped me here, she thought. Decisions. To cut or not to cut. No time to ponder. Other men waiting. Do it now. 'I may look as if I had,' she said, 'but it isn't possible. I'm pregnant.' They walked on for a yard or two before he stopped, turned her towards him and gripped her by the forearms.

'Say that again.'

'I'm pregnant. That's what all the fuss was about, not battle exhaustion. Grief, fear and cowardice. I've got over the exhaustion.'

'Oh, Ellie . . .' He looked at her for a long time, and then drew her to him as if for comfort for himself. Perhaps he couldn't bear to look at her face. Certainly she could hardly bear to look at his, drained of colour, cheeks fallen, eyes wide with disbelief. It was a bitter blow for him, she could understand that.

'It's a good thing it isn't Sunday,' she said, her face against his shoulder. 'There would be people . . .' He didn't reply. She waited, said, 'We'd better walk on.'

'Yes.' He released her. His face was ravaged, white. 'We'd better walk on. Will you tell me about it, right from the beginning? I want to understand . . .'

They walked past the hump-backed bridge, past her grandfather's fishing pool which he had used so seldom but where Terence had been pushed in by Patrick in that famous fight over Bessie Haddow. Her mind was for some reason full of her grandmother. What would *she* have said? Nothing conventional, that was for sure. She had been ahead of her time. Or that quiet, gentle grandfather she had never known, so like this Kieran beside her who was struggling with his soul. '. . . I have no excuse,' she finished. 'We met in Paris and I knew I loved him. No decision to make. I had hoped we'd be married if his wife would give him a divorce. No, no excuse. I never thought he'd be killed. Non-combatants. He was a surgeon. But they're not exempt from the stupid accidents of war, just less so. Not invulnerable.'

'God, that must have been terrible for you! Why didn't you tell me on the boat?'

'That wasn't me. That was just a . . . lump of suffering flesh, being shepherded home. Home . . . the only place for suffering.'

'Have you . . . discussed it with your mother?'

'Do you mean, have I told her officially? No, but she's no fool. I'll tell her and the aunts tonight. I've made up my mind.'

'They're probably thinking it's mine.'

'God, they'd never think that!' She was horrified.

'I'd give anything if it were.' He stopped and turned to her. 'Did you hear me? Would you, Ellie? Would you consider marrying me?'

'To give it a name?' She was bitter.

'It's a good enough reason, but it isn't the only one. You know I've been in love with you for a long time. I asked you to marry me in Paris too, remember?' Now he was bitter. 'You said when the War was over you'd see . . . Well, yours is. You can't go back.'

'That's true enough.' She felt a sharp sorrow at that. There had been so much satisfaction. She knew now what Charlie had got from it. Dedication. Even abnegation.

Something which made you feel good when you got time to think of it. Not wasting your life. But now . . .

'I know you're worried about your mother. She'll stand by you whatever you do but, oh, I'm not trying to bribe you, I've always wanted you, but you could make it easier for her.'

'Think of yourself! How would you feel being father to a child who wasn't your own? Marrying a woman who had someone else's child in her? If you hadn't been first?' She could be as crude as Belle. Maybe all doctors were like that.

'I'd take you on any terms if you'd have me.'

She said she would let him know. They wouldn't talk about it any more. They turned for home because suddenly her strength had gone and she knew she would have to get to bed again. He delivered her into the hands of Susan. 'Make this girl lie down till supper-time,' he said.

'Huh!' Susan looked down her nose. 'We've another doactor on the premises, have we? Between nurses and doactors a don't know whether a'm comin' or goin'.'

But she came up with a stone pig wrapped in an old piece of blanket and put it at Ellie's feet where she lay, and went away without saying a word.

The four of them sat round the table that evening. It wasn't roast pork – a bit of grey brisket, and custard with stewed prunes. Food was definitely getting scarcer. But the custard was made with eggs from Susan's flock of hens round the back which she cootered as if they were fighting cocks, and it had a brown nutmeg skin on it.

'How are you feeling today?' Aunt Isobel said, picking daintily at her food. She always cut off every morsel of fat, 'a finicky eater', mother called her.

'I'm fine, Aunt Isobel. But there's nothing wrong with me. You all know it. Unless being pregnant makes you ill.' She rushed on before she lost her courage, 'I'm sorry I've caused you all so much worry, you especially, Mother.' She had noticed earlier how drawn her mother's face was. 'I know you don't deserve this, considering all the love and attention you've always given me, Mother. It's not as if I was a young, silly lass. I met an American . . . Joe Gould . . .' Her mother turned away as if she couldn't bear to listen. There was a long silence.

'Have you nothing to say, Maevy!' Kate said at last.

'Maybe I should give her a good skelping.' Ellie wanted to weep at the sight of her mother's face. She looked old, defeated.

'You and father expected better of me, I know.'

'Maybe we expected too much. Never mind.' Maevy pulled herself straight, sniffed, there was a queer little stifled moan from her. 'Have you made any plans? Whatever they are,' she looked at her two sisters, 'we'll back you up.'

'We don't care a doo's dab about the village folks,' Isobel said, surprisingly, considering she had spent her life toadying to them along with her husband, John Craigie. 'You suit yourself. It's the War. Things are different. We were working towards things being different in the Movement, weren't we, Maevy?'

'Aye, but not going as far as having a baby by anyone you meet!'

'For goodness sake!' Kate said, and looking at Ellie, 'Don't mind her. She has to get her win' oot first. Her bark's always been worse than her bite.'

Ellie found herself smiling, the first real smile since Joe had been killed. 'She's not half hard enough on me. But Aunt Isobel's right. The War changed things. I . . . have to tell you. I met Joe at Emily's. He's a surgeon. We . . . fell in love.' She looked at her mother, 'I think it was the same as you and Charlie, or would have been. There was only one snag. He was married. And because of the War, and the feeling that there was no future, I . . . we . . . well, you know the result. The day he got word from his wife that she would give him a divorce he was killed. Well, that's the story of my life. It's still no excuse, I know.' There was a look of shock on the three faces. She saw her mother was weeping. She got up and put her arms round her. 'Don't cry, oh, please, don't cry. It's *my* problem.'

'It's *our* problem.' Her voice was impatient. 'Don't *hug* me against you like that, Ellie, I can't get my breath.' She emerged, smoothing her hair, wiping her eyes, 'This is your home.'

Aunt Isobel, who seemed to be excelling herself these days, nodded. 'And she could join the Movement with us!'

Ellie went and sat down at her place again. 'I'm going to make a home for myself with Kieran. He's asked me to marry him.' She saw Kate's face light up.

'Did you accept him, Ellie?'

'I'm going to. I'm very lucky. I've always loved Kieran . . . in my own way. We'll get on fine.'

Susan came in with her tray, her nose in the air. 'I knew it, I knew it. Blethering away when you should be eating up your dinners. It's hard enough to get it, a can tell ye. A was black burning ashamed to put that puir wee scart o' brisket on a plate. The sooner this War's over the better.'

'Stop girnin' and bring in some glasses, Susan,' Maevy said. 'And one for yourself. We're going to drink Ellie's health. She and Kieran are going to get married.'

'Oor Ellie, and Kieran! Your lad!' she said to Kate. 'My, my!' She wiped her hand on her apron and came round the table, offering it to Ellie. 'This is a prood day for aw o' us. Your faither wid hae been right pleased.'

Ellie put her hands on the woman's shoulders and kissed her cheek. 'Thanks, Susan.' And, seeing her confusion, 'It's all right. I promise not to do that for another twenty-six years.'

20

Ernest and Lizzie had left ahead of the others so that they would be at the Hall to receive the wedding guests. Ellie and Kieran had stipulated, 'No fuss, please,' and the table was laid in the adjoining room with a cold collation, the wedding cake in pride of place.

'Have a sherry, darling, it will buck you up.' He filled and brought a glass to Lizzie, kissing her as he handed it over.

'You and your wicked ways! I must admit I need it. I had a terrible desire to weep in the church.'

'Mercifully, Peter Kennedy kept it short. I warned him beforehand.'

'You were clever to get the ceremony rushed on. You're becoming quite a string-puller, my lad.' She looked sad, 'I wish you could have pulled a few to keep you in London.'

'I didn't try. Don't think I want to be farther away from you, but I'd hate to feel I'd been holed up in a cushy job when I know what the others . . .'

'Yes, I know, but . . .'

'They're in great need of men to interview German prisoners after the last fighting at Beaumont Hamel.' He sipped his sherry. 'Names to conjure with, these – High Wood, Delville Wood, Mametz Wood, Thiepval. I want them to be more than names to me.'

'Maybe you'll get time to look in and see your sister in Paris.'

'I hope so.'

'I'll worry about you.' Her eyes filled.

'Don't. Keep busy. The sovereign remedy that cures all ills. Except death.' He was thinking of that American surgeon, Joe Gould. Nothing would ever bring back *him* to Ellie.

'I wish Jonty could find that out. Ernest, I thought perhaps you could have a serious chat with him while you're at home. He's unsettled.'

'Don't worry too much, my darling. Any young man of sensibility would be unsettled in these unsettling times. And he has puberty to contend with as well. Ah, that's a time and a half!' He grinned at her. 'Yes, after this is over, Jonty and I will confide in each other, I promise you . . .' There were voices in the hall downstairs, distant clapping.

'There they are!' Lizzie put down her glass.

'What's the clapping?'

'Oh, that will be Ginny's doing. She'll have organized the walking patients, not to mention those in wheelchairs.' She tut-tutted. 'And Ellie wanted it to be kept quiet.'

'Ah, come on, you can't deny those lads any little excitement that's going. Don't be too hard on Ginny.'

'I'm not, but she's wilful . . . Oh, here you are! Come along in!' Kieran and Ellie came in together, followed by the rest of the family. There were no outsiders, with the exception of Peter Kennedy, the minister. Terence and Honor had not come because they had persuaded the newly-married couple to spend their honeymoon with them. She kissed Ellie, then Kieran. 'Well, how does it feel?'

'I don't know yet,' Ellie laughed. 'I'm in a daze.'

'Short and sweet anyhow.' Kieran shook hands with Ernest. 'Thanks for your good efforts on our behalf. It's useful to have as a brother the most important man in the county.'

'Ah, get away with you!' Ernest took Ellie's hands. 'Let

me look at this beautiful bride of yours.' How pale she is, he thought. I would never have called her fragile before, but it's the fragility of deep-seated grief. Strange to think they would never see the father of her coming child. Belle Geddes had said to him, 'She wants you to know. I know you won't talk.' Except to Lizzie. She, of all people, could understand.

'I want to thank you,' Ellie was saying. 'Both of you . . . for everything. I can't tell you how grateful we both are.' She smiled, and Ernest thought he'd never seen her more beautiful, but the sadness . . . Hard on Kieran, he thought, to be second-best. 'We'll never forget it.'

'It was nothing.' Keep it light. 'When are you off?'

'In about an hour's time.' Kieran had his arm round Ellie. 'We're driving up to Stranraer to catch the last afternoon boat.'

He heard the chatter of voices behind him. 'Excuse me.' He turned. 'Here they all are! Aunt Isobel!' He went forward to greet her. 'How charming you look. And here's the mother of the bridegroom, no less.' He kissed Kate. 'And mine, too. But where's the mother of the bride?'

'She's retired for a second, Ernest. Don't say anything. She was a . . . bit overcome. It's not like Maevy.' He nodded, his eyes understanding. 'And here's the beautiful bridesmaid!' He laughed at Ginny who had joined them, looking very fetching, he thought, in her lemon organza, a silver band on her brow, silver slippers. But could you ever ignore that red McGrath hair? Grandmother Maeve had passed on a fine legacy, not to mention that air of the world being her oyster.

'When I get married I want a service as short as that!' Ginny said. 'What do you say, everybody?' She looked round with that radiant smile which saved her from being brash.

'Was it you who organized the men downstairs? I heard the noise, you wicked girl!'

'What's wicked about that? You can't let weddings pass unnoticed . . . as if there was something to be ashamed of. Oh, Ellie, you looked beautiful in church!' She embraced her cousin. 'I'm just saying to Ernest, what's all the secrecy about, for goodness sake! I'd want to shout it from the housetops! I'm sure if Aunt Maevy had had her way she'd have had you dressed in white with a veil a mile long.'

'I didn't want . . .' Ernest took over for her.

'I don't know what we're going to do about this rumbustious creature. Really, Ginny, you have no sense of what's fitting. It's a little . . . ostentatious, don't you think, to go in for that kind of thing with a War on?'

'Oh, blow the old War! We're entitled to some fun . . .'

He shook his head smilingly and turned to Jonty who was beside them. He had the feeling he was seeing a different Jonty, a young man, no longer a schoolboy. How quickly they changed. And how handsome he was, with all his true father's elegance. Lizzie said he wrote poems. 'There's a bit of a beanfeast next door, old chap. Maybe you could take Ginny in and start the ball rolling. Ellie and Kieran have only a short time with us.'

'Right-oh! The only way to stop this one chattering is to stuff her mouth with food!' It wasn't exactly a poet's reply.

'Oh, the rudeness of it!' Ginny tweaked his cheek. 'Is that what they teach you at Eton, little boy?'

'You'd be surprised what they teach us at Eton,' he said.

Yes, Ernest thought, I'll have a talk with him tonight, see if he'll open up. He didn't know quite what he meant.

He escorted Maevy into the dining-room when she appeared with a white haze of powder on her nose. She'd been crying. He pretended not to notice. 'It's a happy day for you, Maevy,' he said, as they stood in a corner of the dining-room while the others helped themselves to the buffet.

'Very happy.'

'We know everything, Lizzie and I.' He lowered his voice. 'It's better that way.' He put a hand on her wrist.

'Belle?'

'It was Ellie's wish. We're family. Don't worry too much. You know your daughter. She'll put everything into this marriage to make it a success.'

'Except perhaps love.' She had lowered her voice, too. 'She's devastated, Ernest. Her life is shattered. You aren't seeing the real Ellie in that calm, smiling face.' She half-turned to look at Ellie talking to her Aunt Isobel. 'I hear her at nights, walking up and down her room, weeping. Once or twice I know she's slipped into the garden in all that cold. I've . . . feared for her . . . the Sholtie . . .'

'No, that would never be Ellie's way. She'll work through it.'

'I'm her mother. I can't help her . . .'

'No one can help her in the end. Just be there. Now she has Kieran. Her love will grow, it's already there, a different kind, but no less worthy.'

'He's so steadfast. Always has been.'

'Don't forget he loved Lizzie for years.'

'Yes,' she looked at him. 'Yes, I'd forgotten that.'

'Because Charlie was the one man for you. You're probably the exception that proves the rule. A one-man woman.' He wanted to make her smile.

'No, you're wrong, Ernest. I fell deeply and passionately in love with John Craigie when I was a girl. I couldn't see that it was Isobel he wanted.' She smiled at him. 'I can see *that* shakes you a bit! Yes, John Craigie, rest his soul. And I know without asking you that you had a few . . . experiences in New York before you ever fell in love with Lizzie.'

'My, you're a clever one!' He laughed at her. 'You're not the "heid yin" at McGrath's for nothing! But it all proves my point. I think the future is rosy for Kieran and Ellie. The mutual trust and affection is there already. That's the main thing.'

But he couldn't help wondering if he were right, as the little family gathering saw them off later for their drive to Stranraer. Such grief in the girl's face! Did the others notice it? The contradiction of the smile with the haunted eyes. He noticed Kieran's arm was round her as they drove away. If *he* was aware of Ellie's unhappiness, Kieran certainly was. He was sensitive, perhaps too sensitive for a man. Yes, it would be all right, but he knew he would be haunted for a few nights by the memory of Ellie's pale face, and especially that smile . . .

'So that's that,' Jonty said. He was standing beside Ernest in the drive. He was still clutching some unused confetti. 'Some wedding! Over before it begun. I hate the aftermaths of weddings, don't you, Ernest? They leave you feeling like . . . a knotless thread.'

Ernest put an arm round his shoulders. 'I've got a cure for that. Let's change out of this stuff and get into some sensible clothes. You and I will have a good walk. I want to have a talk with you.'

'What about?'

'Cabbages and kings, love, life, you, me. You're growing up, Jonty. It's time to get things straight.'

'I hope it's not a pi-jaw. I get enough of that at school. All right. Race you upstairs!' He was away like a gazelle. Ernest's eyes sought and found Lizzie. She was talking to the aunts. 'Taking Jonty for a walk,' he mouthed. She nodded. She understood.

21

It was fortunate that Honor had the temperament she had. Kieran knew her daughters laughed at her, her capacity for slipping away to her study, her absent-mindedness. She had a rich interior existence. There were no coy glances from her, no honeymoon nonsense.

When they arrived the following day, having spent the night in Larne, she welcomed them with a straightforward warmth and took them up to their room, the large bedroom which Maeve, Ellie's grandmother, had always occupied.

'You can do either of two things,' she said. 'Have a rest and then come down for dinner, or have a walk to stretch your legs. If you do go out, take a daunder round to the stables and say hello to Terence. His latest pet of a horse has got a cut on its hoof. You'd think the end of the world was nigh.'

'Giselle and Terence are still here?' Ellie asked. She had taken off her hat, stuck the hatpins into it and walked over to the window. 'Beautiful, and peaceful.'

''Deed they are, but they've gone to visit Clare and Aidan, and they're staying the night. They've struck up a rare friendship. It was better than Clare and Aidan coming here with their two. All hell let loose!' I wonder if she's arranged it so that we'll be quiet our first evening, Kieran thought. He crossed to the window and stood beside Ellie.

'Yes, peaceful. Different from Scotland, a subtle difference, greener, more spacious. And the light's different.'

'Ah, sure and it's altogether different,' Honor

enthused. 'Opal green, young Terence says, and silver grey in Paris. If you were to let me have the merest peep I could tell in half-a-minute where I was, says the clever boyo.'

'Sometimes you can smell the smoke from Glasgow in Sholton now,' Ellie said. 'I noticed it when I came back from . . .' Kieran noticed how her voice faltered for a second, 'but only when the wind's blowing a certain way . . .'

'It's a rip-roaring place now with all those factories doing their bit. Now, Edna's going to bring you up some tea.' Honor nodded. 'I always think travelling's a wearisome business and you can unpack or have a bath or do whatever the devil you like.' What an Irish beauty she is, Kieran thought. Age had enriched her, added character to her beauty, the rich black hair, the moist rose complexion 'But Terence says I've to make an appointment with you for six-thirty P.M. at the fireside in the hall and a drop o' the hard stuff before dinner.'

'We've sampled your poteen in Larne,' Ellie said. 'I was cold when I came off the boat.'

'Now what did you think of Larne?' Honor stopped on her way to the door. 'A something-or-nothing kind of place, wouldn't you think? A place to pass through.'

'We didn't see too much of it. It was dark. We had a nice hotel, though, the Royal, I think it was called. Kieran had booked a room . . .'

She went on to describe her impressions and Kieran, half-listening, thought of last night. There had been no grand passion. He'd been scared even to touch her – the barrier of her grief was stronger than a chastity belt – but when they had lain together for ten minutes or so, chatting desultorily as if they had met in the street, she had said, 'Don't hold back, Kieran, we're man and wife.'

'Oh, God,' he had said, as unmoved as she was, because of her, 'there's to be no feeling of it being a duty.'

'I didn't mean it like that.' She'd touched his arm. 'I understand . . . I want you to enjoy me . . .'

He'd taken her in his arms. There was no passion in him. It would have been like seducing his sister. His mind was full of the other man who had been in bed with her and whose seed was in her, was growing in her womb at this minute. It would be more than an intrusion on his part, it would be a desecration. 'I'm tired,' he'd said. 'So are you. Don't mistake me. I'm full of happiness that you're my wife, but I don't need the bargain sealed. We've a long way to go yet. All I ask is that you never pretend with me. That would be an insult.' He'd held her until she went to sleep, or was that a pretence? Her breathing was far too regular.

They sat at the window and talked companionably after the tea came. They talked of Maeve, their grandmother. 'There's a faint perfume of her yet,' he said, 'don't you get it? A lemony lily smell, subtle.'

'Yes,' she said, 'her essence.'

'My mother told me that she could remember long ago in that little house in Colliers Row, how Grandmother would spread her newly-washed hair on a towel round her shoulders and ask Kate to brush it. She remembered it as a very special pleasure, a closeness.' She nodded. 'And the firelight would be gleaming on it. Ginny has the same hair. Lizzie's is more copper.'

'Lizzie always says it was Grandmother who taught her how to wear clothes. She was a fastidious woman.'

'Yes. Mother's memories come back to me. Once, when Grandmother was going to visit a cousin – the one she bought the nucleus of the present McGrath's from – she dressed herself up in her finest, right down to the last detail, in order to impress, or entice, this Duncan, a poor sort of man, not used to fine ladies. She must have dazzled him. I think she dazzled Grandfather till the day he died.'

'And this would be the room where she sat waiting for him when they eloped to Scotland.' She looked around. 'It's doing me good already, being here.'

They visited their uncle in the stables, and he enveloped her in a warm hug, a horsy embrace, Kieran thought. The smell was rich, pungent but pleasing. How like Great-uncle Terence he'd become! Now both he and Great-aunt Caroline had gone. The American connection, he thought. I'm a representative of it, we are. But this white-faced girl wasn't joined to him yet, except by the marriage ceremony.

He showed them his prize mare with the lame foot. Its eyes and Terence's had the same look, soft, melting, the man and beast were as close as a man and a woman. He patted the blanket on its back. 'Horses do with a bit of spoiling as well as us. That's what you must do with Ellie, Kieran, spoil her. She's had a hard blow.' Oh, unwise . . . 'I have to say it, Ellie,' he took her hand, 'I'm not one for keeping things to myself. When Lizzie was born, I tell you the hardest thing I had to do was to keep out of the road although she was mine . . . so you see I have a special kind of understanding of what you're going through. Now Kieran here will be at hand to help you.' He spoke briskly. 'You're better placed than I was, lad, with Catherine. Now can you tell me what your plans are?'

'We're going to America to get settled in Wolf House. I'll see how the business is running. I've got a good man there, one who was too old for active service of any kind. I'll have to sever my connection with the Ambulance Service, but I'll see after that if I'll go back . . . Ellie would have plenty of relations to keep an eye on her if I do – Robert and Edie over at Springhill, as well as Aunt

Maria and Sarah and Uncle Patrick, not to mention George and Abbie and Victoria and Jason.'

'I'd be all right if he went,' Ellie said, 'I'll maybe take up some work for a time. War work.'

'Ah, sure you've had enough of that, Ellie.' Kieran saw her face close, go bleak at her uncle's remark.

'There's no rush,' he said.

They had a pleasant evening with their aunt and uncle and they all retired early. Terence had to be up at six to go to the stables, and Honor said she had got into the same habit. 'It gives me more time to write. Mornings are best.' Tomorrow they would begin a round of visits after lunch to see Honor's girls and the grandchildren. And the scenery. They would see what came first.

Ellie chattered almost gaily in their room as if to show him how well and happy she was, but when she got into bed she lay stiff and straight, her back to him. 'Excuse me, Kieran,' she said. He had a feeling that if he touched her something dreadful would happen, a single scream, a violent paroxysm of some kind. When his father died he hadn't known grief like this. It had been a conquerable grief, soothing, almost, a good man laid to rest at the appropriate time.

In the middle of the night he woke and saw that she was sitting at the window. He saw the spread of fair hair on her shoulders, saw that her hands were on either side of her head in such an attitude of classic grief that he knew he couldn't go to her. God knows I'd bear it for her if I could, he thought. He lay on his back. He was surprised he had not felt any jealousy for this unknown Joe Gould. Jealousy was a trivial emotion, of no account here. He was powerless, useless.

Tomorrow Giselle and Terence would be here. She had said she had a rare affection for both of them, and she would be interested, professionally at least, in Terence's condition. She had her father's keen medical mind. His bronchitis was responding to the Irish air, Honor had said. 'It was like a poultice.' 'It's good on the heart too, Ellie, if you'll let it.' That, Kieran noticed, was the only reference she made to Joe Gould – a real writer's remark.

And there would be the children. Who could resist children? Clovis and Jaime in the house. She could hold little Jaime in her arms. No one minded if you wept over children. We'll take each day as it comes, he thought, and ahead of us is our new life together at Wanapeake. He would be glad when the farewells were over and they were on the boat going home. It was his home. Maybe she could come to think of it as hers.

When she came back to bed he took her in his arms and held her.

'Would you take me?' she said. 'Please, please . . . I have to forget . . .' She was shuddering, and yet rigid.

It was in its way an insult but his lust came instantly at her words. She was his wife and he wanted her. Never mind if she was thinking of the dead man all the time. He would have her. He had waited long enough.

He wasn't gentle. He was unlike himself. He used her because he knew she was using him. Her head rolled on the pillow with the force of him. But when it was over and he apologized, she said, 'Nothing else would have done. The gentleness is for when we're sure of each other.'

He helped her to put on her nightgown again over her pregnant body. Her thinness seemed to emphasize it. He was ashamed when he saw the torn lace, but he kept it to himself. There were many sides to every human being and there could be no real harmony until you knew all the sides, good and bad. Sometime in the future they would find the right way for the two of them, a strength and gentleness without the coarseness, and a sweetness.

Maybe the child would help. He was prepared to love Joe Gould's child. That was the main thing.

'We'll be all right, Ellie,' he said, turning her away from him, tucking the clothes round her. 'Now, go to sleep.'

BOOK TWO

The American Connection 1917–1919

1

Of course, the place was not strange to her. She remembered her first visit with Grandmother after the tragedy of the shooting – Gaylord dead and Kieran badly injured, the warmth of Wolf House compared with Claremont. Aunt Kate had the capacity, shared by Lizzie and her own mother, of making a house into a home, while Claremont, Uncle Patrick's house, had seemed like a great mausoleum of stonework, inside and out.

Mrs Vanaressi was still installed, still black-haired, with the bright black eyes of the true Italian, and giving her a welcome which fell neatly between that of a temporary mistress and a servant. She had been a devoted caretaker since Uncle James' death and Kate's and Kieran's departure for Scotland and the Field Ambulance. 'You are what the house needs,' she said. 'Ever since Kieran's mother went away I've tried to keep it in order, but there should be a mistress. It makes a house live.'

'You've kept it beautifully at any rate,' Ellie said, looking round. She was glad it resembled neither the Hall nor Braidholme, a straight up-and-down dignified French-seeming kind of house with its mansards and shuttered windows; but the porch was pure American, furnished with comfortable sofas and chairs like welcoming arms at the top of the wide flight of steps. It had been a favourite place of Uncle James' when he couldn't walk as far as the garden, since it commanded a good view of the Hudson, especially in leafless winter. She recalled him taking pleasure in pointing out Springhill on the opposite bank, where Robert and Edie McGrath now lived.

'It was a sad occasion when you last came to Wolf House,' Mrs Vanaressi said, 'that poor young man gone and Mr Kieran so ill, but now Wolf House is happy with a new bride.' Her look, nevertheless was doubtful, and no wonder, Ellie thought. She had seen her eyes in a mirror at Grand Central Station and thought they were haunted. Memories and regret. Eyes gave everything away, try as one might. What would the woman think when a baby arrived sooner than one could logically expect? Were Italians more tolerant in their outlook? She remembered it was Mrs Vanaressi who had told Aunt Kate that Gaylord had been taking laudanum.

'It must have been quiet for you with my aunt and Kieran gone.' That was safe enough.

'Ah, but I like the quietness! It is friendly here. You will find it so, madam. Your aunt and uncle created a happy atmosphere which still lingers. Besides, if I want to be *un*quiet, I go to visit my daughter, Maria, down by the railway station. Three children already! Still the Italian way and her born here in America. All boys, so her husband is pleased.'

It was Maria who had worked in the Paradise Inn, that 'fast place' Lizzie had once told her about, which Gaylord had frequented. 'He picked up Bohemian ideas there,' Lizzie had said, 'and drank too much. I happen to know that to my cost.' She had changed the subject quickly, as if she regretted what she had said. Lizzie, although an easy talker, never gave much away.

In their room later she said, 'This was yours, Kieran. I remember sitting with you after the accident.' She remembered she had been curious to see the 'hole as big as a fist' in his side, caused by the shot. What a keen medical student she must have been. Now she *had* seen it, or at least felt it that night they had made love at Woodlea. Her curious fingers had followed the hollow like a small crater in the puckered skin. Had it been an inch or so nearer the spine he would have been paralysed. He was bound to have continuous residual sciatica in his leg, but he never complained. Had *she* taken over that monopoly? Once she had been bright and full of fun. 'Do you remember,' she said, 'your father, you and I, discussing the War, and how we agreed it couldn't be avoided? At least we were right there.'

'You didn't know your life would be wrecked by it,' he said quietly. She was sitting at the dressing-table brushing her hair, and she saw his grim face. Grief is selfish, she thought, a continuing self-interest. It could be destructive of any relationship if indulged in for too long. The other person could know nothing of the ecstasy which had preceded the grief.

'None of us knew what the War would do to us, but we went in spite of knowing it was evil. We've both seen terrible sights – you even before. You'd seen Gaylord on that terrible day. You told me about you both lying there in the wood, and how his head was half blown away, the grass spattered with blood and . . .'

'Why do you bring that up? There's no need.'

'It's for my own good. To remember that I'm not the only one to suffer . . .' He was sitting on the bed and she got up and crossed the room to sit beside him. 'It's working out a philosophy that's the difficult part, to stop the inward-looking. Everybody has to live with something. Uncle Patrick and Aunt Maria with their two tragedies, Uncle Terence in Ireland with his . . . Did you know it was my mother who was with him when they found Aunt Catherine in that bath filled with blood? My mother's tragedy of losing her husband in his prime, so cruelly and needlessly. And yet they don't go around looking like death.' She put her arm round him awkwardly. 'I promise you I'll try to become a good wife. I'll never forget what you've done for me, and I hope if I have Joe's child you'll never regret sheltering us.'

He put his head on her shoulder, a touching gesture. 'It's a privilege for me, Ellie. I know I can never take this man's place, but I hope I can become a father to his child. It's I who am selfish. I know you only accepted me because of it, and perhaps for your family, but I've taken advantage of the situation. I don't feel . . . anyone special. I'm very humble.' She heard his voice shake.

She gave herself to him freely that night. Joe was still with her, even more so now that she was in his country, but there was balm in having a man love her and making him happy. But she lied in her responses. She had said she would never pretend, and it was 'Joe . . . Joe . . .' her heart was saying, Joe she was imagining, his dark body, the high cheekbones with the shadows, the smooth dark hair which grew down his spine, those almond eyes, all the time. And when Kieran groaned, it was a strange, absent woman who stroked his back and replied with lies to his broken words of love.

But there was no doubt America was doing something to her and for her even from the first day. There was a new vitality in the air. The snow was deep and white in the garden of Wolf House, and when she walked in her boots and wearing her warm fur coat, hat and muff to the shops, the sight of the children sliding past her on their toboggans made her smile and wave to them.

She enjoyed getting to know the shop people, and being head of a household with Mrs Vanaressi in the kitchen and Irma, the Polish maid who looked like twenty until you were close to her and saw the lines round her eyes. She had married in 1911, just after Ellie had last seen her, but so far was childless and had been happy to come each day to help in the house.

She paid a visit to Claremont and met her aunt and

uncle and Sarah, now thirty-four, small, dark-haired, but with a serenity of expression. She seemed to have lost all interest in clothes and was unbecomingly dressed in dark grey. Kieran said it was because she had become religious.

Aunt Maria and Uncle Patrick were as she remembered them, except that strangely enough Aunt Maria, as if to counteract her daughter's plainness of dress, had taken to dressing as fussily as her own mother, with a preponderance of buttons and bows. There was even a velvet bow in her hair. Her face was too square and broadchinned for that.

Uncle Patrick was quite white-haired and quite pompous – a strange characteristic, Ellie thought, since that was a word which certainly could not be applied to his brother, Terence. Perhaps it was a convenient cloak which hid his disappointment in so many aspects of his life.

They were eager to hear all about Ginny. They spoke of her as if she were some rare being who did not belong to them, and who constantly surprised them. It was a pity that this indulgence had not extended to Sarah when Robert had wanted to marry her and Uncle Patrick had forbidden it. 'That's Ginny for you,' they said, when Ellie told them of her organizing ability, her popularity, her intrepidity. What would they say if she married Magnus Muir, the son of Lord Muir of Muirkirk, Inverness, Scotland?

But from a purely selfish point of view it was a good thing Sarah and Robert had not married because she found a friend in Edie, his wife. She and Kieran crossed the Hudson to see them a few days after they arrived. Grandmother had always said Springhill was the gem of the three houses, and even in the depths of winter it had a rightness and a spaciousness which were beguiling. There was the wide curving staircase which Aunt Isobel and Aunt Maria had come down on Aunt Isobel's twenty-first birthday, with its great landing window looking on to the Hudson, and its golden carpeting. And the large white drawing-room made even lighter by the reflection from the river. The sloping, snow-covered lawns made it seem bluer than ever.

Edie Barnes, that was, looked like a girl who had done the proposing except for the actual words; a quick, bright, dark girl with a flashing smile, a deep cleft in her left cheek. Robert was solid, quiet, but with a sense of humour, as different from his younger brother, Terence, as night from day. He patently adored his young wife who seemed to rule the roost, but Kieran, when Ellie made this remark, said that Robert's word was law.

'He's determined,' he said, 'and he's done a great deal for McGrath's. It's he who's pushed on the shipping side of the business here, and I know he and your mother saw eye to eye in many things when he worked in the Glasgow office. Indeed, they're very like each other. Ernest is the entrepreneur, the committee man. He had more scope in McGrath's early days than he would have had in our father's export business which is solid and long-established. He'd grace any board, as he's now proved with this merger, but you still need people like Robert in the background.'

He welcomed Ellie quietly but sincerely. 'You look as if you've been working hard. Terence has written singing your praises, and it's my turn to thank you for all you did for them. Now you must relax. When Kieran and I are up in New York every day you must visit here often. Edie's longing for female company.'

'Don't take that too literally,' Edie said, laughing. 'There are Priscilla and Polly, the only two unmarrieds in the Vogel and Murray-Hyslop clans. The others are very involved in bringing up their children.' She had been married over a year now, Ellie thought, and Robert already looked like a family man. Perhaps she would find herself in the same position soon.

While Kieran and Robert went round to the stables, Edie and Ellie sat comfortably at the fire. 'I hope you're not one of those horsy people,' Edie said. 'We've a lot of them here. Their conversation is rather limiting.'

'No.' Ellie shook her head. 'Where do your interests lie?'

'I don't know yet. Everywhere. Lenin, the Russian Revolution, people starving all over the world . . . a thousand calories per person a day in Germany. Did you know that? The slowness of Woodrow Wilson, especially now that Germany has announced to neutrals unrestricted naval warfare. Charlie Chaplin . . .' She laughed, 'I had a good education at Vassar, but I'm fighting against the general idea that I should stay at home and fulfil my natural function. I do a lot of voluntary work, of course, and I suppose if a baby comes along I'll settle into motherhood, but I'm not like my mother. I don't feel that's the be-all and end-all of life.'

'You're a different generation. That's natural. My upbringing was different, almost a boy's,' she smiled. 'I suppose because my parents were disappointed I wasn't. Then Mother found out she couldn't have any more, so I became a substitute and followed in my father's footsteps, even to joining up. Besides, my mother, like my grandmother, works in the firm.'

'Robert is a great admirer of hers. Did you know?'

'Robert?' She laughed. 'I always stood rather in awe of him if I went to the Glasgow office as a girl. I remember when he came to work there. He was so serious and businesslike, but then he was at least ten years older than me.'

'He's not so serious when you get to know him. He's quite cosmopolitan when you think of it, born in Glasgow then switched to Ireland when his father remarried, university in Dublin, back to Glasgow to work in McGrath's then exchanged for Ernest and brought here to the American branch. He's adaptable, my Robert, and strong, I mean strong-minded. If you ever have a problem, Ellie, he's the one to go to. I say that as a very satisfied wife.'

'I'm sure he's just as satisfied.'

'He couldn't be more in love with me than Kieran is with you.' What a relief it would be, she thought, to open my heart to this girl, to say, 'This isn't me, it's a sad ghost. I left the true Ellie in France with Joe. He didn't even have a grave . . .' To her dismay she felt her eyes fill with tears.

'Excuse me,' she said, taking out a handkerchief from her pocket, 'I'm a bit . . . run down.' What a puny, unmedical remark.

'No wonder!' Edie was vigorous. 'I'm lost in admiration at what you did in France! Was it terrible?'

'No,' she said, 'it was the happiest time of my life. I wish I were still there. I wish I were getting up at half-past four in the morning and working all day, falling into bed exhausted at night, oh, I wish I felt that urgency! I feel I've let everybody down, taken the easy way out, but there was no alternative, Edie, I had to give it up . . .' She heard her voice breaking and was ashamed. 'No alternative . . .' It was a wail. She saw the girl's shocked face, tried to pull herself together. 'But don't think I'm not happy with Kieran. If I hadn't gone to France I could have married him earlier and then . . .' She was gaining control of herself. 'I tell you, Edie, girls like us are at the crossroads. We want to go out into the world, and when we do we have to take on more than work; there are different problems, different relationships which wouldn't occur if we were safely in our homes, queens of our little castles. There's joy out there, but sometimes terrible, terrible sorrow. You can't have it both ways.'

Edie bent forward and took her hands. Her brown eyes were direct. 'I'm not so enclosed in my little world not to see that you're unhappy. When you want to confide in me, I'm here. I'd like to be your friend. Will you let me come and visit you, and will you promise to come here when you can? Don't think I want to pry. I just feel you need an anchor.'

She had never had a close woman friend. Jean, the girl with whom she had shared the Glasgow flat, had not shared her life. They had both been too strongly motivated in their own careers to concern themselves with the other. There was Belle Geddes, of course, but she was older. 'You're good,' she said, 'and I'm over-emotional. I'm not . . . me. Normally I would have looked for a job in a hospital while Kieran worked. He understands that. But it isn't possible at the moment.' She couldn't bring herself to tell her about the baby yet. She would weep. 'But, yes, I feel I have a friend in you, Edie. We'll have good times together. Now, you must tell me all about you for a change, about your parents and whether you have sisters and brothers, and what it was like to go to a girls' college. I want you to teach me the American way of life, since I'm going to live here . . .'

Robert and Kieran came into the room, rubbing their hands from the cold. 'By Jove, it's fierce out there,' Kieran said, 'but I'd forgotten how dry the atmosphere is, how invigorating. I bet you don't miss damp, drizzly Glasgow, Robert.'

'Sometimes I do. Glasgow is . . . Glasgow, each city has its own ambience. York Street offices and the continual hooting of the ships on the Clyde, especially when it was foggy – what an eerie sound that was. Crossing busy Argyle Street's tram-lines at night and making my way under the Hielanman's Umbrella to catch the Great Western Road "caur".' He laughed. 'I haven't forgotten the dialect. I take off my hat to the man who worked out the brilliant idea of colouring the tramcars according to their destination. It was easy to spot your own even in the fog. Many a good run I've had chasing mine, and the conductor telling me off when I jumped on to the platform when it was gathering speed.'

'They've women conductors now with tartan skirts,' Ellie said, 'to replace the men who've gone overseas. They're far fiercer than the men. I'd rather face a raging bull!'

Kieran laughed. 'Oh, it's a grand city! Strangely like New York, the same vitality. Maybe it's because they're both polyglot, Highlanders (foreigners to the Glaswegians), Jews, Irishmen, Poles, Belgians, Italians and a scattering of the English. It's a racy, noisy city and their tearooms are wonderful.'

'Miss Cranston and James Dalrymple, the Tramways Manager, are our folk heroes,' Ellie said to Edie.

'I'd like to go.' Edie had been following the conversation with lively interest, 'but meantime Ellie and I are going to have a day up in New York and maybe go to the theatre!'

'Are we?' Ellie looked at her, smiling.

'And you two men when you've finished your labours will meet us and give us dinner. I want to see *The Cherry Orchard*.'

'Well, the sooner I get back to work, the better,' Kieran said, 'if I have to earn enough money to pay for all this jollification.'

'I should make it next week.' Robert smiled, 'I don't mean it will take that time, Kieran, but Ellie needs to put her feet up first. Remember, she's been through a lot.' Had Kieran told him about Joe? she wondered.

'Don't treat me like an invalid, Robert,' she said, 'I'm used to attending people in bed, not the other way round.'

'Well, a little of your own medicine won't do you any harm.'

On the way home Kieran asked her if she had enjoyed herself. 'Yes, very much,' she said. 'I like them both. They're . . . dependable.'

'Yes, they're well-matched. It's difficult to remember that Robert is only thirty-five compared with my half-brother, George, who's fifty-two. He's the eldest of father's first family. You get a double advantage with Robert. He can be as solemn as George, but as young as Edie, although she's ten years younger, I think, around your age.'

'What a spread of ages there is in all your families,' she said, feeling for a second her previous general interest in facts. 'I can hardly believe George is only three years younger than my own mother. And what about Victoria and her husband, Jason?'

'She's fifty-seven, he's three years older. Emily's a couple of years younger than her sister. You'll find more in common with their families, I imagine. We would need a family tree to get them all straight! You'll meet them in due course, but, you know, you don't have to feel you must find your friends only in relatives. There will be lots of people dying to meet you in Wanapeake.'

'I can't see myself falling into a routine of visiting, Kieran. I know I'll have to try. I can't . . . I can't make plans yet . . .'

'I understand. Take it easy. Let me look after you for a change. You're lucky. Your kind of work will always be there. All I want is to make you happy.'

She knew she was very lucky. If only this ghostly feeling would go and she could become Ellie Murray-Hyslop, Wolf House, Wanapeake, and not one-time lover of Joe Gould who had been killed by a German bomb.

2

Her medical curiosity saw her through her labour which was long but fortunately uncomplicated. The nurse was efficient, the doctor, she thought, less so, but then he was young and rather in awe of her status as a surgeon.

She showed off a little to begin with in turning down his offer of ether, but towards the end seized the rubber cup gratefully and took long, pain-relieving draughts from it like any ordinary frightened girl.

It was a boy, 'a little beauty', Nurse Everley said, as she put him in Ellie's arms, with long dark hair remarkable in one so new-born. As for the rest, how could you determine any features in the little squashed red face which she immediately adored. It was Joe's baby and hers, not Kieran's, a piece of him from that terrible bombing to treasure and to hold.

Kieran was all that a new father could be, admiring and loving, but she detected in him a greater anxiety for her than for the welfare of the child. He declared him a 'fine little chap' and went on immediately to talk of her. What else could she expect?

She lay in bed for a week, trying to put her thoughts in order. This was Joe's baby, but she must remember that Kieran had taken on the role of father. She must be sure that she made no difference in her attitude to him, that he should never feel left out because of this interloper . . . did he secretly think of little James as that? They had decided to give him Kieran's father's name.

The only solution, she knew, was that she should have another child, this time Kieran's, but for the time being she allowed herself to be besottedly, tearfully, in love with this one she held in her arms.

She lived over in detail her first meeting with Joe in Emily's house in Paris, their visit to the *Jardin des Plantes*, the shivering delight as his personality took hold of her, the overwhelming quality of her love for him. She had no regrets about that night in La Hirondelle, only thankfulness that it had occurred

Her lovemaking with Kieran was like a pleasant habit compared with the tumultuous, traitorous feeling which she could still recapture as she lay in her room upstairs in Wolf House, the only noise that of a steamer on the river and the hum of the air-conditioning box on the window-sill. Summers in the Hudson Valley could be humid and stifling.

The first visitor who was allowed was Edie. They had become firm friends over the last few months, and she welcomed her with open arms. 'Edie! It's good you've come! I'm lying here in a dreamlike state. You can bring me news of the outside world.'

'Well, it suits you at any rate.' Edie laid down the flowers and basket of fruit she had brought and went to look at the baby who was sleeping in a cot beside the bed. 'Perfect,' she said, 'really perfect.' She looked up with her bright quick smile, her deeply-flecked cheek. 'Just what I expected of you because you *are* a perfectionist. But I ought to congratulate Kieran too since he's taken part in it.'

Because her mind was full of Joe she heard herself saying, 'He's not Kieran's. He's . . . someone else's.' How often she had planned how to tell Edie and shirked it. Now it was out.

Edie did not reply. She pulled out her hatpins, lifted her hat from her dark hair, and laid it on top of the basket of fruit, an added nosegay, sat down and took Ellie's hands. 'I'm not a moron. Anyone can count. But I presumed like everyone else the baby was premature.' Her dark eyes were on her. 'You didn't *have* to tell me this.'

'I know,' she said. 'But I feel like a traitor lying here. I've thought of nothing else but Joe since the baby was born. It must be on my face. Is it? Kieran sees it, I'm sure. He's sensitive. He knows he can't really . . . share the joy.'

'Let me get this straight.' Edie released Ellie's hands. 'You had an affair with . . . someone called Joe . . .'

'Joe Gould.'

'. . . You became pregnant and Kieran married you. Why did *he*, Joe, not . . .?'

'He was killed.' She winced, hearing the words. 'He was an American surgeon. He had volunteered. He was in a ward, a tented ward, attending to the soldiers, and a German bomb hit it.' She had to go on. 'A friend of his, another surgeon, came and told me, Jacob Cohen. Jewish. Jewish American. I wonder where he is now . . . This family of ours and its . . . American connections. It's strange . . .' She was in a daze of remembering, saw the concerned Jewish face.

'Did Joe know you were going to have his child?'

'No. I'd kept it from him. You see, he was married . . . Oh, don't look like that, Edie. I knew, I was in full possession of my senses, I'm culpable, but this love we had . . . and in war you have such heightened sensibilities that there is so little time left . . . There's no need to make excuses because I've never felt ashamed. It was inevitable. Then, when I knew I was pregnant but hadn't told him, I had a letter from him telling me his wife was giving him a divorce and we'd be married right away . . . and then Jacob Cohen came . . .'

Edie got up and put her arms round her shoulders. 'My

God,' she said, 'you've lived at least, Ellie. I almost envy you.'

'Envy! If you knew the . . . unfathomable grief. I was married in a daze of pain . . .

'So Kieran offered to take you both on?' Edie's voice was almost light. She was glad of that. All her tears had been shed long ago.

'Yes. He'd asked me to marry him often before. I'd said I *might*, only might, after the War. I was in no hurry, you see . . . and then Joe came along.'

'And now there's Joe's baby.' She left her and turned to the cot. She carefully pulled aside the shawl from the little face. 'Very dark. Was Joe dark?'

'Yes. A dark-toned skin, but golden. Silky hair, even on his body. James has the same. When I nurse him, and run my hand down the little spine . . . oh, God forgive me, Edie.'

'Don't apologize to me. So he's going to be a constant reminder.' She sighed, tucked the baby in and sat down again. 'Well, my dear,' she said, 'you have your work cut out . . .' She stopped speaking suddenly, then said, 'Do you know, I've just had a flash of what immortality means, what the whole business of people coming together means, making babies. Oh, I knew it academically, but here's living proof of it. Joe's not dead. James will grow up and no doubt marry and he'll go on through him. It's so . . . neat!'

Ellie smiled. 'Yes, it's neat all right, but there's Kieran. I married him as an . . . atonement, because of the family. That's not neat, it's mean. My mother took care of me through the . . . aftermath. God knows what I looked like when I arrived home from France, shepherded by Kieran. She has strict moral principles, she's as straight as a die, but she took care of me like . . . a mother, hardly a word of reproach except once when she said I needed a good skelp! You'll have to visit Scotland to understand that one, Edie, but it's not a pat on the back. I owe a lot to her and the rest of them, so understanding, too understanding – Kieran's mother, Aunt Isobel, Lizzie and Ernest, Belle Geddes, our doctor. Maybe I took the easy way out but at least I was making them happy.'

'Did Kieran realize that?'

'He realized he was getting what he wanted but not in the way he wanted it. Does that sound crude? He'd always wanted to marry me.'

'But not necessarily to father another man's child.'

'He said he understood that.'

'He *said*. It couldn't have been easy for him.'

'We've got along very well.' She bridled. 'You've seen us. We've been happy. I've always loved Kieran.'

'In your own fashion. But this is a new phase. Oh, I'm not trying to scare you, Ellie, but you'll have to be careful that you give him as much love as you give little James.'

This girl was spoiling the haze she'd been in. She resented it. 'I've already thought of that. I'm not stupid.'

Edie laughed. 'No, you aren't stupid.' She looked at her, smiling. 'I'm going to tell you something because we're good friends. When you came here so pale and remote, I could see you were unhappy. I thought it was homesickness plus the tension of having done so much in France. I thought you were exquisite, perfect, you had done all the things I'd never done, had a career, succeeded in it at a remarkably young age, gone to Europe without a qualm, worked like a man . . . oh, your fame spread here, I can tell you, from those adoring aunts! I envied you. I'd had a good education but not a practical one, not trained for any profession. I'm not blaming my parents for that. I hadn't any ideas myself. Then I fell in love with Robert and got married but . . . I didn't want to settle down to motherhood like all the wealthy young matrons around here, like Deborah and Judith . . .'

'Priscilla and Polly aren't married . . .'

'Give them time. And then, when I knew you were pregnant I thought, this will be done to perfection, a trouble-free labour – it was, wasn't it? – and the most beautiful baby in the world . . . and soon you'd become a perfect surgeon in our local hospital in between producing more perfect babies . . .'

'You're talking a load of rubbish and I don't agree with a word of it, but are you saying I've let you down?'

'Oh, no! Don't mistake me . . .' She leaned forward and took Ellie's hands. 'You're human and I think all the more of you. You had the courage of your convictions, and that I truly admire. And whatever happens you have something to show for your lost love . . .' She glanced at the baby.

'But . . . there's Kieran.'

'Of course there's Kieran! Oh, I see it all now! You're a passionate girl, not an ice-maiden, and I'm glad. Well, passionate girls ought to have love to spare . . .'

'If he'll accept it now.' She lay back on her pillows, and now the tears were in her throat, clogging it. It was going to be difficult. This was the real beginning of her marriage. Edie was right about Kieran. He was sensitive, but there was another side to him, a tendency to retire into himself, to refuse stubbornly to say what he was thinking or feeling.

For the first time she really saw what he had done for her. As well as giving her and the child his name, he had come out of the Field Ambulance because of her. There had been formalities, papers which had arrived. She remembered him poring over them. It must have left him with a sense of failure, a feeling of a job half-done. It had all been for her, and he would have to be a saint not to resent Joe's child.

'Yes,' she said, and this time she wept, 'it's going to be difficult.'

'Look at little James,' Edie said, her own voice thick, 'lying there without a care in the world.'

'They come when you grow up.' She put her face in her hands. She knew Edie had got up and was pinning on her hat – there was a side vision of lifted arms.

'I'm with you, Ellie,' she said, 'all the way, but, knowing you, you'll find a solution.' She knew she was bending over the cot again. 'My goodness,' she heard her say, 'he's a beauty, worth it all . . .'

3

Jonty was in his room on the second floor of the Hall, where he had been established since Lizzie reorganized the bedrooms. He liked it. The view over the fields right up to the woods was more expansive than his former one on the floor beneath. On a clear day he could make out the ruined tower of the monastery against the skyline, and beyond that the gently sloping hills, a familiar view which spelled home.

He was packing a small Gladstone bag which still had his father's initials on it, N.G.C. His trunk had gone a week before, carefully packed by Lizzie, name tags checked and sewn on the new games clothes. 'Next spring,' she had said, 'you'll need a new cricket sweater. You've grown so much. You don't look like a schoolboy any more.'

At the memory of the words he got up and stood in front of the pier glass on the far wall. Six feet one inch. He'd been measured by Matron before the end of term. 'The height of nonsense,' Aunt Maevy had said when she saw him. He was fond of Aunt Maevy. She was reliable. He divided people into two categories, 'Variable' and 'Non-variable'. She was definitely in the latter. 'And now you've another cousin in little James,' she had said. He could see how proud she was of Ellie's new baby.

'Are you sure I'm not its uncle?' he had asked her. He should have liked to think of himself as an uncle. It gave a feeling of maturity. 'Uncle Jonty', or even 'Uncle Jonathan'. He fingered his upper lip regretfully. He would have liked to grow a moustache, but Mother would have been horrified, as well as thinking he was doing it behind Ernest's back. He could see that she tended to indulge him to make up for Father being dead.

Annabel and Kit, now travelling each day to Hutcheson's School and the Glasgow Academy, said he was 'Mammy's pet'. If they had gone to English schools they would have said 'Mummy'. She had told him it had been a difficult decision to make about their education, but that Ernest had taken the initiative in the end.

'Jonathan is a Crawford, and following in his father's and his grandfather's footsteps which is right and proper. Annabel and Kit are Scottish born and bred and should follow *their* parents.' She had reported Ernest's words, and added, 'But I went to a finishing school near Paris. Grandmother sent me. Ernest has no objection to that or to English universities when the time comes.' He had said that he thought they had made the right decision, and in any case it was pretty difficult travelling in trains when they were full of soldiers.

Was that what had first influenced him, the sight of those rowdy men coming home on leave – of course, he didn't see the wounded ones on the train – and the quieter ones going to the Front? Perhaps, but the idea had been there long ago, ever since he could remember. Father had died after the siege of Ladysmith, in a hospital in a place called Intombi, Uncle Charlie had cut off his leg in an effort to save his life. If either of them had been alive, they would want him to be fighting for King and country.

And Ellie had been in France until she decided to marry Kieran. That was a funny thing. He had always admired her for her strength of character just like her mother. Why had she given up in the middle when she had such a wonderful post in that Scottish Women's Hospital and had been operating every day, like Uncle Charlie? It didn't make sense.

And then the baby coming along so soon. Well, of course, he knew all about babies and the bit that went before and that they could be premature, but Ellie was so efficient in everything she did that he couldn't see her having a premature baby. Had she and Kieran . . . before they were married . . . or had there been someone else? You couldn't help thinking.

He took another look at himself, thrusting out his chest, smoothing his hair with both hands. He saw his father, or his father's likeness from that photograph Mother kept downstairs, the shape, the look. It was impossible to pin down characteristics, except that he was his father over again. But not the eyes. Nature had slipped up there. Father's were almond-shaped and dark in the photograph, secretive eyes; his were what Mother called 'true McGrath blue'. He remembered the brilliance of Great-grandmother's almost up to the day she died.

He went back to packing the bag. Just the minimum requirements. He had told Mother he was spending this last fortnight with Craven in Buckinghamshire and that they would go back together for the Michaelmas term – his first lie to her in his whole life.

She had accepted that without a qualm. She knew that sometimes he was at a loss during the long summer vacation, too old to join in Annabel and Kit's capers, too inexperienced to be downstairs helping in the hospital. And Ginny, who was always good for a laugh, was up in Inverness staying wlth Magnus Muir's parents – 'the Scion', she called him. He had taught her that word, saying that scions were ten a penny at Eton. She had written him a letter. He fished it out of his pocket and spread it out to read it.

Sorry to miss you. You and I could have had some rare *tares* together. Magnus is on leave and his parents have invited me to their stately pile. I feel I'm an imposter. I don't want to live up amongst the heather and the midges, but Magnus is besotted, poor soul. He's only on leave for a week, but they want me to stay on longer, or his older brother does. Maybe I will.

Hamish, the elder brother, has been invalided out of the Army – nothing very serious as far as I can see. You'd think it would have put him off shooting, but not a bit of it. He's at it morning, noon and night and then plonking dead feathered or furry things in the kitchen which land up on the dining-table every night. He's quite different from the Scion. I call him the Laird o' Cockpen, and since you're going to be a poet, I'll quote a few lines for your edification which were written by a certain Lady Nairn. I found some old music sheets lying about here.

> The Laird o' Cockpen,
> He's prood and he's great,
> His mind is ta'en up,
> Wi' things o' the State . . .

Improve on that, if you can, Rabbie Burns!

Oh, I get fed up here, now that the Scion has gone, but 'the parents', as Magnus calls them, hang on to me like grim death. I wish I were older, then I'd do a bunk to France – you've to be twenty-three for the VAD – or maybe I'll just marry the Laird behind the Scion's back. 'Cheerio', as they say in Glesca, and I hope you have a good time with your friend in the Home Counties. Why don't *you* do a bunk?

He put the letter away, and rummaging in the bottom of the bag, took out a notebook and leafed through the pages. He'd worked through all his indecision, doubts and fears in his poetry, if she only knew. 'Shall I be too late to join the fray?' He read the words. He'd never finished that one. Just as well.

'If I should die on foreign soil. . .' Well, everyone must worry about that. Not during battle, but before. A soldier he had spoken to on the train had told him that he 'wet himself' before going over the top, but that when he had downed his tot of rum, got on the firestep and climbed over, he was filled with blood lust, even felt it flooding in his eyes.

'What price glory . . .?' He saw the words on the paper and thought they had a familiar look. That was the trouble with writing poems. You found that half of what you wrote had belonged to someone else, that the words were 'used', meaningless. But you had to work through that, keep on discarding until you found your own way. That was it, finding your own way, your own *fresh* words.

'Anyhow,' the soldier had said, 'if you have a sergeant and the officer of your platoon cursing at you and urging you on, you bloody well *have* to go on. They'd shoot you in the back if you didn't. I've seen a few lying dead like that.' Was that true?

First there had been the asking around, and the letters, and the choice. 'Lochiel' was a grand name. Ginny had inspired him there with her Highland connections. It was an easy step to the Cameronians, Lochiel's own. It was a Scottish regiment. He would not have considered anything else. Maybe they would not have considered *him*, but they had drawn many of their men from the Lowland Scots because of the kilt. His father's regiment, the Royal Scottish Fusiliers, had been out from the beginning because of the possibility of discovery when they checked his name.

There was an Enlisting Office at Crannach – he had seen it when he had cycled past, and the posters with the Kitchener finger pointing at him – shame about him being drowned because of one of those bloody German U-boats – but that would have been too near home. They would have known him right away as the young lord of Sholton Hall. Sometimes he didn't recognize himself in that title.

He had gone off one day on a long cycle run – Mother was very good and did not ask him where he was going – and in a market town twenty miles away had found another Enlistment Office with its garishly coloured posters. He had waited until five o'clock and then joined the small queue – young men like himself, some with black faces straight from working in the pits. He was not surprised at them wanting to get away from that!

He saw one or two looking curiously at him and thought it must have been because of his height. Grandmother would have called them 'wee shilpit things', but they could not have been all that small or they would have joined the Bantams. 'Jolly good idea, this,' he said to the boy nearest him, and was surprised when he looked amazed, then of all things, guffawed in his face and turned away as if embarrassed.

It was surprisingly easy. He had not shaved for two days and there was a faint stubble on his lip (he would have to remove it before dinner, he thought), and he had squared his shoulders as he went up to the desk.

Perhaps the Enlisting Officer had gone for his tea. The one at the desk was old, a bit doddery, and seemingly half-blind, and in five minutes the deed was done. He had to report to headquarters in three days' time. He was glad that he hadn't been told to march to Central Station that night *en route* for training. He had often seen the HLI doing that in the early days of the War. He remembered himself and Ginny taking the train to Glasgow to watch them swinging into the station with their 'cocky wee swagger'.

'If it were done when 'tis done, then 'twere well it were done quickly . . .' And quietly. All his plans were made. 'Now the cock doth crow and this is the telling hour . . .' Who said that? As far as mother and the rest of them were concerned, he was going to spend a fortnight with Craven at Reredon Lacey. He had that time in hand before they would expect to hear from him.

Of course, there was his trunk, no doubt blundering on

its way to Windsor, or already in the school basement waiting for 'the young gentlemen' to arrive. That would be the giveaway when the school porters started complaining to the masters. Would they get in touch with Mother right away? And then buttonhole Craven? Would he manage to stall them off? He had suggested to old Craven that to make the plan foolproof he should join up at his end in Bucks, but he had said he wasn't *that* crazy!

'Oh, to hell with them all!' he said aloud, feeling grown-up immediately he said it. Why was he bothering about an old bashed-up trunk when he might get killed in France?

In Passchendaele. What an ominous-sounding word that was! He had followed The Shiny Ones all through the War since he had first chosen them – the Somme (Ellie had been surprised how knowledgeable he was about the disposition of the troops), Arras, Polygon Wood, and now Passchendaele, the Fifth/Sixth Battalion, Thirty-third Division, east of Messines.

He knew everything. Everything was marked on his map. His lot had been in the Front Line, and now they were improving the roads and tracks between Ypres and Passchendaele (someone at school who had an older brother there had told him), preparing for Something Big. Another Push.

How he loved that word! Not a very poetical word, not a 'breathless-hush-in-the-close-tonight' kind of word. 'There's a Big Push on in Messines tonight' did not sound very musical, but you could make anything into a poem if you approached it in the right way.

That was what he would like to do, write about ordinary things, using ordinary words in their *right* place so that he could get to the heart of the matter, so that everybody could understand it, even that black-faced boy in the enlisting queue, so that there was a revolution in the hearts and minds of ordinary men and boys and they did not have to rely on jingles like:

> Ta-ta Bella! I'll no' say good-bye,
> Although I'm leavin' Glesca wi' the HLI

Not that there was anything wrong with that – it had a 'cocky wee swagger', but something which interpreted what was deep in their hearts would be better.

Maybe this was the last time he would see this room. He crossed to the window and looked out over the familiar fields. He had ridden over or walked over every yard of them as his father and mother had done – his real father, Nigel. Mother had once told him the ruined tower of the monastery was a special place, had been for his grandfather too, Alastair. 'Someday I'll tell you everything about us,' she had said, 'when you are in love yourself.'

He never thought of love. He had to get this War over first. But did Mother miss that young lover even yet? Was she happy with Ernest? Ernest was damned cool, but all right. Non-variable. He couldn't have had a better stepfather. Was it fair of him, with such good parents, to put his life in jeopardy? Would Ernest be furious or would he understand, since he was in France himself, doing his bit? There were so many questions with no answers, but this wasn't a time for thought, it was a time for action.

He went back to his chair, took up his notebook and started writing.

> Good-bye, green sloping fields,
> The blotted dark of woods,
> The grey tooth of the ruined tower . . .

Words crowded in his brain, thoughts on leaving home. He brushed his sleeve across his eyes . . .

4

'I feel terrible leaving you in charge,' Maevy said to Dan Johnson. She had asked him to come to her room at York Street so that they could go over the last details together before she left.

'Why should you feel terrible, Maevy?' Dan, now a newly-married man, had a faint mist about him, she thought, an exudation of moisture on his rosy face, hardly noticeable, but to her acute eye the outward sign of a sexually-satisfied man. Neither he nor Ruby were young, but that would make them all the more eager to sample the hidden delights of the connubial bed. But it wouldn't be like it had been for her and Charlie . . . What a miserable thing to think, she chided herself, *you* had no monopoly on love. Each couple's love and the first expression of it was the most important thing that ever happened to them.

'Well,' she said, smiling, 'you'll be wanting to run home to Ruby as soon as you can every night.' She saw him pull his lips together – there was to be no 'bedroom' talk – and said quickly, 'What a grand wedding it was, Dan!'

'Aye, despite the rationing.' He relaxed. 'Ruby's mother is in with Cooper's and she managed to get a few delicacies, that smoked ham, for instance. And she also knows Sir Tommy.' He tapped the side of his nose.

'I didn't notice a preponderance of Lipton's tea!' she laughed.

'No, I grant you it isn't the stuff for weddings, but he can pull a few strings here and there.'

'Well, give Ruby my love.' That was enough of that.

'I've had a talk with Jack and he has a list of everything in hand at the moment. I know you two work well together.'

'Yes, there's no trouble there. Of course we miss Ernest, but on the other hand, there isn't the same amount of work here compared with when we were running the whole show. Ernest tends to work at board-room level now but he never forgets our interests, I'll say that of him. Have you heard from him lately?'

'Lizzie has. He's still in France, interrogating prisoners. And maybe he'll manage to find out more about Jonty.'

'Now, that's a terrible worry for them. Whatever possessed a young lad with all his advantages to go away for a soldier?'

'It's the young ones that do. Older ones have more sense.'

'They wouldn't accept me because of my bad eyesight,' he said quickly.

'Oh, I know that, Dan, and you're far too valuable here. I'm thankful to have you and Jack to carry on for me while I'm in America.'

'I can't think of you as a granny.'

'I can't think of myself as a granny, but no doubt I'll feel more like it when I see wee James. Oh, it's a fine prospect!'

'Of course it is, and I hope a fine rest for you, too. Between this place and working weekends at Lizzie's hospital I sometimes think you overdo it, but I know you're like your mother. You've an infinite capacity for work.'

'It makes for happiness, or maybe contentment, I don't know which. Now, I know Jack will see to the running of the office. Will you keep an eye on that stuff in the storeroom? It's listed here.' She pushed a sheet of paper across the desk to him. 'That's a complete run-down of all the pieces I bought at the last auction of unclaimed property. To tell you the truth, it makes me feel a bit like a vulture,' she laughed shamefacedly, 'picking over a dead person's remains, but the widow didn't want any of it when her husband was killed over there. My business instincts won.'

'Leave it to me. Do you want it resold in individual pieces, or do you intend to keep it?'

'We'll keep it. No 3 storeroom. It's dry and well aired. I'm looking ahead.'

'Are you going into the antique business?'

'No, not me. But there's a future for auctioneers and valuators, especially in antiques. I'm thinking of Jonty. He's a sensitive lad, loves beautiful things, nature, like his great-grandmother. He writes poetry . . .'

Dan looked dumbfounded. '*Poems?*'

'Yes, he's shown them to Ginny. Once on his hols – that's what he calls his holidays – he went with me to Parkhead, and the way he stroked the wood of some of that old stuff and enthused over it, well . . . "I wouldn't mind having something to do with this, Aunt," he said, "something to do with beauty."'

'He won't be getting much beauty now. Lizzie and Ernest must be out of their minds with worry.'

'Oh, they're that all right. But Ernest was sensible. He said they would shame him if they attempted to bring him back, that it was his choice. Maybe he's trying to pull a few strings to keep him out of the firing line. I wouldn't know and Ernest would never tell you. They're . . . proud of him, or proud of his courage, because he was never a rumbustious type, which makes it all the more courageous to do what he did.'

'He'd be thinking of his father.'

'Yes. Nigel.' She looked at him. 'It couldn't happen twice, Dan, could it?'

He sighed. 'Anything can happen in this War. And now there are those tanks. Everybody's fed up with it. They're throwing men in like old dolls, the lame and the halt and the blind. There are no battle songs now. No cheering of the troops when they march away. Men who march away and never . . .' He left the words unspoken.

'Jonty will come back. That's why I'm building up this side of the business for him. Crawford's holds no appeal for him, and in any case it's a huge combine now. There's no place for him. Sir Edward saw to that.'

'I'll say this for you, you've a positive spirit. You look ahead like your mother. "No regrets, Dan," she used to say to me, "a waste of energy." That's what made McGrath's. So you go off and have a good holiday with Ellie and Kieran and the new baby, and don't look over your shoulder. Everything will be fine here.'

'Nothing could have been done without the Carters and the Johnsons, that's for sure. Well, Dan,' she smiled at him, 'I'll say thanks, and before I end up by weeping on your shoulder, away you go and get on with your work.'

He got up. 'Right oh. Then I'll rush awa' hame tae ma wee wifie.' Getting married had taken years off him. As well as giving him a sense of humour.

As she had always known, the baby was beautiful, but what she feared was there. He bore no resemblance to either Ellie or Kieran. He was golden-skinned and dark, they were pale-skinned and fair, two different breeds from different parts of the world.

'How has Kieran taken to him?' she asked Ellie when she had settled with a cup of tea after her arrival. She had stayed overnight in a New York hotel in order to be fresh. Kieran had called at her hotel for her and seen her on to the train for Wanapeake. He would be late getting home.

'Kieran's essentially kind, essentially fair.' She didn't

think Ellie looked like a tremulous young mother. The awful signs of grief had gone, she had put on a little weight, but there was no vitality in her, no sparkle.

'But . . .?'

'It's too apparent that the child isn't his. No one remarks on it, which is worse. He's found he cannot quite accept it. He tries to hide his feelings, but they're there. James isn't going to unite us. He's going to divide us.'

Maevy looked at this only daughter of hers. She was remote. You couldn't cuddle her, she couldn't cuddle you as in the old days. She was a woman who had had to come to some sort of terms with life. 'That will come. And don't forget babies change. Their colour changes, even their features.'

Ellie ignored this. 'When America went into the War in April it unsettled Kieran. He has a strong patriotic conscience. That's why he joined the Field Ambulance right away. He came out of that because of me, and again, because of me, he didn't enlist. But he's reorganized their firm so that it's working solely for the Government, exporting to Europe all the time, munitions, food, equipment. He's turned the whole business into a machine to further the War. I know George doesn't approve, and Abigail tells me they're on bad terms. It's as if Kieran is obsessed. He works till all hours. Sometimes he stays up in New York in the apartment we have there.'

'It won't last. The general opinion is that another year will see it over. Everybody's tired of it and working flat out towards its end. And now that the Americans have joined forces with us it's going to be over sooner than ever, and indeed I hope so, before something happens to Jonty. That doesn't bear thinking about.'

'Oh, yes, Jonty . . . I keep talking about myself. How is Lizzie bearing up?'

'Lizzie is remarkable. She's planning for the future, a

future which includes everybody. She has plans for the Hall when it ceases to be a hospital. I don't think she intends to live there again. And she has plans for the stables which she keeps to herself meantime. She agrees with me about extending our side of the business into auctioneering and valuating, which would include Jonty if he wanted it . . . I'm also looking into the idea of an antique business. I've started buying choice pieces and laying them aside. There will be plenty of empty property in Sauchiehall Street or Buchanan Street when this War's over. I've already got my eye on one . . .' she smiled at Ellie. 'He's like his great-grandmother, Annabel Crawford. On one of the nights when I wasn't sleeping . . .'

'Are you still bothered with that? You should take a sedative . . .'

'I don't want a sedative. It's a legacy from Charlie. I think of him, and I make plans. I do all my best planning then. I thought of Lady Crawford, and how fond your grandmother was of her, and how fond she was of beauty. I think Jonty's the same. And if he isn't interested, Ginny might take his place. She's brimming over with ideas. That's why she doesn't settle on any man. She's . . . creative, doesn't want to get married for the sake of marrying.' She shook her head, smiling. 'Yes, Mother left us a fine legacy, a wish for independence. But you're fighting against the tide all the time. The joy I've had out of the Movement! Finding that other women felt as I did . . . Oh, yes, Ellie, you have to think ahead, and when you're getting on and it isn't worth planning for yourself, you can do it for the younger generation.'

'You're wonderful, Mother. You haven't one single plan for yourself?'

'Maybe aye, maybe hooch aye.' She laughed. 'Any plans in that direction would include Kate and Isobel.

We'll stick together, three sisters. I get a real pleasure out of that. I never realized there would be so much.'

'You make me feel ashamed. What do you think I should do since you're so clever?'

'Do you really want to know?'

'I wouldn't be asking you if I didn't.'

'Well, for a start I'd stop fretting about who the baby looks like and stop fretting about Kieran as well. He has to work out his own salvation in his own way, and he's chosen the best way, work, work, till you drop from exhaustion. You know all about that. You said, "since you're so clever . . ." Well, it isn't I who am clever, it's you. You were so clever that you became a surgeon like Charlie and went to France, turning down Kieran for that. Now you have James, but that hasn't altered your cleverness, and you must face the fact that for the time being Kieran doesn't want you – no, that's wrong, Kieran will always want you, but he's trying to want you *and* another man's child and that's more difficult. Get back to work. You have plenty of money to employ someone who'll take care of James. Mrs Vanaressi would keep an eagle eye on anyone who had that job. Use your skills. Let some young man in a hospital away to fight for his country and take his place. They'd welcome you with open arms, a clever girl like you.'

Ellie stared at her, her eyes full. 'Oh, Mother I'm so unhappy.' It was the universal cry, Maevy thought. Ellie was in her arms. She still needed a cuddle.

'Aren't we all? Push it to one side. Get on with something which absorbs you, as Kieran's doing . . .'

'But the baby . . .'

'I've said my piece about that. Don't tell me a baby takes all day with a staff like yours. Get back to surgery and you'll find things will come right by themselves . . .'

'I've to go to the hospital tomorrow for a checkup. I could see how the land lies . . .'

'That's my Ellie.' She stroked her head, her fair head. Had that dark Joe loved this fair hair in faraway Normandy? Spread on the pillow? Yes, life was sad all right. She pushed her gently away. 'Before you fix anything, I've a letter for you.' She took it from her pocket, handed it over and got up. 'I'm going to leave you while you read it.'

'Oh, Mother,' she hadn't looked at the envelope,'you're tired and I haven't thought . . .'

'Don't fuss me. I'm not tired. I told you I had a good sleep in New York.'

Her eyes were on the envelope now. 'Who's it from?' She was turning it over. 'Funny. It's got an American stamp on it. And it's addressed to Braidholme . . .'

'I don't know, except that it's yours. I'm going to unpack.'

She left the room. It was something to do with Joe, perhaps from his family. Maybe not. Anyhow, it was none of her business, and besides, Ellie would tell her. She was pretty sure of that.

5

Dear Miss McNab,

You don't know me, but Joe talked a lot about you in his letters. I'm his sister, Holly, Holly Payne since 1913, and living in Long Island, America. I know how much he thought about you, and now that he's dead, I thought you would like to have the photograph I'm enclosing. His former wife sent me on all his effects.

Once, in a letter to me, he said, 'Holly, I've met the one girl who'll ever mean anything to me, too late, Ellie McNab . . .'

I feel I should tell you about Gilda, his wife. When Joe was at Harvard he led the life of any undergraduate in those happy years before the War, lots of parties, lots of girl-friends. She wasn't at the university – she lived with her parents in Cambridge, a town quite near it, and they seemed to do a lot of entertaining of young Harvard men. She was pretty and clinging, an only child, and she became Joe's girlfriend.

She was soon coming home with him and going with us to our summer house at Boothbay. Dad particularly liked young people around. Nothing pleased him better than to take us out in the boat exploring the coves and harbours. We picnicked and swam and fished together through those long summers, and looking back it was the happiest time of my life.

Maybe Joe talked about these days with you, and I guess we were all in love with Boothbay. Even here, with the broad, calm ocean, I can conjure up those rocky coves and islands, Townshead Gut, Spruce Point, Squirrel Island, Robin Hood Cove . . . the names have a kind of magic for me.

And I can remember the seals, those smooth black heads and their whiskered smiling faces. I was the photographer of the family. I still have my Kodak, and my 'sitter' now is my little girl, Charmian, just two.

Joe liked lobster fishing, but I hated to see them turning pink when they were being boiled, and as a little girl I remember weeping bitterly because they were being 'burned'. He was a fine fisherman. We used to say that if we saw another mackerel we'd throw up, but I think that's where he got his first taste of surgery! No one could gut and prepare a fish for cooking on a wood fire on the beach quicker than he could.

Even when he was working in the Boston General he always came to our summer house on the shore when he could, and we used to tease him about bringing a different girl each time. He was popular and girls liked him. He laughed when I called him the Gay Lothario. He was quite unaware of his appeal . . .

I was never unaware of it, she thought, laying down the letter to look at the photograph. The eyes met hers, those eyes which had looked down on her in that bed in the Normandy farmhouse. There had been an oil lamp in the room which they had kept on. Now she was glad of that. His eyes had been long, bright, liquid bright in the smooth, golden-skinned face; the mouth had been thin and fine-shaped like the eyes, the high cheek bones had looked in the lamp glow like bruises. He was a person of long, smooth curves, not overtly muscular, his body had a running smoothness under her hands; there had been the silky feel of the dark hair which grew down his spine . . .

Then I began to notice it was Gilda, and I remember complaining to Mother that she was a bit of a bore because she *squealed* when anything happened, whether it was someone diving off the end of the boat or someone else landing a fish. 'She's an "Ooh!" girl,' I complained to Mother, and she told me to keep my opinions to myself. She was his girl, and if he continued to bring her along in spite of the squealing, it must be because he liked her that way. But I could see she was disappointed.

And then we heard that both her parents had been killed in a motor car crash. They belonged to a smart set who went to Rhode Island a lot and enjoyed cocktails and dancing. They had sounded very sophisticated to us. I think he married her out of pity.

By the time the War came I was married to Bob and living

here, Joe was working as an assistant surgeon in Boston, my Dad had died and Mother had gone to live with her sister in Washington, DC. Isn't it funny how you think things will go on for ever, and then one day you look around and it has all disintegrated. I think many people must feel that about pre-War times. My other brothers, Irv and Bill, kept the family firm going in Boston, but things had changed.

The sad fact was that we had all grown up. Father, who had been the catalyst, was gone, and we had all grown-up problems, setting up jobs, homes and families.

Well, as you know, when the War started we had nothing much to do with it, but Joe was interested right from the beginning. He wanted America in. He joined committees, he worked tirelessly, and sometimes I thought it was to get away from Gilda. Right from the beginning the marriage wasn't a success. She wouldn't entertain his friends, she couldn't or wouldn't have children, she was a dead loss. I think that's why he volunteered for the Harvard Medical Unit. And then he met you.

Why am I writing all this? Well, I came across the photograph when I was cleaning out a drawer. There he was, smiling up at me in that old way. Even I, his sister, felt his attraction. I thought of you, and how perhaps you and he hadn't time to find out much about each other before he was killed. He told me you were a surgeon in a women's hospital, and how he admired you. I can tell you he was a grand man, full of life but not obstreperous – he radiated a quiet, balanced happiness – he was interested in everything that went on, reliable in an emergency, a dream to look at . . . he could have had any girl he wanted although he honestly never believed that, he was as stubborn as hell.

I'm sure that's one of the reasons why he married Gilda, because he knew we weren't enthusiastic about her, that and pity. He was gullible, vulnerable. Mother always said he could never keep anything of his own. What was his was anybody's who cared to ask for it, from his fishing rods to his time, and he was truly loved by all his colleagues as well as all of us. My mother died two months after he was killed. I think she never really got over his death.

You were right for him. That's the sad part. My husband is in France just now, and I know what you must have felt when he was killed. For some reason I remembered where you lived.

We're supposed to have Scottish ancestors – what American hasn't – and that's why your address stayed in my memory. I remembered saying to Joe in a letter, 'Braidholme? Is that Scottish for Broadholme?' And somehow or other I remembered the village was Sholton. I hope this reaches you.

I also wanted you to know that when I knew about you and Joe I went to see Gilda and asked her if she would give him his freedom. He didn't ask me to do this, and it's been on my conscience ever since. Someone had told me that there was a man paying her some attention, and when I called on her he was there. She asked him to stay in the room while we talked, and I think he influenced her. He was a friend of her parents, more their age than hers, but he was rich. Anyhow, she said she would think about it, and just after that Joe was killed. I never knew if she wrote to him.

But I'm glad I've written to you. I don't expect you'll ever be in America. But if it ever should happen I would truly like it if you could come and see me. You could get a train from Grand Central in New York. It's not that far. If you're married and Joe is in your past, just ignore this. I'll understand. 'Trust Holly,' Joe used to say, 'to go gallumphing in where angels fear to tread.' Oh, he was a grand brother, and I loved him!

Holly Payne

She told Maevy about the letter and that Holly had invited her to visit her. She showed her the photograph. 'I'm hungry for details about him,' she said. 'We had such a short time together. Do you think I should go?'

'Please yourself,' her mother said. (Ellie would have liked to say to her, 'Sometimes you carry non-intervention to extremes.') 'Better than keeping that photograph under your pillow with Kieran lying beside you.'

She went red and said, 'Trust you, Mother,'; and it was like the old days when they had quarrelled about Colin Thomson.

'Yes,' Maevy agreed, 'I am getting a bit nebby in my old age, but it's good advice all the same.'

'I'd be happier going while you're here so that you could keep an eye on James. I'd go pretty soon because they've promised to let me know if a vacancy comes up at the hospital.'

She wrote a note to Holly Payne thanking her for writing. 'My mother is staying with me just now and I thought it would be a good opportunity to see you while she's here as she can take charge.' She paused for a long minute, then went on:

I'm married and, as you see, living sixty miles from New York. My husband's people settled here a long time ago (they're Scottish), and he runs his father's export business along with his brother.

I have one child, who is Joe's. He never knew. I thought if I came to see you and talked about Joe to you I would have something to pass on to his son when he's old enough. Some day, perhaps, you would come and visit us.

Don't worry about Kieran, my husband. He knows he is not the father of James, my little boy.

I loved Joe very much. I don't think I'll ever get over loving him, but perhaps in time I can put it in its proper perspective. Thank you for writing.

Ellie Murray-Hyslop.

6

It was strange to be travelling alone. From the time of her marriage to Kieran she had been accompanied by him on any journey they had made – an occasional trip to New York, the occasional evening visit in the environs of Wanapeake if they received an invitation from any of his friends for dinner.

There were, of course, her own afternoon visits to Claremont, where Aunt Maria and Sarah always welcomed her, and to Deborah Sandburg and Judith King, the Vogel daughters who, once they knew of the pregnancy, had been anxious to give her their advice born of their own experience. The young marrieds she met in their respective houses were alien to her, both in their culture and outlook. They hadn't had careers, having, it seemed, gone straight into marriage from school, and she imagined they discoursed freely on house and baby management because that was the only territory in which they felt secure. They tended to skirt the fact that she was medically qualified, far less a surgeon.

The unmarried children of the Vogels and the Murray-Hyslops did not come into this category, of course, but they seemed to be rather in awe of her because she was different from their married brothers and sisters. She saw that she fell uneasily between two stools.

But now she was on her own. She had no need to worry about James. Mother was in charge, and there was certainly no one more competent than Mother. From her seat, as the train bore her swiftly to New York, she compared the broad, slow sweep of the Hudson with their own Sholtie, its occasional quiet pools and the busyness and fussiness of a small river as it ran over its pebbled bed.

Rivers, she thought, mark the course of my life. There was the Oise which had bent in a smooth looping curve near the Abbey hospital on its way to the Seine, the little Thève which ran through the grounds and had been the only source of water for the monks who had once lived there, and the Epte behind La Hirondelle, which had been quieter and greener than the Sholtie.

She remembered that warm autumnal day when she had slipped off her clothes and bathed in the cool water, and the happiness inside her because she knew she would see Joe. That particular moment was the happiest of my entire life, she thought, because I didn't know then that it would be the last time I would see him.

She had been honest with Kieran before she left him. 'I've had a letter from Joe's sister,' she told him. 'She would like me to visit her. Would you mind if I went while Mother is here?'

Now, sitting in the swaying train as it followed the Hudson like a tracing pen, she realized the enormity of what she had asked of him. Love is blind, she thought. I've been obsessed by the memory of Joe ever since his sister sent me the photograph. My eagerness to see her because she is his sister, to pick up any crumbs of knowledge about him like a beggar at a table, has made me heartless.

Kieran had been quiet, but then he had been quiet and withdrawn since the arrival of James, or was it since he had taken on Government work for their firm? 'Where does she live?'

'Long Island.' She had waited.

'I could take a day off if you like.' She remembered the conversation word for word.

'Oh, there's no need!' Instead of being appreciative she had resented his offer immediately. Was he trying to make her into a dependent young matron like Deborah and Judith, cosseted by their husbands wherever they went? Hadn't she been a person in her own right, a surgeon in France, doing a man's job? 'I'm quite capable of travelling on my own.'

'Of course you are, Ellie. I didn't mean it that way. But I thought you might like my company.'

'Well, it would be nice, but you're so busy, and perhaps it would be . . . difficult for you.' Embarrassing.

'She knows that I know about James?'

'Oh, yes, I told her in my reply. I said I was happily married and living quite near her. Maybe she'll visit us later. Her husband is fighting in France.'

'Are you happily married?' He had looked across at her, and the shadows from the dancing flames made his eyes seem sunken. Or perhaps they *were* sunken. He had come in late and tired from New York, too tired to eat, he'd said. Maevy was in bed.

'You know I am. Kieran . . .' She had seen him quicken at the appeal in her voice. 'Perhaps I haven't been very . . . loving, but it's natural after a baby. And you're busy, working so hard in that old office all the time.' She was wifely, playful. She knew it didn't become her.

'At least I stay alive there,' he had said. She knew what he meant.

'You don't still reproach yourself for not enlisting do you? You've done your bit. Besides, it's not men your age they want, thank goodness.'

'I didn't wait to be asked when I went with the Field Ambulance.'

'No, nor did I. But we've *been* there.' She had bent forward and touched his hand. 'I know how the War changes people's lives. It's changed ours, but I'm trying, I'm really trying, to be everything to you.'

'Then why are you going to see his sister?' He had got up so quickly that her hand had fallen away from him. 'I'm going to take a walk round the garden. I'm starved . . . of fresh air.' He had turned before he opened the door, 'I'm sorry, Ellie, sorry I said that.' Kieran would always accuse himself in the end, she thought. Some men would have forbidden her to go.

She caught a train easily in the Grand Central Station, and for the first half-hour was only aware of the long dreary suburbs as they crawled through New Jersey and Queens; but soon the houses and factories were left behind and she caught glimpses of the sea – she must remember to call it 'the ocean'. It would have been better to see Boothbay. This was too flat and smooth, and she disliked its signs of wealth and urbanity. She imagined Boothbay would have had a stern 'Scottish' feel about it with which she would have been familiar – rocks, rough, tussocky grass and a tossing, playful kind of sea. But Boothbay had become a dream to Joe. Perhaps it was better that it should be the same for her.

Holly Payne did not resemble Joe at all. She would not have recognized the plump young woman who came towards her wearing a loose, pale coat, her head bare. Mother always said you should put on your gloves and hat before you left the house. This young woman wasn't wearing either. 'I'm Holly,' she said, putting her arms round Ellie, 'I would have known you anywhere. You're just as I imagined.' Her face was freckled. So different from Joe.

'Would you?' She was shy. 'It's good of you to ask me to visit.'

'It's good of you to come. I wondered if you would bring your husband.'

'No, he's too busy these days.' That sounded rude. 'And he might have been embarrassed knowing your husband was overseas with the troops.'

'Is he like that? The motor's over here.' They were walking out of the station. Holly was a head shorter than her. So different. 'Well, I could have set his mind at rest. Bob is stationed in a depot (she pronounced it "deepot"), seeing to transport? He says there are as many men there as in the Front Line – don't they say an army marches on its stomach – but that it's a lot safer. My Bob fancies being a veteran and boring the family with his exploits. "What did you do in the Great War, Daddy?"'

She drove Ellie in a big, shabby Buick, so expertly that it made her decide it would be the first thing she would do when she got home. Perhaps she could get a motor car of her own when she started to work at the local hospital.

She was an easy girl to talk to, or rather to listen to, for she kept up a flow of chatter as she drove along the coastal road. 'I liked this place immediately when I came. It had a feeling of Boothbay, seafaring? You know what I mean?' Her voice rose at the end of sentences. 'But I'm adaptable. I don't let environment influence me too much?' That was like Joe. 'Boston and Boothbay are in the past now. My life is with Bob and Charmian and any more who come along. I'm already active in all sorts of committees in connection with the War? And I show parties round Shag Harbour? I've discovered hidden talents. I think life goes in phases, don't you?'

'Oh, yes, I think so. I'm in the domestic phase just now, the hen on its nest phase.' She laughed.

'You sound as if you didn't like it.'

'I do and I don't. I have a loving husband, no financial worries, a lovely child, but it isn't enough. I have to contribute, but unlike you, I'd make a terrible committee woman.'

'You don't think child rearing and home-making is a sufficient contribution?'

'Oh, I don't decry them.' How strange to get into this kind of conversation on their first meeting. 'It's just that there's still some of me unused. My mother has always worked and my grandmother before her, and they also coped with homes and families. I think it's in my blood.'

'Well, if I were you I'd follow my instincts.'

'I have. I've applied to the local hospital, and I may get a chance of a vacancy quite soon.'

Holly's house was like herself, busy, untidy, the porch littered with toys. The fat little girl who came towards them with a black woman behind her was like her mother, round-faced and freckled. 'Momma! Momma! Did you bring the lady back?'

'Yes, here she is. Say "Hello" to her.' She bent to lift the little girl in her arms.

'Hello, Charmian,' Ellie said, kissing one fat cheek.

'What's her name, Momma?'

'It's far too difficult for you to say, poppet.'

'Say Aunt Ellie.' Ellie smiled at the child. 'I have a baby called James. You must come and see him.'

'When?' She wriggled in her mother's arms and she put her down.

'Whenever you're free.'

'When are we free, Momma, when? When?' She danced up and down.

'We'll look at the calendar and decide.' Holly smiled at Ellie. 'Now you go with Nancy and we'll pick you up later.'

'She looks like a good nurse,' Ellie said when they had gone.

'Nancy? Oh, she isn't Charmian's *nurse*! We don't live in any great style. Can't afford it? Nancy's head cook and bottle washer, but she offered to take care of her today. She's at a demanding age. Everything is "now" with her.'

They drove to the village, Holly pointing out with pride the Masonic Temple, a white Greek Revival building which Ellie thought stuck out like a sore thumb amongst the other buildings. 'Greek' Thomson's churches in Glasgow seemed more at home in *their* setting.

She much preferred the American Hotel where Holly had ordered lunch for them. 'I thought it would give us a chance to talk,' she said, 'without a two-year-old chattering all the time.' And when they were seated opposite each other and had ordered the sea bass which Holly had recommended, she leaned forward and said, 'Can I say that I think you're beautiful? I know now why Joe fell in love with you.'

Ellie shook her head, embarrassed. 'It was nothing to do with looks,' but it *had* been partly in her case, she thought, remembering the pleasure she had got out of looking at him. 'We were right for each other. We were so sure. I still am. We didn't waste any time because that's how the War affects you. But I didn't mean . . . no, that's not true. I have no regrets about my love, about James, our little boy. But, oh, Holly, how I miss him, day and night I miss him. It tears at my . . .' She knew Holly had waved away the hovering waiter.

'Just let it come out, hon. I'm his sister. I understand. I loved him too. Let it all come . . .'

She had had to keep quiet for so long that she opened her heart. About her love and her loss. She wept at first – fortunately they were in an alcove by the window – broken sentences, the ache, the constant ache which she thought she had conquered. And then, when she was able to speak normally, 'I have to be fair to Kieran. I never talk about Joe, or hardly ever, but now that James is here, he's a constant reminder. He's so like him. A niece of mine by marriage, Priscilla, said that if he had a feather in his hair he'd look like a little Indian.'

'That's Joe. Like father. Smooth darkness. That smile won everybody. Mother was Dutch. That's where I get my . . . solidity from.' She glanced at Ellie. 'And then a sylph like you comes along.'

'Oh, that's not permanent, I assure you! It's . . . this and that. My mother is what you call a "handsome" woman. I'll probably become like her.'

'I'm sorry for your husband,' Holly said, 'damned sorry. Even if he's a saint it's difficult for him?'

'I know that. I torture myself by thinking I shouldn't have married him, but my family . . . well you won't have any idea what Scottish families are like. "Bastard" isn't a word they like to hear.'

'I wonder . . . maybe some of your relatives, but I wonder about your mother? From what you tell me I can't see her wanting you to marry just to give Joe's child a name. Did you confide in her?'

'I didn't *ask* her if I should marry Kieran, but she knew I was pregnant. She was a nurse. In any case, Kieran and I had an understanding. "After the War," I used to say, "I'll see . . ." So she wasn't too surprised at my decision, I suppose . . .' She stopped, overwhelmed by the memory of that terrible time.

'Could you face the fish, now?' Holly asked. 'The waiter's hovering again.'

She smiled. 'What's more to the point, could the fish face me?'

Holly beckoned the man. 'Sorry to keep you waiting. And a bottle of Chablis, please.' She said to Ellie, 'You're all right. You've a sense of humour. But as well as facing the fish you have to face the fact that you're married now – oh, I know you've done that, but I mean, really face it, accept it. Both of you. You're in it now, and nobody gets everything they want, believe me. You don't like my lecturing style, hon, and me the secretary of the Historical Association in little old Shagg Harbour with two "g"s? Oh, I'm sorry,' her round face was creased, 'I never had a sister, I don't know how to talk right. I'm great on the Federal times but no good at this . . .'

She stretched her hand to Ellie, and she took it.

The waiter arrived with the fish, served it with pride and poured the wine. 'Caught this morning, Mrs Payne. As nice a sea bass as you ever did see. Now you go ahead and enjoy it.'

'Thanks,' Holly said, and to Ellie, 'Eat up.' She watched Ellie anxiously as she took up a forkful. 'You just wait until your little boy gets into trousers. He'll be his own little man. With babies, all you see is their face surrounded by white shawl. Mannerisms maketh the man. He'll probably walk and talk like you or your husband. They're copy-cats. Joe used to put his hands in his pockets the way Dad did, when he was four!'

'Did he?' She was enchanted at the thought. A miniature Joe with miniature trousers, hands thrust in his pockets.

'It's true. Charmian was a puny, dark-haired baby. Look at her now, as fat as a butter ball.'

'She's an adorable little girl.'

'Sometimes . . . There's the other solution. Have another child.' She sipped her wine. Her round brown eyes on Ellie were shrewd.

'But I'm going to work.'

'Ah, well, that's something you must sort out between you. How's the fish going down?'

'It's lovely, but I'm sorry, Holly. I couldn't eat any more.'

'Never mind. Have another glass of wine. It'll relax

you, then we'll have a walk by the ocean. The sea wind's great for sad hearts. I know.'

'I'm sorry I'm like this. Burdening you. I thought it was over.'

'It will never be over, but I think the thought of Joe will give you joy eventually. He was that kind of man.'

They drove towards the ocean to what Holly said was the rich part, to a place called Maidstone. 'Bob says he'll buy me a house here sometime. He's a clerk with a real estate broker. Some hope! Look at the village green, Ellie! Isn't it neat? And the ducks on the pond. Like Maidstone, Kent, England. Have you been there?'

'No, I don't know England well.' It seemed strange to her that Americans in a new country should want to harp back to the old. Harp back . . . wasn't that what she had been doing?

They walked on the soft white sand of the beach and she felt unable to say any more about Joe. 'Do you still find whales here?' she asked.

'Only occasional glimpses of the humpback, but in Bob's grandfather's time – he was a whaler? – the big ones. We have dolphins nowadays, the bottlenose, the pilot whale . . .'

'Wasn't there a book called *Moby Dick*? Melville?'

'Yes, Herman Melville wrote about the humpback whale . . . I'm hoping we'll have a son to read it to. He said it was the most gamesome and light-hearted of all the whales. Then there's the MolaMola, all head and no body. Now that's the queerest creature you ever did see . . .' She recognized Holly's kindness in her chatter which passed over her head.

She was overcome with the sense of loss, as keen as it had ever been. The sea wind whipped her face, the beach was deserted perhaps because of it. Holly's voice went on, drawing shadowy figures as if to people it – Fijians,

Sandwich Islanders, Portuguese, Chinese, Montauks, Shinnecocks . . . Indians. Joe . . . love . . . smooth movement of your body on top of me, those smooth brown flanks, the loving depth in your eyes as you entered the loving depth of me . . . why did I come here . . . ? 'Coopers, pump-makers,' Holly's voice was tossed by the wind, 'ship chandlers, boat builders. Have you heard of Queequeg? He was the pagan harpooner in *Moby Dick* . . .'

'Was he?' Such *fresh* agony. She was drowned in tears. Don't meet her eyes. Look seawards, oceanwards . . . the girl's voice was suddenly loud in her ear, she felt her arm round her shoulders.

'I'm a fool. Yapping on about this place and its old inhabitants. I was giving you time . . . it's only adopted anyhow, second-best . . .' Second-best, like Kieran . . . 'I'll always prefer Maine.' She guided her to a tussock of marram grass, made her sit down, and took her in her arms like a child. 'Cry away. Maybe this is the last of it. There's only the old seagulls to hear you. Cry away, Joe's girl . . .'

She wept for a long time in the shelter of Joe's sister's arms. She had a soft bosom and there was a sweet, hay-like smell from her hair. There was love and understanding in her comforting. 'Go right down to the depths. Search out every sore corner. You'll never get a better place than this . . . this . . . this . . .'

She was right. There was the sound of the sea breaking on the shore, and the sound of her weeping, one drowning the other. Sometimes there was the dragging rattle of pebbles as the waves receded, like the coarse sound of her weeping which came and went like the waves as a new stab of memory lacerated her.

And then it seemed to grow quieter, the sea-noise and her weeping, and she could hear Holly's voice crooning, some sea-song perhaps, since this was Shagg Harbour with two 'g's' – a half-smile pulled at her mouth and she sat up and wiped her eyes, shaking her head at herself and saying to Holly in some kind of apology, 'Wails and whales . . . I'm ashamed of myself.'

'It'll do you good.' She looked at Ellie wryly. 'Come on back home with me now . . .'

When they were having tea, Holly produced a box which contained what she called 'the Boothbay photographs'. She spread them on the table between them, and while they drank she showed her photographs of Joe there – 'I think they're more Joe than the one I sent you. That was a studio portrait taken before he went to France – ' On his pony, fishing, swimming, rowing, jumping, standing. She saw the different phases of him, from a child, to a schoolboy, to a young man at Harvard. The strange thing was that he never changed. The dark eyes were always there, the thin curved mouth, the smooth dark hair. It was in the almond-shaped eyes that she saw most clearly that composite she called 'Joe'.

'Now I'm not so sure that this was a good idea,' Holly had been watching her, 'looking at your face.'

'What's wrong with my face?' She tried to smile.

'It's haunted by Joe. If you go back looking like that your husband will never forgive me.'

'I've time to reshape my face,' she said. 'I'm glad I've seen them.'

'Take any you like.'

'Could I? Just one, then.' She took one where he was standing beside his father, 'aged about four, I think,' Holly said. Both of them had their hands in their pockets. Joe's chin was raised, his shoulders were nearly up to his ears. It looked as if he'd just taken a deep breath, to look manly. 'Perhaps in years to come I might ask for some, for James.'

'You can decide if that's a good idea in years to come. You and I will stay friends, won't we?'

'Oh, yes, we'll stay friends.' She touched the girl's hand. 'You're part of him.'

Holly saw her off from the station, this time with Charmian. Nancy had had to go off to make tea for her own children. They stood waving to her as the train drew away from the platform, Holly, bareheaded in her pale coat, stolid, Dutch. She could imagine her in Dutch costume – pointed hat, apron, wooden clogs. What a wonderful mixture of people America was, and now the McGrath and McNab blood had met American-Indian and Dutch blood in James, a rich inheritance. That was something to cling to, to be proud of. She watched the little girl jumping up and down beside the pale coat until she was no more than a dancing dot.

Maybe Charmian and James would get to know each other some day. They were cousins. Maybe they would marry as she and Kieran had done. She was surprised at the madness of her thoughts. She spent the rest of the journey reshaping her face, and when Kieran met her in New York as they had arranged, she kissed him and said, 'Glad to be back.'

'Was it worthwhile?' He looked tired and no longer young.

'Yes, it was worthwhile. I enjoyed seeing Long Island. And meeting Holly Payne. I liked her. She talks in question marks?' He didn't smile, and she talked determinedly about Long Island and its ocean during the drive home.

7

The Canadians had done it. They had captured the main ridge east of Passchendaele and handed it over. Now it was up to him – and the rest, of course. He had to subdue his enthusiasm and not walk with too much of a 'cocky wee swagger'. The kilt helped. The march to Strazeele was the first time he had *really* felt like a soldier, or felt like a *real* soldier, swinging along with the men, singing, learning parodies of all the marching songs he had ever known. Someone walking beside him told him not to be so bloody cheerful, and that warned him. He might give away his age.

But he was soon not so bloody cheerful. The cold ate into his bones, chapped his knees, made his groin ache. His fingers holding the rifle seemed to be welded to it – they would never straighten again – and the pain behind his ears was excruciating. Some of the men had pulled their tammies down over their faces, but he could not have raised his arms to do that. They weren't arms, they were rods of ice. Snot from his nose ran into his mouth. He stopped midsong, '"Take me back to dear old . . ."'

But they had no sooner settled down – dug themselves in, got up a bit of a fug and had some bully beef and a swig of tea – than they were off again, this time in motor buses to Ypres. He felt like a puppet, with sawdust where his brains should have been. The War had seemed much more orderly at school, with flags and maps and communiqués in *The Times*, than when you were in the thick of it. Here it simply degenerated into marching, sometimes piling on to motor buses, bivouacking, billeting, setting up camp then breaking camp, all in the most random manner. You had to spare a thought for those chaps at HQ. It must be a nightmare, a gigantic jigsaw puzzle which someone had dropped out of its box on to the floor.

He was surprised how quickly each man cornered his own little patch when they stopped for a bit. *Homo sapiens*, the homemaker, he thought, but dared not say that out loud. They would think he was daft. He had had enough teasing already because of his accent. He had made a conscious effort to 'talk Glasgow', to forget consonants, to mutter, to blaspheme, and he looked out for any nannying by older men. They brought back Jane, their nurse, to his mind, who long ago had lost her Billy Boy and had wakened Annabel in the nursery by her weeping. Dear little Mouse.

Meantime he tried to fit in with the rest, to wash his socks if he got a chance, to pick between his toes, (an army marches on its feet), swipe lice on his shirt, to knock on farm doors if there was time and try to buy some eggs. His smattering of French came in useful. So far his principal sensation was not fear but hunger, and he found himself sucking up shamelessly to anyone who had a parcel from home. It was like school and tuck boxes all over again.

'How long do you think we'll be here?' He was rolled in his blanket beside Jimmy McAlpine, a lad from Luss, on Loch Lomond. They were in an encampment off the Menin Road. 'Where *is* the bloody War, anyhow?' he asked, feeling warm and comfortable and completely grown-up. And yet he recognized his own bravado, and knew from the distant noise of gunfire that he was only temporarily in a quiet eye of the storm.

'Will you chust not tempt fate?' Jimmy said. 'A'm thankin' ma lucky . . .' they were both out of their blankets and on their feet in a second at the intensity and fearfulness of the noise rushing towards them. They cowered together, terrified at the final tearing 'Whoosh!', listened to the nearby crump with immediate thankfulness that it had missed them, then they were full of dread again at the whistle blowing and the shouting and the squealing of horses. 'Somebody's bought it!' Jimmy said in a hushed voice. 'Come on!'

They blundered with the rest of the men out of the tent, propelled by the sergeant's barked commands. 'At the double, quick! All hands needed!' And as they emerged in a heap into the darkness Jonty heard someone shouting above the din, 'My God! The officers' tent's had it!'

With the others he ran towards the heap of tattered canvas, the twisted struts and ropes, from which a spiral of black smoke laced with flames was coming. He stumbled and fell full-length over what he thought was a bag. In the glow from the flames he saw it was a man with no head, a man with no . . . 'a headless torso,' he found himself muttering, he'd call it that, it was better . . .

Everyone was shouting together now, tearing in a frenzy at the flaps and pieces of torn canvas, like hounds at the kill. He saw bodies being carried out on stretchers. Near him there was a table, quite intact, which had been lifted and set down by the blast. All around there were broken pieces of chairs, broken pieces of bodies. It was carnage. Inside it would be worse. 'Inside, lads!' the sergeant was shouting as if reading his thoughts. 'Inside, and look slippy!'

He began clawing at the debris, found he was clutching an arm, and with someone else managed to free one of the officers, a man he recognized: 'Mac' something or other (there were a lot of 'Macs'). This one was fair-haired, high-coloured, *had* been high-coloured, not now. He was making a high keening sound, almost worse than the sound the shell had made. It was a relief when the fair head fell sideways, and the keening stopped. The hands with the splayed fingers were still. Every part of him was still. There were no legs under the kilt to move.

Someone put a fire bucket in his hand and said, 'I'll take care of this' – it was the doctor – and he climbed over the piles of limp canvas and began throwing water into the hole of the crater, pointlessly. There was only a thin spiral of black smoke. The fire was almost out.

He climbed back and stood to attention at the shouted command. Names were being called out. 'Company Commander . . .?'

'Captain . . .?' 'Lieutenant . . .?' The silence was terrible. Nobody looked at each other. Had they all been having a nightcap round the table when they heard that 'whoosh!'? Had they hardly had time to put down their glasses before they were thrown into the air? The table was intact. *It* had all its legs. It just did not make sense.

Maybe if he searched he would find the whisky tumblers unbroken, maybe a pack of cards if they'd been playing . . . a nice cosy scene, candles flickering, men having a game of pontoon while they had a drink . . . all wiped out, here one minute, gone the next.

Back inside his blanket, he lay and listened to the men cursing and swearing as they discussed the incident, retracting, embellishing, quarrelling over details, replaying it over and over again like a phonograph record – 'The Company Commander killed, three officers seriously wounded . . .' They talked out their own fear.

When everyone had quietened down, he got out his black notebook and wrote in it: '18 November 1917. Saw death at close quarters tonight. The soldiers who've been in it from the beginning at Ypres are fed up. All they want is to get a "comfortable one" and be sent home. I'm not like that, but I wouldn't like to lose two legs. I'd rather die . . .'

His thoughts went to home and Mother's hospital and the amputees who propelled themselves about in their wheelchairs, their stumps sticking out. What would she say if he came home like that? For the first time since joining up he felt lonely and not so sure that he had done the right thing. He tried making up poetry in his head, but it would not come, especially about what had happened tonight It could not be done 'hot'. It was a major discovery.

He became calmer, told himself that he was in an unique situation and he must match the hour. He must not allow himself to forget, not the big things, like tonight – that would never leave him – but the smaller things. He would call his black notebook his 'Commonplace Book' and enter in it every night descriptions, ideas, any lines of poetry which came into his head, the effect of the landscape . . . What landscape? he asked himself. A grey plain like an old junk yard with shell holes filled with water? Feelings, then. The feeling of overwhelming sadness when he watched the patient plodding of the men through that landscape, heads down, how it made him want to weep . . .

The next morning they were on the march again towards the Ypres-Roulers railway. He had an odd lightness of heart which made him feel ashamed as he walked along the duckboards. He was in one piece at least, full complement of arms and legs, only the bloody rain now to contend with. (He liked saying 'bloody' and thinking it. It made him feel one of them.)

As they took up support positions they talked about it always raining in Glasgow, and indeed his memories of it at this moment were of black, shining pavements which reflected the street lamps; but this drenched, chewed-up, water-logged place with the gaunt sticks of trees was like nothing he had ever seen there, even in the slums.

'Give me the cold rather than this,' he said to Jimmy McAlpine, marching with him towards the Front Line, 'Does it rain a lot in Luss?'

'Och aye!' He was sanguine. 'Especially at the Fair Fortnight. But it's good for trade. Ma folks have a baker's, and they crowd in for cups of tea and cakes when it's pourin'. They have an awful appetite for fancies, the Glasgow folk. Our takings double on a wet fortnight.'

He stopped thinking about rain in Glasgow when the shells began to fall. It was one thing marching 'fair drookit', as they said, and another lying down in the mud to shelter from the never-ending fire of artillery. Jimmy said the three-mile approach to Passchendaele had been photographed by the Germans from the air and they knew every inch of it.

At school, after running or playing rugby and getting muddy, you could have a shower. Morning showers . . . The reluctance to leave your bed for the cold needles of water on the skin, then the good feeling when you ran out, dripping. You had to keep a lookout when you were naked. There was always some oaf ready to flip his towel at you, and you felt such a fool covering your thing with your hands like a girl. Still, you didn't want it to get damaged . . .

That made him think of the time some of the men spent writing to their sweethearts and wives. And how they sometimes moved and groaned in bed. He had never had a girlfriend, never thought of it much, but perhaps he would write to Ginny, just to be the same. He could open out to her, but strangely enough not to Mother, for fear of upsetting her. The letters he sent home were short and circumspect, almost like the ones he had written from school. Some chaps wrote screeds, but he did not have that gift. And yet he could write poetry, or try . . . it came anywhere, like that time he had lain in the fitful sunlight in the Hall grounds, looking up into the flickering heart of the chestnut . . .

> They weren't real birds in the tree,
> Only bird shadows darting through the branches,
> Darkening, lightening, pie-balding them . . .

He couldn't remember the rest. Just as well. Different from this, though, this . . . shambles. He looked round: 'All the way, the dead lay . . .' That would be a good beginning. He turned to Jimmy. 'Wonder what this river's called?' It had flooded over the hill, filling the craters. The dead were floating in it, bloated, discoloured, and he had an absurd memory of being taken to Hengler's Circus at Christmas and the water scene at the end, the floating, funny policeman . . . this wasn't funny, it was obscene. Ravebeek. That was the name of the river . . .

'Get that,' Jimmy said, holding his nose and grimacing.

'It's the bodies.' He turned away from the sight.

'Plus the gas. Mustard's the worst. Here, catch!' The rope which the platoon commander was passing down the line had reached them. 'Ma feet's sinkin'. Ur yours? Don't want to join them!'

Jonty passed the rope round his waist. If she could see him now, yoked like a beast in a sea of rotting corpses, her one ewe lamb . . . she was decent, Mother, never kept you short, and Ernest was the same. And if they came down to school they always gave him a slap-up meal in Windsor, bring a friend and no expense spared. Still, maybe they would understand how he had wanted so much to do his bit, as Father had done. Or were they disappointed at his underhand methods, especially covering his tracks with that lie about staying with Craven? Well, he was being paid back . . .

It went on and on, day after day, the noise of aircraft flying low, the heavy shelling, the mud and filth, it was a walking nightmare. If he was actually fighting it had not registered, but he thought not. That, surely, would have shaken him out of the nightmare. Or maybe it was because he had been told to join the Pioneers and help to turn an abandoned German pill-box into a dressing station. He seemed to have been born with a shovel in his hand, digging graves, endless graves, endless bodies, on and on; once he found himself in the pouring rain leading a mule laden with supplies and the beast gave him a look from its yellow eye as if to say, 'This is the bloody limit . . .'

And then he was marching, marching towards Steenvoorde, away from it all to a billet, and it was coming near Christmas. He rewarded himself, lying snugly rolled in his blanket, by taking out his Commonplace Book, the candle flickering on the white sheet, blue-lined . . .

> Will they be proud of me,
> When broken-bodied,
> I'm labelled and sent back home,
> To sadden their declining years . . . ?

He became absorbed. He scored out the words. What sentimental rubbish that was! Maybe he should read a book about syntax and metre and all that, but he had avoided doing so in case it would put him off for good. It was such a fragile thing, the wish to put words down, that you couldn't risk breaking it. Better not to understand, just to let it go as a release, the way he couldn't in letters home, for fear of worrying them too much.

They would be sorry for him if they knew what it was like. Even Ludendorff, he had read somewhere, called the living and fighting conditions 'mere unspeakable suffering'. The miracle was that he was still alive and had not disgraced himself. Of course there were things seared in his brain for ever, the terrain and the corpses – you couldn't think of one without the other. Nor think of shell holes without dead bodies floating in them, like poisoned fish.

And he wasn't so cheerful, not so bloody cheerful by a long chalk. He had thought, for instance, that he might get leave, but he had not. That was for the wounded. And the dead *had* it, for ever. He took his mind off things by trying to imagine how they would be spending Christmas at home, or even in Ellie and Kieran's house in America, or again in Ireland, in that happy house Great-grandmother had come from, Woodlea. Maybe his wish to write poetry came from Great-grandfather McGrath who was gentle, she had said, and good with words.

More and more, as they rested up, he lost interest in his surroundings and escaped into his head. Jimmy said the bloody War had got to him at last and he wasn't as bloody cheerful now. But he thought, better wooden and withdrawn than going off his rocker and bashing his head against the wall of the trench as that chap McGilivray had done. Blubbering, too. No one blubbered at school. He had once, at the Dragon, when he was eight, because it was his first night away from home. But he had quickly learnt to put his head under the blanket.

Just before Christmas they got a new Commander, a man who had left an eye in High Wood.

8

From the window of her bedroom she saw tracks of birds on the snow, ptarmigan, Magnus had told her, little arrows like those on convicts' clothes. Thank goodness for the Ball, the Taquair Ball, Ginny thought, a welcome change. Magnus and Hamish were obsessed with birds and shooting them. You wouldn't find Ernest ploughing through heather and bracken most of the day in dripping moleskins.

She looked back with longing to Lizzie's elegant upstairs drawing-room and the civilized Christmas they would be having with the aunts and some of the ambulatory patients from downstairs, probably Annabel and Kit dressed up to kill for their first grown-up Christmas dinner. Jane no longer ruled in the nursery. She had gone to work in a Glasgow shop where it would be 'brighter' for her since the death of her Billy Boy.

Lizzie and Ernest wouldn't let Jonty's absence spoil other people's Christmas. They were too civilized for that. But she would be grieving all the same. Jonty was her darling, her first-born, the living embodiment of that young husband of hers who had marched away and never come back.

What an interesting life Lizzie had led, a child of illicit passion to begin with (what an exciting thought!), then marrying the Honourable Nigel Garston Crawford killed off in the Boer War, worse luck, but then having the good fortune to have Ernest fall in love with her, a man of the world but lending his intelligence at the moment to the

Government to help them with this old War. Love and war, that seemed to be what life was all about these days.

In a way she was glad she wasn't taking part in their Christmas festivities because of old Jonty not being there. They got on so well together with their fond teasing. It was interesting how at first, because she was three years older, she had patronized him, treated him as a child, and how quickly the gap had closed and their relationship had changed into friends and confidants. Such a relief to have a friend without all that 'love' nonsense!

He had told her a lot about himself which Lizzie didn't know, how he had felt hurt when she had married Ernest so soon after his father's death, and yet how almost against his will he had grown to like Ernest so much. 'You get a protective feeling about your mother,' he had said. 'I, especially, since I was the fruit of their love' (she had kept her face straight there), and then, 'I admire her enormously, always have. I'd hate to do anything to hurt her.'

'You aren't likely to do that,' she had said, 'you're the apple of her eye. I admire her too, especially for never making you feel you come second in her affections.'

'Yes,' he had said, 'you're right, Ginny.' She had seen tears come into his eyes, my eyes, she had thought, so familiar in their deep sea-blueness, McGrath eyes. 'That's why I feel so sad . . .' He had looked into space in his moony way.

She remembered that conversation when she had heard about him running away from school and joining up. She had not been surprised, only in one way because she did not think he had the guts – all that poetry stuff of his – but again not surprised because she knew he had made a hero of his father and he would have to get it out of his system before he could get on with his life.

And she missed the aunts, the Three Musketeers –

sweet Aunt Kate, fragile Aunt Isobel, resolute Aunt Maevy who sometimes reminded you of Britannia on the back of a penny . . . '"Rule Britannia, Britannia rules the waves,"' she hummed, '"Britons never, never, never shall be slaves . . .".' She turned away from the window. She must get on with her dressing.

This stately pile, as she called it in her letter to Jonty on the field of battle, was as cold as charity. Did Lady Muir wear woollen drawers summer and winter? She had often wanted to ask her (would have said 'underwear'), but she was far too stately to be thus approached, the Laird o' Cockpen's Lady!

How was *she* going to manage at the Ball tonight when she wore that dream of a dress in white chiffon with its lovely fichu deliberately slipping off her shoulders, although there were hidden straps to prevent the final exposure of her all. Would *she* have to wear woollen drawers under it? Mother always thought her underwear was most *un*sensible. Sarah said it was 'frothy', but she quite liked it if she was given a birthday present of the same kind from one of the New York stores – although she tried hard not to show it.

That stone hall, with its halberds and shields and crossed swords and antlers, was as cold as a sheep pen on the moors, and draughtier. She had had a lot of experience of sheep pens since she had come up here, cowering in them as she followed the shoot. She sometimes wondered if they had been built for humans rather than the woolly creatures which proliferated on the moors of the Taquair Estate. And, thinking about that, did the *men* wear wool under their kilts? No one had ever told her. 'To the devil with it,' as Aunt Honor would say. She lifted a frothy lace petticoat and put it over her head.

* * *

She need not have worried. There was a roaring fire at each end of the hall, and so many people, which meant so many breaths, and so many reels and strathspeys and quadrilles and Flowers of Edinburghs, that she was soon as warm as toast. Lady Muir had given her a tartan scarf to wear over one shoulder like the other young ladies, and although she felt it spoiled the line of her dress she had thanked her, saying, 'Is it *your* tartan, Lady Muir?' '*Of* course,' she had said. Her smile had been as frosty as the air outside.

She knew Lady Muir did not like her much. There were several reasons. She had gone over them in bed last night while she had waited for the ice-cold sheets to warm up enough to allow her to go to sleep.

One was because Lord Muir liked her *too* much. She had written in her letter to Jonty, 'I'm having a rare time up here fighting off the advances of three hairy Highlanders, the Laird o' Cockpen and his two sons.'

But it was true. The laird took the opportunity whenever it presented itself of putting his arm round her when he was explaining some point of protocol, such as keeping out of the way of the guns, but before he took the arm away he always gave her waist a good squeeze. What his puir lady wife must have to put up with once he's persuaded her to take off those woolly drawers! she had thought.

Jonty, although he was so elegant and high-born himself, was still a young boy and inclined to giggle at risqué remarks like that, especially incarcerated as he was in that school . . . but what would the lad be hearing now amongst those men so much older than he, not to mention the sights he must be seeing? Sometimes she wept for old Jonty in those terrible trenches amongst the rats and filth, remembering how fastidious he was. And more than anything else, the daily danger he was in. Once in the

Sholton butchers she had overheard the women discussing some village lad who had been called up. 'It'll make a man oot o' him.' 'Maybe a dead one,' she had wanted to say to them, but had stopped herself in time. They could be real targes if their blood was up. That was a Scottish word she had heard the Bantams use in Lizzie's hospital.

Then there were the two sons. Magnus was a bit of a Lothario – she had known that before she'd accepted his invitation – but he was likeable. Hamish, on the other hand, had an eye as wicked as an eagle and as predatory. It did not seem to make a scrap of difference to him that she had come as his brother's girlfriend. He had even had the temerity to pull rank, as Jonty would say, inferring that since he was the elder brother he should come first in her favours. The attraction she felt for Magnus – because he was attractive in his aristocratic, narrow-nosed, sloping-chinned way – was not standing up very well now that she was on his territory.

The reason, and it had taken her a few days to find this out, was that the Muirs were not a loving family. Lady Muir cared only for appearances, her standing with the other big houses, and going out with the guns in her heavy tweed suits and no doubt her woollen drawers, and for her dogs. Yes, certainly for her dogs who spilled all over the place with their smelliness and their lolling tongues and dirty coats and tripping you up with every step you took.

Lord Muir was small-minded and lascivious. She had not liked him since she had overheard him browbeat and threaten a poor young lad who was the beater's assistant, and then turn to her with a smile on his face, spoiled by the fading turkey red of his anger, 'Where were we, my dear?'

The two brothers quarrelled incessantly about everything, and now it seemed about her. Hamish treated

Magnus with a constant sneering disdain, and tried, sometimes succeeding, to make him look ridiculous. Magnus gave back as good as he got, but was always ousted in the end because Lady Muir took Hamish's side in any argument. The heir to Taquair must not be spoken to like that . . .

To the devil with them, she thought again, dancing the night away with abandon. There were kilted giants in plenty who had come out of their glens and eyries to attend the Taquair Ball, and she was maliciously pleased to see that they made a beeline for her, leaving the lumpy lassies of noble estate high and dry, and no doubt wishing she would be struck dead or go back to that terrible place called Glasgow where the keelies came from.

Hamish scored a heavy point when he took her in to supper, or rather it was Lady Muir, resplendent in acres of black velvet, who arranged Ginny on his arm, patting and tweaking her here and there and then standing back as if she had just painted them for the Academy. 'Yes, very nice. Keep your shoulders up, Hamish.' She waved an imperious hand backwards towards the band and there was a dreadful skirl from the bagpipes, 'The Lament of the Muirs' or something like that, which made Ginny jump a foot in the air. 'Move!' Hamish shouted in her ear. 'We're leading the procession since I'm the elder son!'

She saw Magnus glaring at her at the supper table, and waved prettily, then delightedly, when she saw the dreadful lump in white with carroty hair with whom he was settled, probably the daughter of one of Lady Muir's bosom friends, and bosom was certainly the word, she thought, remembering the vast black cliff with the mile or so of tartan scarf draped across it.

Her card was filled to overflowing. She was inundated by eager young men in kilts, all of whom wanted to dance with her. She was whirled from one to the other, sometimes their skirts flying higher than hers. Every second man was Hamish, every third, Magnus. In a more sedate two-step he spoke in her ear. 'I don't like how you're allowing my brother to monopolize you, Ginny.' She saw his little moustache quiver, smelled the odour of malt whisky on his breath. Both brothers drank the way they shot, purposefully.

'*I'm* allowing!' she said. 'I'm only an onlooker in this. It was your mother who arranged the supper dance, for instance . . .'

'He's got a hell of a cheek, sorry, Ginny, but I mean, he *has*, commandeering my girl.' His voice whined. 'It's nothing new. I can't tell you what I've had to suffer since infancy as the younger son. The best goes to Hamish, *always*. I'm just a . . .'

'Scion?'

'What?' he said.

'That's what my second cousin, Jonty calls you. It's not an insult, Magnus. It means the shoot of a plant, the young member of a noble family, a sprig. You can't object to that?'

'Never heard of it. Thought you meant a *skian dhu*.'

'What's that?'

'A dirk. Every true Highlander keeps one in his stocking. Originally it was meant for gutting animals, that kind of thing.'

'Oh, I see,' she said. Sooner or later, the conversation in this household got back to hunting and killing. Did both of them, Magnus and Hamish, talk about putting Germans 'up' when they were in the Front Line?

For a change she tried to fraternize with the young ladies who tended to gather at one end of the hall in a lumpy bunch, but they looked at her with suspicion in their bullet eyes and drew closer together to exclude her.

The laird himself asked her for a waltz, and held her so tightly against his sporran that she could feel its long hairs tickling her legs through the chiffon of her dress.

Dancing with someone with a nameless face, she had an acute sense of homesickness, and even more, of unreality. What was she *doing* here? Claremont, although it was also built of stone, was well-heated and comfortable. Mother, Father and Sarah *loved* her. Sometimes they did not understand her, her waywardness, her flightiness, which was often just an effort on her part to brighten them up a little. They were circumspect, they did nothing on impulse, but what did that matter? They loved her, they had permitted her to go and help Lizzie so far away. They had always her welfare at heart. And similarly in Lizzie's house, and Aunt Maevy's, there was love, and caring.

I'm a wicked girl, she thought. I should marry and settle down or take up good works like Sarah, but she knew she wouldn't. Not yet.

Hamish bagged her for the quadrilles, a long, intricate set of measures where they whirled like dervishes to the eerie screeching of the bagpipes. In the half-hour of its length her feet scarcely touched the floor. It was a sign of prowess in the kilted gentry to 'burl' their partners until they nearly had a heart attack. She was certainly breathless when it was over, and made the mistake of saying to Hamish, 'What wouldn't I give for a cool drink . . . !'

'No sooner said than done,' he said, casting a predatory eye around and leading her away in his green velvet jacket, his flounced jabot and cuffs, his swinging kilt, sure of the attention on him, to the conservatory.

There, there were tired palms, and tired couples, long-skirted and short-skirted respectively (that was the men), and subdued lighting, a few dowagers gossiping, and a few lords, judging by the smell of cigar smoke; but there were also quiet corners, and Hamish, having the advantage of being a resident, led her into some leafy arbour where they were practically hidden from the others. 'Enjoying yourself, Ginny?' he said.

'Yes,' she said sweetly, 'it's my first Highland Ball.' And my last, she thought. 'I'll never forget it.'

He leaned forward. 'It could be the first of many, if you like. I know you came with Magnus, but you don't want to waste time on *him*.' She was sitting on a plush-covered sofa and he sat down beside her, sideways and very close. He also smelled of malt whisky, if anything more strongly than Magnus, since the night was later.

She tried not to lean back and away from him. 'Isn't that a little unfair, Hamish, going behind your brother's back?'

'God, no,' he was unrepentant, 'he'd do the same to me any time. We've always fought. There's a tradition, actually,' he said, looking proud, 'that the Muir brothers always fight.'

'I hope not to the death,' she laughed, still leaning away. This seemed to irritate Hamish.

'You're acting as if you didn't like me, Ginny! You know you've flirted with me from the moment you came to Taquair. I've seen those glances of yours . . .' She was incensed.

'What nonsense! That's how I am! I'm bright, vivacious with everyone, haven't you noticed? I don't try! I'd do the same with your father . . .' That had been a mistake.

'Yes, I've seen you,' he said, 'you'll have the old man in a lather if you aren't careful . . .' She was speechless and he was nearer than ever to her, cornering her. She could feel his bare, bony knee pressing against her leg, and then his arms with the dripping lace which belied their strength were squeezing her, harder than ever his father had done.

She could not move. Nor could she move when he kissed her, an impossible kiss from a girl's point of view, she thought, giving her no chance to respond because of its fierceness and strength. She would certainly have a bruise on her lip tomorrow because he had somehow managed to clamp the bottom one between his and was sucking vigorously . . . the next moment he was being lifted from her like a limpet being prised from a rock, and she saw Magnus rearing above her, dark-faced, moustache quivering.

Hamish was sprawling on the floor, she saw, but only for a second. He jumped to his feet, and then the two brothers were locked, like wrestlers on Glasgow Green, swaying, knocking over palm trees in tubs, ferns in pots, iron chairs in their path. There was an audience, too, she realized, horrified, the old lords with their cigars trembling in their mouths, old ladies with hands to their faces, screaming lumps of girls and some kilted giants who were vainly trying to separate the two men.

It was no use, it was a tartan whirl of heaving humanity, of bare knees and bare thighs and bare . . . no, she couldn't look; and then there was a terrible shout from Hamish and she saw he was hopping about and clutching his leg, his face contorted. 'I'll get you for this, Magnus! I'll kill you if it's the last thing I do!' He was sobbing. His friends were helping him to a chair and Magnus, yes, he was sobbing too was beside him and saying, 'I didn't mean it, Hamish, you annoyed me, you annoyed me, you've done it since we were children . . .' She saw he was holding a bloody dirk (or *skian dhu*) in his hand.

She was packed with her cases in the hall at eight o'clock the following morning. She breakfasted with a stern Lady Muir, a surprisingly unaffected husband, judging by how quickly he had shifted his porridge – ambulant, of course

– and then sat down to a huge plateful of scrambled eggs, kidneys and bacon. Magnus was also there, a sullen Magnus.

'You don't have to leave because of last night, Ginny,' he was saying. 'It was only horseplay. There's nothing much wrong with old Hamish, just a flesh wound.'

'If Miss McGrath feels she has to go, leave it at that,' his mother said. Lord Muir, munching his kidneys, looked at her reflectively. 'Don't you agree, Roderick?' she said.

'What?' he said.

'Last night. The *fracas* with the boys. Miss McGrath feels she has to go.'

'What *fracas*?' he said, dabbing his mouth with a napkin the size of the snow-covered field outside the window.

'You weren't there. I don't know where you were. You never are there when you're needed.'

He laughed and said to Ginny, 'There you are, then. I'm never there when I'm needed. Anyhow, I can safely say I've never interfered with the running of this house, and boys will be boys, eh, whatever it was. Who's getting you to the station?'

'I've arranged that, Father,' Magnus said. 'MacDuff will drive her.'

'But he's our best beater!'

'He was under the servant's table when I found him this morning. He'll not be fit for that.'

'Well . . . in that case . . .'

'I'll walk,' Ginny said quickly.

'I doubt that. It's five miles.'

'I thought three.' Lord Muir looked hopeful for a moment, then subsided into his kidneys.

'Then I'll manage alone,' she said, 'don't any of you come with me.'

'*There's* MacDuff.' Lady Muir looked high-nosed towards the window where a man seemed to be *weaving* his way towards the front door. 'Settle it in the hall. I'll say good-bye, Miss McGrath.' She inclined her head, regally.

Magnus said in the hall, sulkily, 'I take a poor view of you going away like this in the middle of everything. I didn't think you were so thin-skinned.'

'Neither did I.' She was determined to be like Lizzie, or Grandmother, to show them all how the real gentry behaved. She had said polite thank-yous to her host and hostess, saying that it had been a wonderful experience to be at Taquair.

'You'll come back?' Magnus pleaded. 'I'll get leave again, soon . . .'

She felt sudden desperate sorrow for this young man who was so willing yet again to be thrown back into that maelstrom, into what must surely now be the final bloody onslaught. She knew how *she* felt about her home and Lizzie's. This was his. 'I hope you're home again soon, Magnus, and that until then you lead a charmed life . . . out there. But, thank you, no. I won't come back. It's not . . . my cup of tea . . .'

She waved with teeth clenched as the old Daimler was steered erratically down the drive by MacDuff – his nose had seemed to be too red to be the result solely of the frosty morning. If she arrived in one piece at Inverness Station she would spend a few days with Lizzie and Ernest, and then take leave herself. She would go back to America and see her 'ain folk'. She turned and waved for the last time as MacDuff made a lunge at the bend in the drive. He was all right, Magnus, but not for her.

9

They were all 'over the water' for Christmas, as Uncle Patrick called it, at Springhill, Robert and Edie's home now. Ellie and Kieran were staying overnight because of James who was safely tucked upstairs in their bedroom. It must give Aunt Maria pleasure to see her childhood home used like this, Ellie thought, as they sat in the great drawing-room with the curtains undrawn because of the view of the Hudson.

When she had come from the dining-room she had looked across and seen the lights twinkling at Wolf House where Mrs Vanaressi would be having it to herself again. There was nothing she liked better, she had assured Ellie, and after she and Mr Kieran came back with the *bambino*, if suitable, she would have a few days off to visit her three sons in New York.

The dinner had been excellent. Edie was a wonderful cook – or had a wonderful cook – it was the same thing, for she had the same gift as Lizzie, that of saying in the splendid table arrangements, the food, the glowing fires in every room, her warm, smiling face, 'My home is yours.' And Robert, while not so urbane as Ernest, had a nice sense of humour which kept everyone in good spirits, almost like that of his Uncle James.

She had sat down beside Sarah, demure in bottle green velvet which seemed to bring out a hidden copper tone in her hair. She was not too old to be married yet. Why didn't she give her good works the 'go-by' (that was an expression of her mother's), and meet some man who would cherish her? There must be plenty of them in

Wanapeake. 'I didn't know your father sang, Sarah,' she said, for he was standing at the piano beside his wife who was turning over the pages of a song book.

'Oh, yes. So does Mother. And Gaylord had a lovely tenor voice. It was the accepted thing here when we visited Grandfather and Grandmother.' She smiled at Ellie, 'My grandfather was very jolly, very Irish, and didn't let anyone off, and my grandmother loved entertaining. I think of her as fluffy and pink and girlish, not what she was like when she died.'

'That's best.' She remembered the sad visit with her mother after Gaylord's death. 'Springhill certainly lends itself to that sort of thing,' she said, thinking of the grand staircase with its golden carpet and the wide landing window.

'Mother was married from here. She came down the staircase on Grandfather's arm. I suppose that's why she wanted the house to stay in the family.'

'She did a wise thing. You couldn't get a better mistress of it than Edie.' She thought of the girl's many kindnesses to her since she had arrived, and what good friends they had become. Like Mother and Belle Geddes. Friendship between women wasn't sung about, but it could be a benison.

Her visit to see Joe's sister had acted as a catharsis. Memories could be talked about with almost a sad pleasure, and Edie made an ideal confidante. She told her of that day she and Joe had spent in the *Jardin des Plantes*, and the ease which had been between them from the start; how they had talked and talked in the dark, secret café over the small coffee cups, but how words had failed them when they were having lunch. 'It was a question of *looking*, finding in each other's eyes more than we could say. I never thought you could make love simply with eyes, Edie . . . And when he walked away from me on the Pont D'Austerlitz, oh, that easy stride of his, I knew this was going to be the most important thing in my life. Do you mind me talking to you like this? It would be an insult to Kieran.'

She had shaken her head, her eyes smiling, and afterwards had told her of her own life, of her happy girlhood in Wanapeake and her college days at Vassar. 'Uneventful; There's not much to say about happiness. It just is . . .'

Patrick rapped on the piano, peremptorily. At sixty-four he was still a fine figure of a man, rather like their Abraham Lincoln, Ellie thought, with his luxurious whiskers. He was inclined to 'go on a bit', as the younger members of the family put it.

'I'm sure you'd rather be chatting to each other than listening to Maria and me, but you have to blame Edie for this. She said she wanted to keep the traditions of this old house, and I'm afraid we're one of them.' That at least showed a sense of humour.

'But just a few words before we inflict ourselves on you. First of all, sincere thanks to Robert and Edie for sharing their hearth and home with us at Christmas. It's an especial pleasure to my dear wife to be here tonight in the home of her childhood.' Ellie looked at her aunt, her face softened with emotion, her grey hair and grey gown with its velvet bows of petunia pink. She was too substantial to be called a grey wraith, but for a moment she looked like a figure from the past, an older version of that dark, striking girl who had come down the staircase with its golden carpet so long ago.

'We send our Christmas wishes to all those younger Murray-Hyslops and Vogels back there,' Patrick waved his hand towards the window, 'whom we understand are at a Christmas Ball, but we do have with us those two pillars of Wanapeake society with their beautiful wives,

George and Jason.' George looked dignified, Jason self-important, Abigail buxom, Victoria housewifely like the late Queen and not at all like her glamorous sister in Paris. 'And we *do* have one representative of the younger members of our family here sleeping peacefully, I hope, upstairs.' His eyes rested on Ellie for a moment. Of course he knew. They all knew whose son James was. He bowed to her. 'Kieran and Ellie's son.

'Then there are our relatives far across the water in Scotland, my dear sister and Kieran's mother, Kate, who is striving to forget her grief by helping Lizzie in her hospital. We send our love to her, to Isobel, a valiant little soul, and especially to Maevy, who as well as lending a hand in the hospital, still looks after our interests in the firm so well and ably, taking the place of Ernest who is doing his duty in the Intelligence Service.

'And we send our love to beautiful Lizzie and the two younger children, Annabel and Kit, and to our own dear Ginny who we understand is spending Christmas in some fine castle in the Highlands. Trust our Ginny!' he said, shaking his head. Everyone laughed.

'Trust Ginny . . .' they echoed. They all expected something different from Ginny, Ellie thought, they weren't quite sure what, but at least, something different from Patrick and Maria.

'But,' Patrick said, raising his hand, 'I'll have you know that Ginny's . . . adventurousness doesn't blind us to the virtues of our dear daughter, Sarah, who has been a support to her mother and me through so many trials, especially the loss of our son, Gaylord.' Ellie, glancing at the girl, saw the softness of her expression. It was good he had singled her out. 'Who would have thought we had such a large family to cover!' Patrick smiled. 'I doubt if I'll have enough puff left to sing with, and that'll be a good thing, I hear you saying . . .' There was laughter.

'But I'm back over the water again in my mind, to that narrow stretch between home and France where young Jonty is fighting as his father did, for us. I hear he's been in active service already, in the thick of the battle in Ypres, a young lad like that. God keep him safe . . . We know how Lizzie must have felt when he ran away from that fine school to join up and him under age, but she and Ernest showed great strength of character in not attempting to bring him back. What a decision that must have been, considering she lost her first husband in the field of battle. But we all know our Lizzie. She's never been lacking in courage or beauty, like my dear mother whose presence is with us tonight . . .' That was true enough, Ellie thought. You never forgot Grandmother, and she would have been proud of her son tonight standing up, speechifying, and *she* well knew the reason for him being a bit long-winded. Shyness, it was. He had always felt himself overshadowed by that elder brother, that boyo, Terence, with his roguish smile, whom girls preferred. Oh, that was a terrible thing with Bessie Haddow, Patrick loving her from a boy and her loving Terence . . . 'Well done, Patrick,' Grandmother was saying. It was a minute before he spoke.

'Something got into me this evening, standing here amongst my loved ones, and realizing how fortunate I've been. And thinking of those other loved ones far away . . . across another stretch of water, the Irish sea this time. There's my dear brother, Terence, with his family around him, and Honor's family, that lovely wife of his. Her books have pride of place on my shelves, as I'm sure they have on yours. And there's his young son, Terence, Robert's brother, married to Giselle Barthe and, I believe, doing well after having been wounded and gassed at Verdun. Isn't that right Robert?' He looked round.

Robert called out. 'Yes, Uncle. They're back in Paris

for Christmas, he and Giselle with their two little ones. He's almost well and thinks he'll soon be able to paint again. He's permanently invalided out of the French Army because of his chest.'

'Well, there you are, now,' Patrick said. 'I don't think I've left anyone out . . .'

'Well, what about your song, then?' Maria said, 'I'm beginning to feel like an ornament sitting at this piano!' Everyone laughed and clapped appreciatively. Ellie noticed the glance Sarah's parents exchanged. A marriage was useless without love . . .

Patrick had his head up, one hand on his chest in an old-fashioned pose. 'What else after all that talk about over the water but "Over the sea to Skye" . . .?' They were all quiet as Maria struck a few opening chords, then his strong baritone filled the room, not a bit weakened by all that talking.

> 'Speed, bonny boat like a bird on the wing,
> Over the sea to Skye . . .'

Ellie listened, thinking, yes, it had the necessary melancholy ring about it, the necessary prerequisite for any Scottish song. Even people who had never seen its misty glens and mountains could weep soft tears. She realized her own eyes were swimming. How sad and yet how beautiful life was . . .

James was fretful, perhaps because of the change of bed, and Ellie took him into theirs and sat rocking him in her arms. 'Hush-a-bye baby,' she sang, smiling at Kieran. 'I'm not too good at hushing songs for babies. Do you know any?'

'I ought to. Mother was . . . motherly . . . let me. Let's see . . . There's "Go to sleep my baby" . . .' He croaked it rather than sang. '"... Close your pretty eye ..."' The baby howled and Ellie held him close to her, laughing.

'No, no, Kieran! You'll have to take singing lessons from Uncle Patrick first.'

'It wasn't the songs so much as the ... pleasure she took in nursing. You could feel it in her arms. That's what I remember, a feeling of safety, and comfort, and ... a warmth.'

'Yes, I suppose that's it. You can sing absolute rubbish, it's only the sound of your voice to a baby, and the smell of you, and the warmth, and the closeness ... see, he's going to sleep already.' She looked down on the dark eyelashes sweeping the baby cheeks, not pink and white, but golden ...

'It's important.' Kieran had undressed, but he had put on his dressing-gown and was standing at the wide window looking across the Hudson.

'Is our house still there?' She was playful.

'Yes,' he said.

'Are you thinking that I won't be around to give all those sights and sounds and smells to James if I'm working in the hospital?' She couldn't prevent the edge in her voice and was immediately guilty.

'We've talked about this before. You must do what you feel is right for you.'

'Your mother never left *you* when you were a baby.'

'But yours did.'

'No, I was at school before she did. She waited for that. I have the same memories as you, the warmth, the comfort ...' She looked down again on the now sleeping baby, the dark sleeping baby so like Joe, and she said, tormented, 'Oh, God, it isn't any use ...'

'What do you mean?' He had turned from the window.

'My leaving him. Always there are choices. That's the

difficult part. I've missed my work. I can't tell you how much, the satisfaction in that hospital in the French abbey, the feeling of doing something to help the War, continuing Charlie's work. The War's still on. The man whose place I'm taking in Wanapeake is going to Serbia with a medical unit.'

'Don't torture yourself.' He didn't come towards her. 'You're doing what your heart and mind tell you to do. In your case one can't work without the other. Your intellect will always rule your heart.'

It didn't always . . . she bent to the baby and kissed its forehead. Did Kieran know that she was kissing Joe? She straightened, hating herself and the hurt she was inflicting on him. 'He's fast asleep, the lamb. I'll put him in his cot.' She took her time settling the baby, tucking him in, giving herself time to recover, to let the longing go from her face. But it isn't working, she thought. Joe is always between us, always will be. It's no use . . .

When she got in beside Kieran he said, 'We must talk, Ellie. *You* must.' Why did she forget how sensitive he was? 'Maybe it's the wrong time. We're in Edie's and Robert's house, we've had a grand evening with them all and we've felt part of it, part of a loving family. Isn't that so?'

'Oh, yes, yes,' she said, 'but . . .'

'You have to talk. I know you do to Edie, and I'm pleased you've found a friend in her, and perhaps you did in Mrs Payne too. You've never told me about that visit. I tried to get you to talk. I heard all about Long Island but not what she said. You have to talk with me, otherwise . . .'

'It isn't that I don't want to, Kieran,' she turned to him, 'but it's . . . tactless . . . talking about a man I . . . loved . . . to the man I'm married to.'

'I'm willing to bring him into our marriage.'

'But he *is* in, in James. I know you see it. I've seen you look at him with a . . . sadness. You rarely touch him. He isn't yours. You haven't taken *him* into the marriage.'

'I try . . .'

'You ask about my visit. How could I talk about Joe's sister to you! Someone as close as that. She showed me photographs of him at every age and stage. They . . . shattered me, brought it all back . . .'

'That's how it should be. You have to work through the hurt and welcome him, not push him away into a private corner . . .' he stopped. '*I'm* telling you what to do. I'm not managing very well myself.'

'I know. But Holly said what you're saying. "The next stage is acceptance," she said, "for both of you."' But what about the hurt?' Oh, that still terrible pull at her heart at times, in spite of all the talking, the unbearable pain of it. She closed her eyes, willing it to go away . . . 'The way I see it – ' she said, making herself speak calmly, 'I know through my intellect it's the only way – is to take pressure off, off you, off James, go to work, concern myself with the people who need me, whom I can help, stop . . . *crucifying* myself, and you. I know that's the way. It might not be other people's, but when you think of it, it is. Your mother, for instance, knew it intuitively when she took herself off to help Lizzie instead of sitting weeping here. Grandmother went travelling . . .' He slipped down in the bed and lay on his back, his eyes open. 'I'm a great disappointment to you, I know,' she said. Her throat hurt to speak. 'I'm not loving and comfortable to be with. I'm not even a good nurse to James. When I'm working I'll be too busy to entertain your friends – I shall be on call, even have to stay overnight in an emergency. Surgery's like that.'

'Tell me one thing, Ellie,' he said, 'have you regretted marrying me?'

She wanted to give him a truthful answer. 'No,' she said at last, 'not even in my dreariest moments. You've been beside me. We were friends long before you were my husband. I'm grateful for that, and so much more.' She smiled sadly, 'Mother used to talk about being Today's Woman. I thought I was one too, but when the time came I wasn't able to face life alone as an unmarried mother. I came willingly to you . . . for shelter . . .' When she looked at him she saw tears running down his face. His eyes were still open. She lay down beside him, taking his hand.

10

Ernest was on leave the last two weeks of April, and Lizzie was in what she called privately 'the seventh heaven of delight'. To outsiders' eyes she seemed more beautiful than ever, and Ginny, who was more astute than most, also saw the slight signs of fatigue. She was still at the Hall. There had been a rush of patients all winter and she was needed. Aunt Kate had said she would not dream of going home yet and leaving Lizzie in the lurch.

Ernest, Ginny told herself, is making up for lost time. She had always been pretty sure that her suave cousin was not as cool in bed as he appeared as he went about his day-to-day affairs, overseeing the gardeners, visiting the patients downstairs and going to Glasgow with Maevy to attend to business matters at McGrath's.

She said to him one morning at breakfast, 'If it weren't for Lizzie, Ernest, I'd set my cap at you. I'd forgotten how man-about-town you were. You make everyone else look so slovenly.'

'Do you hear that, Lizzie?' He smiled mischievously at his wife, but he, too, had that slight air of fatigue. 'You'll have to look out.'

'Let her try,' Lizzie said, helping herself to marmalade. She was the only person Ginny knew who always looked beautiful at breakfast time, especially as now, in her peignoir with her hair loose. It was only when Ernest was home on leave that she permitted herself such laxity – almost as if every minute spent in bed was precious. Generally speaking, she appeared trim in her white overall with her rich copper hair topped by a becoming little white cap which she had designed herself.

'What about the laird and his brother?' Ernest said. 'The last thing I heard was that they were both fighting for your favours.'

'Oh, that's a long time ago.' Ginny shook her head. 'The poor lads are fighting somewhere else. Oh, they're "bonny fechters", as they say here. I haven't kept track of them but I hope they're all right. No,' she shook her head again decidedly, 'I'll never go back to Taquair. For one thing, Lady Muir isn't as pretty at breakfast as you, Lizzie.'

'Ah, but she hasn't an Ernest.' Her cousin stretched out her hand to her husband and he took it and kissed it.

'You two are shameless! I'm glad I'm going to stay with Giselle and Terence. Could you bear to tear yourself away and drive me to the station in the Napier, Ernest?'

'With difficulty.' Cool as cucumber. 'You've hours yet. I'm picking up Maevy as well and we'll both see you off at Central. Ah, Paris in the spring!' He put his hand on his heart. 'How I envy you! You must find time for a stroll in Monceau Park, my dear, its beautiful golden gates are just across the road from Emily's house. Such a satisfying French park with its regulation flower-beds and the children playing. And those pretty nurses gossiping on the benches! Look over at Emily's house from the gates, Ginny. My sister goes on about the interior not being to her taste, but no one could criticize its outside elegance. Those balconies everywhere, even in front of the three mansards, if you please, the striped blinds over the great first floor windows, the massive black front door with its curved portico and the intricate wrought-iron on the ground floor windows – and even more balconies! I think the Barthe family must have spent their time on them bowing to the peasants!'

'I'll tell you one thing,' Lizzie said, 'with all those balconies it certainly wouldn't be possible to have a good old Glasgow *hing oot*.' They both looked puzzled. 'You poor souls!' She smiled commiseratingly on them. 'Haven't you ever noticed the open windows of a tenement on a hot summer day and the women at them? It's their way of taking the air. They even put a cushion on the window-sill to make it more comfortable for their elbows.'

'Good gracious!' Ernest said.

'They're queer folk.' Ginny laughed at his expression.

'If you'd never had a garden of your own you wouldn't find it odd.' Lizzie lifted her nose at them as she lifted the teapot. 'More tea?'

'I'll have coffee, please,' Ginny said. 'I'll get it myself.' She went to the sideboard. 'I'll probably stay with Giselle and Terence part of the time. Terence wants me to see what he's working at. He's begun to paint again and Giselle said in her letter we might have a few days at their farmhouse. Where exactly is it?' She appealed to Ernest.

'In Haute-Normande. Just inside it, a little village near Gisors, Chateau-sur-Epte. Gisors is a fine old town. It has a prisoner's tower, much better than our ruined one on the hill, and a seventeenth-century roofed washing place for women, a *lavoir*, in the main street . . . Do you remember, Lizzie?' She looked blank. 'Well, you must remember the old church with the three towers! We visited it on our honeymoon.'

'Did we?' She was too limpid.

'No eye for beauty, my dear wife,' he said. 'We called at the farmhouse, as Emily calls it, to collect the Delaunay-Belville which Charles had kindly loaned us. Next to Lizzie I was in love with the Delaunay-Belville . . . Their house is in the centre of the village, with massive gates on the corner.'

'*Un petit carrefour*,' Lizzie said as she scraped butter on her toast.

'See how well my wife speaks French! You know she went to school there, to gain her exquisite polish?'

'My *je ne sais quoi*,' Lizzie said.

'This farmhouse . . .' Ernest said, 'it's more like a Normandy *gentilhommière*. It has a tower over the main wing, and the drawing-room is in an extension with a flat roof, balconied. One could sit up there and watch the little river Epte which flows through the orchard at the back.'

'Oh, it's such a pretty river, Ginny,' Lizzie said. 'It meanders, and splits up into two or three Eptes, and poplars grow on its banks marking its course . . . there was one place where it split leaving a little island with a bridge leading onto it, and do you remember, Ernest? We went across the little bridge onto the island and spread a rug and . . .'

'Enough, enough!' Ernest said, pretending to be horrified. 'You might offend this young girl's sensibilities.'

'I'll have you know . . .' Ginny said, then laughed. 'Oh, you two, you're incorrigible! You should be ashamed of yourselves at your age. Eat up your breakfasts and bill and coo at each other while I go and say goodbye to Annabel and Kit. At least I'll get some sense out of them.'

Ernest and Maevy stood on the station platform waving goodbye to Ginny until the train rounded the bend to cross the Clyde.

'She's got plenty of go in her,' Maevy said as they walked out of Central Station. 'Setting off for Paris on her own.' She continued as Ernest helped her into the Napier and settled her, took his seat at the wheel, 'My Mother had the same look when she set off for America. She loved a "jaunt", as she called it.'

'Yes, the same zest for life. She'll meet someone within the first five minutes, an officer or a private, it won't matter which, and be as right as rain for the rest of the journey.'

'I hope she doesn't take up with someone unsuitable.'

Ernest laughed as he steered the motor car out of Gordon Street and turned towards Argyle Street. 'Ginny's got her head screwed on the right way. I notice a change in her recently. More mature.'

'Yes, you're right. Of course, nursing does that to you – but I noticed it, too, when she came back from Taquair Castle. Maria and Patrick will see a great difference in her when she goes home with Kate.'

'Will she come back again?'

'It depends if she's needed in the Hospital. If the War goes according to plan the casualties will soon be tailing off. What do you think, Ernest?'

'I think there has to be a decisive push yet. When, is anybody's guess. But, yes, the end is in sight.'

'I hope that lad comes back safe and well.'

'We both hope so. And pray.'

That was all he was going to say about Jonty, and in any case, all conversation on personal topics had to cease when they got into the Board Room. Maevy had convened a meeting whilst Ernest was at home, and she admired how he took charge so ably, as if he had no other concerns on his mind. His work in the Intelligence Service was never mentioned, and was for the time being pushed aside. His keen mind seemed to grasp with ease the points which Jack Richardson, the Secretary, read from the minutes. When Jack had finished he got to his feet.

'I can see I'm not needed here. No, don't smile, Sandy Gregg, nor you, John Drummond, I mean it. The business is running on oiled wheels, and I can tell you that at the Globe Express in London, where I presided at their board meeting before coming up here, they are very pleased with McGrath's. Shipping, heavy cartage, travel and household removals, they said, could be safely left to us for the duration of the War.' Everyone looked pleased as he went on.

'The unexpected competition from Dunlop's hasn't materialized, despite the family fortune there. We had our toe in the door first, and you'll be pleased to know that Globe Express has bought them off.' There were murmurs of pleasure at that.

'But we mustn't think we're invincible. Although in some ways we've benefited by the War, on the other hand, by the War Office Registration Scheme we've had commandeered fifteen hundred men, eighteen hundred horses and eighty-five motors, and that means we've had to buy up smaller firms just to get their motors! Fuel and straw are as scarce as they're expensive. It was a good decision on our part to bring back steam motors and use domestic coal.' He paused to look round, caught Maevy's eye.

'But the War Office didn't reckon on Mrs Maevy McNab. She has not been idle.' He smiled at her. 'She, with the help of our devoted staff here, Dan, Jack, Mr Donaldson, Mr Cross and Miss Boyes who runs an admirable typing department, have all put their shoulders to the wheel. Her keen eye has picked out derelict warehouses which have been turned into repositories as good as the purpose-built ones, and there are tremendous possibilities in those, bearing in mind the amount of goods and furniture we move, which I leave you to turn over in your own fertile minds.

'Now that the War, we hope, is nearing its end, we have restored the parcels business by doing what we dared not do earlier, increasing rates substantially, and it is becoming a profitable concern. I can tell you now, ladies and gentlemen, the backlog of deficits and interest payments have been cleared, and we are able to pay a dividend on ordinary shares.' There was a subdued drumming of hands on the table, which he acknowledged with a smile.

'There's one point which we must bear in mind, however, the possibility that the Government's war-time subsidies might be discontinued after the War. I don't have to tell you that this would be a disaster as far as McGrath's is concerned, and I'm making strenuous efforts to see that these aren't removed. Fortunately I can pull a few strings.

'One thing I must stress while I'm here, and I'm sure Patrick and Robert in America would bear me out: the future lies in motor transport. I've even seen that in the battle lines, motor buses being used to transport the troops. Money must be set aside for the purchase of large numbers of new vehicles. At the moment our stock is well up, but now that we have amalgamated with the local Wharves Carting Company, we'll need more since we'll be handling cold storage materials. It's obvious that wherever our interests lie – on the river, on the street, in the warehouses, *motor transport is the key*.' He looked at Maevy as he emphasized the words.

'I see a lingering regret in Mrs McNab's eye. The end of an era, she's thinking, I'm sure, and so are we all. Perhaps here and now we should pay a tribute to Kieran McGrath, that worthy husband of Mrs Maeve McGrath, later Lady Crawford, whose life centred on the wellbeing of the horses in our old stables in the Gallowgate.

'We have come a long way since then, have survived one War and look like surviving another to go on to bigger and better things. We are looking to the future, as our founders always did, Kieran and Maeve McGrath!' I'm glad he said that, Maevy thought, listening to the applause. And, it'll soon be me . . .

'Before I sit down,' Ernest was saying, 'I want to thank

you all for your steady, faithful work while I'm away enjoying myself . . . no, Dan, don't shake your head. I don't carry one tenth of the responsibility you all carry here. But before long, God willing, I hope to be back amongst you.' He sat down to general applause.

Lizzie had a family dinner party the night before Ernest went back to London, *en route* for France. If they were apprehensive on his account they were not going to allow it to spoil the evening. Besides, how could they show any anxiety about their affairs when they were in anguish about the fighting at Arras where they knew Jonty was.

She had wept in Ernest's arms last night, and then, drying her eyes, had listened attentively to his comforting words. The training was intensive, even near the Front Line, and platoon commanders were human. They would see his youth, (even if they did not know his real age by this time), and bear it in mind. There were thousands of jobs to be done as well as fighting.

Yes, he wouldn't lie to her, the Germans were using phosgene gas, but there were ways of fighting it which they would all be schooled in. Certainly young Terence had been unlucky, but Verdun had been different. The French had not had the might which the Allied Armies had now. Think of it as a machine, he said, a competent machine.

He got out his maps and showed her the terrain, traced the River Lys, La Bassee Canal, the railway line. 'Some of the men have spent more time on the trains than they have on the Front Line,' he told her. 'Then there are all those refugees, sometimes with their cattle driven in front of them. Try and see it in its entirety, Jonty one tiny speck, and how unlikely that one speck would be picked out by either gunfire or gas.' He comforted her the best way he could. He made love to her, and prayed for Jonty while he did so. And he did not tell her of the Special Order of the Day which had been sent to him with other official papers yesterday, and which had made him shudder.

'There is no other course open to us but to fight it out. Every position must be held to the last man; there must be no retirement. With our backs to the wall and believing in the justice of our cause, each one of us must fight on to the end. The safety of our homes and the freedom of mankind alike depend upon the conduct of each one of us at this critical moment.'

The children were not included in the dinner party. They were going to a concert in Sholton Village Hall in aid of the troops, and had had an early supper. There were only Maevy, Kate and Isobel besides themselves, and this was how Lizzie wanted it.

'Isn't this nice?' she asked, 'so cosy. I miss Ginny, of course, but by all accounts she's having the time of her life in Paris – dinner at Maxim's with Emily and her doctor friend, Monsieur Duval. Charles doesn't like dining out. At one of Emily's dinner parties she met Sacha Guitry! Can you believe it?'

'Who is he?' Kate asked.

'He writes plays, doesn't he?' Lizzie appealed to Ernest.

'Yes, very *risqué*. There are generally only three characters in them, the husband, the wife, the lover.'

'Oh, my goodness!' Kate said, laughing, her hand to her mouth. 'What would Maria and Patrick say!'

'That's not the worst of it,' Lizzie went on. 'She says the Casino de Paris is open again and Giselle and Terence are taking her one evening.'

'I believe nude people parade in front of the audience,' Isobel said.

'I don't know where you pick up that kind of information, Isobel.' Maevy turned to look at her.

'I read a lot.' Her sister was bland.

'Evidently,' Lizzie said, exchanging a laughing glance with Ernest. 'Perhaps you could tell us more, if you don't think it might make Ernest faint away.'

'Try me,' Ernest said.

'They go up and down a ladder,' Isobel laid down her knife and fork, 'which is ten metres high, and they wear plumes of feathers on their heads . . .'

'Monumental head-dresses in all the colours of the rainbow,' Ernest put in, 'a ravishing sight!'

'You wicked man, you've been!' Lizzie pointed her finger at him.

'Perhaps in the course of my duties . . .'

'Looking for spies, no doubt . . .'

'The toast of the evening,' Isobel held up her hand to be heard, 'is a lady called Gaby Deslys who has a dancing partner called Harry Pilcher.'

'It sounds an unlikely combination,' Maevy said.

'Oh, her real name is Gabrielle Claire. They're from America. They dance to a jazz band with xylophones and saxophones and banjos, and everyone is so enthusiastic about her in her satin and pearls that once, when the big German gun fired from woods near Paris, most of the people refused to go down to the basement.'

There was a silence, broken by Kate. 'You haven't been wasting your time, Isobel, I'll say that!'

'And something else I'll say,' Maevy was sitting very straight, 'this Gaby whatever-you-call-her was never a suffragette!'

When the laughter had subsided, Kate said, 'As a matter of interest, Isobel, where on earth did you read all this?'

'You know that soldier who came in with the broken

thigh, Donald Colquhoun? Remember, Lizzie? You told him to help me in the office. Well, he used to sit and read his magazines and once or twice he forgot to take them with him.'

Lizzie looked at the three aunts during the laughter. No, they should never be split up. They're happy together, she thought. They started off together in Colliers Row. They ought to stay together for as long as they live. She waited until she had settled them in the drawing-room and they had been served with coffee. Then she took her seat opposite them where they sat on the sofa.

'After all Isobel's disclosures about Gay Paree, maybe what I have to say to you won't be nearly so interesting.' They looked at her expectantly, Maevy dignified, Kate tranquil but with her air of sadness, Isobel still a little impish after her *tour de force*.

'Let's hear it, anyhow,' Maevy said.

'In spite of all our worries and anxieties, and I know you all know how I worry about Jonty,' they murmured sympathetically, 'I'm trying to live up to Grandmother's example, to go forward, to think positively. To make plans which will include all of us. I think you know how proud Ernest and I are of you, how I appreciate all your help and support in the Hospital throughout the last three years.' The three ladies looked primly downwards.

'You're the one with the ideas,' Kate said, 'we just . . .'

'Ideas aren't much good without willing helpers, Aunt Kate,' Lizzie said gently. 'Everyone knows now that it's only a matter of time before the War ends – Ernest thinks towards the end of this year, and I've great faith in his judgement. My dearest wish is that we'll all be here together with Jonty, unharmed.'

'He'll be all right, Lizzie,' Maevy said. 'We're getting ready for him in McGrath's too.'

'Yes, Ernest told me something of that.' She paused.

'I've heard from the War Office that the hospital here will start to run down soon and probably be emptied before the winter. That means that next year we could go back and live as we were, but . . . things will never be the same. And so, I've been making plans . . .'

'Just like Grandmother.' Ernest smiled at her.

'Maybe so. As you know, the Hall is my property until I die and then it goes to Jonty, but even so, I wouldn't like to do anything here he wouldn't approve of. I can't talk it over with him as he's so far away . . .' her voice broke, '. . . but I can write.'

'Oh, don't talk about dying,' Kate said, 'a lovely girl like you.'

'No longer a girl, Aunt Kate. I'm forty and I think that's a good age to change our mode of life. Of course, I've talked it over with Ernest, and he's behind me.'

'She bullied me into it,' Ernest said, smiling. 'No that's not true, I'm behind Lizzie in this one hundred per cent.'

'I'm thinking . . .' she looked at the aunts' faces, at their polite efforts to conceal their curiosity, too prim for words, as they sat in a neat row on the sofa, feet together, their coffee cups raised. '. . . I'm thinking of making the Hall into an hotel, a hydropathic, if you prefer the proper name.'

There was complete silence. Out of it came Isobel's voice, still brash after her earlier disclosures about the nightlife of Paris. 'If it's a hydropathic it has to have healing waters.'

'Let Lizzie go on,' Maevy said.

'Isobel's right. As a matter of fact, there is a spring coming down the hill from the ruined monastery. It's very ancient. It could *well* have healing powers.' She was bland. 'It runs through the grounds, and I thought of channelling it into the hall where there would be a perpetual fountain . . .' She looked innocently around. Ernest broke the silence.

'If Lizzie has anything to do with it, it *will* have healing properties!' He laughed. 'Go on, my dear, tell the aunts more. You can see how interested they are.' The three aunts sat back in the sofa, careful with their coffee cups.

11

'Well,' Lizzie said, 'I've studied several books on the subject, and I've been to look over one or two places when you thought I was up in Glasgow.' Her smile was mischievous. 'The main requirement is what we have plenty of: space inside and spaciousness outside. We have that all right.'

Maevy nodded round the listeners. 'They knew how to build in those days.'

'This idea of mine became my solace when Ernest and Jonty were away. Indeed, it enabled me to keep my sanity, especially as regards my Jonty. After the daily work in the hospital I'd sit up in bed and make plans and drawings, study the brochures I'd brought back with me. I've been to Graveson, the architects in Crannoch, to discuss it, and they agree with me that Sholton Hall is ideally suited to become Sholton Hydropathic, with suitable additions. It's become too big for a private house nowadays.'

'The right distance from Glasgow,' Maevy said, nodding.

'You have a big conservatory,' Kate looked thoughtful. 'They always have that, don't they? Palm houses . . .?'

'And a ballroom,' Isobel said, no doubt still thinking of Gaby Deslys and Harry Pilcher. 'You wouldn't have to build that.'

'No. It's been shut up since before the War. I became engaged to Nigel at a ball in there. I know you don't mind me saying that, Ernest.' Lizzie looked at him. He shook his head. There had never been malice in Ernest.

'You would have to make provision for motor cars somewhere. They would be the principal means of transport.'

'There's plenty of room at the back of the house for that. We don't have to change with the times as much as the older establishments. They had to convey their visitors from the station by coach, with wagonettes for the luggage. It was quite clever.' She smiled. 'What happened was that at the previous junction the porter would go along the train shouting, "Anyone for the Hydropathic!" And then he'd wire ahead so that the conveyances would be waiting for the guests.'

'Clever,' Ernest said, 'as well as giving a certain *cachet.*'

'Of course, I wouldn't *slavishly* follow the old ideas. Some were quite strict. They even fined a visitor a penny if he or she was late for meals, and they had morning and evening prayers! I think a Sunday visit from Peter Kennedy for the infirm would be quite enough, and those who wanted to worship at the kirk could be conveyed there or drive there themselves.'

'That's their spiritual needs disposed of,' Ernest said. 'Now, tell the aunts about the other side of it.'

'You knew all about this?' Maevy asked.

'Vaguely. I didn't enquire too deeply, indeed I couldn't, not being at home. But I know that my dear wife is only happy when she's plotting and scheming, and I was quite happy with the crumbs she threw at me from time to time.'

'I would never do anything without Ernest's approval,' Lizzie said, 'he knows that. What do you think, Aunt Maevy?' She appealed to her. 'You'll know more about the idea behind hydropathics than I do.'

'I wouldn't say that. But I know you, Lizzie, when you get an idea into your head. Now, then, hydrotherapeutics, it's called.' She put down her cup on the table in front of her. 'The water cure. There's nothing wrong with the principle. Plenty of water inside and out, a healthy regime, exercise, good plain food, it's a well-tried formula.'

'That's it. But, as well, I want it to be a family holiday place with games for the young outside or in the ballroom on wet days, planned walks in the grounds for everyone, golf, perhaps – we could lay out a course – riding . . .'

'And swimming,' Ernest said.

'Yes, I realize that's essential. I should have to have a swimming bath made, and a Turkish bath too, but again it's perfectly possible.'

'Would you allow your gentlemen visitors to smoke?' Ernest asked wickedly.

'Now, there's a point! Healthy bodies . . . I think I could get round that by making a billiard room in the tower with a smoking room off it. That would keep the fumes far enough away from the rest of the guests. Oh, I've been over most things in my mind!' She couldn't quite curb her excitement. 'We have tennis courts. We could arrange picnics in the wagonettes for the younger members – Annabel and Kit could give me plenty of ideas there. My aim would be for it to become an *institution* for whole families to come year after year. I'd have a day nursery. There are any number of Sholton women who'd take on the supervision of small children. The young could play tennis and swim and picnic, and dance in the evenings; the fathers and mothers could golf, the men could play billiards if they wished and the older ones could sit in the Palm Court – that's what I'd call our conservatory when it was enlarged.'

'Oh, my!' Isobel said, laughing, her cheeks pink.

'And with the perpetual fountain going in the hall, and the constant drinking from its water in between all the other activities, we'd send them away better in health and spirits, and dying to come back next year!' The aunts had caught her excitement. There was a chorus of approval from them. Isobel clapped her hands.

'I can't see a flaw,' Kate said. 'It sounds like a wonderful idea. We have one or two similar establishments near us at Wanapeake and it was quite the thing to go. Indeed, I've heard it said that many friendships were struck up, not to mention romances.'

'There's a lot of organization in it,' Isobel said, 'but knowing you, Lizzie, you'll have thought of everything or nearly everything. Permission will have to be had for extra water supplies, for instance. The laundry-room will take up a lot. A competent office staff will be essential . . .'

'I'd be glad of your advice, there, Aunt Isobel.' Lizzie knew when to look humble. She had discussed the question of getting in touch with the District Council with Ernest and her architects.

'You'd have to have a doctor on the staff, or at least on tap,' Maevy said. 'On tap!' She giggled and the other two aunts joined in. 'If I were in your shoes, Belle Geddes would be my choice.'

'How right you are, Aunt Maevy, which brings me to my next point which I've talked over with Ernest, for where in all the wide world would I find a better business man . . .?'

'Oh, please . . .' Ernest demurred, smiling.

'You think so, too, so don't look so modest. After the essential work's done and the Hydro is in running order, I don't intend to devote my life to it. Grandmother always said one should learn to delegate, and Ernest, as you know, has always come first with me. He'll have to make frequent trips abroad in his capacity as chairman of Globe Express, and I wouldn't dare let him go off without me,' she laughed at him. 'So, we've come to the conclusion that we should appoint a Board. There would be Ernest and myself, of course, and Jonty – I'm going to get him to help me with the interior decorating, buying pictures, furniture, all that kind of thing, which he's so good at . . .' her voice faltered, '. . . if he comes back safely . . .'

'He'll be back,' Ernest said. 'You know it, my darling. Go on, tell the aunts the rest.'

'About the Board? Oh, yes, Belle, of course, and last but certainly not least, you three, if you're willing.' They looked at each other, solemnly at first, then unable to control their smiles, began all to talk at once.

'Why us? Oh, don't talk rubbish, Lizzie! Three old women!'

'Speak for yourself, Maevy,' Isobel said, 'I'm bound to say that after my experience with the organization of the hospital I could perhaps give a little advice on the office side of things.'

'That's what I thought, Aunt,' Lizzie said. 'Not to work all day as you've been doing so nobly downstairs, but in an advisory capacity.' She looked at Kate. 'And Aunt Kate, you have such experience of people. Everyone loves you about the place. You could see that things were running smoothly with the servants and we'll certainly need a lot. People would come to you with their little problems . . .'

'You mean, a kind of shop-walker?' Kate laughed, her sadness gone momentarily, 'Oh, girls!' She turned to Isobel and Maevy, 'do you remember Mr Wilson's Colosseum and those beautiful gentlemen in their morning clothes . . .?'

'Pin stripes and patent leather hair,' Maevy said.

'You could wear black satin, Mother,' Ernest said. 'Everyone would love you, especially the children. It would be your own big family.'

'But I've no attributes like Maevy, a qualified nurse.'

'You have your own,' Lizzie said. 'I'd like to rely on you for advice on the health side of things, Aunt Maevy. Of course, I'm talking of the future. I know you have more than enough with McGrath's. All I want from the three of you just now is your promise that you'll serve on the Board of the Sholton Hydropathic.' In the silence that followed, Lizzie wondered if they were going to refuse. Maevy spoke first.

'I wouldn't miss the chance for the world!'

'Neither would I,' Kate said, 'as long as I can go back to America occasionally.'

'As often as you like,' Lizzie smiled, 'and bring the family to stay. The members of the Board will, of course, have free holidays there whenever they wish. That's part of the contract.'

'That settles it for me,' Isobel said. 'If there's one thing I dream about, it's to be pampered.'

Ernest laughed, got up and went to the side table where he busied himself with bottles. He came back with five glasses on a tray. 'Since we're not sure yet if Lizzie will make her Hydro completely teetotal, I think we'd better have something while we can, and drink to its success.' The three aunts each accepted a glass, saying, well, they didn't generally take brandy at this time of night but all this excitement put a different complexion on affairs . . . When they had recovered somewhat, Maevy said, 'But where are you going to live yourselves, Lizzie? Surely not still here?'

'No, I was just going to come to that. I intend to convert the stables into two houses, large cottages but with the latest in everything, easy to run but spacious enough to enjoy living in. This is the bit my husband likes.' She gave him a loving glance.

'Yes,' he said, 'I have to agree. For the first time I'll have a place which is really my own, with Lizzie and our family. Not that she hasn't always made me welcome at the Hall.'

'One of the cottages is yours,' Lizzie looked at her aunts, 'whenever you like.'

'You mean leave Braidholme?' Maevy put down her glass. There were spots of colour on her cheeks.

'You've always been one to face up to facts, Aunt,' Ernest said. 'Braidholme is large, Susan won't go on for ever. A smaller house beside us, where we could keep an eye on you, would be ideal, and when you get really old and decrepit – although I can't imagine it because every time I come home you three look younger than ever – you could move into the Hydro and be *cootered*, isn't that the word? and petted by the staff . . .'

'And take the water cure!' Isobel said, spluttering into her glass. 'Oh, excuse me, but what a night it's been! I've never known so much excitement in all my married life!'

'But we'd never leave Braidholme, would we?' Maevy looked from one sister to the other.

'No . . .' They shook their heads. 'There's Susan. It's her home . . .'

'And if we don't get back soon she'll be sending out the village bobby to see what we're up to,' Maevy said.

The three of them got up, and Lizzie, looking at them, felt ready tears in her eyes. 'If you must, Aunts. Ernest will drive you home.'

Maevy had the key of the door. On the step they said goodnight to Ernest, who said, no, thank you, he wouldn't come in with them. He wanted to get back to Lizzie. That they understood.

'We'll have a last cup of tea before we go up to bed,' Maevy said, opening the door and stepping into the hall which was still lit. 'I told Susan to leave this on, although she always grumbles about the expense. I don't know about you two, but I'm still quite mesmerized.' They were taking off their coats and laying them on the settle. 'What a night!'

'It takes some getting used to,' Kate said, 'and besides, there's the sadness. That gracious house for so long, now going to be a hotel, strangers . . . nothing lasts. I know that.'

'Susan's light's still on in the kitchen,' Isobel said. 'She'll be waiting up to give us a row.' She giggled. 'Should we tell her?'

'No,' Maevy said, 'let it settle in our own minds first. And we won't tell her about the cottages. Braidholme is her life and she might jalouse . . . though I'd never think of . . .'

She walked towards the kitchen door and as she opened it Susan's cat dashed across their feet. A hand clutched at her heart. She recognized it, the Precursor. Things went on beautifully from day to day, you thought they could never alter, and then, from one second to the next . . . but it was all right. The hand released its grip. Susan was sitting in her rocking chair, her hands crossed in her lap, asleep.

'Poor soul,' Kate said, 'while we were out enjoying ourselves. She's got tired waiting.'

'We'll have to wake her up, though,' Isobel said, going forward. 'She can't sit there all night.' She put her hand on the woman's shoulder, paused, took it away and turned towards the other two. In Maevy's eyes she was the Isobel after John had died, frail, drained. 'She's . . .'

She was propelled forward. Discipline. Had to be done. She saw the waxen face except for the slight rim of red on the nostrils, the blue lips. There was no need for mirrors, nor for feeling the pulse: she was gone. She had a sudden fierce regret that they had kept her waiting. She looked up at her sisters beside her. 'She's left us.' She straightened her back, drew in her breath.

Kate let out a little cry, put her hand to her mouth. 'The poor soul . . . and us not here!'

'No,' she said fiercely, 'It's as she would have liked it. No fuss. In her favourite chair, sitting, having a wee rest, waiting . . . Are you all right, Isobel? You're not going to faint?'

'No.' She wasn't the frail shadow any longer. She was the Isobel who had found herself when John died. 'I've got a grip on myself.'

'Well, you get into the scullery with Kate and make that cup of tea. I'll go and phone Belle.'

She went into the hall, amazed that her eyes were dry. But that was how she was. She hadn't been able to weep when Charlie died. She had always had to wait for the tears. She lifted the receiver from the hook, glad that they had that 'new-fangled thing' as Susan had called it. Well, she'd gone, as Charlie had gone, quickly, hardly knowing. But different from Charlie in one way. She had gone at the right time, when the Braidholme days were coming to an end. He had left her in its prime. And hers.

12

Ginny spent her last night with Terence and Giselle, not at the Casino watching '*Le Spectacle Nu*' which Isobel knew so much about, but in their little *appartement* in Passy. Their visit to the Casino had been as Terence had laughingly said, purely educational, simply to show her Parisian life in wartime.

'You'll find the audience as interesting as the performers, and some of the ladies of it hardly more clad.' That had been true enough. 'When I compare it with Verdun and the misery of those refugees trudging along the roads, it's hard to believe, and then I tell myself it's the Parisian way of cocking a snook at death. Such style! Can you see me getting the same inspiration in Glasgow, or even Dublin?'

Terence was right about Parisian style, Ginny thought, helping Giselle put the children to bed while he cooked the meal. He had taken over that job during his long convalescence. Little Jaime, now two years of age, was a beauty, dark-eyed and French-looking with Giselle's distinctive nose; Clovis was a strapping boy more in the mould of his grandfather in Ireland. She set up in position again two dolls which had slipped downwards on the mantelpiece.

'What are they called?' she asked.

'Nenette and Rintintin. To guard us from the Gothas.'

'The Gothas?'

'Yes, German aeroplanes. It's a superstition. Don't you believe in superstitions?'

'I hadn't thought about it. But these are pretty. Nenette and Rintintin?'

'And we had Zeppelins, the great dirigible balloons. There were twenty-six people killed in the north-east of Paris. That was in 1916. We have forgotten now with the arrival of the Gothas. We have had over sixty raids since they started at the beginning of the year. We went to live in our farmhouse for the sake of the children, with *Maman*. We aren't long back from there. Terence said Paris *sans Mère* was preferable! And then he has still to attend the hospital for treatment for his arm.'

'It isn't better?'

'No, nor his lungs, but we try not to . . .' she shook her head as if to dismiss the thought. 'And then we have the *grand canon*. It's in the forest of St Gobain and its shells can travel as far as Paris! We call it *Grosse Bertha*! But even in April, when the Germans were only five stops from here, the linen *boutiques* had exhausted all their stocks of blue and red flags . . .'

'The French flag?'

'No, the colours of Nenette and Rintintin!'

Ginny laughed. 'Yes, Terence is right. You have style.'

'But I think we'll have to go back to La Hirondelle, not because of *Grosse Bertha*, but because of this new malady, the Spanish Influenza. Have you heard of it?'

'Oh, yes. It's very virulent. I worry about Jonty.'

'And I about Terence because of his weak chest. As a matter of fact, we have only come to Paris to be vaccinated. Terence says they ought to shut all the schools and forbid meetings, but try telling Parisians that.'

'Well, there's no point in worrying.' She tucked Jaime's small hand under the counterpane, 'I wonder how this one's American counterpart is getting on.'

'Little James Murray-Hyslop?' Giselle was folding napkins. 'I believe very well from all accounts, a fine baby.

Aunt Maevy, of course, sings his praises . . .' She looked up, 'You know he isn't Kieran's child?'

'Yes, I was on the fringe of that when Ellie came home. She looked so sad at times, even on her wedding day. I was her bridesmaid. I behaved like a clown to try and cheer her up.'

'I'm sure the American officer she met at *Maman*'s was the great love of her life.' She put the neatly-folded squares on the top of a chest, 'I think we had better join Terence now. When he cooks his *pommes dauphinées* he becomes quite temperamental.' She laughed.

'That's because he's a true artist.'

Over the candlelit dinner table Giselle said to Terence, 'Ginny and I were talking about Ellie. And her lover who was killed.'

'Were you?' He was dishing up his *poulet fricassée*, 'more *legumes* than *poulet*', he said, 'because of the rationing'. He looked up. 'I'll never forget the radiance of her face when she came to visit me in the hospital at Condé. It was . . . luminous. And she was so sensitive about how I felt, every ache and pain, as if her whole being was tuned . . . maybe this sounds fanciful, like a violin with perfect pitch.'

'She wasn't like that at her wedding,' Ginny said. 'Her eyes . . . I'll never forget them, and yet she smiled, all the time . . .'

'Not exactly the typical bride. Sad, sad . . .' He sighed. 'What do you think of my *fricassée*, Ginny? Is the seasoning all right?'

She tasted. 'Just right. Subtle, not overdone. Like your paintings. If they stop selling you could get a job at Maxim's any day of the week.'

'There isn't much difference between the two. A lot of ingredients on the one hand, a lot of tubes of paint on the other. It's the mixer's hands that count.' He spread his, and she noticed the deformed one, the thinness of the right arm. He saw her look. 'It could have been worse. I'm alive.'

'You are lucky when you think of Ellie's lover,' Giselle said.

'Oh, yes, but it must have been hard for Kieran, too, second choice, and now the father of another man's child.'

'But it was *his* choice.'

'Do you think she's got over the American?' Ginny asked. She had always admired Ellie, her cleverness and her beauty, but had categorized her in her own mind as a bit of an ice maiden . . . until that wedding day.

'No,' Giselle said, 'but she will have to come to terms with it. She has a strong character, and an even stronger sense of duty. She's doing what is right for her now, working in a hospital in Wanapeake. Now me, I'm selfish, I couldn't leave my two babies – my three babies,' she laughed at Terence – 'but Ellie's different. There is a War on, she says. That must come first.'

'Maybe she's selfish, too,' Ginny said. 'Perhaps it's for her own sake as well.'

'Whatever the reason,' Terence said, 'Kieran will understand. I hear from Robert he's working just as hard for the War in his firm, overworking, he says. He and Edie get worried about his long hours. He sounds as if he's working himself into the ground.'

'What does that mean?' Giselle asked.

'*Sans cesse, ma chérie, très, très dur, c'est à dire, comme mineur.*' Three talents, Ginny thought, sampling again the delicious *fricassée*: cooking, painting and a gift of tongues. In the distance they heard a muffled but powerful boom which repeated itself two or three times – a sinister, heavy sound new to Ginny.

'*C'est la Grosse Bertha*,' Giselle said, getting up. 'I'll go and see that the children are all right. Nenette and Rintintin will take care of them,' she said to Terence.

He smiled at her and said to Ginny, 'That's Paris.'

She came back to the Hall ready to knock over a mountain, as she told herself. There had been the feeling before she left for Paris that she was at a crossroads in her life, but being with Giselle and Terence had given her a new impetus and a new slant. They were an ideal couple, she thought, that's how I'd like to be, some day . . .

And being in Paris had been good for her. She had been involved in looking after the casualties of War in Lizzie's hospital, but Glasgow was too far from the centre of things to be attacked. The sight of those beautiful ladies dressed by Chanel strolling down the Champs Élysees was one thing. But it became poignant when she thought of the grief and loss perhaps concealed behind their immaculate exteriors, their silk tunic dresses, their elegant parasols. She would never again see a couple in a chic Parisian boulevard without thinking of Nenette and Rintintin.

She plunged into a rush of work when she started nursing again in Lizzie's hospital. After Ludendorff had called off his spring offensive on the Somme, the full result of the battles became known: two hundred thousand casualties and ninety thousand prisoners. From the end of April the wounded had begun to arrive at the Hall, for the most part those who needed long term treatment or convalescence had been shipped home.

The Lys offensive had been the worst of the lot, one of the patients told her. It was Ludendorff's last fling, a brilliant piece of strategy, but the casualties had been terrible. He was one of them, he said, croaking, with a damaged lung which refused to heal, a 'good Blighty one'. He would never work again.

After the Lys came the Aisne and the Marne. From talking to the patients she became knowledgeable about the location of the French rivers, and the oddly-named *Chemin de Dames*, which seemed from all accounts to be as busy as Argyle Street on a Saturday night. Liddell, of the damaged lung, declared that it was all over bar the shouting, but it was difficult to believe. The wounded came in a steady stream, patients who would need a month or two of care, if they didn't die in the interval.

And her darling Jonty was fighting for his life near Ypres. His letters were still 'jonty' – as she called them. He'd had a fine time recently, he wrote, stuck on a train because the one in front had been hit by a shell, blocking the line. 'If it's not trains it's motor lorries. I spend my time being transported from one battlefield to the other, fraternizing with other regiments like the Royal West Surrey (kiltless, poor souls), and even a New Zealand Entrenching Battalion. You can't say you don't meet the *nicest* people in the War!' And, then, 'A good friend of mine from Luss, on Loch Lomond, Jimmy McAlpine, was killed yesterday . . .'

He never mentioned his poetry.

It was the end of August before she and her Aunt Kate left for America. Lizzie had told her of her plans for the Hall, saying that she expected Ginny would want to return to America for good then. 'I expect so,' she had said. 'This War changes everybody, even me! I have a feeling I ought to get back home, give it another try.' Lizzie had given her a considering look. In spite of her easy manner, Lizzie was close. She remembered an expression of Magnus Muir's, 'playing your cards close to your chest'.

And there was Sarah. She was a faithful correspondent and had written that sometimes their mother looked 'frail'. 'It's a strange thing to say, Ginny, but she begins to resemble Grandmother Caroline. It worries me. Of course they don't look alike, but Mother has taken to a more frivolous mode of dressing, and between you and me, I know she has had her hair dyed . . . I think she fears old age.' To Ginny this disclosure was somehow moving.

She and Kate had plenty of time to talk as the liner took them to America, safely, they hoped. 'Have you made up your mind to return to Scotland, Aunt?' she asked her.

'Yes.' Her sweet face was unusually determined. 'It's a challenge to me, but most of all, I'd like to end my days with my two dear sisters in my own country. Now that Susan's gone, we'll begin to think about moving into one of the stable cottages when they're built. But there's no hurry.'

'Won't you miss seeing your grandchildren?'

'George and Abigail's, and Victoria and Jason's?' She smiled. 'They're no longer children, my dear. Besides, this journey gets easier every time I make it, and they'll soon be setting off for Scotland themselves.'

'It's strange how our family has spread – Ireland, Scotland, France, America . . .'

'That's what makes it interesting. And you're so young, Ginny. You can travel about the world visiting them all . . . unless you have other plans, like going up north?' Her smile was mischievous.

'No, that's over, if you mean Magnus Muir. I should have had to marry his mother as well. And spend my days with the guns! Can you imagine anything worse than squelching about all day in a bog? I don't know what my plans are. I'm waiting for . . . direction. But I'm due to go home first. Maybe they'll think I've matured . . . what a hope!' She looked away. 'And then when I saw Giselle and Terence together, I thought the only thing in life worth having was a happy marriage. And there's Lizzie and Ernest . . .' She laughed. 'Did you ever see the like of them after so many years?'

'Lizzie is . . . Lizzie. Her man is the most important thing in her life, even before Jonty, and we both know how she anguishes over that lad in spite of her brave face.'

'Yes, she's special. But there's Ellie. She's always put her career first.'

'Except once,' Kate said.

'The American officer? What was his name, Aunt?'

'Joe Gould. I hear little James is very like him in features, or rather, unlike Ellie and Kieran.'

'That's hard for Kieran.'

'Hard but not impossible if there's love there. We'll have to see . . . Do you think you might study for something when you get back?'

'No, I'm not academic. But I know only too well I shan't settle down to good works like Sarah. We'll see how the bools run . . . do you remember that saying of Grandma's? For the time being I just want to see Mother and Father.'

'Well, that's the best reason you could have for going home.' She put her arm round her as they sat in the padded lounge. 'You're a grand girl, Ginny, so like my mother with her beauty and her spunk. She used to say you can't put an old head on young shoulders, but I can tell you here and now, there's a brilliant future ahead for you.'

'You have a great capacity for saying the right thing, Aunt Kate.' She laid her head for a moment on Kate's shoulder.

13

She was surprised at how emotional she felt at the first sight of her mother and father and Sarah, when she arrived at Claremont. She ran into her mother's arms, noticing as she did so that Sarah had been right. Her mother was frailer, gaunt even, her curls jet black (wasn't she sixty-six?), her cheeks bright pink, and she had a row of matching pink bows marching down the front of her dress. Her shoes were high-heeled with pointed toes and her fingers were bejewelled.

But it was her own mother, and she went from her arms, the tears running down her cheeks, into her father's. No pretence here, just more grizzled than she remembered him, and perhaps stouter. Sarah was Sarah, she would never change – soberly dressed, her hair in an old-fashioned knot – but she was waiting to put her arms round her as well. They were all laughing and crying at the same time.

'You've changed, Ginny,' Maria said. 'I don't know what it is, you're different somehow.'

'I'm twenty-one now, don't forget, and I've been having porridge for breakfast for the last two years. I'm probably as fat as the side of a house.'

'You know you aren't,' Sarah said, 'you're slimmer than ever, but Mother's right. I know what it is,' she put her head on one side, 'you're more mature.'

'Thank you very much, sister dear. Oh, it's lovely to be home again, and how lovely the house is! And the garden is absolutely beautiful, Father! You must spend a great deal of time in it.'

'We spend a great deal of money keeping two gardeners, but it's worth it. It's always been a great consolation to your mother.' Did he mean because of Gaylord? 'I don't get much chance to enjoy it with going to New York every day.'

'You know I've been asking you to slacken off for a long time, Patrick,' Maria said. 'And so has Robert.'

'Perhaps I will when the War's over. My goodness, it's grand to have you back with us, Ginny. You'll have so much to tell us about your nursing, and about Sholton. Are you going to settle down with us?'

'I don't know yet. Everyone keeps on saying the War's going to be over any minute, but it keeps on going on. Lizzie's hospital was full when I left, and I said she had just to call on me. We're all worried sick about Jonty. He's been lucky so far, but . . .'

'He was a foolish lad to join up at his age.'

'But a brave one, dear,' Maria said. 'You can understand him, his father being in the last one. The Crawfords have a reputation in the county to keep up, a tradition . . .'

'He didn't have to run away from school.' Ginny saw her father's moustache bristle and thought again of Gaylord. He, least of all of them, had been unable to cope with the rigidity in his father's character.

'That grand mansion of theirs,' Sarah was the peacemaker, 'it must make a wonderful hospital.'

'Oh, it does, and Lizzie has plans for it after the War. There's so much to tell you, and so many people to see: Kieran and Ellie, and Edie and Robert, and the Vogels and George and Abigail. And all the cousins. Are Polly and Priscilla married yet? Oh, I can't believe I'm home.'

'Well, first of all you'll go upstairs and get out of your travelling costume – I must say it's very smart. Is that the latest in Paris?'

'Yes, *la tunique. Très decollétée*, but filled in for modesty.' She pulled a face. 'And buckled shoes.' She pointed one in front of her. 'You'd love the fashions, Mother. Some ladies wear their skirts much shorter than this. It's a Women's War, they say, and they've taken over a lot of the men's work. When I was in Emily's house in Normandy I saw three women in the fields drawing a harrow, replacing men *and* horses! But Paris is *très gai* on the surface. Don't look so disapproving, Father. They're too near the War to escape it.'

'You're better off in Glasgow.' His mouth was a straight line.

'Father's going to drive us to Wolf House after we've had lunch,' Maria said, 'and you've had time to collect yourself. It'll let you say hello to Kieran and Ellie and see the baby. They're at home on Sunday afternoons, fortunately. We won't stay long. It's such a busy house with Ellie working in the hospital. We'll have a quiet dinner here together.'

'Yes, that's what I'd like. And you and I, Sarah, might have a little walk round Wanapeake after lunch. I want to see the shops again, and the blacksmiths, and the market gardeners where we used to buy plants, and the recreation ground . . . oh, it's grand to be home! Oh, Sarah!' She put her arms round her sister's waist and whirled her about the room. 'Do you know the latest ragtime song? "Everybody's doing it, doing it . . .".' She sang as they whirled.

'Stop! It's too quick for me!' Sarah was laughing, flushed.

'A Parisian waltz, then? They were playing this one all the time I was there . . .' She hummed, a haunting little refrain. 'It's called "Destiny". Me . . . re, me, re, me, re, me . . .' Paris came back to her, frenetic but sad, so different from here.

'Just look at us, Mother!' Sarah called, her small face alight. 'It's obvious Ginny's back, isn't it?'

'Our Ginny,' her father said. He was smiling and nodding.

After lunch they strolled down the leafy road from Claremont to the centre of the small town. It was much warmer than Scotland, humid, in fact, but Ginny revelled in her light clothes and the sun on her bare arms. Not like grey Glasgow, she thought, where any good day was a benison. The pavement was dry and sandy, and the big houses sat back from the road with their green grass skirts and their striped blinds, their brilliant flowers on the porches. There was a Sunday quietness, and yet it was an American Sunday quietness. The houses, unlike Claremont with its solid stone, were mostly clapboard, the children who passed them occasionally were dressed differently from those in Scotland, with brighter colours and odd-looking peaked cotton caps on their heads, and their speech was different. She heard one boy say to his friend in sing-song Yankee, 'I've been to the swimming hole *every* day . . .'

'Everything is the same,' she said to Sarah, 'and so different from Scotland. It's the density of the trees here and the dirt roads, and the names on those shop fronts. There's Mrs Addams' Kandy Kitchen. Is she still there?'

'No, she gave it up after her son Abe was killed in France. Her daughter runs it.'

'Oh, that's sad. Has the War made an impact on Wanapeake?'

'Oh, yes. We had a grand send-off for the boys who went from here. They marched from the Recreation Ground down the road to the station, and the children went in front carrying the American flag with the town band. At first we watched from the sidewalk and then we all joined in. There were tears that day. I'm helping with sending comforts to the troops and organizing benefits so that there's plenty of money to buy them. And I've adopted a soldier whom I write to, just like the school children.' She laughed shyly.

'Does Mother do anything?'

'Oh, yes, she knits, but you know Mother, everything has to fit round Father. It's always been that way.'

'I see a difference in them. I'm aware of their age for the first time.'

'Yes, and so are they. It makes them . . .' she smiled, 'just a little testy sometimes.'

'Are you happy to stay at home with them, Sarah?' She put her arm through her sister's.

'Yes. It's the life I've chosen. Not without a lot of soul-searching. And then, you see,' her voice dropped, 'I'm happy in our Lord.' Ginny was silent, embarrassed. 'Oh, I know you think it's a dull life and that it would never suit you, but I've discovered that the main thing is to know oneself. People think I must be envious of all those cousins of ours, married with families now. Edie's expecting. And there's little James. We're surrounded by babies!' She laughed. 'In Ireland the three girls have all got children . . .'

'And in France Giselle's brother, Marc, is now a proud father. I didn't see the twins when I was in Paris, but they've always been elusive.'

'There's a place for aunts as well as mothers and fathers. That's how I look at it.'

'You're a contented soul. I couldn't do as you're doing.'

'Why should you? You are you, your temperament is different from mine. I may never get a better chance to say this, Ginny: don't be like me, don't stay here for too long. They'll . . . eat you up.'

'Mother and Father?'

'They haven't changed, only grown older. They have in me a daughter who's going to look after them in their old age, which I've accepted. They're . . . demanding. You know father wouldn't hear of my marrying Robert? Oh, it's a long time ago and you were too young to know, or to know how I wept . . . but I don't bear him any grudge now. Maybe he knew me better than I did myself. And Mother's still the same, devoted to him. She has submerged herself in him. Did you notice her dress today?'

'Yes, quite fancy,' she laughed, 'with all her buttons and bows. And her hair . . . unlike her, somehow.'

'No, I understand her. Did you know Father married Lizzie's mother to give the coming child a name? Lizzie was Uncle Terence's child.'

'Yes, she told me herself one evening. I got the shock of my life.'

'Bessie Haddow was Father's first love, and he had to stand by seeing her always in love with his brother. I think Mother has always felt . . . inferior to Bessie Haddow, his second choice.'

'Hence the buttons and bows as she grows older . . .'

Sarah nodded. 'There's only one person in Mother's life, Father. She submits to his wishes, always has done. It's strange because I understand she was a determined young woman. Families . . .' she squeezed Ginny's arm.

'Maybe you're wise to stay single, Sarah. It isn't all fun.'

'Neither of us really knows. There are the hidden joys . . .' She looked sad for a second. 'You'll see Ellie and Kieran today, see how they look . . . It's lucky it's Sunday, otherwise they wouldn't have been at home.' Was there some hidden meaning in what she said.

'Ellie works in the local hospital?'

'Yes, she's highly thought of already. I know one woman in my church, whom she operated on, and she can't speak highly enough of her . . .' she looked at the watch pinned on her blouse. 'I think we'd better turn now.' They had stopped at a crossroads where the lawns ran down to the intersection. 'That's the new hospital, by the way. Ellie might well be there now. Mrs Vanaressi says that as soon as she serves up the meal Ellie has to jump up and leave it.'

'And leave Kieran?'

'Yes. We'd better hurry. Mother will be agitating. She's always the same if I'm late. That's what I mean, Ginny. It's not for you. It would smother you.'

'It's not for you either.' She was annoyed on her sister's behalf. 'You're subjugating yourself, doing the same as Mother.'

'There's only One to whom I subjugate myself, and I'm happy to do it.' Ginny looked at her sister. Her face was radiant, making her feel humble, and then uncomfortable. Had Sarah travelled further than she ever would by staying in the same place?

Ellie and Kieran had changed. She was thinner, her features more aquiline, which seemed only to have honed her beauty. The pale fineness of her skin and the pale gold of her hair had a luminous quality, like that of an enamelled miniature. Kieran was worn-looking, older than his years, and his slight stoop made him appear less tall than she remembered. Since she's such a good doctor, Ginny found herself thinking, why doesn't she notice that her husband is far from well?

Their greeting, however, couldn't have been warmer, and when they were seated and tea had been served, Ellie plied Ginny with questions about Lizzie's hospital. 'Kieran's mother is tired of answering me, aren't you?' Her glance was fond on Kate, whose greeting had been just as warm.

'No, I'm not.' Kate was her usual tranquil self. 'It's just that I can't give you all the information you want. Your own mother's the one who could, or Ginny here. She's a very good nurse. People are always saying that to me.'

'Oh, Aunt Kate's geese are always swans,' Ginny laughed.

'If her nursing is as good as her looks, then she's in the top priority.' Kieran smiled at Ginny. 'What a tonic you must be to those poor lads coming back from the Front!'

'I try to make them laugh, at least. How's your business going, Kieran? I hear you're doing War work all the time?'

'Yes, much to George's chagrin, but it's only temporary, I tell him. He's washed his hands of me and tries to keep our old customers happy meantime.'

'Kieran's never home before nine o'clock in the evening,' Ellie said.

'But neither are you, my darling.' There was a weariness in his voice which struck Ginny more than if it had been acerbic.

'It's because I'm the junior surgeon, and the nearest.' Ellie spoke generally as if she had to explain herself. 'The dogsbody. But like Kieran, I feel it's only temporary. We're both . . . committed.'

'How does little James get on without you?' She remembered Mother saying to her when she was a young girl, 'Ginny, you're so brash!'

'I think he prefers Rachel. That's his nurse. She's a lovely girl. Have you finished?' She was eager. 'Come up to the nursery and see him, Ginny.'

'I'd like to.' She got up. 'I can compare him with little Jaime in France,' she said as they went out of the room together, 'you know I was there recently?'

'Yes. How is Terence? He was so brave when I visited him in Condé . . .' She stopped, and Ginny remembered what Terence had said about her at that time – her radiance, her exquisite sensibility. She was suddenly professional. 'Did you notice his breathing? Phosgene gas is terrible on the lungs. And then his poor arm. Are the fingers still bent? He was so brave. He has quite a degree of muscle wasting.' Once more she plied Ginny with questions as they went upstairs. Her intellect will always war with her heart, Ginny thought, and was pleased with the profundity of that thought.

The little boy, now a year old, was an exceptional baby. Rachel, the nurse, handed him over to Ginny to hold, and as she cradled him in her arms, she saw Ellie's eyes on him with such love that she turned her head away, feeling she was intruding.

'He's a grand little chap, Ellie. I'm not as good at asking questions as you are, but he seems all right to me!' She laughed. 'What long limbs he has! He's going to be tall. And his eyes!' The baby seemed to be listening to her. Unusual eyes, compelling. She said deliberately, when Rachel had gone out of the room, 'He's not like you, or Kieran.'

'No, he isn't.' Her voice was calm. 'He's restless. Let me take him.' She took him in her arms, and as if recognizing her the child stretched out a hand to her face. 'He knows me, although he doesn't see me as often as I'd like. Don't you, James?' She pretended to bite the small fingers clutching at her cheek.

'You're his mother. Don't you miss him, being away so much?'

'Oh, I *miss* him.' She laid the child in his cot, slowly, reluctantly, tucking him in, 'but it's better for him. I love him so much I might . . . smother him.' The curve of her body over the cot spelled love.

* * *

She said to her parents and Sarah when they got back to Claremont, 'That was nice. They were so welcoming.'

'And especially nice for you to see your dear sister, Patrick,' Maria said.

He had sat down in his winged chair, stretched his legs. 'Sunday visiting. Tiring. Yes, in a changing world Kate never changes. There's real beauty there, inside and out.'

'I thought Ellie and Kieran looked tired, as if they were expending too much time on their efforts for the War . . .' Here I go, she thought, saying it with a rush, '. . . and too little time on their own happiness.'

'They both have a strong social conscience. Isn't that so, Patrick?'

'Yes, but I agree with Ginny. Now that Kate's there she'll perhaps be able to get them to slow down.'

'Aunt Kate won't interfere,' Sarah said.

'Oh, I'm all for interfering,' Ginny heard her own brash voice. But they were right, of course. No one could do anything about it. She would have liked to have said, 'I think the source of the trouble is with that little boy upstairs,' but that would be frowned upon. As were post mortems on visits paid.

When she went to bed that night in her own old room, her thoughts went back to them, and the love in Ellie's eyes when she was holding the baby. How would it affect Kieran? He must have seen that look many times, or had he grown to love James too?

War casualties, she told herself, don't always happen on the battlefield. She composed herself for sleep, her hand under her cheek in the old way, because she was home.

14

The next few weeks were a round of pleasure, and being young and liking pleasure, Ginny enjoyed herself. Her unmarried cousins, Priscilla and Benjamin Vogel (Thomas had followed Kieran's example and was serving in France with an Ambulance Unit), Polly and Sam Hyslop (they had dropped the 'Murray' bit, Sam told her), were delighted to welcome her back into the fold.

The two girls confessed they had never quite understood what had made her go to Scotland and help in a hospital. America had not even been involved in the War then. 'More like Sarah, we thought,' Priscilla said, 'she's very holy.' And you're rather silly, Ginny thought, finding herself surprisingly protective of her sister although she had found she could not join in on Sarah's daily good works and church attendances.

Benjamin and Sam were both at Yale (Benjamin just up), but on vacation, and they had a bevy of friends around Wanapeake who played tennis and swam, and drove gaily from one house to another. In the evening there were tennis club 'hops'and War Fund dances which Priscilla and Polly ran and which involved a great deal of effort – selling tickets for them, raffle tickets, booking bands and arranging catering. Their efforts were laudable but somehow puny to Ginny compared with what she had seen and done in Lizzie's hospital.

When she told them one afternoon at the tennis club about the number of amputees she had nursed in Scotland, they had looked uncomfortable, especially Sam. After the others had gone to play, he spoke to her as they sat in deck-chairs on the Club verandah. 'For two pins I'd throw up Yale and volunteer. When you told me about those men . . .'

'But there's only selective conscription in America, Sam,' she said, 'and it will never come round to you. The feeling in Europe is that now General Pershing has joined forces with us, the War's nearly over.'

'Still, I feel guilty. There's Thomas. He threw up a good job in the city to join an Ambulance Unit. He's a pacifist, a serious sort of bloke, not married yet although he's twenty-eight.'

'And you're only twenty. Don't feel guilty. They're going to need young men like you in America after it's over. Live ones. But, gosh, how I worry about Jonty! He's in the thick of it, only eighteen yet.'

'He skipped school, didn't he? There you are, Ginny, that's what I mean, and here am I enjoying myself! Ben's too young to think about it yet, and Zach's only a kid. Fifteen. It's great to speak to you,' he was an engaging freckle-faced young man, she thought smiling back at him. 'You've seen those poor souls.'

'Only in a Scottish Red Cross Hospital. Ellie's the one who could give you the details, if you like. She operated in France on those poor souls, as you call them, brought straight to her from the battlefield.'

'I'm almost afraid to speak to her. Oh, she's always very nice to me, always very kind, but there's an air of remoteness about her which makes it difficult – not like you.'

'I haven't been through as much as Ellie. That's what makes her remote.' She had lost his attention. He was waving to some young people who were getting out of their motor, the girls in white tennis shirts and blouses, the men in white flannels with striped blazers.

'Here are the Trumbulls. And the Winslows! Yoo-hoo!'

He stood up to wave. 'Good for you! You made it. Come and meet my relation from Scotland!'

The thing is, Ginny thought, getting up with a smile, that I've just left an old country and this is a new one. They're different . . . but she had to admit shortly afterwards that she found Craig Trumbull very fetching, and she couldn't resist teasing him, nor could she resist his invitation to go to the tennis club dance that night, nor even for a spin up the river before that to a little roadhouse he knew. He was different from Magnus or Hamish Muir, fresher, healthier, whiter teeth, newly-minted.

'You're an eye opener, Ginny,' he told her over a long, cool drink. 'Going to Scotland has given you an extra something.' She pouted and said, did he think so? but something was wrong. Two years in Lizzie's hospital had made her ten years older.

She and Sarah generally visited Ellie and Kieran on Sunday afternoon. Ellie liked them to drop in. 'I must make sure Wolf House is still a home and not simply a place to sleep,' she had said to them. 'That's how Kieran's mother made it, a real home, a *foyer*, as they call it in France.'

Kate was still with them, but planning to go back to Scotland again. Meantime she had settled into Wolf House without usurping Ellie's place in any way, but obviously very happy to be back in her old home. On this particular Sunday she was sitting in the kitchen chatting with Mrs Vanaressi.

'We're going over old times, girls,' she said when they arrived. 'Ellie and Kieran are in the garden with James. Too much sun gives me a headache.' She smiled at Ginny. 'Scotland does that to you.'

'I would willingly send them some, wouldn't you? I'll go and say hello. Are you coming, Sarah?'

'No, I'll sit with Aunt Kate. I love to hear of the old days and Uncle James.' Her small face was tender, and Ginny felt a rush of love for this sister of hers who demanded so little of life.

Ellie and Kieran were in the stone loggia, probably because of the heat. The trellised roof which kept the sun from them was heavy with vines and was supported by stone pillars round which roses clambered, leaving the sides open to the air. The floor was of stone as well, but Ellie had spread a rug piled with cushions on which James was crawling. As Ginny came up the stone steps Ellie had just got down on the rug beside the baby in a flurry of white skirts. She looked beautiful, and younger than usual as she looked up to welcome Ginny. Her hair was tied back by a brown velvet bow.

'We were just talking about you. How strange!'

'Were you?' She got down on the rug beside her, holding out to James the rubber dog she had bought for him. 'See, James, it squeaks!' The child grasped it eagerly.

'He's so hungry for new experiences. Did you notice how he grabbed it?' Ellie looked up at Kieran. 'See, he's thrown away his bell. That's kind of you, Ginny. He loves it. Have you come alone?'

'No, Sarah's in the kitchen talking to Aunt Kate.'

'Oh, she and Mrs Vanaressi have great confabs. I think she is one of your mother's best friends, Kieran.'

'Father is the link.' He smiled. He didn't look as tired as before. His shirt was open at the neck, he was wearing thin cotton trousers and light shoes. They both looked well, Ginny thought. Her first impression had modified somewhat: this is how they were, a hard-working young couple who put themselves last.

'You haven't told me what you were saying about me,' she said.

'Oh, nothing but good, I assure you.' Ellie smiled at

her. 'I'm going to a conference in New York next weekend . . .'

'She's been asked to read a paper,' Kieran sounded proud.

'It's just a little interest of mine, about anaesthetics, but it looks as if I'll have to stay up two nights. Kieran's mother had already arranged to stay at Robert and Edie's that weekend. They have invited some friends of Maria's parents to meet her again – old Wallace Point residents who've moved to Albany – and she doesn't like to put them off.'

'So you want me to look after this little lad?' Ginny ruffled the baby's black head. How soft and silky the hair was.

'Oh, no, it's not that. I would never agree to go away unless I'd arranged it first with Rachel. It's my other little lad, Kieran.' She laughed. She's feeling guilty, Ginny thought. She's making plans so that he won't be on his own.

'I'm being disposed of,' Kieran said. His smile was one-sided. 'I was wondering if you'd let me take you a run up the Hudson next Sunday? Sarah's welcome, too. Ellie says I never take time off. We could cross the river at Peekshill and go up the west bank. Have you been to New Paltz, for instance? It originally belonged to the Huguenots who bought it from an Indian tribe in the seventeenth century. I know that's fairly modern by the Scottish standards you've become accustomed to – Robert the Bruce and all that – but it's the best we can offer. I've always wanted Ellie to get up there. There's Mount Mohonk further on and Lake Minnewaska.'

'I've never been to either,' Ginny said. 'Typical, when you've lived close at hand most of your life. I'll get my Indian head-dress ready.' She laughed. 'Seriously, I'd love to go.'

'It must sound dull to you after the fun you've been having with the Vogels and George's Polly and Sam. Has young Zach joined up with you, too?'

'No, he just loafs around making disparaging remarks about his brother and sister.'

'Give him time.'

'Are you sure you don't mind, Ginny?' Ellie said.

'Mind?' Don't insult your husband, she wanted to say. 'We'll have the time of our lives.' She spoke directly to Kieran. 'Do you think we might reach the Catskills?'

'No reason why not. We could always stay the night.' His smile was mischievous.

'So we could. Well, that's that.' Ginny stretched out on the rug, her clasped hands under her head. 'This is bliss. I'd forgotten how *predictable* the weather is at home.' She looked up at Ellie who was now sitting beside Kieran. 'I'll enjoy some intelligent conversation with Kieran for a change. I think I've picked up the Calvinistic disease in Scotland. I'm so used to their "real and earnest" – ' she laughed – 'attitude to life, that I can't take too much now of whizzing around from one tennis party to the other and talking nonsense all the time. It's more wearing than working. I can understand *you* avoiding the social whirl.'

Ellie smiled, making no comment. 'Do you think you'll go back to Scotland?'

'I don't know. I'm torn. I want to please my parents by living at home again, but do you know, Ellie, after the excitement of my arrival I have the feeling that I'm breaking up their routine. They depend on Sarah. They know where they are with her. And she never lets them down. *I'm* not like the weather. I'm *un*predictable. Mother looks at me quite anxiously sometimes as if to say, "And what are we going to do with you now?" And then when I come creeping in from those benefit dances and charity hops I feel I'm disturbing them.'

'You could do temporary work at the hospital in Wanapeake, if you like. We're rushed off our feet just now with this Spanish 'flu. I thought it was going to bypass us.'

'Yes, Giselle and Terence told me about it. The thing is, Ellie, I don't want to tie myself down.'

'Or you could leave home and train properly as a nurse. How about that?'

'That's too committing as well. It was ideal at Lizzie's. I worked hard, very hard at times, but there was no commitment, you see. I could say to her, "Do you mind if I take a few hours off and go to Glasgow?" And I enjoyed those wounded lads, helping them. I think that's what I most miss.'

'But there has to be commitment with most things.' Her pale face had that air of sadness she had noticed before. 'That's the difficulty: making choices. Lizzie's was the exception. You could slide out of it when you wanted to. Though I'm sure you didn't do much of that in spite of what you say. Lizzie was always singing your praises, and Aunt Kate, too. If I were you I'd mark time before you make up your mind whether to go back with her or not. Everything's very fluid just now. The War might be over.'

'Yes, who can tell? I hope it's over soon because of Jonty. Sometimes you feel as if he's been *too* lucky. I think of his father. . .'

On the following Sunday Mrs Vanaressi telephoned her. She was shouting as if there was no receiver in her hand and her voice had to carry from Wolf House to Claremont. 'Miss Ginny, is it?'

'Yes.' The others were at church. 'I was just setting off . . .'

'Mr Kieran didn't want me to do this.' The woman's voice was agitated. 'I've persuaded him to go up to bed.'

'Yes, he's ill, Miss Ginny, although he says it's nothing. What nonsense, with a face like his and his body shaking as if a train passes. He said don't stop her coming. We have an engagement. "Who is this you have an engagement?" I ask. He talks in a peculiar way and always those terrible shakings. "Miss Ginny," he says, "she wants to see the Catskills." "Well, there will be no Catskills for anyone, that I can tell you," I say to him. I go now to fill two hot water bottles . . .!'

'Have you telephoned the doctor?'

'No, he wouldn't hear of it.'

'I'll come right away. When you hang up the receiver, will you telephone and ask the doctor to come right away?'

'Yes. Oh, I am a silly woman! I should have paid no attention. But he can be very stubborn, Mr Kieran, gentle but stubborn . . .'

'Just do it now, Mrs Vanaressi. I'm coming right over.' She hung up.

Sarah and her parents had been driven by the chauffeur, Brewster, since it was Sunday. Her father liked him at the wheel when they went to church. She went quickly to the large coach house which now served as a garage and wheeled out a bicycle from the selection there, the one she used on her visits to the shops with Sarah.

It was five miles to Wolf House, and she arrived flushed and panting. It was even hotter than last Sunday. The great trees bordering the road seemed to prevent any breeze getting through. Sholton with its bleaker landscape was better. There you always got what Aunt Maevy called 'a good blow' from the river.

Mrs Vanaressi was waiting for her. 'Oh, you have been quick, and so hot, aren't you? Come into the kitchen and drink some lemonade.'

'Not just now.' She could see the woman was anxious. 'Did you get the doctor?'

'He was out.' She shook her head. 'His wife will try and find him. Dr Melvin. He is good, and young. He attended well to the master although he died in the end . . .'

'Yes, well, I'll go up right away and see Kieran. You know I did nursing in Scotland? Maybe I'll be able to help.'

'That was my thought. My old mistress sings about you . . . oh, she'll be so distressed that she is at Wallace Point . . .' Ginny was halfway up the stairs.

Kieran had somehow managed to get out of his clothes. They were lying in a tumbled heap half on the chair, half on the floor. He lay flat on his back in the bed, his nightshirt unbuttoned, and she could see the rise and fall of his chest as well as hear the stertorous breathing. She sat down and took his hand.

'Kieran. How are you feeling? Mrs Vanaressi telephoned me.'

'Who is it?' His voice was slurred. She saw the hectic flush of colour on his cheeks, the unfocused eyes. Her fingers were on his racing pulse. She heard a noise behind her. Mrs Vanaressi was at the door carrying a glass on a tray. She heard the clink of ice. She crossed quickly to her and half-shut the door behind them, speaking softly. 'He's ill, Mrs Vanaressi. I'm glad you brought the lemonade. Perhaps he'll sip it. Could you bring me a basin so that I could sponge him down? He has a temperature. We'll fill it here.' Uncle James had had wash-basins fitted in all the bedrooms.

'There is one in the bathroom next door. I will get it.'

She went back into the room, and crossing to the bedside, put her arm under Kieran's head and raised it. 'Sip this, Kieran.' She had the glass in her hand and put it to his lips. 'It'll make you feel cooler.'

He opened his eyes. 'Ginny . . .'

'Come on, swallow.' He gulped the lemonade greedily, spluttered, and when she gently removed her arm, he lay panting.

'I'm sorry . . . Ginny,' he said, 'spoiling things, we were going to . . .'

'It doesn't matter now. We'll do it next Sunday, what do you say? I'm going to sponge you down. You're very hot. And Mrs Vanaressi has telephoned for the doctor.'

'Melvin? No need . . .'

'Well, better safe than sorry.' She regretted that. 'How did this start, Kieran?'

'More . . .' He pointed to his mouth and she helped him to raise his head, holding the glass against his lips. 'Start . . .? Let me see. A splitting headache. It came on quite suddenly . . .' his voice trailed away. 'Ellie will be sad about this . . .'

'Have you her address?'

'Ellie . . . she's sad all the time . . . do you notice? Sad . . . but she smiles.'

'Do you know her address in New York, Kieran?' She spoke distinctly. Mrs Vanaressi was at her side with the basin.

'It's in the kitchen,' the woman said. 'She never forgets anything. It's written on the blackboard, and the telephone number. And the telephone number of Springhill also if I should wish to speak with Mr Kieran's mother. Everything is methodical here. Because of the baby, you see.'

'I'll go down, but first, would you fill the basin with tepid water, please, and bring it to me with a flannel?'

'You sponge him down? That is good.' When she had brought the basin and put it on the chair beside the bed, their eyes met. She knew what it was, Ginny thought. It was in the papers. People didn't talk about it much, preferring not to as long as it didn't spread in Wanapeake. But Ellie was at a hospital every day where germs abounded.

Mrs Vanaressi knew. So did she. It was influenza, the dreadful Spanish variety which the papers said was killing as many men as the War, a special virus which some said originated in Spain, others in France and yet others in places as far apart as China and Kansas. Pandemic. She remembered talking about it with Giselle. And it had found another haven in this thin body which she was uncovering.

She helped Ginny to take the nightshirt over Kieran's head. It was nothing to her, her movements seemed to say. Hadn't she three grown-up sons in New York? She folded the bedclothes well back so that Ginny could sponge his burning body. Steam rose from the flannel although the water was tepid.

'Why . . . are you taking off . . .?' His hand fell on hers as if to dissuade her.

'Because I'm sponging you down and it seems sensible,' Ginny said briskly, 'let me get on.'

'You're . . . cheeky,' he said. 'That's what Ellie calls James sometimes. Cheeky . . . it's Scottish . . . and then she hugs him . . . hugs him . . .'

'Well, he's a lovely little boy. Is that nice? Cooler?'

'Paris . . . it was nice in Paris. We walked in the Bois . . . You're . . . allowed to walk in the Bois . . . anywhere. Under the trees. The leaves . . . scrunched . . . is that a Scottish word? . . . under our . . . feet. She says,' he smiled, 'Ellie . . . "It's all . . . scrunched up. I'll have to iron it" . . . her white dress. That's nice . . . cool, oh, cool . . . fair hair, hasn't she? She's never cut it . . . bobbed . . .' he smiled, 'funny word, bobbed . . . And in the morning . . . when she gets . . . out of bed, she brushes it, so quickly, and *whirls* it up . . . anxious to get away . . . always anxious to get away . . .' The door bell rang.

'That's the door,' Ginny said to Mrs Vanaressi. What on earth was the woman making of Kieran's rambling? She remembered Ellie's mother talking once about Susan, that nice housekeeper who had died, and saying they knew everything, servants . . .

'I go down quickly and bring the doctor,' Mrs Vanaressi said. She was another one who knew everything.

15

Dr Melvin was under forty, judging by his unlined skin and springy gait, but he was prematurely grey and bald on top. All his growth of hair seemed to have concentrated in his eyebrows which were bushy and strangely black.

'I'm sorry to be so long,' he said. 'Wife got me at the Country Club. We don't get many calls on a Sunday afternoon.' He was eyeing Kieran professionally as he spoke. 'Didn't expect to find you here, Ginny.'

'Mrs Vanaressi telephoned me. Kieran and I were going for a motor run but she became alarmed . . .' Dr Melvin was bending over Kieran as he listened to her. He had taken his hand.

'Hello, Kieran. Remember me? Not feeling so well, eh?' Kieran opened his eyes.

'Is it Dr . . .?'

'That's right, Dr Melvin. Your cousin's been looking after you, I hear.' His fingers were on Kieran's pulse as he looked at his watch. Ginny saw his brows draw together. 'Now, I'm going to sound you, old lad, see how your chest's behaving.'

'I sponged him down,' Ginny said, and, seeing a twitch in his eyebrows, 'Mrs Varanessi helped me. He was burning hot.'

'Yes, pretty high temperature.' He replaced his watch in his pocket and began listening to Kieran's chest through his stethoscope. As he tapped she recognized the difference in the sound his fingers made. He straightened, remained as he was, looking down at Kieran.

'What do you think?' Ginny said.

He turned. 'I know you were nursing in Scotland. Have you guessed?' She shaped the word with her lips, and he nodded. 'Spanish variety. The first case in Wanapeake. Have to be notified. We were hoping . . .'

Kieran said distinctly, 'What's all the fuss, Melvin? Can I get up? Ginny's waiting . . .'

'You can't get up, old son.' He put the bedclothes over Kieran's bare chest. 'You're ill. You've picked up Spanish 'flu somewhere.'

'Not in Spain.' She saw the rift at the corner of his mouth.

'It's all over the place now. This is probably the best place to get it, in your own home. You'll need careful nursing. I'll arrange for someone to come in right away.' He said to Ginny, 'Where's Miss McNab?' That would be her professional name here.

'She's giving a paper at a conference of surgeons in New York. That was why . . .'

'I should get in touch with her right away. Tell her to come home. She's better here, take charge.' He bit his lip reflectively, 'Wasn't his mother staying?'

'She's visiting over at Wallace Point.'

'Ah. Well, could you hold the fort until either of them comes?'

'Yes, of course. If you tell me what to do.'

'We'll have to fight it, that's for sure. It can be . . .' 'Lethal'? she wondered. 'We'll set up steam inhalations, plenty of fluids, of course, and plenty of sponging down. Nourishing fluids, if you can get them into him. Build him up and sponge him down, that's the trick. It's his chest that's worrying me . . .' He looked down at Kieran who lay with his eyes closed. Was it her imagination, or was there a thin thread of blue outlining his lips? 'But, there's the congestion.' He straightened as if he had made up his mind. 'We'll try cupping. Have you ever seen it done?'

'No.'

'Well, here's your chance.' He lifted his bag from the floor, opened it and produced a heavy glass cup which he placed on the bedside table. 'That's it. Now we need . . .' He rummaged again in his bag and brought out a glass rod and some cotton, plunged once more and placed a small bottle of alcohol beside the rest, and a box of matches. 'Sometimes it's necessary to make a cross-cut on the skin before the cupping but we'll leave that out for the first time.'

'Does it . . . cupping . . . help?'

'Oh, yes, I've seen good results with congestion. Now, I want you to get as close to Kieran with me as you can. Take up that glass rod with the cotton, that's right, dip it into the alcohol and light it. Have you got that?'

'Yes.'

'Speed is of the essence. Right. Now, light your rod, pop it into the cup,' he was holding it, 'withdraw it right away . . . good girl!' He pressed the cup firmly on Kieran's thorax.

Kieran submitted to the process without complaint. He seemed to have gone away from them, except for a slight start when the cup pressed on his chest, and she saw Dr Melvin was grim-faced.

'Is it bad?' she asked him after a time when she felt they could talk.

'Bad.' He nodded. 'It's fortuitous that he's semi-conscious while this is being done, but that won't last. The pain's going to be terrible, all over his body, sore throat, sickening headache, especially the back of his head. Oh, yes, he's going to know all about it, poor lad. It's a battle. I only hope his wife gets here soon.'

Kieran stirred, moaned. 'Ellie . . .' he said.

'Your cousin's just going to get her, Kieran.'

'Keep James away.' He had become agitated. 'And Rachel. That's his nurse. Don't let them in! Maybe there should be a sheet across the door . . . for the plague. She'd never forgive me if James . . . where's Ginny?'

'I'm here, Kieran.' She bent over him and the odour from the poison in his body sickened her for a moment. 'Dr Melvin's leaving now. I'm going to send up Mrs Vanaressi to sit with you for a few minutes while I telephone to Ellie and Aunt Kate . . .'

'Aunt Kate? Who's Aunt Kate?'

'Your mother, silly.' She took his hand. It was burning.

'On you go.' Dr Melvin's eyebrows indicated the door. 'I'll wait till the housekeeper comes up. Remember, plenty of fluids and call me if there's any change. I'll look in again later.'

'Thanks.' She went running down the stairs, thinking of the randomness of life – one minute the Catskills, next minute this . . .

She telephoned to Kieran's mother first since she was nearer, but her heart fell when Edie told her she was not there.

'That's terrible news about Kieran,' she said. 'So sudden! But Aunt Kate's gone off with those friends from Albany for a few days. They were so insistent. I could see she didn't really want to go, but she said to me – you know Aunt Kate – that perhaps she should since it would give Ellie and Kieran some time on their own.'

'She wasn't to know. I'll try to get Ellie now.'

'You need some support. I'll come over by the next ferry.'

'Definitely not in your condition. Pregnant women are particularly vulnerable. Ellie will be here soon. She won't be able to get home fast enough.'

Again she was unlucky. Ellie had given her lecture, the

clerk at the Conference Centre told her, and had been persuaded to join a tour of hospitals in Long Island. They didn't know where exactly she would be at this minute, but rest assured, they would get in touch with her as soon as possible since it was a matter of such urgency.

She hung up the receiver. There was no doubt about it, she would have to hold the fort until Ellie or Aunt Kate arrived, or the nurse whom Dr Melvin was going to provide.

She ran quickly upstairs and when she opened the door she saw that Mrs Vanaressi was trying to hold Kieran down in the bed. She turned a worried face to her. 'He gets very excited, Miss Ginny. And saying terrible things, hard things . . .'

She took Mrs Vanaressi's place, bending over Kieran and holding him firmly by the shoulders while he struggled. 'Kieran,' she said, 'it's Ginny. Nothing's going to happen to you. Ellie's on her way here . . .'

'You shouldn't have brought her from her conference!' His face was livid. 'It was important . . . and who's that woman? The black-haired one? She wants to bring James in! There's no sheet . . . no sheet . . .!'

'He talks all the time about a sheet!' Mrs Vanaressi was nearly in tears.

'It's all right, Kieran, all right. No one's going to harm James. You know how we all love him. Try and be calm. You're not doing yourself a bit of good . . .'

'It doesn't matter about me. Maybe I should die. That would solve things . . .'

'What nonsense you talk! You just want people to feel sorry for you. Dr Melvin says you have to drink plenty of fluids. Try and sip this.' He seemed calmer, and she helped him to partially sit up while he drank from the glass of water she held out to him. She had brought a large jug from the kitchen.

'Ah, that was good!' He sighed.'There's a fire inside me . . . raging . . . burning . . . is my head still on?'

'Of course it's on.' She laughed.

'It doesn't feel as if it is.' He closed his eyes.

She said to Mrs Vanaressi as she straightened the bedclothes, 'Go down and have a rest now. And I don't think you should come up any more than you can help. I'll fetch iced water from the kitchen myself.'

'Do you mean because of the infection?'

'Yes. You cook for the staff, Mrs Vanaressi and we can't be too careful. A small child is very vulnerable.'

The woman nodded. 'Did you find the young mistress?'

'No, but they'll pass the message on to her. She'll be on her way by now. But his mother has gone to Albany with friends. Perhaps it's as well. Now, on you go and have a rest.' She was probably as old as Aunt Kate.

'A rest! Pooh!' She shrugged her shoulders. 'But, yes, you are right. We must be careful not to carry infection to the little one. And you must eat. I'll bring up a tray. If you think it wise, I'll leave it outside the door.'

'Don't bother about me. The main thing is plenty of water for Kieran. I'll get tepid water for sponging him here.'

'It's what we thought, then?'

'Yes, I'm afraid so.'

She looked at Kieran, seemingly asleep, his head jerking sometimes on the pillow, his brows drawn in pain, his face devoid of colour. 'He wasn't well before he got this. I've watched him. He'll have to fight.'

The waiting time was a nightmare while she wrestled with Kieran in his delirium, soothed him with words, even silly songs, induced him to drink (there was no trouble there. He had a raging thirst), and continually sponged him down. He was incontinent, and she had to call on Mrs Vanaressi to find him fresh sheets.

No nurse arrived, but Dr Melvin did around seven o'clock, harassed, his eyebrows bunched together over his eyes. 'The worst possible day to get anyone. I'll manage it by Monday morning, I doubt before. No word from Miss McNab?' He was still formal in his reference to Ellie, a professional colleague first and foremost.

'Not yet, but she'll be here as soon as they can find her. I can manage.'

'You'll have to, I'm afraid, Ginny.' He cupped Kieran again and went away, having left a sedative for him, if she thought he needed it. But it was difficult to decide. He seemed to alternate between delirium and a state of semi-consciousness.

At three o'clock in the morning, when Ginny was dozing in a chair, she heard the sound of an engine outside, the slam of a motor car door, someone entering the hall and then come running upstairs. Ellie was in the doorway, hatless, pale. 'Ginny! Oh, how is he?'

'Sleeping just now . . .'

'I got your message when we were at Southampton. It followed me there.'

'Ellie . . .' It was Kieran. She went to the bedside, and bending over him, kissed his brow.

'I wouldn't have left you for the world.' There was anguish in her voice, and then Ginny saw her professionalism take over as she felt his pulse, put her head down on his chest to listen to it, ask him questions. 'How often has the doctor been?' she said to Ginny over her shoulder.

'Twice. He'll be here again first thing in the morning.'

'Good.' She sat down on the bed. Kieran had relapsed into a semi-conscious state again. She looked wretched, hollow-eyed with tiredness and anxiety, but fully in command of herself. 'He's pretty bad.' She had dropped her voice. 'Do you know if the doctor took swabs of his throat?'

'No, I don't think so. But he cupped him.'

'It might help. Has he been incontinent?'

'Yes.'

'What was his temperature when you took it last?'

'One hundred and five.'

'It's still up. You've been giving him plenty of fluids?'

'Yes, I've even wakened him up and made him drink. I know how important it is.' She could suddenly have yawned in her cousin's face with tiredness. It was the relief of seeing her.

'Ginny,' Ellie's voice was gentle, 'forgive me. I haven't even thanked you for all you've done. You've been that kind. Weren't they able to get Kieran's mother?'

'No, she's gone to Albany with friends.'

'Perhaps it's as well. It would only have distressed her. Now we'll not talk any more.' She got up. 'Come along with me.'

'Where to?' She got up, feeling stupid with fatigue.

'I'm going to show you where to sleep. You're dropping on your feet.' She looked at Kieran, then got up and went quickly out of the room, Ginny following at her heels. She opened a door at the end of the corridor. 'Here you are. There's a bathroom, too. Have a bath if you can be bothered, if not, just tumble into bed. There are night-gowns in the top drawer.'

'You're tired, too . . .'

'No, I'm not. I must get back to him.'

'Try not to worry, Ellie.' She would have liked to say more, but could hardly stand with tiredness. She saw how her cousin's face twisted at her words.

'I blame myself. It's those . . . choices . . .' She went quickly out of the room.

She didn't mention James, Ginny thought, the moment before sleep engulfed her.

The next morning, when Ginny dressed and went downstairs, she found Ellie in the dining-room. She was as pale as a sheet, but immaculate. Her hair was freshly brushed. 'How is Kieran?' she asked. She felt it must be a good sign her being here.

'No change. The nurse arrived this morning and she insisted on me going down for breakfast. She's the officious type but I didn't like to put her back up right away. I think I'll tell Dr Melvin I can manage quite well without her.'

'Did you get any sleep last night?'

'No, but I'm used to it.'

Ginny poured herself some coffee. 'I shouldn't get rid of the nurse, Ellie. She'll take charge of Kieran while you're at the hospital, and then you can take over at night, if it's needed.'

'Oh, I'm not going back to the hospital! Not while Kieran's ill. I've already asked for leave of absence.'

'Oh!'

'I'll do it the other way round. I'll be with Kieran during the day and then if Dr Melvin can get me a night nurse that would be better.'

'You and I could do it together,' Ginny said. She was having one of Mrs Vanaressi's waffles with maple syrup. Nothing had ever tasted so good.

'I'd love that, but your parents might object. You know it's infectious.'

'Well, if it is I've got it.'

'But there's no point in compounding the felony. That would be irresponsible on my part.' She smiled wanly. 'I have enough on my conscience. No, what you can give me, Ginny, is your moral support. Come round and see me from time to time and have a peep in at Kieran, no more. I'm hoping in a few days he'll be on the mend.' Was that a considered medical opinion (she must know the incidence of fatalities better than she did), or a deliberate shutting of her eyes?

'I'd like to. But remember if the nurse lets you down I'm your man, and available at any hour of the day or night, distance no object.' She laughed.

'I didn't thank you properly last night. You're a grand girl.' Her eyes were moist as she looked up. 'Now, get on with your breakfast and report back to Claremont. I've phoned your mother to say you'll soon be home. Mrs Vanaressi let her know last night you were staying.'

'Yes, she told me.'

'I'm going to have a little look at James, from afar.' She got up, leaving her toast untouched, her coffee half-drunk, and went quickly out of the room.

There's something about her, Ginny thought later, riding home in the comparative cool of the morning, something very touching, a sadness, Kieran had said. She must be worried out of her mind.

She called each day and there was no change. And then the third day when she arrived, she met Dr Melvin on the steps. 'Is he getting better?' she asked him.

He shook his head. 'No. It's high time he did. Away and talk to that cousin of yours and cheer her up a bit. She's worrying her heart out.'

They spoke through the open doorway. He wasn't rallying, she told Ginny, her voice calm. The chest infection was the chief worry. And his bones ached, poor Kieran, they ached *that* badly. He was getting aspirin for that.

'It's always like this with those foreign bugs,' Ginny

said jauntily, her eyes on Kieran lying motionless in the bed. 'They're invaders. You have to fight them.'

'Do you hear that, Kieran?' She watched Ellie bend over him and saw the aquilinity of her profile, the seared circles under her eyes, 'Ginny says you have to fight. Isn't that what I've been telling you?'

'Fight?' She heard his voice. It was weaker. 'I'm tired . . . leave me be . . .'

'I'll not leave you be.' Her voice was shaking. 'You're wicked to say that, to punish me. You can get better if you try. Aren't you listening to me, my darling? It's Ellie speaking to you, your wife. You must get better for me, please . . .' Ginny slipped away.

16

He missed Jimmy to laugh with. There was no one in the platoon near his age, and he objected to being treated as the baby. One of the men had discovered that he was called 'Jonty' at home (he'd slipped up there), and it seemed to amuse them. It was so un-Scottish, not sturdy like Alastair or Calum or Donald. If they had known that it was Nigel Jonathan they would have had a fit.

He and Jimmy would have laughed at the latest Army Order which decreed that a salute should be made always with the right hand and never with the left. 'God knows whit Gerry wid hae said aboot that!' He had a recurring nightmare where Jimmy raised himself from the mud, his face bloody, his right arm blown off, a look of agony in his eyes, not for the loss of his arm but for the fact that it was his saluting one.

He no longer felt noble and ready to die for his country, the nearer to death he came. He no longer wrote any poetry.

The objective was a sunken road known as Gloucester Road, overlooked on the left from Villers Guislain. It might have been overlooked, but at five-forty in the morning, as well as a creeping barrage as they advanced, there was a creeping mist which obliterated the village and clung to the fields.

On such a morning at home he might have gone out with one of the gamekeepers to shoot rabbits, more because it was expected of him than because he liked it. He had always felt shameful when he laid the fur-blooded carcasses on the kitchen table and saw the respectful pleasure on Cook's face – The Young Lord Fulfilling His Role, subject for a poem.

He missed the support of the tanks. They were like father figures blundering along in front of them, he felt somehow rejected without them, and perhaps so did the others because the artillery fire was weak and ineffective.

Not so that of the Germans. He saw Joseph Connolly, a Glasgow keelie, dangling grotesquely on the barbed wire, or rather his corpse, as if it was there for target practice. He would never see his back court again where he'd climbed over ('dreeped ower', they said) the wash-house roofs with his pals as a boy, his kingdom. It was strange how often grown men talked about their boyhood and not their wives and children.

There were others now, dangling, lying, hopping on one foot, cursing. Gerry was picking them off like Aunt Sallies at the Sholton Fair. They didn't seem to want to pick *him* off, for some reason. He crept along with the last two platoons, even when the Major had been wounded. 'The buggers are trigger-happy,' a man said beside him. If the War was going to be over as soon as they all said, the Germans were showing the courage of desperation.

They reached Gloucester Road and they were still being sniped at. Two new recruits who had joined the battalion the previous week fell together beside him, their bodies forming a cross. He had the odd feeling of taking part in a spectacle but not being part of it, like being in a school play. 'The slings and arrows of outrageous fortune . . .' They were all around him here, too, but he was impervious. It couldn't last . . . he had been saying that for ages, but it had.

Maybe it was because he never felt fear. Before they started, yes, mostly in the bowels so that he was running to the latrine up to the last minute (it had been the same in the school play), but never when he was in the middle of things. It seemed like one of those early morning stalkings at the Hall, and with the same lack of danger.

He had worked it out that he was so afraid that he had gone through some barrier of fear into a state where he could feel nothing. And that he was encased as if in armour. 'What did you do in the Great War, Jonty?' 'I don't know. I was in a state of shock . . .'

Even when they were driven back without gaining a foothold and he saw Gloucester Road full of corpses, he felt nothing. The state of shock was so deep and had lasted so long that you could have driven a sliver into his heart and he would have felt nothing. He had a brief stab that perhaps that had happened, and this was his ghost . . . and then, nothing again. Even the disembowelled body he tripped over, with the mince-like entrails in a stinking heap, did not make him turn away.

Over their canteens of stew that night he took part in a conversation about why dead Germans had bayonet wounds and the British mostly head wounds. 'The significance is,' he said . . . and someone called out, 'Watch it, Crawford. They'll make you a bloody officer if you're not careful!' It was all more or less the equivalent of bashing your head against a brick wall, he told himself. It wasn't time yet to feel anything.

They were at it again the following night, creeping towards Meath Post which they had to capture. That was a walkover. He didn't know how it was done. All in half-an-hour. They must be getting good at it, even to the extent of taking quite a lot of German prisoners. They looked quite decent men, relieved, apologetic. He thought of shaking hands with them and saying, 'Enough of this, don't you think? Let's go home.' When his hand was half-way out he retrieved it, thinking that for a moment he had taken leave of his senses.

Then, on to Gloucester Road. The bodies were stinking now. There was machine gun fire from the direction of Villers-Guislain but none of it found him. *Christ Walking On The Battlefield. Me*. Poem. But every soldier felt like Christ walking on the water until a German bullet found him. And those who might have been feeling omnipotent at that moment were being disabused of the idea. Summarily.

A group of Germans who had been missed at the Post had come out and opened fire with good results. Jonty saw his own lieutenant lie down gently and die. The state of shock, if that was what it was, deepened. After that he found himself constructing blocks in the sunken road and realized that he had hands and arms and feet and legs and his head hadn't been bashed in or lifted from his shoulders. *Headless Man Helps To Construct Blocks*. He didn't feel invincible, only impervious.

By the twenty-second September the new Front was consolidated, the blocks were constructed and they had withdrawn to Meath Post. All prisoners and wounded had been evacuated. Neat, QED. They set off, kilts swinging round their thighs, to their bivouacs. It was only then that he climbed out of the state of shock and the shaking began. He decided to write to Ginny.

One thing a man will never know (he felt grown-up writing that), is the agony of childbirth. You'll think I've gone off my nut when you read a sentence like that, but the situations we get into here, or the situations we are sent into, must be the same. You must go forward. If you turn you'd be shot in the back. You're in a vice, and it's then I say to myself, 'Well, you walked into it, Jonty, straight into the snare,' the snare of disillusion because that's what it's become.

I'm sick of the sight of rotting corpses, mutilated corpses; sometimes I want to be one of them just to get it over with. And yet I know I'll do what I'm told, I'll walk into enemy fire, I'll put up with the mud and the rats and the miserable food and the dirty jokes. People talk about the wonderful camaraderie. I felt it with Jimmy who was killed, and I might have felt it with the two new recruits who were killed yesterday. But most of the men treat me as a kid, pull my leg. They know I ran away from school and they think I'm crazy. The only thing they envy me for is that I haven't 'bought one' yet. They rub themselves against me for luck when they go up the firestep, say, 'Stick to wee Jonty. He'll see you through.' It's a race between my luck holding out and the end of the War. I don't want to die. I want to come back to Sholton and see Mother and Ernest, to go to university perhaps, or take on that job Aunt Maevy wrote to me about. 'This is something for you to hold on to, Jonty', she said. 'You have to think positively. I did and I've now got the Vote!' She's a grand lady, isn't she? Non-variable.

I'm sorry to hear about Kieran having caught the Spanish 'flu. Thousands have died out here, especially the Americans, though strangely enough, no one I know. He must have been run down to get it. You sound very despondent about him. Yes, I agree. It would be terrible for Ellie if he died. You don't expect that in your own home. Give them my love . . .

They had to reach Villers-Guislain and the high ground overlooking the Canal. Everyone understood that on both sides, and it became a ding-dong battle. What was more difficult to accept the following morning was the regular lines of dead soldiers, headed by their officers, covering the slope of the hill. They had been mown down by machine gun fire. The sight got through to him, making him turn away, sickened and defeated by it all. 'By God, they had courage!' the orderly whom he was helping said to him. It didn't excuse it. *Horizontal Lines*. Poem.

Headquarters were established while they talked about the next move. So you presumed. You could let them get on with it. He was happy where he was, having gained a certain amount of popularity by his ability to cadge eggs from the farmer's daughter. There were plenty of rude jokes about payment, but he was used to that. It was mild compared to some of the stuff they came away with.

The farmer's daugher was all right, reminding him a little of Giselle, but because of her gender rather than her femininity, which was practically non-existent. He realized that his mother supplied something essential in his life with her beauty, her engaging mannerisms, her perfume – the whole concept of her in his mind gave him pleasure; and although the girl didn't even smell nice, the sight of her tight cotton dress buttoned over her full bosom and the black hair pulled back from her face to reveal small, feminine ears, was like a breath of fresh air, or as fresh as you could get it here. But he would never have dreamt of touching her. She was simply there to look at and to smell, if you could separate her feminine odour from the farmyard one.

But he lost that pleasure when they moved on to Honnecourt Wood and there were no farm doors to knock on. The news was good. The Canal had been crossed successfully and, along with his battalion, Jonty went over at Honnecourt. They were now part of the Hindenburg Support Line, and once again he was working like a navvy, helping to build bridges this time. He noticed how hard and strong his muscles were and he felt fit, and apologetic about being fit.

Now it became a race with death. *He Ran an Even Race With Death* . . .? No, throw that one out as an idea. Too banal. Still, it would be a shame if he were killed off so near the end. He knew it was near the end. The feeling ran through the men, made them snappy, and careful, but somehow much friendlier. It was the few days before school broke up all over again, when you promised your friends you would write and felt that on the whole that chap you'd hated wasn't so bad after all. Now, when it was almost too late, he was beginning to fit in, the others were beginning to accept his being different, his youth, his speech.

Clary was the objective. Third Army Orders for the ninth October provided for a continuation of operations. Aubencheulaux-Bois, Villers Outreaux, Malincourt. Would those names be engraved on his memory till the day he died? There was the feeling of a great, swinging movement now, nothing could go wrong. The Might of The Allied Armies, he thought of it in capitals, of which he was a part, was sweeping all before it.

They walked into the *Place de la Mairie* with bagpipes playing and the place alive with cheering people waving French flags. They crowded round to give them flowers, to kiss them; somewhere in the background a tinny gramophone was playing *La Marseillaise*. You could almost tell yourself that nothing bad had happened to you, that it had been 'See the Conquering Hero Comes' all the time, marching and singing all the way from Villers-Guislain through the undulating countryside, the deep valleys with the dark woods on the ridges, the rivers, the blue ribbon of the Scheldt Canal . . . No festering blisters, no fear in your guts, no limbo; everybody friendly, the larks singing, a soldier's idyll. No decomposing bodies in the ditches, no blasted trees, mud, filth, rats: it had been all a play, a charade, with the people of Clary now playing their part as a triumphant chorus. There was even a little girr who hung a daisy chain round his neck, '*Merci, monsieur*.'

Battalion Headquarters moved in and established themselves in the village, everyone went around looking very important, and there was peace in the land for a day and a night. The next day they were swinging out of Clary and towards Troisvilles. Sholton, here I come! Mother, kill the fatted calf. Have a party. Ask up all the soldiers, the blind, the halt and the lame. Or perhaps the hospital was already closed and Mother had started on her Great Plan.

But the Germans did not seem to know when to lay

down their arms, although the whole of the battalion was assaulting them. Even when they were chased down Le Cateau-Inchy road and were kept under fire by a howitzer battery. The hunt was up. Everybody lost their tiredness as they followed the retreating Germans in Pied Piper fashion into a nest of machine gunfire beside the river. Jonty was beside the captain when he was killed. That was useless, a bloody useless death so near the end. Or was it so near the end? They did not swing so jauntily as they marched back to Troisvilles behind the NCO.

The euphoria was over. Now it was a business-like arrangement of setting off on the 22 October to cross the Selle and establish an outpost line prior to attacking the next day. The men talked that night about what they would do to the Germans at the Big Kill. The smaller the man the bigger the talk.

Zero hour was fixed at 2 A.M., and because he was dozing against a wall in full battle-dress waiting to go, his nightmare came back. Jimmy struggled up from the mud, his face agonized, the bloody stem of his arm quivering. When he wakened he could not shake off the unease as they marched off to take up the position of assembly.

Maybe it was because they were all tense that there was a good deal of confusion when the barrage hit them. The sight of men lying dead before they had even started, others screaming in agony, disheartened everybody. It was an augury. 'Had bloody well enough of this,' a man said beside him. 'Who said the War was bloody well over bar the shouting?'

Perhaps it was because they were anxious to get away from the assembly point that they went through the resistance towards their next objective 'like a knife through butter', as Forbes said, a Glasgow man in his thirties, bow-legged through rickets. He's going to stick to me like a leech, Jonty thought, and give me his considered opinion all the time. Maybe they would lose each other. That was an euphemistic way of putting it.

The village lads at Sholton played rounders at school. It was a good game. He often wished they had played it at the Dragon. This advance became like a game of rounders also, bounding towards their objective, waiting until the barrage died down, bounding towards the next. Everybody was pleased when they reached the one near Ovillers without any trouble, pleased also with the booty, the prisoners, the guns, the trench mortars, and the big prize, fifty machine guns.

The following day it was the same game again. 'Like takin' toffee aff a wean.' Forbes had surfaced again, unluckily. But he retracted that, feeling ashamed. He was a fine wee man, the salt of the earth. The euphoria was back.

Vendegies Wood now. Mother would never find those places unless she had a large-scale map. But in any case it was Paris she liked, for its smartness. He was lucky to have a mother like her, truly sophisticated, the envy of all the other boys when she came to visit him at school . . .

Running up towards the crest. 'Mind the wire, lads!' The Platoon Commander shouting. It was the euphoria to blame. He got caught by it as he was bending down, and as he struggled to free himself he felt a searing pain in his shoulder and a noise in his ears far louder than the noise from the German machine guns. He'd been hit. He'd been *hit*!

He was still conscious enough to realize that in his predicament there were only two alternatives: to be shot again which would finish him, or to be taken prisoner. The ignominy of the second came over him, making him sweat. He twisted his neck round but it increased the pain so much that the shout for help was strangled in his throat.

Two men from another platoon began clambering through on either side of him. 'Get me off this wire!' he shouted to them, but a louder shout behind them drowned his and the men were through and away without a backward glance.

Anyone caught in the wire was a sitting target. The next man who was climbing through obviously realized that to keep on the move was the only way to stay alive – for the time being. They had all seen the scarecrows which had once been men, dangling.

This time he was taking no chances. Besides, he had just caught sight of Forbes who seemed always to be bobbing along at his elbow. He gathered the strength to shout but it turned into a piercing yell. 'Git me aff this bliddy wire, ya wee bastard!'

Forbes stopped in his tracks and stared, his little rabbit chin working, then his face cleared. 'Ach, sonny, whit ur ye daein there, for Pete's sake?' He extricated him speedily and none too carefully, tearing the flesh of one of his buttocks in the process, and dragged him to the side, making him speechless now with the double pain. 'The Rid Croass'll be alang in a meenute. Ta-ta, Bella!' He louped, the only word for it, over the wire, and was gone.

He tried to crawl towards a tree, but the jarring made tears come into his eyes. He rested and went on, and had made about ten yards when two orderlies appeared with a stretcher. They bundled him onto it and set off, joggling him cruelly.

'Where did it get you?' one asked him kindly. He put his hand on his shoulder, speechless with the pain. It came away sticky and he held it up.

'In the shoother, wis it, eh sonny?' the man said. The anger increased his pain. 'Sonny', and he a veteran, wounded in battle!

Getting back to the ADS was pretty bad. It was the *shooglin*. When it came to the bit the Scottish words couldn't be beaten. Onomatopoeic. He was surprised he remembered the word. And then he drifted into a state of semi-consciousness which was partly self-induced.

He thought of home and the family, of Annabel and Kit. Mouse would now be twelve. He saw her clearly, her sweet pointed face and that wispy hair of hers, so unlike Mother's. And Kit, ten, with his good looks, the McGrath good looks, Mother had once said: the reddish fair hair, the brilliant eyes, the fine complexion. 'He'll make many a lass sigh at her supper,' she had said.

Would *he*? Would he meet some beautiful girl, something between Ginny and Ellie, and live in one of the stable cottages which Mother was going to have altered? They would be special. She had a flair. Of course, once he was in the antique business he would travel to Paris and New York. Indeed, he might have a *pied-à-terre* in either or both of them . . . he was brought back to reality by the sound of snipping scissors as his jacket was torn from him. 'Oh God!' He tried not to screw up his face.

He heard the doctor's voice, felt the sting of disinfectant, the rough cleansing of the wound. He wouldn't make a good GP, that was for sure. Not like Belle Geddes . . . those strange eyes 'Compound fracture of the scapula,' he heard him say to the ambulance orderly. Then there was a period of such pain while they put adhesive plaster on and put his arm in a sling, that he felt small explosions in his brain and hung in a sea of pain. Pain was coloured. Red. Pulsing red.

'There's a bit oot o' his bum,' he heard the orderly say, but fortunately the dressing of that hardly hurt. All pain was relative.

'Send him up the line for hospitalization.' He saw through half-closed eyes the doctor write out a card and tie it to his wrist, felt the jar in the broken shoulder as he slapped the other one. 'Well, you've been a clever lad. Bought a nice one. I think it should see you through to the end.' He didn't feel sorry about that. He remembered he had had his moment of glory at Clary.

On the eleventh of November at eleven o'clock, the hospital ship steamed out of Le Havre, bound for Portsmouth. His arm was in a sling, he still had a plaster on his backside, but he felt good. He had all his limbs and the War was over.

17

Giselle clung to Terence's arm. It would be terrible if she lost him in the crowds in the Champs-Elysées after nearly losing him at Verdun. 'Everyone's delirious with excitement,' she said to him. 'So am I. The War's over and you're getting better . . .'

'*C'est vrai*,' he smiled at her.

'And really, our whole family have been very lucky, although Marc and Oliver were never in a great deal of danger. But then they are diplomats!' She laughed. 'And now the good news of Jonty! He will be on his way home.'

He nodded. 'That would have been the cruellest blow of fate for Lizzie. But I think he's born lucky, that young man, just as some people are born unlucky.'

'Not yourself?' She looked up at him. He would never be really well again. They both knew that. The gas had ruined his chest. But, fortunately, he was not a labourer. His painting did not demand great physical strength from him, only moral and artistic fibre, and surely he had plenty of that? Of course, he had his 'down' times, as she called them to herself. Who wouldn't after what he had been through?

'Oh, I'm lucky. I've got you, and the two babies, and still a desire to paint if this old arm will let me.' And if the desire leaves him the arm will be the excuse, she thought, with insight . . . no, she wasn't going to spoil this great day. 'I'm counting on everyone wanting their portraits painted now.'

'If they can afford your prices!' She laughed.

'Yes, there's that.' I wasn't being *literal*, Terence.

'Don't let's be gloomy!' She squeezed his arm. 'The War's over, and look at those flags! Shall we walk on to see the booty taken from the Huns?'

'"Huns"!' She had made him smile. 'All right, let's gloat.' He bent and kissed her. 'Everybody's allowed a little gloat, wouldn't you say? Keep tight hold of my good arm. I don't want to lose you.'

Bands were playing, people were singing 'Le Madelon', soldiers were being kissed, at one stage they linked arms with a crowd of people and danced a farandole down the middle of the street.

The Avenue Alexander II was lined with field artillery right up to the Pont Alexandre and on either side of the Champs-Elysées, about fifteen feet apart, as far as the Place de la Concorde. Another crowd of people had yoked themselves to a cannon and were pulling it along the middle of the street. The soldiers sitting on top of it were waving bottles of champagne which had been pushed into their hands.

'*Vive Clemenceau!*' they shouted. '*Vive Joffre!*' a rival faction responded, to be drowned by an ever louder shout, '*Vive Foch!*'

'Listen to them!' Terence said.

'*Merveilleux!* It's even better than Mistinguette's high kicks at the Casino! Look at that huge tank! And the Krupps Cannon! They've captured that beast at last!'

'And the German helmets covering those monuments! What a pity Clovis and Jaime weren't here to see the fun.'

'They might have been jostled. Besides, it's our own celebration. Afterwards we'll go to our little café at Passy and join in the singing. *Mon Dieu!*' She hid against his shoulder at the noise above them. 'That aeroplane! He's doing stunts above our heads. Wouldn't it be too dreadful if he were killed in the hour of victory?'

'He knows what he's doing. Come on, let's join in. You take the bad arm.' They ran into the middle of the street to join on to a long line of people dancing down the middle of it. The woman whose hand Giselle was holding turned to her, tears streaming down her face.

'I lost my son, but I thought, why be selfish? Go out and celebrate with the others.' Giselle smelled the wine on her breath, saw her flushed cheeks. 'I'm celebrating for the dead, you know. *Vive les Morts!*' she shouted, dropping Giselle's hand to wave her own in the air. '*Vive les Morts!*'

Her joy went. We're dancing on graves, she thought. She looked at Terence. His chest was heaving, his face grey with the effort of keeping up with the others. 'Let's go back now,' she said to him.

They sat over their Pernods in the little café which was no less busy than the streets. People spilled out on to the pavement, and the waiters ran in and out, smiling, bearing trays of drinks. 'They're making a fortune tonight,' Terence said.

'What a cynic!'

'No, a realist. There are always those who grow fat because of wars. We know plenty, don't we?'

'Yes.' She thought of her mother's friends whom she met occasionally, rich industrialists with factories making munitions, even Dr Duval who said he had never been busier. 'So many of my ladies suffer from *la nervosité*,' he had said to Giselle. 'Probably too much nightlife,' she had wanted to say. She had long since given up trying to understand her mother in her endless search for pleasure, or her father, for that matter. She had a private theory which she had confided to Terence that he no longer had a mistress, simply a *pied-à-terre* somewhere, where he could escape from *Maman*.

'I wonder how they celebrate in Scotland,' she said. 'Do you think they'll go to church?'

'If they do they'll have a good dram, as they call it, when they get back. I know my father will at Woodlea. I mean the dram.'

'It would be nice to visit Ireland again. Perhaps next summer. Do you think he feels . . . self-conscious about this War, or . . . self-conscious for Ireland?'

'I don't know. He's certainly more Irish than the Irish now. It's only the beginning of trouble there, just you wait and see. I don't want to be pessimistic, but the end of a war is often the beginning of trouble, peace at a price. Britain, France and America are going to squabble over the settlements, Ireland is going to bear a grudge, the millions of dead will be forgotten in their squabbles and people will begin to wonder what they died for.'

'It's not like you, *chéri*, to speak like that.'

'It is like me. Artists can see better from the wings. The only problem is, should they stay out of the fight or join in?'

'Stay with what makes you happy.'

His grimness left him. 'How did I find a wife like you? Do you know what would make me happy right now?'

She drank the last of her Pernod. 'I have a good idea.' She smiled at him as she put down the glass. 'I think we should go home now. Madeline will want to get away.'

'You're a wonderful wife,' he said, 'you anticipate my every wish.'

Later in bed they made love, a historic love-making, Terence said. They would tell Clovis and Jaime when they grew up that their parents had made love on the night of the Armistice. She lay content, her mind ranging happily – Jonty's homecoming at the Hall, the three aunts who were becoming characters as well as aunts, the insouciance of Ernest (he should really have been a Frenchman),

Terence's parents and those three cousins who amused her with their Irishness, Ginny, whose visit she had enjoyed so much, Ellie and Kieran.

Was Joe Gould still coming between them in the shape of little James? Or had Kieran's brush with death made her realize that you couldn't go on loving ghosts? There was an element in the Scottish character which clung to ghosts. Although they said that *L'Alliance Ancienne* gave them a lot in common, Frenchwomen were much more practical than their Scottish counterparts.

Ellie should stop being so conscientious, become more self-indulgent. Hair shirts were not becoming, and Chanel or Patou would never design such garments. Still, they were an interesting *mélange*, the Scots. She remembered that adorable grandmother, Maeve, who knew how to combine practicality with self-indulgence in the right proportions. A good cook.

And Lizzie who resembled her and would gladden any man's heart, particularly Ernest's, had the same happy combination. Look at her plans for the hotel she intended to make of that great mausoleum of a house, like the Natural History Museum in the *Jardin des Plates*! Look at Lizzie herself, the beauty of her, the seductiveness of her. She had got the mixture right.

Perhaps the secret of the Scottish temperament lay in its heritage. What a background of poetry and song they had, that wonderful Mr Robert Burns, for instance, whom Kieran had told her about, and who knew so well how to appreciate women. And in this man at her side were all those attributes, the poetry, the romance, and yet the hard-headedness. And the soft heart. Sometimes the melancholy.

Yes, she thought, going back to Ellie, she had the wrong proportions, too much romanticism because she had had to repress it for so long when she was studying.

Joe Gould, however satisfying he had been, would have to be relegated to his proper place. Now Ginny had it right, a light-heartedness which would never be in Ellie. The French admired *insouciance*. Ginny was the New Woman, the Post-War one. Ellie belonged to the years before it.

Should she waken up Terence and tell him about all those wonderful thoughts she had been having? Tell him again how much she loved him? No, her love would be better shown in letting him rest. She could hear the rattle in his chest which they had both learned to live with – 'my orchestra', he called it. It would always be with him.

18

It was the first time that Kieran had visited Edie and Robert since his illness, and Ellie was doubtful if they should go when she saw the cold, blustery day it was.

'I'm quite well,' he told her. 'The wind will blow away the cobwebs. I was in that sick-room far too long.'

She had not told him that there was one night when she thought he would never come out of it alive. It was the nurse's night off, and while she was sitting with him he had coughed, mildly at first, but then it had developed into a paroxysm, his face blue, his eyes staring out of his head.

She had pulled him upright against his pillows, unable to do anything for him except hold him, and eventually he was sick, black, evil-looking bile which confirmed her opinion that this particular type of influenza resembled a plague. Eventually, the retching over, he lay back exhausted, looking like death.

She had sat quietly, waiting for him to recover. He must not be further taxed. Thousands were still dying all over the world, and Kieran had never been the most robust of men. She stroked his hand, feeling in herself a deepseated fear. Was she to lose two men in this War? Joe's had been a violent, random death, but never could be blamed on her. Would she be able to think the same about Kieran's, if it happened?

Dr Melvin was worried about his lack of will to live. Kieran, of course, had been run down before the onset of the infection – long hours, not eating properly, worry. 'What is it,' he had said to her one night when he had called, 'that could be worrying him, a healthy man with a beautiful wife and child, and no money problems? I can't understand it.'

She made up her mind. 'I never told you,' she had said, 'I should have. James is not his child.'

His bushy eyebrows had shot upwards. 'Isn't he?' Was he playing the innocent? Rumour spread, and she had a great respect for his shrewdness.

'Didn't you guess? He's not like either of us.'

'That's nothing to go by.' He'd been dismissive. 'I've seen quite a few throwbacks even in my short medical career. I knew he wasn't a premature baby – he was too well-formed for that – but the War was on, I knew you and Kieran had been in France together, I knew . . . these things happen.'

'The exigencies of war?'

'To tell you the truth, Miss McNab,' he had looked rueful, 'I stood a little in awe of you. You came here with such a fine reputation, a surgeon in France at your age! I might have said something to an ordinary young girl, but . . .' he had smiled, 'I wouldn't have dared to question *your* behaviour.'

'You're making a mistake,' she had told him, 'I *am* an ordinary young girl – not so young now – with an ordinary girl's passions. I fell in love with someone else in France, and James is the result.'

'But in the end you chose Kieran?'

'No, Kieran chose me. My . . . Joe was killed.'

She remembered the look almost of admiration which had come over his face, and how his eyebrows had pulled together as if he was having to make a rapid re-assessment of her. 'Well, well,' he had said, 'you surprise me.'

'I'm sorry I've knocked myself off the pedestal you'd put me on.' She had smiled. 'But I assure you it was totally undeserved. Kieran and I . . . well, we've both suffered a lot, he more than me. I didn't stay at home to work it out. I ran away . . . to Wanapeake, to the hospital.'

'But you were needed there, Miss McNab.'

'Not as much as I was needed at home.' She had said impatiently, 'Could you call me Ellie? We're not in the hospital.'

'All right. Try Ron. Mary says I'm not particularly like a doctor anyhow.'

'You've acted like one as far as Kieran is concerned. No one could have done more than you . . .' Her thoughts left him and went back again to the memory of that night when she had been in the grip of fear – and realization had come with it. The scene was crystal clear. Perhaps it would never leave her.

'Ellie . . .' The weak voice.

'Yes. Oh, I thought you were asleep. That coughing took it out of you.' Cradling him, an arm round his shoulders, 'Can I get you anything?'

'What time is it?'

'Four . . . in the morning.'

'That accounts for it.' The hardly audible voice.

'Accounts for what?' The first close grip of fear.

'The feeling that I'm . . . about to die.'

Now the terror beating strongly in her as she looked at him. His closed eyes. The blue tinge to his lips. The terror-beat stifling her as she bent forward so that he could hear.

'You are not going to die, Kieran. That bout of coughing weakened you. Everyone feels low in the morning. I'm going to get you some beef tea. . .'

'No, don't go.' Still the closed eyes, the voice weaker. 'How long have I been ill?'

'Five weeks. That's why you're weak. Ron Melvin was going to try to get you up tomorrow. He's right. You lose your strength in bed . . .' How had she spoken so professionally with the fear stifling her, making her heart ache sickeningly? It would be just punishment indeed if he died. Then she would have nothing or no one to get between her and Joe. That was what he was thinking. She bent over the pain, finding it unbearable. How could she tell him how she was suffering when she had made him suffer for so long?

'Kieran.' His hand was cold, unresponsive. 'You mustn't leave me, please.' Steady the trembling in her voice. 'That would be too cruel. You know I can't do without you.' Was that a faint smile on his blue lips? 'Oh, I can see you're smiling at that, but it's true. I'm not pretending, God knows. Don't you believe me?' Waiting, waiting. She had seen men brought into her like this in France, drained of blood, no life in them. Sometimes you found a spark . . . 'You're punishing me, lying there! I want you to know I've been doing a lot of thinking since you were ill. I was going to tell you when you were better, not when you were . . . You've been my support for a long, long time. I hadn't realized it, how much I'd relied on you. You were . . . a yardstick to me in many ways. Oh, I admit I thought it was all too easy, someone whom I liked and admired, just to marry him. When Joe came along . . . I see now, he was my knight on a white charger. There was a craving in me for romance. I never had time to read stories when I was young. I had to study. Charlie wouldn't have let that happen. He used to read to me, wonderful books, but then when he died I felt I had to work hard to take his place, to . . . comfort Mother. Maybe it was best that Joe died. No, that's a stupid thing to say. It's never "best" that any young man should die, but maybe our love wouldn't have lasted . . .'

'But you don't love me.' The voice as cold as his hand.

'Love? What is love? Love is discovery over a long

period as well as instantaneous. Love is suffering and pain and realization. Some loves have to die. Others are constant, have a growth of their own, are profound, there is a feeling of ease and rightness. That's always been there with us. You'd . . . destroy me if you left me!' The relief of tears, her head in her hands, such bitter tears.

'I'm not blackmailing you. Don't think that. But I've tried for so long to remove your sadness. I can't live any more with the sense of failure.'

'Give up trying then!' Tears running through her fingers. 'Everybody has had sadness in this War. I'm not alone in that. You had sadness on that ambulance at Verdun picking up those poor men, I had sadness every time a mutilated body was carried in to me. Some people are better at hiding it than others . . . I envy them. Look at Giselle, knowing that Terence will never be really fit again. Look at Lizzie, her husband killed in the one war, her son in daily danger in this one, and any time I've seen her she's looked radiant. I haven't a face like that . . .'

'You have a beautiful face.' She laughed in the midst of her tears.

'Joe,' raising her head, 'let's bring him into this because he's here. He left an imprint on my personality as well as leaving me with his child. There was pre-Joe Ellie and after-Joe Ellie. If he'd lived, perhaps we shouldn't have had a long-term happiness, perhaps we should. Who's to know? But he's dead and you and I are here. Oh, Kieran, stay with me . . .'

He was tired of all this emotion. She could tell by his voice. 'I'd do anything to please you, Ellie. You've always known that . . . if it matters . . .'

'Oh, it matters!'

'I love you so much . . .' Did she love him in the same way? It didn't matter. If Kieran was to live, she would have to let Joe die.

She had let him sleep. When he wakened at eight o'clock he had said he would like some tea and toast at the table by the window. Mrs Vanaressi helped her to get him out of bed and into the chair. He was painfully thin in his thick plaid dressing-gown. She told him he looked like a waif.

'Have breakfast, then, with a waif,' he said, and she sat down with him. They were there when Ron Melvin arrived.

'What is this?' he had said, his eyebrows working overtime, 'a party in the morning?'

'I thought it was high time I got up.' Kieran smiled at him.

'Well, you're the patient. May I join you? This chair?' He sat down at the table. 'Is there any coffee in that pot Ellie?' He beamed on both of them.

The drawing room at Springhill was warm and welcoming as were Robert and Edie. She was well gone in pregnancy now, but still light on her feet, and she ran to find a comfortable chair for Kieran.

'Now, don't treat me as an invalid, Edie,' he said. 'You're the one who should be molly-coddled. When is the baby due?'

'We're hoping for a Christmas one, although that might be a bit unfair on him, or her.'

'I'd call it a double celebration. Well, Robert,' they shook hands, 'still making millions for MacGrath's?'

'We're not doing too badly. It will be a difficult time post-war, but now that we have Ernest at the helm again he'll take care of things – not that Aunt Maevy wasn't a good enough substitute.'

'Lizzie will be in the seventh heaven of delight. That's her favourite expression.' Ellie laughed. 'Both Ernest and Jonty back home.'

'Yes, and full of plans. The Hall is emptied now of patients, and the building of the additions has begun. Jonty's greatly in favour of her idea. They'll be able to remain there or stay at Braidholme – Aunt Maevy has offered that – while the stables are being turned into two desirable residences. Have you ever seen the stables, Kieran?'

'Perhaps. I can't say I remember them. They're some distance from the house, aren't they?'

'Yes, about a quarter of a mile away, over a small bridge. They're built round a square courtyard, and as there are stables, hayloft, a coach-house and two cottages on either side of the arch, the whole thing just lends itself to alteration. Trust Lizzie! Where else would you get a castellated parapet thrown in, not to mention a beaded cornice and pointed windows with drip moulds, no less!'

'You haven't missed much,' Ellie smiled at him.

'Architecture is one of my little hobbies.'

'Your husband is full of surprises, Edie.'

'I'm constantly finding that.'

'Is that why you look so blooming?'

'Perhaps. But there's nothing like being pregnant to dampen down one's ambition. When do you intend to go back to the hospital, Ellie?'

'I don't quite know.' She was bland. 'The young doctor whom I replaced is back now, and although they say I can be appointed to another post at any time, I'm in no hurry. Kieran and I are making plans . . .' she caught Edie's eye . . . 'to travel. Not in the winter but in the spring, perhaps.'

'To Scotland?'

'Certainly Scotland. Aunt Kate's going back then, when they hope the rebuilding will be completed. There will have to be a decision made about Braidholme as well. Anyhow, we hope to accompany her.'

'And no doubt include Paris and Ireland at the same time?'

Kieran smiled. 'Our family has had the good sense to spread itself. Visiting them all is as good as a Cook's Tour.'

Back at Wolf House in their bedroom they said to each other it had been a good day.

'And Edie looks wonderfully well,' she said.

'In time you might . . .' He was nonchalant as he pulled his shirt over his head.

'In time I might . . .' she said. 'There's no rush. That's what I have to learn, there's no rush. I don't have to set myself constant goals or make commitments. I intend to be less conscientious, less obsessive, lazier, more loving . . .'

'In a word, less Scottish?' Kieran was in bed. 'There's only one department where I'd like you to show more alacrity.'

'And what is that?' she said, smiling at him in the mirror.

'In getting into bed. You've been brushing that hair of yours for at least ten minutes.'

'Well, isn't it my crowning glory? But, since you insist.' She got up, threw off her robe, and laughing, ran to him like a child. 'Is that quick enough for you?' she said, snuggling down at his side.

'Yes. I'm glad to see you're so dutiful.' He put his arm round her. 'Ellie, this will be the first time for a long time. Have you forgotten how?' He sounded wistful.

'That's a thing you never forget. You'll be all right, I'll be all right. I'm speaking as your medical adviser.'

'Well, in that case . . .'

The strength in his arms surprised her. Or was it the strength of his love? In any case, it made her happy as long as she didn't think.

19

'Too harsh for some, too soft for others.' Ernest was at the head of the board-room table on a bright day in May. 'And, of course, it won't please President Wilson. There's no room for idealists in this world.' He was referring to the Treaty of Versailles which had been approved in plenary session the day before. There had been a general discussion of its various points before he called the meeting to order.

'First of all,' he said, 'I'm pleased to welcome Lord Crawford, my step-son, whom you will all agree is going to add lustre to our future dealings. We shan't see much of him as he is going to study at the Sorbonne, then Fine Art in Florence. Isn't that right, Jonty?'

Jonty nodded, trying to look important and dignified in his pinstriped suiting which Mother had insisted on. Of course, he would only be a co-opted member until he was twenty-one, but both she and Ernest wanted him to get his 'toe in the door', as they put it. 'I want you to be my little spy,' she had said, flicking a speck of dust from his lapel, standing back to admire. Fortunately he had succeeded in persuading her not to stick a carnation in his buttonhole. 'I've always longed to be a fly on the wall at one of those board meetings. You know Ernest, how secretive he is about everything.'

Well, he would be able to tell her that Ernest comported himself very well. In spite of his frequent trips to London to the Globe Express offices, his knowledge of what went on here couldn't be faulted. Of course he had a good team in Mr Johnson, Mr Richardson, and most important of all, Aunt Maevy, but even so, he did it all so effortlessly. That was what he would most of all like to emulate, Ernest's effortlessness.

It was strange to think that you could go through all that fighting, all that danger and horror, and emerge just as self-conscious at certain times, just as unsure of yourself. There was no one here who had seen the sights he had seen, even Aunt Maevy as a nurse, although she had always looked quite unflappable. 'Omnipotent Aunt Maevy', Ernest had begun to call her.

But what they had been saying about this Treaty of Versailles made him wonder why he had gone to fight at all. They were going to beggar Germany with all those reparations and make them so downright angry that they would start another war. People who bore a grudge always broke out in the end. The only good thing from the German point of view was that their boundaries were kept intact, whereas Austria-Hungary's and the others, the Poles, Rumanians and Italians, were all to pot.

Well, next time he would not fly to arms. He had marched away and had the good luck to march back, but never again. Were there thousands of men like him saying the same thing? But then the ones who had come home had set about having children, and it would be those children who would be called upon . . . it all did not bear thinking about. Better to listen to Ernest.

'We have had in our time to come to terms with Canal competition and Railway competition, and we have done this by throwing in our lot with them rather than throwing in the sponge. There are always gaps to be filled in by carting firms – feeder traffic, as it's called. We have done this with horses and now with motor transport. When war came we put our facilities at the disposal of the country. We have not shirked our responsibility.

'When things were black we looked around and joined

forces with a rival instead of fighting them, hence Globe Express Deliveries, of which we are a proud part, and which is playing such an important part in the economy of the company.

'But as well as acorns growing into large trees, it is possible to pick up the acorns which fall, and that's what we have done. We have some of the finest cold storage facilities in the country, we have furniture repositories second to none, we have a thriving sideline in our Auctioneering and Valuators Department, and that's why my stepson is here today to be introduced to you : . . although none of you need that introduction . . .' All eyes on him. He looked down his nose, hiding his shyness.

'We have a good staff in our new department, but we need new blood and someone who is university trained in the Fine Arts to help us. That Jonty has the presence to match that, no one looking at him need doubt.' All eyes again turned on him. Thank God for the pin-stripe suiting. This time he tried a wry smile.

'He's always been interested in that side of things. You won't find Jonty in the changing house. He has a fine sense of beauty, like his great-grandmother and his mother, and is a poet of some note. Some of you might like to know that his first volume has just been published . . . what is it called, Jonty?' He knew perfectly well, old Ernest, but he responded in a strong voice. Mother had said to speak up. Some of the members of the board, like Mr Drummond and Mr Gregg, were getting on.

'*Horizontal Lines*. It's the title of the first poem in the book.' He thought of pointing out that there was a *double entendre*, that lines on a page could be called that, as well as lines of dead men . . . No, he wouldn't. 'Thank you for the spot of free advertising, Ernest.' Laughter was sweet.

'We stick together in this family,' Ernest said, amidst the laughter. 'And, ladies and gentlemen, we have another member of that family and the firm here today whom I know you have already met but I'd like you to welcome officially, Robert McGrath, grandson of Kieran and Maeve McGrath, the founders of our firm. I'm sure you've all noticed her portrait hanging in the boardroom here, which has been kindly given to us by Terence in Ireland. It was painted by his son, and I think you will all agree that it is a fitting tribute to her beauty . . .'

Pretty good, Jonty thought, looking at it critically as befitted a future fine art dealer. He particularly admired, from where he was sitting, how Terence had painted the gleaming folds of the gold gown, as well as captured the striking pose of Great-grandmother's head. Not a sloucher, Great-grandmother, straight as a ramrod.

He really must get together with Terence when he was at the Sorbonne. He could teach him a lot about art. Ginny had said he would like Giselle, too, that she was keen on family ties. It was good to think that Ginny had come over with Ellie and Kieran and Aunt Kate. It was Mother who had invited her. Knowing Mother, she must have something up her sleeve.

'Thank you for your welcome.' Uncle Robert was on his feet. 'Unfortunately my wife wasn't able to travel with me because of our small daughter, Sophie, who arrived on Christmas Day, nor was my Uncle Patrick, who now finds long distance travelling a bit arduous. But he's still travelling daily to the New York office, you'll be pleased to hear, which at sixty-six is no mean achievement. I can't persuade him to stop. He says he wants to die in harness – a chip off the old block.' He smiled round the table, the strong lines of his face relaxing. He's like a rock, Jonty thought.

'But be sure the American side of the business goes from strength to strength. Ours is a young country and a big country, and although shipping is our main interest, we follow the railway network closely. There's plenty of work. We have invested heavily in large vehicles, and we're thinking of a new sideline: travel. Some of the younger members of the family, such as Benjamin Vogel and Sam Murray-Hyslop, are interested in this side of things, and I'm hoping to get it off the ground soon. You'll see my plans in the papers before you.' He looked round the table. 'Let me finish by saying that the ties which bind us are close. Long may they continue that way.' The applause was warm and prolonged as he sat down.

Ernest got to his feet. 'Thank you, Robert. It's good to feel that we're international, and that the young are going to bring new blood and new ideas into the firm – Jonty here, and Ben and Sam on the other side of the water.

'This is the age of the motor, the post-war era. We have travelled a long way since we had stables in the Gallowgate for our fleet of horses. Kieran McGrath was the expert there, but fortunately we have in the firm a young man of the same calibre who is going to lead us into the new age, Iain Pearson, and I am going to propose today that he should join the Board.' There was a murmur of assent. 'I gather that is to your liking. Those in favour raise your hands, please.' Everybody's hand went up, Jonty saw. Was a co-opted member entitled to vote? He would risk it.

'Unanimous.' Ernest looked pleased. 'He began in the motor repair section, went on to motor haulage, covering both steam and petrol. He is the perfect combination, a good engineer with a business head. He is the right age, thirty-two, and my considered opinion is that he should be appointed as General Manager of McGrath's as of from now.

'You'll all know that John Drummond is retiring. We can't replace you, John,' he smiled across the table at him, 'but at least we have done the next best thing, found someone with the same name, only the Highland version, so that's a step in the right direction.'

Jonty was impressed. He had met Iain Pearson at one of Mother's dinner parties, a seemingly taciturn youngish man who had blossomed as the meal progressed. He had fought with the HLI on the Somme and had, like him, escaped serious injury. They had found a lot in common.

With Iain Pearson, himself, and the two cousins in America, there were going to be people in the firm nearer his own age. Even Ernest was getting on. He had had his fiftieth birthday recently – 'sucking the half lemon', he called it.

He didn't look fifty, Jonty thought, watching him as he made some graceful concluding remarks about the ongoing prosperity of the firm and and its prospects for the future. He was lithe and thin, his sandy hair had not a touch of grey in it. He was always urbane, never peevish or bad-tempered.

Was there something in being married to the right woman, he wondered? When he came to choose someone he would try to find a girl as like Mother as possible. She would make anyone happy, both in their private life and their public one. He was not so naïve as to miss the glances she and Ernest sometimes exchanged at the breakfast table.

It was quite a nice prospect, a job that he liked doing and a girl he could love every night if he wanted to or if she wanted to. But he must watch that he did not become too contented. He had noticed that he had written no poetry since he had come home. There had to be stress or danger or unhappiness. Poetry never came out of contentment. But he consoled himself. There was Paris and Italy ahead of him. Anything could happen.

* * *

He travelled home in style with Ernest and Robert, driven by the chauffeur. Mother had promised him a run-about for himself this summer, and he had his eye on an Aston Martin. Still, this was very nice, the grey velvet interior, the pinstriped suiting, the smell of Ernest's cigar.

And Uncle Robert grew on you. At first he had seemed very serious and dull, but he turned out to be interesting to talk to. 'You must come to America sometime and study the pictures in the Museum of Modern Art,' he said. 'You can stay with us at Springhill and go up to New York every day. It would take you a week to see all their stuff. Edie's very interested in it. She knows all those painters like Monet, Matisse, Mondrian . . .' he laughed. 'I only remember the ones beginning with "M", but our house is littered with books about them. Is modern stuff to your fancy?'

'Yes, that or very old. I'm fascinated by Piero della Francesca. It's his perspective, you see. I'd like to do a tour of all the places where his pictures are hung.'

'Well, that's the beauty of going to Paris and Italy. You'll find other students to talk to, perhaps tours to take part in. Take my advice and enjoy yourself, Jonty. I regret I neglected that side of my education in my hurry to get into the business world. But Edie's doing her best with me!'

Yes, he liked Uncle Robert very much. Especially when he said, 'I'm speaking to you as if you were a young man straight from school, and then I remember that you experienced in one year more than I have in the whole of my lifetime.' And he added, almost shyly, 'I shall be proud to be associated with you.'

He demurred, embarrassed, but touched. 'Oh, you quickly forget once you're home.'

But it wasn't strictly true. He still occasionally had that nightmare of Jimmy rising up from the mud, the anguished face, the stump of red, angry flesh which quivered sickeningly as he raised it.

Once he had shouted out in terror and Mother had come running into his room. 'What is it, Jonty?' She had on a thin silk night robe and her hair was about her shoulders, rich, copper, Burns-Jonesien. He had been shamefaced, sullen.

'Nothing. Just a bad dream.'

She sat on the bed beside him. 'You should talk about it.' Had taken his hand. 'Don't bury it.'

'I can't.' He had drawn away his hand. 'Some of it's . . . in the poems.'

'But not all of it?'

'No.' He shook his head. He was afraid she would hug him and then he would burst into tears.

'Perhaps later on, when you least expect it. . .' How brilliantly blue her eyes were against the ivory silk.

'I don't know. If I do they'll be different. Recollected in tranquillity.' He heard himself guffaw. How could you recollect any of that in tranquillity?

'You should speak to Ellie. You know what happened to her.'

'Yes . . . but you can't just *speak* to her. It has to . . . come *up*.'

'Yes, I see that.' She sighed. 'Would you like me to make you a hot drink? Or anything?'

'God, no! I'm not Annabel or Kit!' He was impatient with her.

'But you're my son.' She bent and kissed him. 'My very dear son.' He had buried his head in the pillow when she went.

20

She had laid on quite a spread for them all, 'in your mother's inimitable fashion,' Ernest remarked when they peeped into the dining-room at Lizzie's request. She wasn't downstairs yet. She liked to make her entrance just before the guests arrived. 'The table's positively groaning,' Jonty said, and Ernest agreed.

'Your mother is a generous woman. When the day comes that she can't lay on "spreads" like this, I'll know she's lost her zest for life. Come into the hall, sorry, the Pump Room, and I'll give you a drink. They'll soon be here.'

There was no doubt about its magnificence. 'The first impact is important,' she had said, when he had questioned the necessity to knock down so many walls. The area was huge, but broken up by groups of easy chairs and sofas arranged round small tables. Flowers were everywhere. A log fire crackled in the marble fireplace with its wide chimneypiece and the pair of antlers hanging over it.

The *pièce de resistance* was, of course, the marble fountain from which the water gushed through lions' mouths into a marble basin. 'Would you rather have some holy water?' Ernest said, laughing.

'No, thanks. When I think what it cost to lead it here! Trust Mother!' He seemed to be saying that quite a lot. 'Do you really think it has medicinal properties?'

'Who knows? Spring water can't be bad for you. You can bet before Lizzie's finished with it, it will be curing everything from dyspepsia to housemaid's knee.' He had filled two glasses with sherry and given one to Jonty. 'Do you mind losing your home like this?'

'No, I don't think so. When Mother wrote to me in France about it, it seemed so . . . unimportant. Houses were the last thing you thought about. You were more concerned with just staying alive. Besides, I was chivvied a bit – I never told you – I became guilty about the privileges I had. Maybe if I'd been an officer it would have been different. No, if I thought about here at all it was about my childhood years in it, my very young childhood, really, because after that I was away at school most of the time. And I knew that if I ever got back alive nothing would make me become a country gentleman like Father might have been. And as for going into the family firm, Sir Edward put paid to that by making it a public company.'

'We never see him now.'

'No great loss. No, my heart was never in the market-place, nor in the changing houses, as you said today. I wanted to see the world but not in a *dilettante* fashion, I wanted to *absorb* places and pictures, to fill my mind with . . . beauty. Does that sound soft?'

'Why should it? It's admirable.'

'I think it was the *ugliness* of the War that made me long for beauty. There was nothing redeeming about it, only in the spirit of the men. I say, Ernest,' he looked at his glass, 'this must be potent stuff. I'm talking my head off!'

'No, you're not. You're describing the man we recognized in you. You're right. The role of the country gentleman is played out here; a thing of the past. It's no longer even country. And you've never been an enthusiastic sportsman, banging away at things. You've had more discrimination than that. As long as you don't bear her any grudge. I know my Lizzie.' His face became tender.

'She's inclined to sweep other people along in her enthusiasms.'

'No, she didn't do that with me. She said right from the start that she would never do anything against my wishes. But she's right, unerringly right. Big houses like this, twelve miles from a city, are an anachronism. And,' he said, 'I think the way she's done the cottages is superb.'

'Don't be modest. I know you've had quite a hand in them.'

'Well, who could resist it? There's so much there to use, to incorporate. That hipped slate roof, early nineteenth century. I've had great fun there. I've even designed a private suite for myself in the attic as a *pied-à-terre*.'

'Yes, and taken the best view! But you'll have the other cottage for yourself eventually. That is, if you want it. The aunts will move in there first, but if and when they get frailer, Lizzie will have them in the main building so that they don't have any housekeeping to do. Maybe,' he said smiling wickedly, 'that'll coincide with you marrying and wanting a place of your own. Does the idea appeal to you?'

'Not immediately. I've got a lot to do.'

'Good chap. I was thirty-six when I married your mother. She was worth waiting for.' He turned as Lizzie came into the room. 'Wouldn't you agree?'

'Agree to what?' Lizzie said.

'That you were worth waiting for?'

She smiled as she twirled around. 'I'm the last person to *sprouse*. Now, what do you think of this? I thought it suited the marble elegance here.' The tunic of her dress was banded in silver, as was the square neckline; her hair was done up in Grecian fashion on the top of her head and tied with a knot of silver ribbon. There were curled tendrils escaping from it.

'Are you going to parade like that every evening when your guests are here?' Jonty said.

'With a jar on one shoulder?' She mimicked a Grecian pose, her eyes dancing. 'Why not if it's good for business?' There was a noise outside of tyres rolling on the gravel. 'Here they are. That's right, Redfern.' The butler had appeared and gone towards the door. Lizzie whispered to them. 'I've said he can come any time he likes. He misses the kitchen talk in his cottage.'

'Bit of a comedown for poor old Redfern,' Jonty whispered back. 'A hydro instead of a stately home.'

Isobel, Kate and Maevy came in first, followed by Robert, Ellie, Kieran, and last of all, Ginny. Maevy had insisted on them all staying at Braidholme. The transformation of the Hall was to be a surprise for them, and in any case she had said she liked Braidholme being packed to the attics. It might be the last time. They had discussed the idea of it being used as an annexe for the Hydro, if it should be needed.

In the midst of the talking and the laughter and the expressions of surprise from the American contingent, Jonty found his way to Ginny's side. He had seen her when she arrived two days ago, but not since then. 'Hello!' he said, kissing her, 'your dress is marvellous.'

'Thanks. This is the latest American fashion, I'll have you know. Shorter than worn in bonnie Scotland. Shall I scandalize the village worthies?'

'I should think delight them. It's nothing to what I saw in Paris. You haven't changed a bit, Ginny. Not to look at.'

'But I'm different inside. Oh, there were some fun and games when I was home. I have all sort of things to tell you. But I'm so glad you're back in one piece! I never thought . . .'

'I'd make it? Sometimes I wondered myself.'

'We've got so much to talk about, but I must go and speak to your mother first. Doesn't she look gorgeous?' She dashed off and he went to greet Ellie and Kieran.

They had changed, he thought. Kieran looked older, thinner, but still with that essential sweetness of expression. There were very few men who could look like that and still be *manly*. And Ellie, whom he had always thought of as a rather remote beauty, seemed to have a new softness in her face. Well, of course, everyone had thought Kieran was going to die. That would have been two deaths for her. Maybe Mother was right when she said he ought to have a talk with Ellie about the War. He had thought at the time it was an outlandish thing to say, but now, strangely enough, he could imagine it.

'Isn't it wonderful, Jonty?' she said, 'all that . . . terrible business behind you. Is your shoulder quite healed?'

'As right as rain.'

'*My* war was over before yours.'

'Yes.' What could he say to that?

'I see the good parts of it now. Do you?'

'Yes . . .' It was awkward with Kieran standing there, and the thought of Ellie's dead lover in his mind. He did not look perturbed.

'I hear you're going to study in Paris and Florence, you lucky chap,' he said.

'Yes, I'm looking forward to it. Are you all right now, Kieran? You had a bad time.'

'Ellie had a worse one.' He smiled at her. 'It's all behind us now. Stupid of me to pick up a bug when I wasn't even in the War. But it's great to see you back safe and sound. Be sure to look up my sister in Paris. Remind her the War's over now. I don't think she's noticed!'

'Is she still having her salons?' That was a stupid thing

to say. Hadn't Ginny told him that Ellie had met Joe Gould at one of them?

'Oh, yes. They're her life's blood. And Charles' *bête-noir*, I'm afraid.'

The aunts were enthusing as they sipped the water from the fountain. At least Isobel and Kate were. Maevy looked more sceptical. 'Here's Jonty!' She kissed him. 'Second time today I've seen this young man. We decided to be teetotal and try some of this magic potion, but I'm inclined to think I'd rather have a sherry. What do you think, girls?' He looked at them fondly. 'Girls'!

'I believe I can feel it doing me good already,' Isobel said, her mouth pulled down to hide a smile.

'Water is cleansing to the system, of course,' Kate said seriously, and then laughed at herself. 'Hark at me! Lizzie has already put her spell on us. When I think how we used to wander about that hillside when we were weans and have a drink at the well free! And now it's going to cost the earth!'

'Never to you.' Lizzie was beside them. 'You mustn't make fun of my magic potion. Jonty, get them a decent drink, for goodness sake! Are you all terribly hungry?'

'Not me,' Kate said. 'We had an enormous Scottish tea. I'd forgotten how filling they could be and I made a pig of myself.'

'Well, that's good because I thought we could have a tour of inspection first, principally for the benefit of Ellie, Kieran and Robert. Shall we start with the lounge – we don't call it the drawing-room any more – and then go through to the Palm Court?' Jonty, arriving with Redfern in tow with their glasses of sherry on a silver tray, was amused at the glances the three aunts exchanged. They were at the delightful age, he decided, when they could afford to laugh at foibles, laugh at life. Was life the biggest foible of them all? What a thought! He followed in Lizzie's entourage.

The 'lounge', as it was to be now called had been enlarged to twice its size and seemed even larger because of the vista of glass and greenery at one end, Lizzie's famous Palm Court. The lounge itself seemed to be suffused with golden light, partly because the late sun of a fine May day was filling it, and partly because the huge windows were draped with gleaming gold curtains whose colour was repeated in the carpet. Great bowls of white lilac stood everywhere, and the expanse of the carpet was broken up by groups of easy chairs placed round low tables.

'It should be called "The Sunshine Lounge",' Ernest said dryly when they had all admired the general effect and were going through the glass doors into what had been the former conservatory but now was scarcely recognizable with its white-painted wrought iron tables and chairs, its hanging plants, its banks and pots of flowers – the gardeners had excelled themselves – and, of course, the palm trees. There was a podium in one corner also banked with flowers, and Lizzie indicated it casually. 'I thought on grand nights we might have a small orchestra playing. It adds to the atmosphere.' They were all agreed on the atmosphere. Jonty, who had seen it before, basked at second-hand in their admiration.

'Mother thought this place might appeal to the older people when they just want to sit and chat. There's going to be plenty laid on to keep the younger ones occupied.'

'Jonty gave me lots of ideas there,' Lizzie said. 'What do you think of it, Ellie?'

'I don't know what to think except that it's wonderful, but, knowing you, Lizzie, I'm not surprised. Mother's always said you had a gift for organization once you found out what you wanted to organize. This is it. Don't you think so, Kieran?'

'I can't wait to be old enough to come and sit here. And listen to "The Blue Danube",' he said, laughing. 'You're to be congratulated, Lizzie. I can organize bales of cotton at the Battery docks in New York, but I couldn't do this in a hundred years.'

'You haven't seen it all yet. Now, if we go through this door,' she opened one which was set into the glass, 'it leads you by a covered walkway to the new swimming bath.'

That had been his idea. 'Take account of the Scottish weather, Mother,' he had said. He ran ahead to open the door of the large building, stood aside and ushered them in, concealing his pride. 'I'm rather pleased with this,' Lizzie said, 'but it's thanks to Jonty.'

The water of the swimming bath was aquamarine and it lapped silkily against its tiled walls. All round it there were mahogany-doored changing cubicles. The small sound of the water which lay in a gleaming sheet, undisturbed, seemed to make it a place of mystery, strange, oriental even.

'Shades of the Middle East,' Ernest said. He must have felt the atmosphere as well. 'I can just see a sheik sitting on his silken cushions here while his harem disport themselves in the water for his benefit.'

'Through that door there,' Lizzie said, 'are the Turkish baths . . .'

'What did I tell you?' Ernest said.

'And I've engaged a *Swedish* gymnast. He's starting next week. Very handsome, and Ernest's madly jealous!' She gave him a teasing look.

Jonty was standing beside Ginny. 'You and your mother have thought of everything,' she said, smiling at him.

'Almost.' He was pleased. 'There's a croquet lawn just outside. We might have a game later.'

'Or a swim. We had swimming parties in Wanapeake in the summer. There are restaurants with pools now.'

'I remember hearing that the uncle who died, Uncle Gaylord, went in for that kind of thing.'

'Yes, it was the death of him eventually. Not the swimming, but the people he associated with. Or maybe that was just part of it . . .' He didn't know what she was driving at. 'He took drugs. Did you know?'

'I knew there was something suspicious. I was too young when it was all going on to be told much. This place gives me the same kind of feeling, delicious, but kind of . . . decadent.' They were in the Turkish bath now, a place of flat wooden benches, Moorish arches, dark, multi-coloured tiles on the walls and the floor – he had had difficulty in finding the correct colours. Mother had given him that job and the Glasgow shops had not understood his rejection of their pale greens and whites in favour of something of Islamic persuasion. He had found stained glass lamps which exactly repeated the dark, rich colours. He had thought of burning incense but Mother had drawn the line there.

'You're going to have the use of all this,' Ginny said. 'Aren't you lucky?'

'Not for long. I start in September at the Sorbonne, and I may go to Paris earlier.'

'I might join you there. I've no plans made. I haven't plans made for anything.'

'Not even to get married?'

'No, I'm proving hard to please.' She must be inundated with offers, he thought, looking at her. She reminded him of great-grandmother – everybody said that, he knew – or grandmother as she would have been when she was young: the rich red hair, those brilliant, lively eyes, the depth of their blueness. The men were probably afraid to ask her. She was different from Mother although there was a strong family resemblance. Mother employed wiles. He had seen her using them. Ginny was more direct. 'I've a feeling,' she was saying, 'that if I stay any longer at Claremont I'll become like Sarah, sing in the choir.' She pulled a face.

'Oh, no, you're totally different. Everyone says so.'

'Not nearly as good. Here we go again!' Lizzie was moving forward, followed by her train of the aunts, Robert, Ellie and Kieran.

Certainly the tour was thorough; the rebuilt kitchen with its gleaming copper pans, its huge ovens, the ice-house – catering was a job in itself, Lizzie informed them – the refurbished ballroom, the children's crèche; then outside to see the putting green, the vista of fields beyond the house which were to be turned into a nine-hole golf-course, the riding stables built nearer the house now, the tennis courts, the greenhouses – since it was to be a health establishment they would grow all their own vegetables and fruit.

The enthusiasm for Lizzie's accomplishment did not falter, but weary feet did. When they were led back to the Palm Court where a buffet supper was to be served, they settled down with sighs of relief. The maids circled with champagne, Ernest toasted Lizzie and Jonty and wished the Sholton Hydro every success. They all drank to that.

Soon the maids were again going round with smoked salmon *vol-au-vents*, anchovy *croûtes*, caviare pancakes, grouse pie, ham and turkey on silver platters, macedoine of vegetables, Russian salad. Jonty, who had a good memory, ate sparingly, with a picture of all the puddings on the dining-room table in his mind – the almond castles, the crème caramels, the chocolate soufflés and the trifles.

He had found himself by chance sitting in a sheltered

corner of the Palm Court with Ellie. Kieran was with Ginny. He would have liked someone else at their table – a *tête-à-tête* was always more difficult.

'You must be as proud of your mother, Jonty,' she said, 'as she is of you.'

'Oh, I don't think she's very proud of me, really.' He sipped his champagne. 'She wasn't at all pleased at me running away from school and joining up. Looking back, I'm just as surprised at myself.'

'Do you regret it?'

'I don't know . . . no,' he said decisively, putting down his knife and fork. 'I couldn't have borne to be at Eton with the War going on. I should never have forgiven myself if I'd missed it, thinking of my father. And it could have been over if I'd gone about it in the ordinary way because there would have been officer's training first.'

'These are your reasons for going. Were there any good bits when you were there?'

He shook his head. 'Nothing to do with the War, no. The great camaraderie that everyone talks about wasn't there, for a start. Have you read some of the poems that are coming out? "Swinging to glory together . . ." That sort of thing. People behave the same way in war as out of it. The good things were the simple things that I didn't have to fight in mud and filth for, the dawn chorus although it was pretty scanty since there were hardly any trees left; *stopping* marching when you'd been marching for days and days. Once I was offered a bath in a farmhouse and I jumped at it. To feel lousy all the time is worse than feeling fear. The silkiness and the seduction of the water . . . that's me being a poet again.' He grinned at her, feeling at ease.

'You wrote it down.'

'Yes, it's in the book. That's another thrill, getting the right words down to express the feeling – but you can get that at home, too. I remember they gave me a white towel in that farmhouse to dry myself with and I stood staring at it for ages, its whiteness, its *depth* of whiteness, held it up to my face . . . well, it's all there.'

'Yes, I know. I've read it. Liked it.'

He was pleased. 'I had only one friend, Jimmy McAlpine, and he was killed. His people had a baker's shop in Luss, and he used to make me salivate by describing the meat pies his father made. And he'd tell me the names of the loaves: the cob, the crusty, the pan, the sultana brown, the white currant with caraway seeds, the wholemeal. We'd talk about eating slices of them thick with fresh butter and strawberry jam. He liked what he called the "heel" of the loaf, the crust, and burned black. Once, when I was laughing myself silly, I looked at him and the tears were running down his face. I asked him what was wrong. "It's the tattie scoanes," he said, "A've just minded them."' He looked at Ellie. 'Potato scones, he meant.'

'I know.' She smiled at him. 'I'm Scottish.'

'So am I but I didn't. That's the fault of an English education. "It's the brown blisters on them," Jimmy said, "when they come off the griddle, and you pit a lump o' butter in them and roll them up to keep it frae runnin' through your fingers . . ."'

'You probably felt like crying, too.'

He nodded. He had. 'Tattie scoanes', while they were walking along the muddy road with all the detritus of war in the ditches – old belt buckles, old clothes, old boots, old bits of men. He had told Jimmy about the eggs, to make up for the scones . . . the ones the farmer's daughter had given him, warm, brown, with bits of straw stuck to them by hen shit. They had talked about bird-nesting, and the thrill of discovery, how the eggs *cooried* together.

And how the bird flew squawking away when you put your hand through the thorns to touch them . . .

'He was killed,' he said. All the time he had been speaking he had been sipping the champagne because of his throat. It had become hoarse, not with emotion, but with talking too much. Champagne was a good way of clearing it. 'I still weep about it,' he said. 'I have nightmares about him struggling out of the mud. I think of him never getting back to Luss to get the heel of the loaf or his tattie scoanes, of the sadness of his father. He was an only son and was going to take his place. I think of the laughs we had and his kindness, but most of all I think of what he looked like when he died beside me, riddled by machine gun fire, a travesty of the Jimmy I knew, a bloody travesty.' He took up his knife and fork and cut the game pie into small pieces but he didn't touch it.

'It's early days,' she said, 'it'll go. You'll only remember the good bits eventually, the tattie scoanes, his face when he laughed. What did he look like?'

'Dead or alive?' he wanted to say. 'Look like? Freckle-faced, curly hair, buck teeth. But kind eyes. He saw into me.'

'Try and change the image,' she said.

'That could be the first line of a poem. "Try and change the image," she said . . . Try . . .?' He raised his eyebrows.

'Put that one in the place of the one that disturbs you. Do it during the day. Imprint it. Then *that's* the one you'll dream of . . . eventually.'

'Yes . . . eventually.' He saw the bloody stump while he was speaking, and he *wasn't* sleeping.

'It's not impossible. *I* had to do it.'

'I know,' he said, embarrassed. 'Ginny . . . or Mother . . . told me.'

'I didn't see him die. That was almost worse. A bomb

dropped on the hospital tent where he was looking after patients. I thought of him in . . . bits . . . all over the place. In my dreams I was trying to piece him together . . . "You're a surgeon," I'd say in my dream, but it was no good. They wouldn't . . . *fit*. You're the first person I've told, Jonty, because we both know . . .'

'Has it stopped?'

'Yes.'

'How?'

'I went to see his sister. She was a wise girl, quite different in appearance from Joe, "solid" she called herself, but she was wise. "Go right down to the depths," she said, so I did, and then something happened . . . a trauma.'

'You mean when Kieran got ill?' He was quite pleased with himself for saying that. He must be intuitive.

'Good for you.' He was even more pleased by her pleased admiration. 'They come into everyone's life sooner or later. I knew that if I went on being obsessed by Joe that Kieran would die. It was as simple as that. So I gave it up.'

'That couldn't have been easy.'

'It's the decision that's hard. The doing's easy. Do you know what I'm going to tell you?' She leaned forward, 'James, Joe's little boy, is two now and very like his father, and I can look at him sometimes, not always but sometimes, and not even *remember* Joe.'

'So, do I have to have something traumatic?' he said. How had he ever thought she was remote? Beautiful, yes, but not remote. Now he saw the extra dimension in her beauty, the fineness, the warmth of expression in her eyes.

'Life's traumatic,' she said, smiling at him, 'just living it. Or you could make your own trauma. Why don't you take a trip to Luss and see Jimmy's folks? It would do *them* good at least. And think how they'd be able to boast about their Jimmy's friend, Lord Crawford.'

He grinned at her. 'First time, then, it would be any good to me. Now why did I never think of going to see them? I've plenty of time before I go off to Paris.'

'You can't think of everything,' she said, laughing now, 'you're only young yet.'

'You cheeky thing,' he was laughing with her, 'I'm a veteran!'

21

Lizzie had asked Ginny to come and visit her on the afternoon before she returned to America. Ellie and Kieran had gone to Glasgow with Kieran's mother. She had wanted them to see the house in Blythswood Square where she had been nurse to the four Murray-Hyslop children. Ernest had suggested teasingly that she should arrange for a plaque to be put up. 'And never to a better man than your father,' she had said, and he had kissed her fondly. 'You're right, Mother. He's still green in my memory.' She had noticed he had said 'Mother', and not 'Kate'.

Robert was also in Glasgow, at the McGrath's office, going over business affairs with Maevy and Ernest prior to his return. He had, as he said, a list as long as his arm of items from Uncle Patrick which had to be gone into, and he wouldn't dare go back without having seen to them all.

And Jonty had taken himself off to Luss to visit the parents of an Army chum. He had apologized when he was saying good-bye to her. 'You'll be gone before I get back, but I should have done this long ago. Sometimes you have to have things pointed out to you.'

She had told him she had seen him having a long talk with Ellie at the 'Hydro-warming' – this being the name they had laughingly decided on for the tour of inspection Lizzie had laid on. 'Were you comparing notes about the War?' she had asked.

'In a kind of a way. Ginny,' he had said, 'I can ask you

this. How do you think Ellie and Kieran get on together? Are they happy?'

'They look it. There's nothing like nearly losing someone to make you realize their worth. That's what's been wrong with me so far. Everything has gone too smoothly.'

'You've plenty of time yet,' he had said. Sometimes she had to look twice at Jonty, disabuse herself of the idea that he was no longer her boyish young cousin, but a man who had been close to death many times. She had given him a hug.

'Do you know, Jonty, I almost envy you. Not yet twenty, and you've been through the Great War.'

'The War to end all wars,' he had said, and that hadn't sounded like the boyish young cousin either.

Lizzie was sitting in the Palm Court with a silver tea-tray on the wrought-iron table beside her. She was like someone who, having discovered a favourite garment, couldn't stop wearing it.

'Excuse this,' she said, waving at her smart purple costume, her paler chiffon blouse whose fichu was frothing over the front of the peplumed jacket (a comprehensive wave), putting her hand to her small toque which showed the right amount of her shining copper hair. All her hats were designed with that purpose in mind. (As Aunt Maevy was wont to say, 'Lizzie knew how many beans made five'.) 'I've just got back from shopping in Glasgow. Did you walk over from Braidholme?'

'Yes.' She regretted her sensible shoes, her fawn linen skirt and white blouse, her knitted cardigan. 'All my clothes are packed. I'm leaving this,' she spread her hands, still in the pockets of the cardigan, 'with Aunt Maevy for the deserving poor.' Lizzie's look said, 'And so you should.'

'Sit down, Ginny. You'll be ready for a drink. Will you have your tea with lemon or cream?'

'Lemon, please.'

'There you are.' She handed over the cup. 'A French cake?'

'Yes, please. While the going's good. You can't get fancies like those in Wanapeake.'

'I'm going to make a feature of afternoon teas here when the Hydro opens, for non-residents. Keep them pricey. Two and sixpence each, I think, to keep out the riff-raff.'

'Oh, Lizzie!' She laughed. 'How can you be so snobbish?'

'Easily. This place isn't intended for the *hoi polloi*, make no mistake. I do plenty for the deserving poor in other ways. It's a business concern. There will be big overheads and it's got to pay its way and make a profit, otherwise it's all been a waste of time.'

'But you'll soon get fed up with it! You'll have to work like Aunty Maevy, and I don't see you doing that at all.' She bit into the chocolate 'fancy' which was flavoured with rum. 'Delicious. Ernest has to travel a lot – he told me himself – and after being in the Army for so long he'll want you to go with him. You like travel. You're like Grandmother.'

'You know me through and through, don't you?' Her eyes sparkled as brightly as the diamond brooch pinning her fichu. 'Well, you're quite right. I enjoyed creating this place, planning it, but the day-to-day running of it isn't for me. Aunt Isobel will keep an eye on the office side of things, but, of course, I'll have a well-trained girl in the office as well. As a matter of fact, I've got Miss Porter coming from McGrath's. She wanted a change and she's a grand shorthand typewriter, Aunt Maevy says. Aunt Kate's good with the domestic staff, and she's willing to help there, but I don't want them to feel tied in any way. They're getting on. It's Ernest's idea to put them on the

Board. He says more people die from not being wanted than from old age.'

'So you'll just . . . swan about?'

'Preside.' She lifted her chin. 'Grandmother always said you had to learn to delegate. I'll be on the premises every day when I'm at home, but I'll need someone who'll be a resident manager, or manageress, a general factotum, someone who'll hold the reins, who by her appearance will be an asset to the place, give it . . . tone.' She wiped her lips delicately with her napkin. There had been a tiny crumb of chocolate on the top one.

'A stand-in, in other words.'

'Oh, I don't flatter myself I'm unique, although I have a husband who's always telling me I am.' She laughed, showing the tip of a pink tongue. 'More tea?'

'Thanks. You have lovely tea in Scotland.'

'It's not Scottish, it's from Jackson's in Piccadilly, Earl Grey. It's popular in the best houses.' She lifted the teapot, having first added water from the silver jug, filled up Ginny's cup, and handing it over, said, 'We haven't had time for a chat since you came, with all the comings and goings. Tell me about your life in Wanapeake.'

'My life?' She had to think. Until the War was over she had done her best to help with voluntary work. No one could pretend it was exciting sitting in Wanapeake Town Hall packing comforts for the soldiers or rolling bandages at the local hospital. She had accompanied Sarah on her door-to-door charity collections, feeling like an imposter.

She had found herself quite unable to enrol for a full course in nursing. She did not see it as her role, and the commitment frightened her. Nursing as a contribution to the War effort had been attractive, but not as a long-term prospect. She knew she would never have the dedication of Ellie. That would have to start in the cradle – she had a suspicion in Ellie's case she would be rocking another kind of cradle before long. Ellie was logical. James was two. Kieran was fit and well. Now was the time. She could see the list of reasons she would give herself as if they were written on a piece of paper in front of her. Maybe. She had not always been logical. There was James to prove it.

'My life?' she repeated. 'Mostly trying not to annoy Mother and Father. A little of Ginny goes a long way with them. I'm better away from them, then they can boast about me from afar.'

'You're sharp, Ginny. No *beaux*?'

'Plenty. But I'd never marry for the sake of marrying. I nearly did it once with Magnus Muir. The two brothers had to have a good go at each other to save me from a fate worse than death. And them.' She laughed.

'Ellie did – marry for the sake of marrying.'

'She did it for James. But I think it's working now. Haven't you seen them looking at each other? I'm an expert on exchanged glances between married couples.' She smiled at Lizzie.

'Yes, you're right. In another year or so she'll realize how lucky she is with Kieran. He's the salt of the earth. He was in love with me once, you know.'

'Was he? I'm not surprised.'

'Yes, but Ernest swept me off my feet. Kieran's a slow maturer. All he needs is a happy marriage and a child or children of his own and he'll blossom like a may tree.'

'Still, I'd rather be in love first.'

'It's the *state* that's important, whether it comes before or after. It's natural and right. I'll give you a piece of advice, Ginny. Don't be too independent, or at least, don't show it.'

'So you want me to go back to Wanapeake and put on a soulful air and twist my wrists and find a suitor?'

'Nothing of the kind. That was just by the way. What

I'd like you to do is manage this place for me, become what they call in France a *Directrice*.'

'Me?' she said, and then, laughingly, '*Moi?*'

'*Pourquoi pas?* You look even better than I do because you're younger. You have assurance, a good brain, which you need to use, you'd help to build up this place for Jonty and me, you'd be amongst your family . . . and I'd pay you well.'

'How much?'

'Five hundred a year, and six weeks' holiday. I'd want you to travel. It would be good for our reputation, and let you see how similar establishments are run in other countries.'

Ginny laughed. 'Well, well! Who would have believed it? Still plotting!'

'I have unerring discrimination.' She looked haughty. 'Jonty and Ernest think so. They think you're right for the job. I've already asked them.'

'See, I was right. Plotting behind my back. Do they think I'll accept?'

'They weren't sure.' Lizzie laughed. 'That's the beauty of you. You aren't cut-and-dried. There's a kind of mystery about you, a . . . promise. No one can say which way you'll jump. You could make a brilliant marriage, or a disastrous one, because in the end your heart will always rule your head. You could run this place like a dream. That, at least, the three of us are agreed on. What do you say, Ginny?' She looked away as footsteps sounded on the tiled floor. Ginny turned her head, too. 'Why, Iain!' Lizzie was saying with her brilliant smile. A youngish dark-haired man was weaving his way through the greenery towards them. He looked slightly irascible as he flicked back a spray of fern which bent near his head.

'They told me I'd find you here,' he said, glancing at Ginny. 'I've been looking at the drains.'

'Oh, yes, the drains!' Lizzie looked enchanted. 'Ernest mentioned he's asked you . . . this is my cousin, Miss Ginny McGrath. Mr Iain Pearson, Ginny, general manager in the firm.'

Ginny held out her hand gingerly. He must have interpreted her look because he withdrew his. 'I couldn't find the downstairs cloakroom.' He turned to Lizzie accusingly. 'You've changed everything.'

'That was the general idea. Here, wipe your hands on this.' She held out a napkin. 'Will you have a cup of tea?'

'No, thank you. I've got to get back to York Street.'

'Sit down, then, for goodness sake! You're like a hen on a hot griddle.'

'All right.' He smiled and sat down on the edge of one of the wrought-iron chairs. 'You can channel the waste water to the village. They'll be glad to have it. But you'll have to get in touch with the Hydro-Electric Company. You're going to run short of water with your swimming bath and your Turkish bath and your baths for everybody . . . which engineers are looking after your interests?'

'Scobie in High Street.'

'Didn't they give you plans?'

'Yes, I'm sure they did. Do you think you could call in and see them on your way back, Iain? Explain . . .? You're good at it.' Her eyes were appealing, her voice limpid. This was how it was done, Ginny thought, watching her.

'I'm a bit rushed. I wouldn't have come out today, only Ernest . . .'

'They'll take it much better, coming from you.' Humbly.

'All right. I'll go and see them.' He turned to Ginny, the question of the drains now out of the way. 'You're from America? Robert McGrath's cousin as well?'

'Yes,' she said. She knew his kind. She wasn't going to

make conversation with someone who spoke to her like a teacher to his pupil.

'When do you go back?'

'Tomorrow.'

'Ah, that's a pity.'

'Why is it a pity?' she said sweetly

'Well . . .' he was at a loss. 'Your visit's been . . . short, and the weather has been . . . inclement.'

She raised her eyebrows. 'We've had one day of rain in the fortnight I've been here.'

'Ah, well . . .'

'She's teasing you, Iain,' Lizzie said.'That's her American way.'

'Is it?' He got up.'Well, I must get on *my* way if I'm to catch Scobie before they close. Good-bye, Miss McGrath.' He bowed this time. 'I hope you have a pleasant trip home.'

'Thank you, Mr Pearson. Good-bye.' She liked lean men. Ernest was her model. And he had an advantage over Ernest in that he was taller. And younger. But he had none of Ernest's insouciance, oh, dear no. Still, if you messed about in drains all the time . . . She watched him walk quickly out of the Palm Court, this time dodging the waving fern neatly.

'You're a tease,' Lizzie said. 'You should have told him you're coming back to be Lady Manageress.'

'Who said I was?'

'You know you have no intention of turning it down. Come on, confess it.'

'We'll see.' She laughed. 'I hate to admit it, but I believe you've managed me the way you do everyone else.'

Lizzie shook her head and the little toque went awry. Even like that she looked beautiful. 'How can you say such a thing?' she said.